About w

Valerie Blumenthal was born in Hampstead, London in 1950 and was educated in London and Switzerland. She worked in the wine trade for eight years whilst writing for her own pleasure, but is now writing full-time. She lives in a small village near Henley-on-Thames. *'To Anna' – about whom nothing is known* is her first novel. Her second, *The Colours of Her Days* (Collins, 1989), is set in the art world of the nineteenth century.

VALERIE BLUMENTHAL

'TO ANNA'
About whom nothing is known

FONTANA/Collins

First published by William Collins Sons & Co. Ltd 1988
First issued in Fontana Paperbacks 1989
Second impression July 1989

Copyright © Valerie Blumenthal 1988

Printed and bound in Great Britain by
William Collins Sons & Co. Ltd, Glasgow

To my Father –
with special love

Prologue

Prologue

The voice on the radio announced: 'Next, we have a work by Sir Bernard Foligno. It is his concerto for piano and violin, popularly known as the Summer Concerto, and was written in late 1883 when the composer was forty-three.

'The first performance was given in April of 1884 at the Royal Albert Hall, in the presence of Queen Victoria, with Douglas Hamilton, the Victorian virtuoso and friend of the composer, taking the solo violin and Foligno himself at the piano. Sir Charles Hallé conducted the work. According to Bernard Shaw:

'"The ovation continued for some nineteen minutes, the audience rising like a monumental wave, and the occasion was one of the most memorable of my life."

'It is the best-known and longest of Foligno's concertos, and unquestionably the most moving. This richly descriptive work is unusual in that it has four movements instead of the more normal three.

'It was dedicated "To Anna" – about whom nothing is known.'

PART ONE

Chapter One

The year was 1852; summer. The place was Bayswater, close to Hyde Park where one could enjoy a boat ride on the Serpentine, or a simple stroll on a fine day. Then, all the latest fashions would be paraded – women in wide skirts over voluminous petticoats, men sporting the new look in low-crowned hats and lounging jackets. On a fine day the road through the park would grumble with the constant wheels of carriages and the sounds of horses' hooves against the hard surface.

But at nights Hyde Park was a place to avoid: then vagrants, drunks, and other low-life prowled; and the affluent people living within its perimeters made certain to lock their doors well.

In Bayswater, at that time, there was a fashionable Jewish community; and one Friday evening, in a white-terraced house just out of sight of the park, the Folignos were celebrating the entry of the Jewish Sabbath.

'Bernard, please will you put that pen down. Shabat has entered. Your mother is about to light the candles.'

'Papa, I have just one more line. I shall forget it. It must be on paper.'

'And are you to forget those other written lines? This minute, Bernard.'

'I could almost have written it by now.'

'Bernard, do not provoke me. You are warned.'

Pouting, the eleven-year-old child stroked the inky nib lingeringly in a provocative show of rebellion, then followed his father through the large family room and into the adjoining oak-pannelled dining-room. The heavy drapes patterned with a dark, swirling William Morris design were pulled, and the gas-lamps were low as his mother performed the ritual lighting of candles. Bernard and his father put coverings on their heads and tulets around their shoulders, and his father said Kiddush, enunciating each word clearly and lovingly in his resonant voice. Then the Chollah was passed, twisted like his mother's looped plait and crusty and dotted with seeds, and inside tender and soft, tasting slightly of honey; and afterwards the sweet red wine, thick in its small silver cup, to be shared between the four of them. His younger sister took a great gulp.

'That is not fair,' Bernard complained. 'You have left almost nothing for me.'

'You should not mind,' his sister taunted. 'You always say music is your drink.'

'Well, and so it is, but that does not quench my thirst.'

'Nor does wine, does it, Papa?'

'I will not be arbitrator in your disputes, children.'

'Mama, Rachel is a selfish cow.'

'Bernard, I dislike that expression,' Helen reprimanded him mildly.

'I am not a selfish cow.'

'But she is *selfish* nonetheless.'

'Rachel, you should not have taken more than your fair share.'

Mollified by this small concession to justice, the boy glowered at his sister and sat down, whilst the new young housemaid, who at fifteen embarrassed him with her flushed skin and bold brown eyes, helped his mother dish out food and serve it to each member of the family.

The line of music sang in Bernard's head and taunted him with its unwritten presence, transposing itself into a different key and inverting.

'That is interesting. That could be really fine.'

'What could be, dear?' his mother enquired gently.

'He's talking to himself again,' observed Rachel scornfully.

Bernard ignored them both, hearing only the melody in his head, which had progressed from one line until it was like arteries from a main vein, flowing with life and branching out with intricate twists and turns.

12

I have to write it down. I shall burst with it. By Sunday, when Shabat is over, it will be lost to me.

'Mama, Papa, I wish to be excused from the table.'

'Why, Bernard?'

'I have to answer Nature's call.'

He ran up the dimly-lit staircase to his bedroom, the melody now throbbing so forcefully that he could barely spare the time to sit on the chair before his pedestal desk. But he picked up his pen as though it might contain poison.

'Shabat has entered . . . Do not provoke me. You are warned.'

Who was he worried about, God or his father? He shut his eyes, took a great breath and dipped the nib in ink. He had never done such a thing before: blasphemed on Shabat. It had always been unthinkable, but inspiration did not pick its moments; when it attacked, it had to be acquiesced and dealt with. It knew no rules or discipline as yet.

In the privacy of his room, Bernard forgot time and the awaiting meal downstairs. He scratched the back of his head and the kuppel slipped to the ground unnoticed and unmissed.

Joseph stood in the open doorway watching the slender, hunched form of his son for several minutes. He was a kind man who did not consider himself extreme in his religious attitudes. At first he felt anger at catching Bernard in this combined act of disobedience and blasphemy, but then he saw that his son was transported to some other environment where the ordinary did not exist and therefore no rules could be flouted, and the anger dissipated and was replaced by an almost painful tenderness.

Nonetheless, protocol had to be observed. He picked up the boy's kuppel and set it on his head. Bernard adjusted it absently and then started with realization, dropping his pen so that ink splattered his clean trousers. He span round, his cheeks divested of colour, and the music in his head was a tower of notes toppling all about him.

'Papa!'

'Bernard.'

They confronted each other across the iron bed: startled dismay and reproachful gravity. Joseph was sad; he would have to inflict punishment – and on Shabat. To write once the sacred

13

darkness had descended was not permitted in this family. It was not merely a question of religion. It transcended even that: heritage, pride, morality, tradition. For hundreds of years whilst the Jews had wandered, the Talmud had remained constant: and Bernard had been raised with that knowledge and had no excuse to stray.

'You will return to the dinner table now, Bernard, and afterwards, afterwards . . .' His eyes sought forgiveness from his son for what was to come.

'Yes, Papa. I am sorry, Papa.'

'Apologize to God, Bernard.'

But surely it was God who filled my head with such wonderful music, thought the boy. *He sent me the music on Shabat. And since it was He who sent it, how can writing it clash against His Will? At my age, Wolfgang Amadeus Mozart had written his first opera.*

Throughout the meal of clear soup with small matzoh dumplings floating on the surface, followed by the inevitable Friday-night fish, the boy could think only of his composition. He was alternately hot and cold, and kept wriggling his shoulders in frustration. The others chatted around him; familiar voices which contributed to the fabric of his environment. The family was always there; the music was not. There were the sounds of cutlery against china plates; the dim glow of reflected candle-flames and the lace of the tablecloth; the smell of wax and sweet wine and cooking. All these things he often delighted in. When he returned from school, weary from the perpetual battles with his classmates, emotionally drained, the solid reassurance offered by his home appeased him. Now it stood in the path of his creativity.

Because it was Shabat. When God had supposedly rested from His creativity, and Abraham had decreed that all Jews must follow his example.

At the table his mother glanced worriedly at him; his father with pain in anticipation of the forthcoming punishment, and Rachel with scorn; but Bernard was only aware of the music in his head.

Later, when everybody was asleep, and the gas-lights were

14

turned off, he defied God and his family once again. He lit his candle and wrote until the notes danced like miniature black witches before his reddened eyes, his head ached, and he fell asleep at his creation – to be discovered the following morning, and further reprimanded for this appalling repeat performance of blasphemy and disobedience. Then they all walked to the synagogue in Wigmore Street as if nothing had happened.

Around him the men nodded and swayed, prayed and mumbled and adjusted their tulets, whilst the cantor's nasal tenor rang out in a thin, monotonous whine. The choir sang ancient Sephardic melodies, and the women in the gallery above the men gazed about: at the stained-glass windows with their vivid blue and green birds, red lions and gold-striped tigers; at each other's finery; and, once in a while, at their prayerbooks.

Downstairs, Bernard – on the edge of his seat because of his sore bottom – buried his head in his book. He saw only clefs and notes and rows of five lines, and heard only his composition. In this way he was blaspheming as surely as if he were dipping his pen in ink and covering pages with writing.

Rachel spotted him, and sensed his remoteness. *How odd and pale he looks*, she thought, watching him standing now, almost as tall as their father. *He always looks as though he is in pain.*

I shall end the coda with an imperfect cadence, Bernard thought triumphantly, *as though the piece would wish to continue, but may not. And I shall call the work* Summer Overture. *It will make you think of dusty roads and performing bears, of moist grass and speckled leaves and ladies in pretty dresses.*

He glanced up and saw Rachel watching him. *How pretty she is.* And he smiled.

In that instant Rachel became aware of her older brother's uniqueness, and in a flash of insight which was gone before she could interpret it, all her opinions of him changed. From that moment, when he smiled up at her, Rachel revered her brother. Nobody in the family could understand this sudden and extraordinary behaviour reversal, least of all Bernard, who at first was suspicious, thinking it a kind of trick. When the strange idolatry persisted he treated her gently, as he had always done, but remained distant and preoccupied.

Undaunted, Rachel followed him about, ran errands for him and turned the pages of his music when he practised the piano. He was only grateful that he could apply himself to his music with one problem removed – that of Rachel teasing him for his efforts.

'Bernard?'

'Yes, my love?'

'You were talking in your sleep.'

'Was I? I did not even know I slept. You see how lovemaking affects me nowadays! What was I saying?'

'It was something to do with your childhood. I cannot imagine you as a small child.'

'Perhaps I never was in the true sense of the word. I was never light-hearted or mischievous. I was ungainly and ridiculously tall and thin. And prone to sulking and brooding.'

'Well, that at least has not changed!'

'You are harsh on me.'

'However you are no longer ungainly, and I do love you, regardless.'

'And I, you, my Anna. But is it not strange I should dream of my childhood?'

'Tell me about it. In all our years together you have scarcely mentioned it.'

'I fear I shall bore you, Anna.'

'You are incapable of boring me. And you have three hours in which to try.'

'Very well, then I shall attempt to recall. I shall tell you about the family room to begin with. . . .'

The family room had tall windows framed by thick velvet curtains, and the walls were crowded with pictures. The room

16

always seemed to be cluttered with sewing. There were patterns and swatches of material, and frills of lace and bright silk thread; there was his mother's embroidery and petit point, and Rachel's samplers, and needles and scissors and silver thimbles. Against one wall was the Hawkins iron-framed piano, a dark mahogany upright with barley-twisted brass candlesticks either side of the musicstand and, stacked high on top, sheets and sheets of music, mostly torn in odd places and dogeared from so much use. Against the opposite wall was the Folignos' pride and joy – a fine Georgian drop-leaf table, and around it six balloon-back leather-seated chairs. Dotted about the room were other easy chairs, contemporary in style, and a chaise-longue upholstered in dark-blue, plush velvet. On either side of the chaise-longue were a pair of matching embroidered foot-stools and, beside the grate, a papier-mâché lacquered screen. A pretty work-table with drawer and bag held the sewing, on top of which was always a vase of flowers surrounded by small ornaments. There was also a tall cheval-mirror in front of which Rachel would prance, fluffing her fair hair and stroking her tilted nose to reassure herself of its pert smallness. Rachel could have been Christian. Between brother and sister there was not a trace of physical resemblance.

It was in this room that the four of them spent their leisure-time, each pursuing his own affairs. Bernard played his music that no one heard any more, because he had played since he was three, his mother sewed, Rachel read a book and Joseph gazed down columns of figures, grunted occasionally, or read the paper and duly commented on fragments of the news to nobody in particular.

Sometimes in the evenings his parents and sister would gather round the piano and sing to Bernard's accompaniment the old Sephardic ballads they had always sung and knew by heart. Their voices would merge and fill the room joyously whilst, his face averted from them, Bernard's eyes would brim and spill over with the very goodness of it all.

The days passed and Bernard's 'Summer Overture' grew and developed and ruled his life. He had never known a feeling like it – a germination that was within him and spread beyond. Night after night when the rest of the house slept he worked on his composition, and what had begun as the skeleton of a melody was now a complete work written in proper sonata form, and he could not leave it alone . . . Here was Rachel portrayed by the flute, and here his parents, solidly together in the guise of a lone cello. And himself – the piano, naturally. And in between were threaded his impressions of summer.

Bernard spoke to nobody about what he was doing. Almost as wonderful as writing this work was the fact that it was secret, and he guarded it to himself proprietorially.

Twice a week he visited his music master, once for piano lessons, and once for composition and theory. His teacher was the famous Johann Baptist Cramer, himself a pupil of the great Muzio Clementi. Beethoven had said of him: 'Next to Cramer all the rest count for nothing.'

The old man lived in Kensington and was now eighty, but he was as sharp in his mind as ever, and dapper in his dress with his stiff-winged collar and narrow cane. Cramer loved Bernard and was always gently firm with him, trying to coax from the boy the true passion he knew was there.

'When I was half a year younger than you I was touring, giving concerts. The way you hold your fingers like rods, you will never be more than fair. How can they move quickly and be flexible when they are straight? Your fingers, my young sir, should be furled like autumn leaves; or curled as a bird's claws on a perch. *Curl* them, young sir. Now *play*. Again and again. It is no use *feeling* if the technique is not there. For the moment forget feeling. Be aware, that is all.'

'Liszt is impossible,' Bernard argued, frustrated.

'But magnificent,' Cramer counteracted. 'He is your hero, no?'

'Yes, yes. Oh yes.' His voice was fervent.

'Then *learn* to play him. The most rewarding experiences are not easily understood.'

'Will I ever learn to play him?' He looked up entreatingly at his teacher, and the old man softened:

'One day I dare think *you* might be magnificent.'

18

'Really?'

Cramer did not repeat his compliment. However Bernard wished to perpetuate the discussion.

'But my father expects me to become a stockbroker, like him. He is one of the few Jews allowed in the Stock Exchange. He is proud. He says I must regard my music in perspective.'

'And who is to say how that perspective is? It depends from what angle it is cast.'

'But he is my *father*.'

'Ah, and one must do as one's father desires, mustn't one, young sir? So meanwhile we learn. He pays. You practise and learn and progress. And as a man, when your business day is over then you will be able to impress and entertain young ladies in drawing-rooms with the assurance of a professional. You will have long left me then, and I shall be dead, and your battles will be your own.'

'I do not wish to be a drawing-room dandy. I do not wish to provide enjoyment for young ladies. Sir – I want to be a musician, not a stockbroker. I am not interested in figures and shares and statistics.'

There. The words were formed at last, spoken. And with their emphatic reality there came a wonderment at his own sudden feeling of direction.

'Sir – you will not tell my father?'

'We are friends, are we not?'

'I believe so.'

'Then enough is said on that matter. Now we continue with the Chopin nocturne – and curl your fingers. If you do not learn to do so your choice of career will be extremely simple.'

Each day at Milton Hall School in Hammersmith was one of endurance for Bernard. He had been selected by the other boys as their prey, and having latched on to him they gave him not a moment's peace.

'Jesus's murderer.'

'The murderers were the Romans.'

'Alerted by a Jew.'

He tried again, tall and pale in the middle of their circle: 'Benjamin Disraeli is a Jew.'

'Baptized at thirteen, you skinny miser.'

'But –'

'There is no case to answer. You have no case to speak for, Jew-boy.'

He was tired of always being on the defensive. It was different for Rachel as a girl. She had a governess, and each morning they sat talking gently with books resting on their laps. Bernard had a locker seat and a desk with a thick wooden lid bearing the engraved initials of anonymous boys, and he must remain at school until he was almost eighteen; six and a half more years. And they must be borne stoically in order to repay his father for the rare privilege of attending a public school, of benefiting from a middle-class education. That he would remain until his final year – this was the greatest privilege of all; and he simply did not know how he would bear it.

He never spoke to anyone of his unhappiness, half-blaming himself, thinking perhaps he was strange with his black, black hair and silences. Only the prospect of those two afternoons a week with Cramer helped him through his early schooldays.

Bernard enjoyed the walk to Kensington from Hammersmith. He noticed the way the sun glinted through the dappled leaves of trees; observed the carriages gleaming with reflected light, the horses' ears pricked keenly forward, their coats polished and fine; and the ladies – they were so beautiful in pastel colours and holding their parasols. On the way to Cramer's home he would be so immersed in reverie that he could be jostled by passers-by and not even notice. Tall and gawky, he loped along with his arms dangling at his sides as if his own limbs bothered him.

And then he would arrive, and would feel an enormous pleasure at seeing the old man – and a sense of pride that such a person should be his teacher.

At Cramer's, the real work that mattered took place.

'You *cannot* ignore the viola.' His teacher raised his voice in frustration. 'It exists.'

'But I cannot write in that clef. It is so muddling. I forget. I have a forgetful mind,' Bernard shouted back, anguished.

Cramer was scornful and imitated a falsetto: 'I cannot write in the alto clef. I cannot curl my fingers . . . Go to your stockbroking future, child. Your vocabulary is too limited for a musician.'

When his master was harsh to him, Bernard seemed to wither inside. Now his lower lip trembled babyishly. He said: 'I – feel.'

'So act upon it. Learn to deal with it.'

The day came when he wrote a passable part for the viola *and* the clarinet, and they celebrated with a small glass of port which went straight to his head. For the remainder of the week Bernard lived in an elevated state of self-importance.

Cramer, more than anyone, knew and understood Bernard, and at the end of their lessons they would have tea together and talk. Cramer would subtly try to draw the boy out of his introversion, to learn his thoughts. He spoke of his own life and related it to Bernard's.

'I was travelling at your age. You could also.'

'With my *music*?'

'How else, young sir?'

'Would I be ready?'

'I believe so. How old will you be in a year and a half? Thirteen?'

'Yes.'

'You are so tall now, aren't you? And so pale and serious. Ah Bernard, life is not easy, is it?'

'No; and I can never tour. There is my schooling, which I hate now, and then there is stockbroking which I hate in the future.' His jaw clenched and he spoke with quiet vehemence.

'But one can dream,' the other said gently.

'Yes?'

'Yes, and pleasantly so. And perhaps our dreams can help us pass the time, young sir, when the actuality is not what we would wish it to be.'

'*I* wish . . .'

'Yes?'

'Oh I just wish, that is all.' His eyes searched Cramer's for assurance.

21

Cramer obliged: 'The delightful thing is not knowing, is it not? You are adamant about what you may or may not do. But you cannot know for sure, young sir, because any single incident can occur to devastate our most orderly of plans. And that is the joy. The key to life. So continue to wish. It is as good a way as any of wittling away the time.'

Chapter Two

School term ended and Helen took the children to Weymouth. They went to Weymouth unfailingly each August, and stayed in the same boarding house where the proprietor understood their dietary requirements.

On the beach there were pony and donkey rides, side-shows, and men with pet monkeys and hurdy-gurdies . . . Newspaper vendors hoarsely crying out; cockles sold from little stalls with striped canopies; ices and sticks of rock; boats like painted bananas; and the pervading smell of freshly-caught fish.

Some women went in the sea, their garments flapping like giant wings, alternately ballooning and clinging to their legs. Helen did not venture into the sea. She was too self-conscious and instead sat fanning herself in a chair beneath a tilted umbrella, watching her children and making sure they did not go out beyond waist-level. Since their waists were at different heights they stood apart, shouting to one another above all the other cries, and their conversation floated back to her.

'See, Bernard,' Rachel called, 'on tiptoe I am not so much more shallow than you.'

'There is a sudden dip, Rachel,' he called back. 'Be careful.'

At this brotherly concern Helen's heart warmed.

'No matter – I bet that I could swim if I had to. A puppy swims as soon as it is put in water.'

'You are not a puppy.' Bernard's tone held slight scorn.

'Oh Bernard,' she pleaded. 'Come over here. It is not fair – I cannot come to you. Come to me and we can throw the ball.'

'For a few moments, then.'

Afterwards he stood alone at the sea's edge – the tide lapping in to form twin wrinkles around his ankles and then, with a hiss, retreating, leaving them naked and tingling, before creeping up once more and encircling them with the old cold-warmth around the little faded tide-marks.

At four o'clock, with absolute precision according to Helen's watch, they returned to the boarding house to relax and prepare for the evening, and, after supper, they retired to the privacy of Helen's room where she read from the Old Testament.

At the end of the second week Joseph arrived with city-worn eyes and a jaunty boater to bely them. He immediately entered into the holiday spirit and became gay and lighthearted, and was liable to creep up unexpectedly behind one and tickle one's neck, or go 'boo'. He teased them and told jokes and determinedly – almost heroically – discarded his stockbroker's formality. He sat on a pony to please Rachel, and went into the sea to please Bernard, and took them on family outings.

Then suddenly they were packing up again, and it was time for the journey home.

They took a carriage to Southampton, and from there the train to London. They had a compartment to themselves, and Bernard sat on one side of his mother whilst Rachel sat on the other. Joseph was opposite them, concealed by a newspaper, but his legs were outstretched, and one foot deliberately rested by Bernard's and would occasionally rub his ankle in a gesture of affection. Every so often his pale blue eyes would rise above the paper to appraise the trio sitting opposite him, and a look of pure satisfaction would cross his face, before he inclined his head once more and gave himself up to the pleasures of his reading.

Bernard felt the soft touch of his father's foot, whilst his arm was against his mother's. Little Rachel's head lolled against Helen's breast and her breathing was heavy with sleep.

'My little one gets so sleepy,' Helen murmured. 'I do hope she is not ailing.'

Joseph glanced up sharply. He was never so profoundly engrossed in his reading that he was unaware of the conversation about him; and when it concerned the welfare of his family he was immediately alert.

'Why should she be ailing?'

'Dear, I did not say she was ailing. I said I *hoped* she was *not* ailing.' Helen spoke in a soothing tone and stroked the silkiness of her sleeping daughter's hair.

'But do you think she *could* be ailing?' he persisted anxiously.

'I expect she is just tired after the excitement of the holiday, that is all.'

'You are certain that is all?' Joseph relied on her every word.

'Yes dear,' Helen answered, although a moment ago she had expressed her own doubts.

And Joseph, grunting his satisfaction, hid himself once more.

Bernard, looking out of the window, felt a great sense of well-being. He watched the countryside appearing and disappearing – stretching and re-shaping itself like a rolling caterpillar – and listened to the wheels of the train as they rasped against the track. The chugging became a melody, and he thought with a sudden flash of inspiration, *I shall include the train journey in my 'Summer Overture'.*

'So it was still not finished?'

'No, oh no. It was weeks before it was finished . . . We returned home and London seemed eaten away by the heat. The drains stank. Everybody was irritable. Rachel and I would go and sit by the Serpentine. We would remove our shoes and dangle our feet in the water and watch the little boats drift past with lovers in them. Rachel giggled at the lovers. She was so small next to me, so fair beside my darkness, and so impossibly lively besides my reticence. She challenged me, I remember, about feeding the ducks and swans.

'"They will peck you," I cautioned her. "And their beaks are strong."

'She looked at me provocatively. "Then I am brave, aren't I?"

'"Not brave, foolish."

'"Would you care if they pecked me?" she asked, her fingers outstretched still whilst the birds tugged at the crusts.

'I told her I would, and she drew her fingers back immediately and with some relief. She was like that. Poor little Rachel. Her tiredness became more pronounced, and sometimes I noticed that she would clasp her tummy . . . Am I boring you?'

'No, my love. I want to hear it. All of it.'

'Well, snuggle up to me then. Oh, it is so good lying beside the woman you love, with the curtains billowing and the rain outside.'

'We are sinners, you and I.'

'Hush, darling, we will not speak of that now.'

'But it is true.'

'And has been for years. It is so old an issue as to be historical. Do you want me to go on?'

'Yes.'

'On one of our walks, Rachel bought her spinning top with her. I remember I remarked it was like a planet that went round and round. She did not realize planets went round, so I explained a little to her. She was sad. She said she would have preferred them to remain still and to serve no purpose other than to be distant and sparkling. And so we got on to the subject of Heaven.'

'Do you believe in Heaven?' Rachel asked.

'Of course,' Bernard answered her impatiently. 'We are taught to believe it.'

'But Bernard, you must believe it because you want to, not because you are taught.' Rachel gave a scornful little laugh. 'How stupid you are sometimes. You do so much what is expected of you. Anyway, I believe in Heaven.'

'Good,' he answered irritably.

'Do you know why?'

'No.' Bernard sighed, wishing he were on his own.

'Because I see things,' she said in a voice full of mystery.

'What things?' He was interested now, despite himself, and looked into her bright little face.

'I cannot explain. Funny things. Feelings that become pictures. Places I have not been to but which are not just my imaginings.'

'You can tell people's fortunes when you grow up,' Bernard teased.

And then Rachel said something astonishing: 'I don't think I shall grow up, Bernard.' She spoke perfectly calmly.

'You mean you don't *want* to grow up.'

'No, I don't mean that.'

'What then?' When she did not reply, he asked again on a more insistent note: 'What then?'

But she would not elaborate and said instead: 'Bernard, will you write a serenade for my favourite doll?'

'Oh Rachel, one doesn't wrote serenades for dolls. Don't be so babyish.'

'I am not babyish. And I know you are writing something else very important.'

'How do you know?'

'I *know*,' she answered almost patronizingly, adding: 'it is in your head,' as if that explained everything.

Bernard was lost for words. He could not understand her. He threw a stone across the water and watched it bounce.

'Am I right?' she persisted.

'You've been spying on me.' He turned on her, suddenly angry.

She shrank away from his anger. 'No I haven't. I promise. I just know.'

Her eyes shone with hurt tears and Bernard put his arm around her. 'I did not mean to shout. It is just so hard to believe.'

'Well, it is true.'

'You will not tell Mama and Papa about what I am doing?'

'I promise I will not. What's it called?'

'"Summer Overture."'

'What's an overture?'

'An independent work in a single movement. Mine is unusual because it will have a recapitulation with a new theme mingled with the others.'

'You are too clever for me. I do not know what you're talking about. I think you are too clever for yourself, Bernard!'

'But I am not clever, Rachel. I do not think I will ever

understand the stock market like Papa does. Sometimes he shows me figures and uses words which are frightening, they are so mysterious to me. Rachel – I shall never understand them. How am I to be a stockbroker if I cannot comprehend the simplest things Papa explains to me?' Bernard had never confided his fears before.

'You can understand. You are only not interested,' Rachel said simply.

Of course she was right. Bernard shook his head in amazement. 'Little Rachel.' He hugged her impulsively.

'You are only one year older.' She sounded aggrieved and broke away from him.

'Don't be cross now. And Rachel, I shall write a serenade for your doll.'

'Thank you, Bernard.' She smiled with complacent superiority, before bending to the water and surveying her reflection and losing those strange revealing moments to vanity.

In Bernard's house, tucked away from the Bayswater Road in a small crescent, his parents entertained Jewish friends – intelligent and comfortably-off people who mixed unquestioningly together and knew the unspoken rules and limitations that applied to them. His father discussed the stock market, his quiet voice enthusiastic as he talked of a 'bull' market, and of the price being fetched for raw materials. He would speak of the affluence of Britain, and his certainty that the Jews could contribute so much to it.

Sometimes he introduced Bernard, who loathed these sessions when he was put on display.

'And here – this is Bernard, my son. When he leaves school he will join me at the Stock Exchange.'

'How do you do, Bernard?'

'How do you do?' He stood straight and austere, his eyes expressionless.

'What a tall boy you are, and not yet bar-mitzvaed. So you are to be a stockbroker like your father. You are very privileged, you know. Your father has reached such a respected position. It is not easy, and we must tackle these things.'

That word 'privilege' again. It seemed to crop up all the time. A heavy, cloying word.

Bernard thought: *It is not a privilege to me. To pursue a career in music would be a privilege. You would not understand what I mean. And you cannot imagine what I do each night.* He smiled privately at that.

At nine o'clock exactly his mother would tuck him up in bed and kiss him goodnight, but as soon as he heard her footsteps retreating downstairs, Bernard would leap up and go directly to his desk where his Summer Overture beckoned. He would light his candle, listen anew for any footsteps or voices and begin work.

How he enjoyed the solitariness of writing music. How truly himself he could be, and how amazed his parents would have been had they known he spent part of every night, whilst they presumed him to be asleep, composing a work of Great Importance. But his paleness each morning was attributed to nothing more than rapid growth, and his mental preoccupation and absent-mindedness were no different to usual.

Possibly Helen would have understood, for Bernard's musicality was inherited from her. She had a fine soprano voice and taught singing, and Bernard often accompanied her pupils.

One of these was a Jewish girl of fifteen called Sophie. Sophie was dark and gentle-eyed with a gloriously pure and resonant voice, and Bernard loved to hear her sing, to feel her standing so close as he played for her. He could almost imagine her breath on the back of his neck; certainly he heard every quick, deep little intake between the phrases.

I think I must be in love with her, he reflected seriously at the age of not quite twelve, *or else why should I so look forward to seeing her each week? And I should so like her to hear my Summer Overture, to play it to her and for her to admire it.*

But he scarcely said a word when he saw her. Silently he would take his seat at the piano, feeling his ears redden, and he would play what was required of him, whilst any conversation they had was in his head.

School recommenced, and with it the usual harassment – not only from the boys but also from some of the masters who, aware that it was shortly to be the Jewish New Year, made snide remarks. Bernard tried not to take the comments personally, but nonetheless they *were* personal, aimed as they were at his heritage, which was instilled in his soul, and he could not comprehend why he was condemned for what he was, regardless of what he was like. The pride he felt for his race became tainted and distorted, for it was difficult to be confident when everyday someone threw dirt at you and your origins.

But – in just over a year he would be bar-mitzvahed. He would be a man, whilst all his fellow pupils would remain boys. He was being groomed for this event that was every Jewish boy's objective and every parent's joy, and each Sunday morning was occupied with Hebrew lessons and study of the Old Testament.

After the lessons his teacher often remained for lunch, and he and Joseph would talk at length about religion, and about their plans for the approaching festivities.

Helen spoke of the hours of preparation for the huge feasts before and after Yom Kippur, when they must spend almost the entire day in synagogue, not permitted to eat or drink, remembering the dead and repenting of sin.

'What is sin, what have I done?' Bernard had asked once, upon being told he was guilty of it.

'We all sin,' Helen had explained. 'It is a displeasure to another; a misdeed; it is a corruption of ourselves, however minor. When you are disobedient and it causes anguish, then that is your sin. There are serious sins and sins which involve blasphemy, and there are lesser, trifling sins, which might seem inconsequential. We might lose our tempers too quickly, or do a deed that is selfish and unthinking. Hardly a day goes by when we do not sin in one way or another, and so we pray to be better people. Do you understand?'

For several years now he had known the meaning of sin, and yet he had written on Shabat. Which was more of a sin – the fact that he had put pen to paper, or that he could not regret it?

One Sunday Bernard noticed that occasionally his teacher's gaze would follow their young maid who served them, and

Bernard blushed on his behalf. Rachel made cow-eyes of boredom across the table at him, and kept kicking his toe, and later she remarked:

'He has the breath of an old dog, and a voice as tiring as the wheels of a carriage on a long journey! I do not know how you stand him.'

'He is a good teacher,' Bernard replied automatically. 'What he says is interesting.'

'I thought you disliked religion.'

'*I* – dislike religion?'

'Yes. Being Jewish.'

'I am proud to be so. How can you have thought such a thing?'

'I just thought, that was all.'

'Well, you are wrong.'

'Do not shout at me Bernard.'

His sister's hurt eyes looked remorsefully into his intense dark ones. Bernard was disturbed by their conversation, and for several days he could not rid his mind of it.

Summer drew to a close, and with it his overture found its own conclusion. The night before Bernard was due to see Cramer he could neither eat dinner nor sleep. He would slip into a light doze and dream that his teacher was tearing his manuscript into tiny pieces; or a fellow pupil was pouring ink over each page; or his father was standing, huge and forbidding, blocking his doorway, brandishing a giant talmud which shielded his face; or Cramer had died and requested that his body be wrapped in the manuscript. Many times Bernard woke perspiring and bounded immediately from the bed in a panic, to stand by the open window and inhale the nocturnal London air and listen to its sounds until, comforted by the familiar, he would return to bed. Eventually thick grey morning replaced the night, the day passed fairly uneventfully, and at last he was walking the long journey to Cramer's.

Fine drizzle: the pavements glistened with it; and the wheels of carriages splashed him with mud. Summer over. Summer Overture. Summer over . . . Overture. He dragged his feet dismally and thought: *How can I have been so conceited? I am a child, and my work is childish. Do I believe myself to be another*

31

*Mozart? He will laugh – no, he is too considerate. He will be
critical, and I shall not be able to bear that. I wish I were older
and could write with wisdom. I wish I were not me. . . .*

He came finally to the house and stood waiting, feeling much
as a slave thrust into the amphitheatre must have felt whilst
awaiting the arrival of the lions.

Cramer opened the door and greeted him as usual. His face
wore its crevices of age with the gentleness born of time used
wisely. Bernard almost immediately thrust his package at him.
It was bound in plain paper and painstakingly sealed with thick
red wax, in blood-like globules.

'What is this, Bernard?'

'It is something I have written. I should like you to read it,
now please.'

His eyes were shut. Within him the sense of failure already
lodged itself; and against this the slight hope that perhaps the
presentiment might be unfounded.

Cramer touched his shoulder, then his cheek. 'But young sir
– I cannot read it here, now, this moment. *Now* it is our lesson.
Tomorrow I am travelling to Bath, where I shall remain for a
couple of weeks. I must have time to digest the contents of your
work. I presume it was not written lightheartedly, and therefore you would not wish me to study it superficially.'

Bernard opened his eyes slowly. Dots danced in the air
before him. 'I was not thinking.'

'You expected an instant verdict. Bernard, some composers
have to wait until they are dead before they are rewarded with a
favourable verdict.'

'I could not.'

'And I am not asking you to. But they are the greatest: those
who are prepared to dice with unpopularity, write music that is
so rare and extraordinary and innovatory that initially it is
frequently misunderstood, because the listeners' ears are too
naïve . . . Young sir, whatever my verdict, which you know will
be honest, I want you to know that I am intensely proud of you.
And Summer Overture, huh? Was the title before or after the
composition?'

'In the middle, I'm afraid.'

32

Cramer laughed. 'It is as good a place as any. Now Bernard, simple piano pieces today; so simple you can *almost* forget to think. Today you will play for me with great feeling. You will not be Bernard. You will be music.'

The following day Bernard became aware of one of the new boys in the front row. He was short and slightly built, with pouched, rabbit-like cheeks and a small red mouth. He wore glasses and had the habit of peering as though trying to see above their rims, rather than through their lenses. Bernard only knew his surname: Hamilton.

'And so you met dearest Douglas. The pair of you – what a strange couple.'

'Yes, we were. The others diverted their attention to him for several weeks and I was left in relative peace at the poor boy's expense. I suppose we were drawn together by our mutual inadequacies, as it were. And then we discovered so much. It is rare, that feeling of empathy.'

'I know. It is why you and I are so special, and why I value our relationship. And now I am becoming old.'

'*You*? Old? But dearest, you are young still, and so very beautiful.'

'It occurs to me, as you talk, that the years are gone – so many of them, and that they can never be repeated. Even my conscience is unaroused nowadays. And I would like to die old with you and it is not possible.'

'Why this morbid talk of age and death?'

'It is something that bothers me terribly. Enough, now tell me about Douglas as a boy.'

He stood on his own in the playground for the twenty minutes between morning lessons, peering round him, his pale eyebrows twitching, his head tilted at an angle. Every so often another boy would approach him, make a comment, pull an impolite face, tauntingly re-adjust the glasses and laugh the tuneless laughter of mockery. Hamilton appeared impervious,

33

and Bernard could only admire such neutrality. He thought how dismal it all was: the dark prison-like railings with spikes, the ugly red-brick expanses of the school, the tea-coloured sky, the sightless behaviour of the boys; the dour faces of the masters.

Then Hamilton's querying glance met Bernard's and his mouth opened in a humorous and ingenuous smile, and although they did not speak then, each recognized in the other the extending ribbon of friendship.

Later Bernard learned that he was the son of a wealthy Scottish surgeon and an aristocratic mother from an old Gloucestershire family. They lived in a large house in Harley Street which also served as Mr Hamilton's consulting rooms, and their second home was in Gloucestershire where Mrs Hamilton spent most of her time, her main interest during the winter being to hunt.

'What do you mean, hunt?' Bernard asked curiously.

'Do you really not know?' The other was aghast.

'No, else I would not have asked.'

'How extraordinary.'

'Why is it extraordinary? Have you heard of the Talmud?'

'No, what is that?'

'You see.'

'Yes. And if we are to be friends we can find out.'

In stature he came to Bernard's chin. He had a high, rather affected voice, a round intelligent forehead, and a self-assurance that was daunting. Until now there had never been another boy in whom to confide; somebody to share his fears or his yearnings. And now – how wonderful was that gentle sweep of pleasure resultant of commitment to another individual.

'Do you like music?'

'*Like*! It is my passion,' Bernard answered, laughing.

'Mine also! I play the violin. I long to play Paganini perfectly.'

'In league with the devil. And I long to play Lizst, who is the greatest living musician.'

'So you are a pianist.'

'And I like to compose. I have just written something I call "Summer Overture".'

34

In such a way things happen: lives develop and alter like shifting soil, and a fragile platform becomes the plinth upon which other events are built, or possibly from which they topple. In a short space of time three major things happened to Bernard just before his twelfth birthday: he completed his first composition; he met Douglas Hamilton, who not only helped him make some concessions towards normal childhood but would remain his closest friend throughout his life; and his sister Rachel became ill.

Chapter Three

Everywhere the atmosphere of sickness prevailed. It had happened overnight – one day they went about their ordinary routines, the next their lives were in upheaval. Rachel was dying of a wasting disease. Douglas Hamilton's father himself had examined her and had found a large growth in her abdomen, easily discerned beneath his probing fingertips.

The verdict had been given: 'There is no hope.' And by that short sentence the entire structure of their lives was altered, and the little household was submerged in its sorrow. It was devastating, such sorrow. The Folignos could not see past the immense block of their grief, but for Rachel's sake they must maintain a façade of cheerfulness.

Joseph had broken down and cried and it was Helen, always the more stoic, who had told the news to Bernard.

That had been on Sunday, after his Hebrew lesson, and now it was Tuesday, and Cramer had promised he would give his opinion of Bernard's composition. How could Bernard think of music? Music was too emphatic a reminder of all that was vital and alive, whilst his sister lay propped palely against white pillows: hurting, going away. . . .

He stood in Cramer's music room, so large and bright and dominated by the huge piano, waiting for the old man to speak.

'Why a face so sad, young sir? And I have so much that is good to tell you.'

He likes it. He likes it. The words shrieked in his head. For a moment he exulted in a joy that was to the exclusion of everything else.

The moment passed, and his own sense of tragedy was now two-fold. How could matters be so harshly mistimed? Cramer wanted to publish his work. His sister was dying. Those two facts were at such odds. Bernard could not consider Cramer's proposal. He could not even broach it to his parents – his success, his happiness – and then measure it with justification against the failure of death and their grief. He was guilty that he should feel thwarted and know a sense of waste, when back home was waste on such a different scale.

Why so sad? Because his future slipped away before him, already in the past; because he must forget music and the pleasure he derived from it, and the selfish satisfaction gained from having his work published; because Rachel would finally die, and as the sole sibling he must do what was expected of him. It would be his duty.

On his way home from Cramer's there was a man in the street selling clockwork clowns for a penny. They performed antics such as handstands and somersaults. Bernard bought a pair for Rachel. The purchase obviated his guilt a little; guilt caused by unrighteous self-pity.

The festivals passed without cause for celebration, and on Yom Kippur Rachel fasted also, but only because she could not eat without vomiting. In synagogue they all prayed the entire day for her, Joseph rocking backwards and forwards in his seat, his head bowed; and Helen asked God to atone her for all her sins, and begged that he might take her life in place of her daughter's.

Death seemed to play games and, having cornered her, released her again. Rachel made a slight recovery and was allowed downstairs – the first time in five weeks. She was carried tenderly by her father in the morning, and he laid her carefully and lovingly on the chaise-longue in the family room, in front of the fierce-burning fire. Around her body that had lost its soft flesh, blankets swaddled her like a mummy. They were not the same people, they could not be; but when they were with Rachel the pretence must be maintained: smiles and bright voices, whilst they longed to weep. The slowness was the worst; the delaying of dying, the waiting for the inevitable.

Rachel asked one day from her position on the chaise-longue: 'Mama, might I have one of those dresses? You know, those

37

pretty ones with the latest tartan pattern. I have always so fancied them.'

Helen bent to her daughter and enveloped her in her arms. She felt like a chicken, and Helen was overcome with rage. Its violence generated a futile energy through her body, dissipating within a moment and leaving her vulnerable.

She tried to disentangle herself and avert her face from Rachel's, but it was too late and the tear fell on her daughter's cheek. Rachel put down her doll which she had been limply holding and wiped her mother's eyes, whilst Helen tried to regain her composure.

Last night she had said to her husband, 'Please dear, we must behave normally. She must have no inkling that she will not get better.'

She had cradled his head against her as he had kept repeating, 'Little Rachel, little Rachel.'

Her chin resting on his balding crown she had remained dry-eyed, unable to release the ache stretching across her throat. Absurdly she had thought: *when people used to ask how many children I had, I always answered without thinking – two. Now I shall only be able to say I have one child.* She had continued to stroke her husband's head, staring directly in front of her all the while, and when they were in their separate beds, Joseph's hand had reached across the gap between them and clasped hers, pressing and kneeding, bruising her knuckles.

Now she had cried in front of Rachel. Helen stood up straight and forced herself to smile.

'I am sorry, little one. It is only that I hate seeing you ill. But Mr Hamilton says you will be recovered in no time. Why, already you are so much –'

'Mama, I know,' interrupted Rachel.

What do you know, my darling? wondered Helen, gazing at her child's peaked face and sunken eyes. *God, please do not let her know she is dying.*

It was quite late in the afternoon by the time she was ready to go out. She took a cab to Piccadilly, where she was dropped off outside the Old Bath Hotel. Then she walked up and down the length of the street, past Green Park and the cab shelter, past

Devonshire House, and back again towards the Egyptian hall, trying in shop after shop to find a tartan dress for Rachel. Some had the size, and some the style, but only the last and most unlikely shop had both. The material was finest wool, the sleeves billowed out and ended in tight lace cuffs, and under the full skirt edged with plain velvet were layers of broderie anglaise petticoats and frills. A wide velvet sash was attached to the waist. Helen stroked the dress as though it breathed her daughter's breath, knowing it would be the last item of clothing she would ever purchase for her. Next door was a small bookshop, and on an impulse she wandered in and requested a copy of Dickens's *David Copperfield* for Rachel.

It was later than she had thought; outside, daylight was replaced by evening's dreary wall of drab grey, and the smell of fog was in the air. Lamp-lighters with their poles lit the tall street-lights, impatiently pushing away children who swung from them by lengths of rope. Bernard would have finished his music lesson and be wondering where she was, and Rachel, whose mind must be kept constantly occupied, would be lying fretting on her chaise-longue.

At last a vacant cab passed. Helen hailed it to stop, and lifting her enveloping cloak and mass of skirts, climbed the step and entered the small compartment through the flap doors. She sank heavily into the tabaret-upholstered seat, her head fell back and she felt herself drifting into a light doze. Even then the burden of sadness was present.

She was roused abruptly when the driver pulled his horse to a halt from a brisk trot. The carriage swayed slightly.

'What is the matter?' Helen called through the side window to the driver perched high at the rear.

'Bloody kitten shot across the road right in front of the wheels, ma'am. Apologies and all that.'

His whip was lifted in readiness when Helen asked: 'The kitten – is it injured?'

'Don't know, ma'am. Caught its paw a bit, I imagine. Should think that's all. Bloody animal.'

'We must not continue until we have checked. Driver, would you please wait while I go and look.'

39

From her window she could make out a small black and white form huddled under the dull yellow glow of the gaslight. Two youths in ill-fitting clothes were staring dispassionately at it, obviously considering it as possible bait. Helen strode purposefully towards them, lifting her skirts to avoid a puddle. She was more emboldened than usual and picked up the kitten without hesitating. One of the boys nudged his friend before saying, 'You don't want to get yourself all covered in filth from 'im, missus. Scrawny little bastard. Best thing to do would be drown 'im. I'd forget about 'im if I was you.'

His hat was too far back and he pushed it back further still and scratched the front of his head. His friend smiled with a lopsided leer, revealing brown, worn-down teeth. Their breath smelt of stale beer.

Helen ignored both of them and returned to the cab clutching the kitten. The hem of her dress and the edge of her cape trailed in puddles as both her hands were occupied, and she almost tripped climbing up the step into the cab, unassisted by the driver who plainly considered her a little crazy.

Once resettled, Helen examined the creature's bleeding paw, and bound it with her lace handkerchief. It resisted, but not wholeheartedly, and after its initial hissed protestations, fell asleep, purring slightly against her, its head with its small pink nose and comical black moustache resting on the package containing Rachel's dress.

They rattled and swayed their way back without further incident and Helen watched the world from her window. At the junction of the Edgware Road, boys selling newspapers shouted out the latest numbers of dead in Turkey. A ragged beggar ran alongside her cab and she took a penny from her silk purse, leaned out of her window and handed it to him. The air smelt of assorted life, and her daughter was dying.

Back home she found Rachel flushed and crying, with Bernard kneeling beside her trying to comfort her.

'Darling, I'm home. Don't cry, dearest . . . I have a surprise for you.'

'The dress?'

'And more besides.'

She went to the kitchen to fetch the kitten. Helen's old maid had bound its paw and washed its face.

Bernard gasped when he saw her come in with it. 'Hush,' his mother whispered. 'Close your eyes tightly, Rachel,' she called from the doorway.

'Like this?'

'Tighter.' Helen approached the chaise-longue on tiptoe.

'Like this?'

'Yes.'

Helen bent and kissed the squeezed eyelids and set the kitten on top of her.

'Open.'

'Oh. *Oh*. Oh Mama!'

'You like him?'

'I love her. Where did you get her? What's happened to her paw?'

Helen told them the story. Bernard listened enthralled, and his sister's eyes were shining as they had not for several weeks. She looked well, and with her thinness concealed under the covers one could not guess at her wasted body.

She cannot be dying, he told himself. *I will not believe it. I shall go to Cramer and tell him it was all a mistake, and then he will publish my work and I can perform it.*

'Do you want to name it?' Helen asked Rachel. 'It can be yours.'

'Yes.'

'Well, you go to sleep now, and later we will help you into your pretty new dress and you can decide what to call it. We shall have a sort of ceremony with Papa and Bernard present.'

'That would be so lovely. So really lovely. Can she sleep with me now?'

'If she will stay.'

'She is already asleep.'

'Then we must not disturb her, after all her adventures. By the way, darling, how do you know it is a girl?'

'I just do.'

'Oh – I see. Now you get well and strong soon, so you can learn to feed and look after her yourself.'

41

She left the room quietly with Bernard. Outside the door she turned to him and, shaking her head, said: 'Oh Bernard dear, it is so very, very sad. So heartbreakingly sad,' and went downstairs to the kitchen, leaving him with her poignant words ringing in his ears.

That evening the ceremony was held in the family room. Rachel lay on the chaise-longue in her new dress, surrounded by pillows and cushions, her new book on her lap, and declared that she was going to name the cat Anna.

Afterwards Bernard played the piano. He thought of the future Cramer had predicted for him, and of the years of adulthood ahead when his creativity would lie fallow. Then he thought of the years of adulthood Rachel would never know. He remembered her strange pronouncement: 'I don't think I shall grow up, Bernard.' His back was to his parents and sister and the tears trickled down his face.

Something soft landed on his lap. From that moment, Anna the cat became a music lover.

'My namesake; how strange.'
'Even cats must have names.'
'But it is still a curious coincidence. And you have not told me before.'
'I had forgotten.'
'You seem to have forgotten so many things. Am I responsible for the revival of these recollections?'
'You are responsible for more than recollections.'
'Ah!'
'Shall I continue with this – exorcism?'
'Is it an exorcism?'
'In a way.'

Time no longer had any meaning. With its passing Rachel's death was brought closer and became more inevitable. That was its sole significance. The house was a place of hushed voices and stealthy footsteps. It was as if she were already dead. Possibly it was worse, because they could not permit themselves the luxury of mourning.

For Bernard this period was scarcely less traumatic than it was for his parents, and had it not been for Douglas Hamilton he would have despaired.

One day between lessons, Douglas said to him, peering over his glasses, and upwards to meet his friend's unfathomable gaze: 'I say, Foligno, would it be very bad form to call each other by our first names, do you think?'

Bernard felt a sudden sweeping happiness. 'No – no, I don't see that it is,' he answered carefully.

'We could be blood brothers,' continued Douglas, assessing Bernard for a change in his expression. He was rewarded by a white-toothed smile that shone from within.

So with the pricking of fingers and rubbing together of blood they became brothers, and Douglas said: 'I wish you well, Bernard, my brother.'

And Bernard replied: 'I wish you luck, Douglas, my brother.'

'May our strength be combined.'

'And know no boundaries.'

'And the world will bow before the great pianist.'

'And tug impassioned at the sleeve of the great violinist.'

They faced each other gravely as they said this. They took themselves very seriously – even their jest was in earnest. But generally it was a period of gloom and sorrow as Rachel's deterioration continued.

Belatedly Bernard composed a serenade for Rachel's doll. But Rachel was not well enough to be brought downstairs to hear it.

'Please, Mama. If Papa carries her gently to the chaise-longue again. Please let her hear it.'

'No dear, it is not possible.'

But it will make her better, he thought. *It will be magic. Her hair will grow and she will become plump, and it will be my little piece that will have made her recover. I know it.*

'Papa –' he tried his father this time, 'please let Rachel be carried downstairs. I have written something especially for her.'

'Bernard, she must not be moved. Mr Hamilton said.'

'He could be wrong.'

43

'Are you a surgeon suddenly? Have you spent many years without my knowledge becoming erudite in the field of medicine?' Joseph said angrily, flushed with emotion.

'I just thought . . .'

'Well, think again.'

'The music might make her better,' Bernard persisted.

'Music, music –' His father almost choked with his distress. 'It is all you think about, your music. *Morphine* is what Rachel needs. Not music. You understand, Bernard? Music . . . And do not pout like that. You must learn to think of other things besides music. It is of small use in the world of commerce. Music. Oh Bernard, leave me alone. I cannot –'

Joseph stumbled from the family room, fighting back sobs, leaving Bernard limply holding the pages of his composition, knowing for certain life would never be right again, feeling the loneliness of the misunderstood. Standing there in the middle of the room, his long arms hanging uselessly, his shoulders drooping, he had a terrifying moment of identity crisis. His body trembled and his shoulders shook. He must have remained like that for ten minutes, completely unaware of anything about him, until gradually his body ceased to judder and familiar objects became defined once more.

Selina came in to check the fire, and he brushed past her without blushing as usual, and went upstairs to his room. He found a large sheet of paper and wrapped this around his 'Serenade', melted some wax to seal the package, and placed it inside a rosewood box. Another much thicker envelope already lay inside. This contained the outpouring of imaginings and impressions that could have made him a prodigy: his Summer Overture. For a moment he stared sadly at the box, then he locked it and set it on the floor of his mahogany linen press. The box with its precious contents would be put completely out of his mind and remain locked for many years.

'Do you know where it is now?'

'In the attic I imagine – alongside other relics.'

'Then you must find it, dearest. Everyone would be curious to know what you wrote as a child. You must publish it.'

'That would be a kind of vanity, I think. But I shall look for it nonetheless.'

'You promise me?'

'I have said so. I am as curious as you to see into my child's mind again.'

'It is so odd that we have not discussed all this before.'

'Not really. The present has always mattered more.'

Bernard went into Rachel's room. His parents were there; aged and ugly with sorrow. They sat either side of the brass bed like drooping sentries, and only the egg of his sister's head was visible, her arms tucked inside the covers. Bernard remembered her little peals of laughter.

'Hallo, Mama, Papa.'

'Hallo, Bernard dear.' His mother.

'Bernard, I am sorry if I was harsh to you,' his father said gruffly.

'It is all right, Papa.'

'But you must learn to be realistic.'

And isn't music realistic? 'Yes, Papa.'

'I love you, my son.'

It is an odd love – tempered with condition. 'I know, Papa.'

The nurse replaced bowls, her skirts making stiff brushing sounds.

Will her eyes never open again? 'Rachel?' Bernard sat carefully on the edge of the high bed and reached under the covers for her hand. It was like a sparrow's claw.

'Oh Rachel – and I have composed a serenade for your favourite doll. Oh Rachel.'

Extraordinarily he felt a reassuring answering pressure on his hand. Her eyes remained shut.

'Mama – Papa – she pressed my hand.'

'Bernard, she is not conscious dear,' his mother said.

'I tell you, she pressed my hand.'

He could feel it again, the soft pressure. 'I promise –'

45

'Bernard,' Joseph cut in sharply, warning. He had already given up.

Bernard said nothing further. He continued to sit between them on the bed, feeling and silently answering the pressure, drawing reassurance from it and letting his life flow into the veins of his sister. The moments of contact were extraordinary and precious. He had never felt so close to her as he did now, when outwardly she did not appear to know he was there, and her unflickering eyelids remained as smoothly shut as oysters.

She died the night after Bernard's twelfth birthday, at about eleven o'clock. December the second, ten days before Chanukah. She had not pressed his hand again, or shown any further sign of life since that day.

Rachel was washed thoroughly, doused with water and then anointed with spices, before being covered with a white inner shroud. She was buried almost immediately in consecrated ground.

Joseph was inconsolable, and again it was Helen who was the stronger; she had borne a child and now it was taken again. The family was depleted, but it was her duty to keep their unit together, to try and solder their damaged emotions. Gaunt and sallow-skinned, her very soul aching with exhaustion and restrained tears, she was hostess to a never-ending stream of visitors as the family sat 'Shivah' for a week.

Whilst prayers were held Joseph sat on a low stool, as was the tradition for an 'Avel', as such a mourner was known. It was decreed that his upper clothes be torn and his beard untrimmed, and on his feet were velvet slippers since he was not allowed to wear leather. Each evening for seven nights he recited the Kaddish to a packed room – as for the next eleven months he must continue to do so – praising God and begging him for peace and a good life.

'But what life,' he asked Helen, 'what life am I entitled to, when she had none?'

For seven days Joseph did not go to work or Bernard to school, and the atmosphere in the house was stifling. During the day Bernard would lope about silently, not knowing what to do with himself, and at night he would lie awake thinking

46

alternately of Rachel and of music. He thought a great deal of Cramer, who upon hearing Bernard's news had attempted to comfort him. But Bernard had rejected the kind and wise words of solace and advice; he had shrugged and gazed directly over his old master's head, because nothing Cramer said was now relevant.

When they had parted – there had been no lesson, since music was not permitted that week – Cramer had said: 'Do not lose sight, young sir.'

'What of, sir?'

'Remember – perspective?'

'Mine is two straight lines, sir. Now, if you forgive me I must return to my mother.'

The serious high-foreheaded face watching the lanky figure from the window was chagrined and meditative. Cramer sat down at his piano that was of his own design and played.

After seven days Bernard returned to school and Joseph to work. Helen wore black and never again wore another colour. Bernard resumed his musical studies and continued his conquering of Liszt; and whilst his fingers perfected their technique and his concentration absorbed facts, his mind divested itself of passion. He practised mechanically and with almost manic dedication, but the brilliance of his playing had a remote quality about it.

The months passed. Douglas Hamilton was the only person who probed beneath Bernard's veneer; little Douglas who never seemed to grow and was always sheltered by Bernard from the Milton Hall thugs. He forced Bernard to talk, exhausted him with his continual philosophizing and psychoanalysing, and insisted on discussing music.

Late one afternoon after school, Bernard returned with Douglas to his home in Harley Street. His mother was out visiting, his older sister with her, and the two boys had tea alone, served in the parlour by the wide-hipped Italian housemaid who kept ruffling Bernard's curls with exclamations of delight. The china was finest porcelain, and the elaborately engraved silver pot had a bone handle.

Doug takes it all for granted, Bernard thought enviously, *his* family's wealth, his talent – and his future. Why, he even has his father's approval and sees nothing unusual in that. Oh, he is so fortunate . . . His eyes became wistful as he imagined what it must be like.

Douglas set his plate down and delicately wiped the cake crumbs from his lips with the corner of a lace napkin. His violin rested beside him and, picking it up, he announced: 'I shall play you a piece by Vivaldi.'

He adjusted his position in the chair so that his back was upright and his short legs splayed a little, and with his left hand he balanced the violin under his chin. Immediately his expression became tender and he glanced briefly at Bernard, gave him a fleeting, cheery smile and began to play.

Seated across the table from him, Bernard watched his odd little companion rock and rage, caress and saw. He had heard him play before and knew that this twelve-year-old boy's formidable talent matched his own; nevertheless, the sight of his serious face with its changing stream of expressions, and the glasses slipping down his nose made Bernard want to smile. Then he was diverted by those fingers – so stubby, yet impossibly fast and nimble. He watched, fascinated by their precision and deftness.

The piece came to an end, and in true theatrical style Douglas remained poised as he was for a moment or so, before relaxing and setting down his violin. He gave a mock bow in his chair to Bernard.

'I have mastered that piece, I think,' he said modestly, scratching his nose where his glasses had rubbed.

'You are excellent, Doug.' Bernard leaned forward and patted his friend on the shoulder.

'No more so than you. And I cannot compose.'

'Oh – that . . .' Bernard's voice trailed away and he averted his eyes from his friend's piercing gaze. His Summer Overture was in the past.

Douglas changed the subject: 'When I leave school I shall go either to the Vienna Conservatory, or the Conservatoire de Musique et Declamation in Paris.' He spoke with an easy casualness.

'I know someone who is soon going to Paris,' Bernard said reflectively. 'She is a singing pupil of my mother's. Her name is Sophie. She has a fine singing voice.' As he spoke of Sophie, he could hear her voice and imagine her grave eyes staring ahead as she sang. He had not seen her for a while, as his mother had still not recommenced her lessons, and when he thought about her now it was with an intense longing.

Douglas was saying rather grandly: 'I have still not decided which would be better for me. I quite favour studying under Mayseder in Vienna, but is not the idea of Paris enchanting? I shall just have to see.' He gave a neat little shrug. 'I mean to say there is still time, and meanwhile there is so much to master. One day I shall play Bach's Partitas perfectly, especially the Chaconne. I shall make it sound so simple people will wonder what all the fuss is about. And although it is frowned upon, I shall use a chin rest. I shall be a thoroughly modern violinist and I shall shock the world. Wouldn't it be wonderful, Bernard, if you and I could perform together, become famous together?'

'It will not be possible.'

'Why not?'

'Because my future is not as a musician. You *know* that already, Douglas –' His voice rose in frustration and he glared at his friend. 'I have told you so, so many times,' he continued, running his hands through his hair in his agitation. 'I have told you *repeatedly*.'

'And I do not believe you,' the other said with annoying calm.

'Well, you had better, for it is true.' Bernard turned his back in a huff.

'Then,' said Douglas, relentless, 'you are particularly imbecilic – and not fit to be my blood brother.' That was most wounding of all.

But Douglas was the determined defender of Bernard's well-being, the retainer of his soul, and they went everywhere together. When it became apparent that Douglas was intellectually far ahead of the rest of his class and therefore in favour with the masters, because of their friendship, greater interest was taken in Bernard, and as the boy matured his talent could no longer go ignored. Milton Hall was a school with a fine musical reputation, and if there was a child with potential then that child was encouraged and made a member of the school orchestra. Both friends were selected as soloists, and Bernard felt a cynical sense of irony: only a few months ago he would have been mad with delight at such an accolade; now he must not allow the honour to be significant.

How funny, he thought, *one must learn to enjoy what one does not enjoy, and to not enjoy what one does enjoy.*

It was a hard lesson at the age of twelve.

It was autumn – over a year since his Summer Overture. Cramer asked: 'Young sir, is it not time you tried your hand once more at composition?'

Bernard stuttered and flushed and found no words to reply.

'Ah, I see it – you have outgrown your musical passions. Your fingers are mere implements. The rest, it is not sufficiently sophisticated for a future city gentleman.'

He could not bear the sarcasm in his old master's voice, or the recriminating sadness in the eyes. Briefly he felt resentment. His chin quivered and steadied, his lower lip jutted, and he was silent. Cramer had no right to taunt him. He of all people should have understood.

Much later, back home where a semblance of normality had been resumed – his mother had even recommenced her singing tuition – Bernard said to his father: 'Papa, I have a request to make of you.'

'Yes, Bernard, what is that?'

Joseph had aged. He was forty but looked ten years older, and his pale eyes that Rachel had inherited were tired and gentle.

'Papa, I should like to visit the Stock Exchange with you. Soon. Would it be permitted? I should be most interested to do so, and I should appreciate it if you would explain some rudimentary things in connection with the business.'

'My son, come here.'

Bernard got up from his seat and walked over to his father,

who pulled him onto the edge of his own chair and put his arms around him. His eyes watered with emotion as he said:

'You have made me very, very happy. I am so proud to hear you ask what you have asked. You have no idea how happy it has made me. You will become a fine businessman, and it will give me great joy to take you to the Stock Exchange and show you around. It is not for nothing we Jews are successful. We are astute and shrewd in the world of commerce, Bernard. Are the Rothschilds to be sneered at? One day in the future the Jews will be the strongest business force in London. You will be very proud, my son, of your heritage, and to have succeeded despite the odds, and to be amongst such happenings.'

'Yes, Papa.'

'When you are thirteen, my son. I shall take you with me then, I promise.'

Helen looked at them both, understanding each better than they understood themselves. But the important thing was, in that moment of self-delusion there existed harmony and, whatever the reason, one could only be grateful for it and pray it stayed that way.

That night Joseph's hand reached for his wife's. 'He is to be our reward my dear, I feel it.'

'Joseph, you must not attach so much importance to his future. It is unfair to him.'

'My dear, but you have seen. It came from him. Himself. His heart. The words came from his very heart.'

'I hope so.'

'She hopes so! Ah women! Never satisfied unless they can manifest something to worry about. I *know* my boy, Helen. And he has made me so happy. The music – it was a passing phase.'

He slept more soundly than he had done since Rachel's death, secure in the knowledge he would build and build for his son, and his son would build for *his* son, and so it might continue.

The following morning at the school prayers which Bernard always attended alongside the Christian boys, they recited the words:

51

'When I was a child I believeth as a child and spaketh as a child, but when I became a man I spaketh as a man and I put away childish things . . .'

Amen.

Chapter Four

Bernard's voice broke. It seemed to happen almost overnight. His bar-mitzvah, which was so soon, changed from being something he was longing for to a prospect he could only dread. How could he possibly sing his 'portion' from the Torah scroll with a voice that sounded like a burst from a ship's funnel?

'Papa, I refuse to sing it,' Bernard told his father wildly. 'I shall recite it instead. I refuse, I refuse. You must not make me.'

'How harsh you make me seem, Bernard. You speak of my "making you". You attack me in order to defend yourself from the attack you are sure I shall inflict! Before I answer, may I explain something to you? May I ask you something?'

'What?' Bernard replied sulkily.

'"What," he says. You see, you have no faith or trust in your father that you cannot answer an unqualified "yes, Papa."'

'Yes, Papa.'

'The question first and maybe it will render the explanation unnecessary: What, Bernard, is the purpose and meaning of a bar-mitzvah?'

The boy answered without hesitation and in flat monotones, because it was a question his Hebrew master had posed him many times: 'A bar-mitzvah, meaning "Son of the Commandment" is a ceremony to celebrate a thirteen-year-old boy's attainment of maturity, when he must take upon himself the "Yoke of the Commandments".'

'And?'

'It is embarrassing.'

'I am asking you to continue.'

'And the appearance of sexual characteristics is important in deciphering whether or not a boy or girl is truly male or female, in order that he be permitted to marry.'

'And do grown, uncastrated males have female voices like you did just a week ago?'

'No.'

'I am proud of you, my son; of the man you are becoming. I find that I have a great deal to look forward to. I am proud that on the occasion of your bar-mitzvah you will openly be declaring your manhood. I wish, therefore, to hear no more on the subject.'

'Papa, I *want* to recite it.' As he shouted his voice cracked, and he ran from the room, almost crying with shame and the old rage which had never quite left him.

'We always make ourselves out to be different,' he complained to Douglas at school. 'All boys' voices break – why must we make such an issue of everything? Then as soon as a Gentile has the affrontery to accuse us of being different we tell him he is prejudiced.'

'You know, you always say "we" when you talk of the Jews. It is never "them", but "we".'

'So?'

'So you class yourself as Jewish not English.'

'I can be both.'

'No, you cannot. You have to choose.'

'Why?'

'Because you cannot belong to two races. And when you have selected one, then you are apart from the other.'

'But my family has been in England for generations.'

'They have been Jews for longer. If there were a conflict between the English and the Jews, which side would you choose?'

'It would never happen.'

'That is not the point, dear chap. Go on choose.' Douglas looked sternly at Bernard over the rims of his glasses, his funny round face pushed forward like that of a pink-nosed cat.

'You enjoy drilling me, don't you?'

'You raised the subject, and you have not answered my question.'

Bernard hesitated; but he had known the answer all along. Anger filled him, and shame. And shame at his shame. 'All right, then. I would choose the Jews. Us. Yes we are different, different, different. And I *hate* it.'

They did not speak for nearly three days. On the third day a mathematical problem which needed a greater ability than Bernard's seemed like a reasonable excuse to break their unhappy silence. That afternoon, to show good faith, they went once more through the ritual of pricking fingers and mingling blood.

For the fortnight before the great day, Helen made him swallow an entire raw egg each morning, and as it slid down his throat he fought against retching it up directly. She fussed over arrangements: on the Saturday after the service there would be Kiddush, where sweet cakes and biscuits and the garnet-coloured, rich wine would be offered; three days later there was to be a large party with an orchestra. All the family had been invited, and many friends with their children. Helen had two brothers, who did not speak to each other, and she prevaricated over which brother to invite, before finally becoming so impatient with the situation that she asked both.

'It is outrageous that I should have to choose,' she fumed to her husband. 'I will not risk alienating myself from one to please the other. They are petty. Such quarrelling should not happen in families. It is always over money. Where money is concerned, the nicest people become unrecognizable. Even the cousins do not talk, and Harold in particular is exceptionally vindictive. I find him increasingly ungracious. And he is so conceited, strutting about with his aspirations to become a barrister. I always have the feeling when he speaks with one, that he is thinking how best he can use that person. Even at his age. However, he is my nephew, and I must not say such things.'

Every day more presents arrived for the embryo man, and meanwhile, in front of a mirror, Bernard gloomily rehearsed his speech. Finally the day itself arrived, just before the first anniversary of Rachel's death. Yahrzeit and mourning for the dead child; pride and hopes for the living one. Too many hopes.

He dressed with great care and brushed his thick, unruly hair back from his forehead. It was a fine broad forehead, so pale that the black eyebrows were emphatic insects set at obtuse angles. He tied his silk cravat precisely and fixed it with a gold pin which had been one of his presents, and finally slid on his patent pumps. They were new and squeezed his toes. He practised chanting a few notes. He had been perfecting a different technique for the last two weeks, sucking the sound from his stomach so that, whilst the result was rather gruff and jerky, at least its pitch remained balanced.

The synagogue was packed – the women elegant in the gallery above; and around him the men, nodding congratulations, nodding their private prayers, caught his eye to smile. He was hero of the day. Beside him on one side was his Hebrew master, his catarrhal breath reeking hotly; and on the other his father, already much shorter than Bernard and very bald now, which was concealed by the grey tophat. His blue eyes were blatant with pleasure at his grown son, as though no other man had ever watched his child become an adult.

The moment arrived; he was called up to help carry the Torah from the arc, then unveil it and chant his piece. He was already at the front, and he climbed the four shallow steps to the 'bimah', his heart beating fast and his gaze directly forward. He was aware of, rather than saw, everyone's eyes on him. The rabbi smiled encouragingly, and the cantor emulated him routinely with thin dry lips. Bernard moistened his own with the tip of his tongue and cleared his dry throat. He felt disorientated. Carefully he drew back the embroidered curtain draped in front of the arc, and with the rabbi's assistance lifted out the heavy Torah. At this point his feeling of detachedness dissipated and he was overcome with a great surge of unexpected emotion. He felt profoundly honoured, aware of a sense of history; and because he was partaking in this timeless history he was a piece of it, and was therefore immortal.

With trembling hands he removed the two ornate and pointed silver cups which dressed the wooden spires, whilst the rabbi nodded encouragement and held the sacred readings with an experienced, steady grip. Next came the lush blue velvet with its fringing and gold embroidered Hebrew writing. It slid smoothly off like a sensuous woman pulling a dress over her shoulders, and revealed the rolled parchment. This he unrolled and began to read from – those prayers and laws that were unchanged for thousands of years. The letters leaped iniquitously before him, but it did not matter for he knew the words and their significance by heart. He was so gloriously proud. He sucked in his stomach, and in his new, man's voice boldly sung his portion while intermittently other male voices grunted and muttered and chanted. Afterwards, when his father was called up to read, their eyes caught and held, emanating a raw emotion which belonged to a moment that would never be repeated.

Later in the hall there was Kiddush, but it had been decided to withhold the speeches until the party on Tuesday night. Everybody clapped him on the back, and he was pushed forward from person to person, dizzy with his own success and still vaguely disorientated.

The evening of the party arrived. Downstairs in the big drawing-room, which doubled as a ballroom, the expanse of parquet flooring had been cleared of its usual furniture, and gleamed as a result of Selina's early morning toil on her hands and knees. Tables had been set up for more than a hundred guests, and the starched white cloths were like nun's habits. A quartet, consisting of a pianist, violinist, cellist and clarinetist, had already assembled and was organizing sheets of music, stands and stools. Hired staff were adding final touches to the tables, whilst his mother fiddled with the flower arrangements. Her dress, as usual, was black, but she had made the concession of pinning an exquisitely perfect orchid to the dark lace at her breast. Her hair was looped and simply dressed with tortoise-shell combs. Yet the severity of her attire seemed only to emphasize her serenity.

Everything was shining and reflecting, and when Bernard wandered into the room he was amazed by its transfiguration from mundaneness to a place so splendid and enchanting. All this to celebrate his manhood! In fact, only this very evening he had peered closely into his toilet mirror and found a few stray curling hairs grouped round his chin. He had gazed at them with astonished curiosity and tugged at them to ascertain their reality. One had come away between his fingers and he had mourned its loss. Now in this glittering room, decorated fit to celebrate a prince's birthday, he felt somewhat self-important.

Standing tall between his parents, he shook hands and kissed discreetly powdered cheeks. His two estranged uncles arrived almost simultaneously, faced each other appalled, and then turned on Helen.

Joseph told them sternly, 'There will be no scenes to spoil this special occasion. Whoever wishes to depart is free to do so. We will not take sides in private feuds, and we have picked tonight to celebrate, not to perpetuate a quarrel. That is your prerogative, and Helen and I would prefer it if you conducted it elsewhere.'

Bernard noticed his father's hands were clenched in tension. Harold and the other cousins stared at each other disdainfully, and the two wives looked distressed and helpless. Helen's hands were trembling, and one went instinctively towards the smooth orchid and fingered its form. Watching her unconscious reaction Bernard felt a wave of protectiveness towards her, and of respect towards his father for shielding her, and for the first time he thought of them as people and not just as his parents. He stroked his mother's bony wrist, then glared at each uncle in turn, the two bristling, pent-up brothers whose business differences had destroyed their affection and caused them to forget they had once been small boys playing together in the nursery.

Entering the room he could see a face he knew – Sophie's. She was with her parents, and was partially hidden by her father's stoutness. Bernard had not seen her for months – her lessons with his mother had coincided with his own with Cramer – and now at the sight of her almost grown-up, in her ice-blue silk gown cut modestly low, her dark hair shining richly, he felt his heart pounding.

'Excuse me. Excuse me . . . may I pass please . . .' *I have to see her.*

'Hallo, Sophie.' His voice shot upwards in falsetto, and the blood of embarrassment rushed to his cheeks.

'Oh hallo, Bernard.' When she smiled her rather small mouth parted to reveal little, very white, teeth.

'I did not know you would be coming.'

'Why not? Our parents are friends.'

'I had forgotten that.'

He was struck mute, his arms dangling. He fixed his eyes despairingly on her face.

'Congratulations on your bar-mitzvah, Bernard.'

Even her speaking voice was beautifully modulated. A true singer's voice.

'Thank you. The worst is to come.'

'The worst?'

'My speech. I dread it.'

'Oh, you will do well I am sure. I thought you were very good in synagogue on Saturday.'

'You were there?'

'Of course. How is your piano-playing coming along? Are you still studying with Cramer?'

'Yes I am, although there are other things that matter now besides, which keep me busy.'

How Cramer would have sorrowed to hear him speak in such a way.

'Such as?'

She pries so. She makes me feel disquieted . . . Has she not lovely eyes?

'There is school work, which I must take seriously now, as when I leave I shall join my father as a stockbroker.'

'That will be most interesting.'

'Yes it will be. There are only six Jews –'

'These are my parents.'

'How do you do?'

'I remember you when you were a little boy. You are so big now.'

I must ask Sophie to dance. Harold will do so otherwise. I cannot ask her. She seems so adult. . . .

Her parents were talking to some other guests. Sophie was half-smiling at him, almost expectantly it seemed.

'May I . . . Will you dance with me later on?'

'Yes, if you'd like me to. Thank you.'

But before he could dance with her there was the lavish dinner, and then speeches: a toast to him, an emotional speech by his father, and then Bernard's reply. He stumbled heavily to his feet, his notes in his hand trembling like leaves in autumn as they clung to their branches. He tried to clear his throat, but the saliva became a thick block which would not be dislodged. He felt slightly drunk too, and strangely disembodied.

The notes were upside down. Everyone was waiting expectantly, the men remembering how they had felt many years before.

'Thank you Papa, for the kind things you have said . . .' He gazed down at his shining shoes of which he had been so proud, and suddenly thought he had been as vain as Harold. '. . . Mama, for making such a wonderful evening . . .'

He looked up and saw her biting her quivering upper lip. Never had he seen her cry, not even at Rachel's funeral. 'Thank you, Mama,' he whispered, as though there was no one else in the room. Then: 'Ladies and gentlemen –' he forgot to suck in his stomach muscles and his voice cracked. The drunken feeling returned, and with it the departure of his inhibitions. '– As you'll no doubt notice my voice is in the midst of breaking. This is, I'm afraid, unavoidable, so I shall not apologize for what I cannot help . . .'

Amidst laughter he continued, speaking for about ten minutes in all, until there was nothing more to say and he sank into his chair, drained yet exultant.

He danced with Sophie. Her hand was dry and cool in his own, and she held his firmly and almost proprietorially.

'You spoke awfully well.'

'Thank you.'

'You were very witty.'

'Really? Was I really?'

'Yes you were, really. You – look more than thirteen.'

'Do I? It is difficult to tell oneself. How old are you now?'

'Sixteen. I shall be going to the Conservatoire in a year.'

'You are very lucky to be going . . .' He took a deep breath. 'You look very pretty tonight.'

'I am too fat.' She said it without guile.

He had not noticed her body. In his innocence he hadn't thought of her female form at all. Now he was forced to look. She was quite short, and her waist was certainly not well-defined; her breasts although decently concealed, were obviously large, and her bare arms revealed below the elbows were rounded, the flesh soft and creamy. There was grace in her plumpness and whilst she had a prematurely matronly appearance, to Bernard she represented beauty incarnate.

Later he danced with his mother, and when he looked round the room, searching for a glimpse of Sophie, he saw her dancing with Harold. He felt a surge of jealousy and tried to catch her eye. Was she enjoying dancing with Harold more than with him? Then she smiled at him, and it seemed that his heart was clenched and then released slowly.

He meant to dream about her that night, but instead fell into a deep and empty sleep, and when he awoke the following morning it was with a heavy sense of deflation. Nothing was different after all. And when would he see Sophie again? Oh, he was so young. Being thirteen did not set you free.

'So young sir, you have had your bar-mitzvah. How did the occasion fare?'

'I believe it went well.'

'And did you read your speech or memorize it?'

'It sort of happened. Some of it was memorized – the rest just happened.'

'That is how all the best public speakers operate. And if you are to be a successful businessman, then the chances are you may have to make many speeches.'

Bernard studied his old master to see if he was mocking him. Increasingly he began to feel disquieted in his presence, that Cramer was scornful of him and deliberately trying to make him feel uncomfortable. But nothing in the fine, seamed face appeared spurious, and the eyes were benign and caring.

Oh Cramer. Oh sir –

His heart called out and he could not say the words, but the teacher was satisfied to see in that brief moment of unveiled expression the boy he recognized as his old pupil.

'Come, young sir, you might think composition beneath you after your flight of glory, but composition is what we are going to tackle this afternoon; two-part composition. For two instruments. One day you might find it useful . . . Shall we say piano and violin? Shall we pretend it is Liszt playing the piano, and Paganini's ghost the violin?'

'Douglas and I?' the boy murmured.

'What is that, Bernard?'

'My friend Douglas and I sometimes pretend that I am Liszt and he, Paganini.'

'I should like to meet your friend. He is a good friend?'

Bernard hesitated before confiding to Cramer their secret: 'We are blood brothers.'

'I do not understand.' Cramer sat on his music stool surveying the boy standing in front of him. 'How can he be your brother?'

'To become blood brothers you must care very deeply for another person, and then you cut or prick your fingers – each of you – and rub those fingers together to mingle the blood. You will not tell?'

'I shall not tell. But is it wrong then, what you did? Why do you wish it not to be known?'

'It is not in the least wrong. But it is very private.'

'I understand, young sir. Oh yes, I do indeed understand. So – next week why not bring him to your lesson? I should like to hear you play together. Besides, it is good training.'

For what? He tried not to look forward with all his heart to the next week.

'Bernard,' his father said that evening, 'I have a surprise for you.'

'Yes Papa?'

'I have arranged for permission for you to be shown around the Stock Exchange.'

'And – what was it like? How did you react to it all?'

'We travelled by cab together early in the morning, and my father told me for the tenth time how the Stock Exchange had originated in Jonathan's Coffee House in Change Alley eighty years previously. When we at last arrived, other dark-suited men nodded soberly and raised their hats to Papa, and he glanced at me. His eyes said: You see they know I am a Jew and they respect me.

'I was allowed on the "floor" – a rare and almost unheard-of honour for a non-member, and generally I was made much of. But later, in a candid moment, my father said – and I can hear him saying it – "Bernard, these people never forget for a moment you are a Jew. As soon as your back is turned they will discuss you. But your birthright is the key to your ability. Jews are known to be shrewd with money. Gentiles might dislike you, but they will come to you for your business acumen. They will glean all they can and invite you to their club, but never their home. No, never their home."

'Later we went to his office which consisted of two smallish cream-painted rooms above a barber's shop in the city. I met the young assistant, named Arthur, a tall youth with ferocious acne, and was plied with coffee whilst my father rustled through papers and documents and a young messenger handed over information from whichever source he had gleaned it.

'We left the office and had our hair cut downstairs, sitting beside one another, swathed in white towels and discussing share prices and new companies. I have to say I felt puffed with importance and sophistication. After the barber had finished with us my father showed me the Royal Exchange, and then the Bank of England with its fine, pillared façade and statues. I recall it was snowing and the flakes lay trapped in the brim of Papa's hat, like a moat. The pavements were polished and slippery, and he took my arm and we ran until we were finally able to find an unoccupied cab. My father was panting from exertion and I helped him up the steps. He was so small and light.

'We were very close for those hours and it was a great day in my life, yet our closeness was based on deception: my father was joyful because of my apparent interest, and I was joyful because of the way I was being treated as an adult. But there you go – there are more relationships than not which thrive on some kind of deception.

'The following afternoon Douglas and I played together for the first time at Cramer's.'

It was the school holidays and Bernard took a cab from Bayswater to Kensington. He had not told his mother about the afternoon, and when she kissed him goodbye she noticed his cheeks were unexpectedly flushed and hot.

'Bernard dear – your skin feels burning. Perhaps you are ill –'

'I am perfectly well, Mama, truly.' He made an irritable clicking sound with his teeth.

The driver was waiting, but Helen gripped Bernard by the shoulders, possessive now over her remaining child.

'Dear, perhaps you are sickening. You feel feverish.'

'Mama, I promise I am well,' he insisted in a frustrated tone. 'I shall be late . . .' He tried to sound calm. 'Please, Mama.'

'If you are sure.' Her voice was small.

He knew then he had won. He hugged her, 'I shall be fine,' and stepped gladly into the cab.

All the way there he battled against his excitement and the thrilling sense of anticipation at playing with Douglas under Cramer's guidance. He knew it would be a rare musical experience and as such he was fearful of it, not wishing to have music dwelling in him any more. But it was too colossal a thing to fight against.

That afternoon with the three of them in the room, sharing like-thoughts and like-pleasure, whilst the atmosphere of music gnawed at them – that afternoon was quite simply magical to Bernard.

Cramer sat beside him at the piano, frail and wise, and Douglas sat opposite – little and intense, and silenced for once. Outside the rain streamed down the windows in fast-flowing rivulets, and inside the warm condensation misted the glass and hindered their vision. It was, therefore, as though nothing existed beyond that room with its engrossed occupants and delightful air of expectancy. They were totally absorbed, discussing, elaborating upon a point and then emphasizing it by a short phrase on the piano or violin.

'Bernard, it is time you attempted conducting,' Cramer said. 'I have, as you know, always been scornful of conductors, regarding them as superfluous. However, it is necessary for you to learn.'

'But sir, I would never be able to do it.'

'Rubbish, young sir. You are always so very negative. Do you find that, young Douglas?'

'Oh yes, sir,' Douglas agreed disloyally. 'Definitely. And he is so jolly *guilty* the whole time. I have told him it must be a typical streak in –'

'Be quiet, Doug. That is quite untrue and most unfair.'

'Dear chap, I could quote you a dozen examples –'

'All contrived.'

'Boys, boys!' Cramer laughed. 'I refuse to be diverted. Now Bernard, you *are* going to attempt to conduct, whilst your friend plays, and then I shall listen whilst you and he play.'

'And what about Douglas?' Bernard said in a disgruntled tone. 'Are we going to see him conducting?'

'Oh yes, most certainly. His turn will come.'

Douglas groaned.

'Now young man, you may position yourself – so. And Bernard – so. That is very fine. Now for the Mozart. Are you ready?'

Bernard lifted his arms and Douglas began to play. Every so often Bernard would fling his arms too high and Cramer would grab them, calling him a wild man. Douglas would stop his playing, and there was much laughter. But amidst the laughter there was seriousness and single-minded concentration, and Bernard – enjoying himself now – longed to arc his arms wide to encompass the notes, to be part of the sounds his friend was producing; he wanted their span to embrace the entire world which he knew by rights should be his.

'And now it is time to play together. The prepared Beethoven please.'

Cramer watched the two boys with interest; the one introverted, with the height of a grown man and build of a gangling youth; the other underdeveloped but with a rare awareness and self-assurance. And both so talented. What a pleasure it was to hear them! The old man leaned back in his chair and closed his eyes, but even with his eyes closed he could clearly picture them. How valuable music was, he thought; how close it brought people; how tragic his young sir could not make it his career. . . .

But just then Bernard was not thinking of his future; he was immersing himself utterly in these moments and sharing them with Douglas – giving, taking, submitting, asserting – and they would catch one another's eye and smile. Such precious moments.

Outside the light failed. It was time to finish. Unaccountably Bernard was afraid; he was confused, disturbed by the power of his own feelings, and when Cramer suggested a further such meeting the following week, he vehemently refused, hurting Cramer with his rebuff as much as he hurt himself. For with that refusal he denied and negated the superlative afternoon.

'Oh dearest, you were so stubborn! Why could you not just have accepted things as they were?'

'Because I was conditioning myself to become something else. Because I was just what you said – stubborn. And a child . . . Anyway, instead therefore of returning home in the good spirits merited by the afternoon, I was aware of having damaged something terribly special. When I arrived back I was in a muddled and angry mood, and filled with a bitterness directed alternately at Cramer and at my father; at whatever was responsible for the shortcomings of my life.

'To make matters worse, when I went inside I found my cousin Harold already there; Papa was friendly with a barrister and Harold wished to enquire about him. He remained for dinner and talked solidly about himself and his wretched future. During dinner he did not once address me. Only afterwards did he condescend to talk to me, and then it was only in order to find out more about Sophie. . . .'

*

Bernard imagined Harold visiting her, walking across the drawing-room of her house in his squeaky shoes, smiling that self-satisfied smile. He imagined them sitting opposite one another, discussing – what? What did a boy and girl discuss? At thirteen he had little idea. Sophie was three years older or more. And Harold was almost sixteen – still too young to go courting on his own; but the thought of Harold being chaperoned during his wooing efforts did nothing to assuage Bernard's jealousy, and the pain in his chest was so powerful he could not believe it was caused by mere emotion.

He went to bed that night unhappy for several reasons, and lay for a long time gazing upwards at a ring of light on the ceiling. Within that ring he saw first Harold's face, then Sophie's, and then he saw three animated people in a certain room in Kensington. That image lingered longest.

Chapter Five

It was early October, 1857, but cold like winter. Pavements and cobbles were drenched from the continual onslaught of rain, and black water settled in crevices and pits. Trees were already prematurely bereft of leaves, so bad had the gales been, and the skeletal shapes of elms were like the spines of fish.

Recovering from a mild bout of the influenza, a rug wrapped around him up to his armpits, Cramer began a letter to his friend, Sir Edmund Moore, music critic and publisher. In his tremulous old man's hand he wrote:

I do not know what to do: here I have as a student the most gifted young musician I have seen for years – and I am at my wits' end! He is determined to enter the world of commerce, obsessed as he is with the need to gratify his father and assure himself of his 'Britishness' into the bargain. The first is surely a noble and commendable-enough reason, but one that I fear will repercuss badly ultimately.

This boy is a truly complex character, which of course can be advantageous where creativity is concerned, but he will not channel the complexities in the direction they naturally seek. Instead he denounces them. He is determined to re-arrange his own person to conform to a type that will prove acceptable to his father. His name is Bernard Foligno, and he is a Jew. He views this factor as a consideration before all else, being nonetheless obviously confused by the issue of his religion versus day-to-day living. This sort of conflict is so alien to me that

I cannot always keep my patience. It is not the way in which I view God.

As a result of his continual inner war Bernard is inhibited and introverted, although he affects a kind of bravado and has a dry wit. But then one realizes he scarcely smiles; when he does, his smile is so beatific it illuminates his whole face. But it is gone almost directly. Sometimes I long almost to drown him – and afterwards to raise him to the surface laughing with the joy of re-birth.

It is a tragedy. I feel so helpless. I cannot stand to see such great talent go to waste. His piano playing is technically perfect, although at present barren of emotion. But that is there. I know it; for when he was no more than eleven or twelve, he played with the passion of a poet thwarted in love – but then, of course, he lacked the technique. The two combined, my dear Edmund, would be a 'tour de force'. He never needs to use music, and memorizes quite formidably complicated and lengthy pieces. However, I feel it is as a composer that his future lies. Again, as a mere child he wrote some delightful works, in particular one he entitled 'Summer Overture', which I was quite prepared to publish. More recently he has written shorter, quite complicated pieces which are beautifully balanced and considered. They have a harsh melancholy which is certainly most revealing, although I am careful to appear non-committal.

Why now do I write of this boy, whom I once felt was my protégé, and still love almost as a son, despite the fact that he looks upon me nowadays with suspicion? I write because I feel that I have failed, and it bothers me.

We are all mortal (more's the pity), and when one achieves the age of eighty-six, one is increasingly aware of that fact. I should have liked to have seen Bernard established as a leading musician before I died. I have lived in this country since I was three, long enough to know that he is what England needs: a composer with ingenuity, passion, brilliance and accuracy. My life has been varied, full, and by most standards, successful. I have accomplished, by good fortune, more than I set out to, and found much that has been rewarding on the way. But young Bernard Foligno is my thorn in all this, Edmund. I have one hope – that his friend Douglas Hamilton, a violinist about whom I am sure you will one day hear a great deal, might try and sway his opinions, but the problem is that these opinions have their origins as far back as Abraham, and it is difficult to fight with ghosts from the Bible. . . .

Bernard was now almost seventeen, and had grown another three or so inches, standing at just over six feet one inch in his stockinged feet. Sport was greatly favoured at Milton Hall, and his wide shoulders and developed leg muscles were the result of daily physical exercise of one kind or another, but particularly rowing. Despite this he remained a fairly lethargic boy by nature, only exercising because it was expected of him, and not because he derived much enjoyment from it. His facial changes were subtle but distinctive: flesh padded the high broad cheekbones which had previously been too prominent, and now the line from cheek to jaw-bone was strong and smooth. The stubborn cleft chin had become more powerful, balancing his nose and wide brow over which his black hair curled loosely. Nor was his paleness so extreme – perhaps he had been anaemic on account of his rapid rate of growth. And outlining the contours of this rather remarkable face was the dark shadow of early manhood, heavier around his full-lipped mouth and chin where he shaved. It was both a severe and a sensitive face, entirely without lightness of emotion except when he smiled. Only then did the flatness of his dark eyes apparently dissolve so that the irises seemed compounded of softness.

He had finally grown into himself, daily and imperceptively altering, clowning his way through these bodily modulations – a clever-talking boy whose witticisms would be uttered in gravel-like tones and accompanied by an expression that betrayed no hint as to whether or not he was jesting. This was the boy who led the school orchestra brilliantly, and then resigned because he had 'lost interest'. Douglas had been furious – had bullied, nagged and scolded him like a terrier at a quietly stubborn labrador, but Bernard remained obstinate and Douglas himself was given the position.

Bernard loved four people and one cat in his life. The four people were his parents, Douglas, and Cramer. But he was also capable of deep dislike – currently directed at his scripture master who taught Latin besides and was not well-disposed towards Jews, and who had a habit of flicking his black robe angrily around him whenever Bernard addressed him; a fellow-pupil who felt he should be in the first rowing eight instead of Bernard, and finally and more seriously his cousin Harold, who now spent much more time at their home since his father had moved to a house just a block away.

Harold was a solitary, secretive young man. The time had long passed since he had craved friendship and offered his own without an ulterior purpose. He could barely remember – or perhaps he chose to forget – that as a young child he had been eager and tender-hearted and had pursued relationships with other children, desiring only to be liked. But he had unintentionally damaged every potential friendship, one after the other, with his domineering attitude and sudden bouts of spitefulness. And once again he would be on his own. Afterwards Harold was always mortified, failing to comprehend what he had done wrong, and becoming increasingly mistrustful, feeling himself outcast.

In his own home Harold was a different character: there his mother ruled. A short square-set woman with Harold's features, she reigned with unbending dominance, strictness and religious devoutness and Harold was completely in awe of her, constantly seeking her approval and affection and never receiving either.

His father, that avaricious older brother of Helen, was weak and ineffectual. Cowed by his wife's aggression, he deferred absolutely to her and tolerated every insult she levelled at him without complaint. He went on business for longer and longer periods, leaving the boy to the mother's discipline, and the

71

more dependent on her strength Harold became, and the more desirous of her love, the more aloof she was with him.

Harold began to vent his resentment on others. It gave him a heady feeling of power, and he enjoyed watching an expression change from pleasure to bewildered hurt. Away from home he could forget that within it he was a timid, submissive mouse, and he developed a sense of cunning, coupled with an all-consuming need to succeed. Yet, whilst within him festered an instinctive antagonism towards nearly everyone he met, he never rid himself of that deep-rooted longing for a normal family life.

Then his mother died unexpectedly after a brief illness, and Harold was shattered; not a single disloyal thought towards her crossed his mind. He wept for many days and suffered for many weeks, and then like a mole instinctively finding its way, he sought out an alternative home to provide him with his sense of family.

Gone were the intimate Friday nights. Now Harold and his father would join the Folignos for Shabat dinners and afterwards, when they gathered around the piano, Harold always sang louder than anyone, dragging the notes so that they would be heard last. And the choice of songs was always his, for he would launch into one before the others could make a suggestion. During the week he would come on his own, and amble in heavily, short and frog-like in physique, grinning superciliously.

The Folignos were tolerant, pandered to this youth who had just lost his mother and whose father was always travelling, and Harold increasingly spent his time in their home, dictating their ways and directing conversation so that it belonged solely to him. As a barrister he had cast himself well. And this was another thing: he had the advantage over Bernard in that he was already a law student, whereas Bernard was not due to leave Milton Hall until the end of the summer term. He was a schoolboy still, whereas Harold aged nineteen donned his city clothes each day. Bernard had even seen him use a *cane*, one with an ivory handle and a brass-tipped end.

One evening before dinner, feeling pleasantly relaxed after the bath he had taken in his room, Bernard sat before the piano. He was on his own except for the cat curled on his thighs, and the fire crackled and lent an orange warmth to the room. He was rapt in concentration when his cousin walked in. Harold sat down and picked up a copy of *The Times*, proceeding to rustle the pages and bite noisily into an apple he had just taken from the fruitbowl.

'Quite right,' he muttered intermittently, disregarding the angry slump of Bernard's back. 'Who do they think they are?' Then: 'I am heartily weary of Palmerston and the Whigs and their party . . . And Gladstone, the pious preacher – he is giving the country's money away. Disraeli was the perfect Chancellor. That man, mark my words, will be Prime Minister one day. How can a country that is continually growing in terms of technology and attaining new levels of understanding – how can such a country fully exploit and explore every opening available when the government changes every twenty months? To achieve stability there must first be stability behind one!'

His last sentence was almost shouted. He was Harold the Orator, addressing his invisible flock. This was the rehearsal for Things to Come.

Bernard was attempting to compose a complicated piano piece and he could not concentrate with anyone present, least of all Harold. He had heard nothing his cousin had said, only the sound of the conceited voice.

Out of perversity he said flatly, 'I disagree.'

'But how can you not agree? I have merely stated facts.'

'What facts?' Enquired in a disgruntled tone, as he scrawled the initials A.C., and further on, an A sharp in the treble clef.

'The fact is, we need a Conservative government with someone like Disraeli heading it for several years at least.'

'Palmerston is practically a Conservative,' Bernard mumbled, his back still to Harold. 'What is wrong with England the way she is?'

The music was going from him. It was seeping away. He could almost see it, like a mass of treacle. How he hated Harold! To have to discuss politics when he was in a creative mood was practically obscene.

The would-be lawyer could not be repressed. 'Nothing, in answer to your question. However, that is more by good fortune than good judgement. We are living in fortunate times since the Crimean War is over.'

Now Bernard spun round, his eyes smouldering with fury, invoked not so much by his political beliefs as by his intense dislike of this bull-necked youth with his lank, mouse-coloured hair, fat wet lips and reptilian light-brown eyes.

'I suppose the poor, who are become a forgotten breed now that the new middle-class is established – I suppose the poor, the eleven percent unemployed, the families living on five shillings a week, can all be casually waved aside. I suppose all these people consider themselves blessed.'

'My goodness! Quite the young liberal, aren't we? I see you have the romantic ideals peculiar to most schoolboys. In this world, Bernard – the real world – there is always opportunity for the man who is prepared to further himself. Anyone who is self-motivated can forge ahead.'

He stretched his short neck, pleased with himself, and swivelled his head from right to left and back again, before taking a further bite from his apple. Then he sat forward, like a prepared bull.

Bernard only longed for the ridiculous conversation to end, and with worthy restraint said: 'Harold, I accept your condescending attitude to myself, but your presumptious views towards others, namely the under-privileged, I utterly refute.' And he turned back to the piano again and fiddled with the keyboard.

However, Harold would not be brow-beaten. 'What a pampered schoolboy you are.'

At this Bernard whirled round once more, his face alive with emotion. 'And you, who talks of a real world in which he has never tried to live, you will one day be the hypocrite who defends people, knowing they are guilty, and condemns those knowing they are innocent.'

'Do calm down. There is really no need to shout. My dear cousin Bernard, even you must surely know that no man is guilty unless proven so, and that is not for the barrister to decide. He merely presents a case. The decision lies with the jury, comprising people like yourself – when you will be old and wise enough.'

For everything he had his answer, pat and assured and twisted to his gain.

Bernard rose to his feet, his expression thunderous, and just as Harold's face began to register fear, there was a knock at the door.

'Come in,' the older boy answered with some relief, for he had been convinced Bernard was going to hit him.

The fury inside Bernard burst. How dare he? It was not even Harold's house. 'No – *wait*!' he bellowed as the door opened a fraction –

'What the?'

'This is *my* family's house. In this room, in which I was working, I am –'

'Working?' interrupted Harold cuttingly.

'Yes. Working. At the piano.'

'Ah, the maestro.'

The jibe went ignored. 'In this room where I was working,' Bernard repeated in a controlled voice, 'I give permission for someone to enter. Who is it please?'

'Selina sir, to stoke the fire.'

'Come in then,' he ordered authoritatively.

She came in hesitantly, eyes cast downwards, and scurried over to the fireplace.

Harold's gaze rested on her appraisingly as she bent and straightened, her strong arms prodding and lifting. As far as he was concerned the disagreement was over. Bernard was inconsequential to him; a lightweight rival who did not merit too much energy expended on him.

Bernard, too, had forgotten the conversation, and for the same reason as Harold. He was also watching Selina. How old was she? Twenty? Twenty-one? And what had she done in life to make her a woman, besides stoke fires and clean away ashes and scrub and polish and wait at the table, always with a half-smile that just touched her nut-brown eyes? She had remained static, caught behind the starch of her apron, whilst he felt himself to be another person to the tender eleven-year-old he had been when she first entered the family's service.

How interesting, he reflected as he looked at her, *that a five-year interlude can be so differently represented*.

75

Her body was still that of the fifteen year old she had been then: slight of frame, and as she bent, the nape of her neck, with its fair tendrils escaping from her cap, was pink-tinged and delicate. But her breasts contained in their binding uniform were high and full, and Bernard noticed the way the fabric pulled taut there. She turned to go, straightened the skirt of her apron, brushing off some mark, and was about to excuse herself when she stopped under his scrutiny. She did not look away, but her already coloured cheeks flushed a shade darker, and the brightness of her brown eyes seemed to become enhanced. Confused, she stammered something and fled from the room, leaving Harold and Bernard together as before, only now there was not the piano between them, nor could the quarrel be resumed. Selina's aura lingered and they stood like tense puppets at obtuse angles from each other, with clenched fists and awakened sexuality and the embarrassed air of having been caught in the midst of a forbidden act.

Two weeks after this incident Bernard began his affair with Selina.

It was a day in early November and Bernard was at home because of a severe cold. Helen had forbidden him to go to school, and he had battled with her because it meant he would also have to miss his music lesson. But·his mother had been adamant.

'I shall *not* remain in bed,' Bernard had protested. 'That is too tedious for words.'

'Well then, if you insist you may get up. But you must not tax yourself. And remain warm. There has been this awful influenza about, and that can so easily develop into pneumonia, Bernard dear. I am not fussing, but it is true. And it is such a dreadful day that you are best to remain indoors.' She continued, 'I have to go out after lunch. A visiting afternoon. Do you mind?'

'No, of course not. But it is your turn to hear me. You must make certain the cab comes right to the door. I shall hail it for you. The rain is hurtling down.'

'Your cold – I shall worry. Since Rachel . . .'

She let the sentence trail and Bernard took her hand and

76

pressed it to his cheek. 'I know. But nothing will happen to me, I assure you. I shall go straight back to the fire as soon as I have found you a cab. I promise. And you must not give every urchin a penny for the guy. Someone might snatch your purse.'

Helen laughed, enjoying the rôle-reversal and the tenderness in her son's teasing authority. 'I shall heed your advice. Oh, and the servants are all off this afternoon.'

'Then I shall have a delightfully peaceful time of it.'

Sitting at the piano listening to the intermittent spitting of the fire and the hammering of the rain and the muffled voices from the street, Bernard felt a sense of well-being. Anna the cat crept stealthily onto his lap, and Bernard stroked her absently before fingering the piano and playing a few notes. These developed into a few more, and before he knew it, glorious unstructured music was flowing from his fingers. He played with excited flat hands that Cramer would have despaired of, but he played with all the passion he had lacked for the past few years. Excitedly he grabbed the manuscript paper from a shelf by the piano and began to write.

Perspiration formed on his forehead and with one hand he opened the buttons of his waistcoat and loosened his collar and necktie, whilst with the other he contined to write. He did not hear the knock on the door, or Selina entering, and when she appeared suddenly beside the piano he was startled by her presence.

'Goodness, you gave me a fright.'

'Sorry sir. I came to see if you was wanting for anything afore I go out.'

'No, I –' his mood was still euphoric and he could not contain it '– Selina, do you like this?'

Without waiting for an answer he turned back to the piano and played what he had composed so far. He played with the same flat hands and passion, and afterwards, his wild curls stuck to his damp forehead and his eyes running from his cold, he flung himself back on his stool in a gesture of abandonment. The stool rocked precariously, Bernard tossed his head to try and shake away the clinging hair, and when he looked at Selina he was laughing joyously.

Selina stared at him, and as she continued to stare Bernard's laughter died. He noticed that she was dressed to go out, wearing a small blue bonnet which fastened under her chin and revealed no hair except the curly fringe. A Shetland wool shawl was thrown over a paler blue short coat and her old laced boots were brown and highly-polished.

Bernard was self-conscious. 'I didn't intend to –' he began to say.

'That was the most beautiful music I ever heard.'

'You can't mean that.'

'And why can't I?'

He was taken aback by the quick boldness of her retort, and felt himself once more to be the eleven year old discomforted by a young servant's brown eyes. He longed to say something, and thrusting his chin forward nervously, complimented her: 'You look very pretty.'

'Oh . . . Your mother, she gave me the coat when she took to wearing black. I altered it. I'm so little, it was almost to the ground on me. And the bonnet was second-hand. It was trimmed with fur and I liked that, but it was in such poor condition I decided to take it off.'

'Why do you apologize for looking pretty?'

'I'm not. I was just explaining that was all, in case you thought . . .'

'In case I thought, "where does she get the money to dress in such a way?"'

'Yes, well you might've, mightn't you?'

'No.'

'Oh. Well, like I said, I came in to see everything was all right by you, and you wasn't wanting anything.'

'No. But thank you anyway.'

'That's all right. Well, I'll be on my way.'

But she lingered, fiddling with the keyboard of the piano.

Bernard mustered his courage once more. 'You do look pretty.'

'Thank you, sir.' (He could not accustom himself to the idea of

78

her calling him 'sir'.) 'Well, and I like your music. I'm not much of an expert, but I liked it ever so much.'

Her cheeks were scarlet. She fiddled with the piano a moment longer and then left. Bernard went to the window to watch her —saw her take a few steps in the rain, holding her umbrella, and the shawl slide from her shoulders and catch under her booted foot. She tripped and stumbled awkwardly to the ground, her leg under her. He caught her expression of pain, saw the mud splatter the sweet coat, and was instantly out of the room and in the street where she was half-sitting, half-lying, the shawl trapped beneath her heel as she struggled to disentangle it and rise to her feet in a pathetic attempt at dignity. Her face was contorted, and Bernard stood hovering over her uselessly, waving his arms about. A big woman with a huge umbrella stopped:

'I'd carry her indoors somewhere, dearie, what are you waiting for? Can't you see the poor thing's suffering?'

Together they helped Selina upright, and then very coyly he lifted her into his arms and carried her, dripping and muddy into the house.

'Oh Lord, I'm sorry, sir. I'm ever so sorry,' she kept repeating between little intakes of breath.

Seeing her small round face suffused with pain and smudged with rain and dirt, whereas before it had been so fresh and assured, Bernard no longer felt shy. In a tender voice he said: 'But you must stop apologizing, Selina. It is not your fault you fell.'

He held her more tightly; briefly felt the glistening skin of her face against his own, before laying her down on the chaise-longue in the family room. She was shivering and all her features were clenched in the effort not to cry.

'I shall fetch you a brandy,' he announced in a tone of sudden inspiration. And as an afterthought he poured a small glass for himself also, and returned to sit beside her on the edge of the chaise-longue, covering her with a rug.

'You're shivering so much.'

'I know. I cannot stop. Isn't it peculiar?' Her teeth rattled.

'I shall put some more logs on the fire.' He stacked the fire up

79

carefully and for a moment stood watching it blaze, then he sat by her once more. Her expression was less strained and they remained in silence, sipping brandy, the only sounds in the darkened room being the fire crackling and the clock ticking. Bernard made no move to turn on the gas-lights, and the greyness outside made it seem like evening. Shadows from the flames teased the patterned walls. The brandy, too, was like fire down the throat.

'It's the first time I've had brandy,' Selina said hesitantly.

'Me too,' Bernard confided.

'Oh sir, maybe we oughtn't.'

'Nobody will know, I promise. They won't miss that little bit.'

'It is nice though, isn't it? It burns the tongue, then it becomes smooth as it goes down your gullet, if you know what I mean.'

Her face contorted again.

'Is it agony? Perhaps we should get a doctor.'

'Oh no. I hate doctors. Killed my brother the doctors did. No, I'll bind it myself. It's only a sprain.'

She explained to him where the bandages were, and whilst he went to fetch them she removed her stocking. When he returned Bernard found her bare-legged and clasping her ankle. The stocking lay in a dark sensuous coil on the floor, having assumed its own life and a new implication. He stared mesmerized at the pale bared flesh revealed from knee downwards, and she who had not given a moment's consideration to her action was suddenly embarrassed. There was a faint pink mottling to her skin, as though strawberry juice had been spilt and wiped away, and the calf was round and firm.

Bernard broke the strained silence, forcing his voice to sound matter-of-fact as if he had seen a thousand women's bared legs.

'Where does it hurt?'

'Where I'm holding it of course.'

'Perhaps it's broken.'

'No. I broke my wrist once. It feels completely different.'

'But perhaps you do need to see a doctor,' he persisted.

80

'*No*. My brother had coal-dust in his lungs, honest coal-dust. So what does this wizard do? He pours this hot stuff down Johnnie's throat and minutes later he's choking and coughing up blood.'

'That's terrible. I'm sorry.'

Selina shrugged. 'We're dispensable, aren't we? People I mean.'

Bernard could not answer that and was surprised by her cynicism. 'Well, at least unclasp your ankle,' he said after a pause.

She did so and he was taken aback by the swelling and discoloration. 'No wonder it hurts!' he commented, and whistled through his teeth. 'Shall I try and bandage it for you?'

'If you could . . .'

It was while Bernard was clumsily strapping her ankle that the inevitable happened. As he pulled a little on the final knot to fasten the bandage, Selina winced and Bernard placed a reassuring hand on her shoulder. Their faces were perhaps an inch or so apart and they moved instinctively closer to one another and kissed – she with more experience than himself. At first he was hesitant, feeling the strangeness of a woman's lips attached like soft rubber to his, and then as he began to enjoy the sensation there came the appalled shock as his mouth parted and he felt her tongue, quivering and probing. But pleasure surpassed his inhibitions and natural instincts overcame inexperience, and he who had never before been aware of his body now knew only one overwhelming need.

As he pounded gloriously into her he was vaguely conscious of her small, bird-like cries. He stopped, still inside her: 'Your ankle, is it paining you?'

'No, silly. Don't stop.'

'But you were crying out as though in pain.'

'That was pleasure, silly, not pain.'

'Oh I thought . . .'

He began to move once more, understood her cries for what they were and joined in with his own. He gazed into the staring eyes and allowed a tide to overtake him.

Afterwards he could not look at her. The glistening on her

81

thighs which had come from each of them shamed him. He had done what men did, with a man's instincts but with a boy's mind. He stood beside where she lay on the floor, her legs loosely parted to reveal the wet curling hair, her bodice undone and corset loosened, her skirts round her waist, and he carefully buttoned up his trousers and adjusted his clothing. He felt languid and a little dejected.

Selina patted the floor and said softly: 'Come lie down again beside me.'

He did so, austere.

'Why do you look so stern? Are you angry with me?'

'No – no. With myself only.'

His nose was running from his cold and he absently wiped it on his shirtsleeve – a child's action, and one for which he would still have been reprimanded.

'Why?'

She was so simple in her approach, and Bernard appraised her honest little face which bore an expression of puzzlement and hurt, whereas before her eyes had been locked with his in savage pleasure.

'Because . . . It was wrong.'

'But why was it wrong? Didn't it feel right at the time?'

Bernard made no reply, torn between surrendering to the luxury of sensation, and adhering to his Victorian conditioning.

Selina persisted: 'You're so silent. I can't fathom you. You frighten me, sir.'

At that Bernard was contrite. 'Oh Selina, I do not mean to make you unhappy.'

And he turned to comfort her, cuddling her warm body against his, feeling her feminine softness, and before he knew it he was inside her again, guiltlessly and wholeheartedly.

He confided his affair to Douglas one afternoon at tea in the Hamiltons' Harley Street home; such an important transitionary stage in his life could not go unshared with a blood brother. Douglas had wanted to practise a new piece of music, and they were in his bedroom. Bernard watched his friend rock back and forth lovingly, the small pale fingers caressing the bow, his receding chin burrowed into the chin rest which he only ever used at home as his teacher disapproved. His metal-framed glasses were steamed up and he stopped to take them off. His eyes were pale blue and large, and they focused vaguely on Bernard whilst he buffed the thick lenses. At that point Bernard blurted it out.

Douglas replaced the glasses on his face upside down, resited them, removed them, and then replaced them once more on the end of his short nose. He looked at Bernard with an expression of sheer awe. 'Gosh dear chap, it's all frightfully exciting and splendid, but – suppose she were to have a child? That would not be so amusing.'

'There are – ways, Doug.'

'Ways?'

'God! Yes, ways.'

'Oh,' Douglas said dismally, unenlightened, humbled in the face of his friend's new wisdom. Then he put down his Stradivari violin – a birthday present from his father – which he had been clutching rather in the way a baby clutches a dummy for comfort, and looked suddenly cheerful.

'Gosh, dear chap, this is all much more fun than Corelli who can be quite tedious once you've mastered him. Now tell me everything. Absolutely everything.'

'Not everything, Doug. Not even to you.'

'Well, as nearly as is possible then . . .'

For several months Bernard visited Selina almost nightly in her room, creeping up the stairs in case a creaking floorboard should prove his Judas. In fact the third stair did creak, and at first it seemed in the silence that its groan was a roar which would awaken the entire house. Now he knew to avoid that stair and was quite nonchalant about the whole procedure. Bernard became almost obsessed with his unabating need for Selina, and with each lovemaking session he became bolder and more exploratory.

Gradually he began to discover pieces of her life. Little

snippets were revealed, sad fragments that endeared her to him. And Bernard, at that probing age when every new experience was a testing ground, fell in love – if not with Selina herself, then with an image he contrived of her. Newly infatuated with the idea of Socialism, he loved her for what she represented: the glamour of poverty which had surrounded her upbringing in the Midlands – the widowed mother who took in washing, the sisters who had died in babyhood, the brother who had choked. Her tragedies and disadvantages set her apart from others almost as if she had a special talent, and as such he admired it and could see no falsity in his feelings.

During this time Bernard's mind was alive as it had never been before, and he composed prolifically, often after visiting Selina, writing until the washed grey of winter dawn stared through his curtains, and only then would his mind become aware of its deprivation. He ruffled the bed-clothes to make them appear slept in, dressed for school, inspected his winged collar, hardly lighter than the pallor of his face glaring back at him from the mirror, and hurriedly put away the scribbled sheets of music in his chest of drawers. Then he went into the family room for his breakfast which Selina would bring to him on a butler's tray, whilst his parents took theirs later in their room. This little ceremony was always strange to him: the formality of her uniform, the sterility of her job, the small smile that disclosed embarrassment and recognition of the fact that despite everything she was a menial. She would open her legs to him, but she would always call him 'sir'.

Outside their front door one Sunday morning, the third day of snow and ice, there was a commotion and the shrill sounds of rending wood and a horse screaming. They all ran out to see what had happened: the big bay horse, felled like a tree, on its side heaving, having abandoned its attempts to get up. The foam of sweat on its body mingled with snow; the eyes rolled, wild and agonized. The old coachman stood beside the beast weeping, and nobody could help him. Joseph covered Helen's face and led her inside, whilst Bernard remained watching. He was aware of Selina beside him.

'Go inside,' he ordered dully.

'Will you?'

'No. I shall help.'

'Then I'll stay.'

The boy walked hesitantly over to the weeping man; saw the injured horse at close quarters and heard the almost human wheezes of pain.

Distressed, he asked: 'What can I do?'

'Can you unharness t'other one and lead 'im away? 'E's disturbed. I don't like 'im seeing 'is pal shot. Cover 'is eyes with me 'kerchief.'

He sniffed mightily and blew on his handkerchief before handing it to Bernard.

Dismantling the nervous horse was no easy business, and tying the cloth around its head harder still. He fumbled in the cold, inexperienced with the straps and buckles and wary of the animal. But the longer he delayed, the more the animal on the ground would suffer, and he forced himself to be as quick and efficient as possible, noticing from the corner of his eye that the coachman was now crouched on the ground with his arms about his horse like a lamenting lover.

Once Bernard had bound the cloth around the horse's face, covering its vision, the creature immediately seemed to relax, and he led it a hundred yards away and then stopped and stroked its warm silky ears. He had always been rather afraid of horses before, intimidated by their size, but now he saw how naturally timid they were, and as the animal became docile he felt a growing affinity with it. There was a shot, and then another one, and the loud sobbing of the coachman could be heard despite the chattering from the crowd which had gathered.

Bernard held his horse for quite some time before another coachman offered to take it from him, and the boy gave him the reins almost reluctantly.

'What will happen now?' he asked.

'Meat cart's on its way. This 'ole bloody thing'll break old Wally's heart. 'Ad that 'orse since it were a three year old. Broke it to 'arness 'imself. I'd go inside now if I was you. Yer nose is as red as Wally's eyes. Bloody weather. Bloody snow and ice. If it weren't for the bloody ice 'e wouldn't 'ave broken 'is bloody leg.'

Selina was still standing on the step. 'You're crying,' she said softly.

'My eyes are watering with the cold.' He averted his face.

'You're crying,' she insisted.

'Maybe.' He brushed past her, went to his room and wept like the coachman, and wondered why happiness was such an intermittent thing.

It was March 1858, and Cramer's health was deteriorating. Bernard was having a lesson.

'Da – di-da – da-da-da-a-a-a-di. There is no fortissimo on the held note. Mozart was a subtle composer. In fact the forte is on the da-da with the da-a-a-a softer and absolutely level in tone. And peaceful wrists, Bernard. I do not approve of this new-fangled idea of wrist movement. If after all this time your fingers cannot achieve the required dexterity without the wrists' aid, then you should not be playing. Now remember, no forte on that long beat. It has quite sufficient impact in its very unexpectedness. Please go back four bars to the triplet, played pianissimo . . .'

When Bernard had finished, Cramer told him, 'And now you may move your wrists. Pivot them, and your fingers. Stre-etch. Squeeze. Stre-e-e-tch, squeeze . . . Young sir, I look at you sitting at my faithful piano, this dark brown dog, and I see an almost grown man, and it is a shock. I am not sure that you enjoy playing Mozart. Did you know that my reputation as a pianist was founded on performances of Mozart? Mozart and Bach. Your hero is Liszt, a true virtuoso, possibly the greatest pianist the world has seen, but as a composer Mozart in my opinion was second to none. His subtlety, young sir, is part of his brilliance. But youth must have its flamboyance! Play for me, Bernard, and we shall talk afterwards. Young sir, play for me what enters your head. At random.'

Cramer leaned back in the wing chair and placed his hand inside his waistcoat in its habitual pose. His hooded eyes gazed beyond Bernard, watering slightly, fixing their sight on the Kensington street through the window.

Bernard's heart reached out tenderly to his old master. He thought: *Oh Cramer, I want to touch your hands, which once were capable of such legato, and are now such poor things*.

He played the piece he had commenced that afternoon he had begun his affair with Selina, but now it was considerably changed. He had entitled it 'Interlude', and it opened with the right hand playing a repeated quaver beat. Then the left hand came in, in imitation, and an aggressive pattern developed, the right hand at odds with the left; the question and the answer, like a two-part invention by J. S. Bach. But then with an augmented chord the entire mood changed, and thereafter was simple and perfect harmony.

As the notes died, his fingers still resting lightly on the keyboard, Bernard turned to face his teacher challengingly.

'Occasionally, Bernard,' the old man said, stroking his chin to hide emotion, 'you still surprise me. And what do you do with these pieces you compose? These little thought occurrences you so casually invent? Is it like eating food – you desire it, digest it, and then forget it? You have the unfathomable face of a blank wall, as if such things were nothing to you. Do you dislike your talent so very much, Bernard? If this is so, then you are disliking the only self that is honest.'

'Please sir – I do not choose to analyse myself.'

'How then will you ever offer yourself to others? You must know yourself before you may make that offer. But yes, that is your affair, my young sir.'

But he remembered when a boy sat before the piano with fingers like rods that were unable to convey the fierce urgency of his heart.

'We will have tea instead, would that please you? And I shall tell you of my second meeting with your hero Liszt, and of his own doubts and insecurities. Maybe one day you will meet him for yourself, but for that you will have to go to Weimar.

'It was 1841 and I was in Paris for a spell. In that city Liszt was fêted by the world of the Arts. You must remember, he had been thrilling audiences in the capital since childhood. However when I saw him it was a private soirée, and he was there with his friends, the artist Delacroix and the writer Victor Hugo. He was in low spirits and they were doing their best to cheer him; for you see, Bernard, he is never satisfied. Ferencz Liszt is a strangely contradictory creature, on the one hand he thrives on his popularity, revels in fashionable society, and on the other he despises and rejects them. We were discussing his symphonic poems, I recall, when suddenly, and with no consequence to the conversation that I could see, he put his head in his hands and bemoaned: "But I am unable to do justice to Schumann. I must endure repeated failure in my perform-ance of him." He is a kind, sensitive man with a sadly restless spirit, and he has problems. He is never content. Do not be like him, Bernard. That is why I say "know yourself". It is so important for your future – *whatever* you decide to do with it.'

When he spoke for any length of time now Cramer became breathless. Age was an effort; disability an encumbrance. He had done so much, and his mind was still perfectly lucid. It was an annoyance that his body would not co-operate when he willed it.

Bernard stayed no more than half an hour. Cramer was drifting into sleep in the heavy 'grandfather' chair, his hand back in his waistcoat.

The boy gazed at the yellowed face full of character, and felt a wave of love for his old teacher. 'Goodbye, sir.' He did not think he had been heard. He nearly kissed the forehead, so sure was he that Cramer was asleep.

But: 'Goodbye, young Bernard,' came the reply. 'Don't throw your piece away. It is truly innovative and clever. I am rather suspicious as to the origins of the inspiration behind it, but I promise you can trust me not to tell your parents.'

Then he lapsed once more into the benign breathing of a dozing old man, and from the shielding sides of the chair all that could be glimpsed of him were his legs, between which rested his cane.

*

'And I never saw him again. Oh Anna, how I would have grieved if, as I shut the door behind me, I had known that I would never see him again.'

'My love! I do believe you are almost crying, all these years later.'

'I can see him now. Truly. He was unique. And he has influenced my entire life. Anyway, that evening I took a cab home, for it was becoming dark and raining as usual. Besides, two days previously a man had been murdered in Hyde Park for no more than the ten shillings in his pocket.'

'Cramer's face remained in my mind all the journey home. I had an image of his closed eyes masked by scaly hoods, and within me was the brooding sense of shame I habitually felt after leaving him; as if I had declared the sins of my soul. In my head rang my teacher's voice, with his many stories and anecdotes which I never tired of hearing; I feasted vicariously on the lives of great men. Anyway, when I arrived back Harold was there. . . .'

Bernard braced himself to be pleasant to his cousin and, mindful of the pleading in his mother's eyes, sat quietly in a chair whilst Harold continued his soliloquy from the chaiselongue. Meanwhile, Bernard read his notes about scrip issues and options, and various 'case histories', and generally familiarized himself with his father's world.

It was to this apparently cosy scene that Joseph returned: his son engrossed in literature relevant to his future, his wife sewing, and his nephew (whom he regarded nowadays with some tolerance and increasing respect) holding forth with his usual vociferous assurance, and he was almost a happy man. His life was on a delicate equilibrium once more.

That night as usual Bernard crept up the stairs to Selina's room. He was tired and unaccountably depressed, and he longed to be with Selina, to have her massage his neck, and be comforted by her arms.

Without thinking he stepped on the third stair and it groaned. He paused, agonized – before bounding lightly up the remainder of the staircase.

Harold saw his disappearing form. His room was nearest the staircase, and the cold had kept him awake. He had been about to go to the cupboard on the landing where he knew extra blankets to be kept when he heard the creak. His door made no sound as it opened the half-inch that enabled him to see Bernard's back view.

He had wanted Selina for himself.

For weeks he had been plotting how to set about it, fantasizing about sharing a bed with her, envisaging what he would do to her. That schoolboy Bernard had overstepped him. Disappointed and enraged, Harold felt himself close to tears. His eyes narrowed as he planned his revenge.

Three days later Bernard was summoned to the headmaster's room. Fearful, he wondered at the reason for this; the man's expression was too dour for a gratifying explanation. He came directly to the point:

'I have received an anonymous letter of very grave and indicting content, and whilst I abhor the deceit and cowardice of the sender and would on principle normally disregard any matter concerned with a person of such base reasoning, nevertheless I feel compelled to act in this instance. I wish to ascertain the truth because of the gravity of the accusations. Have you, Foligno, been having relations . . .'

The air was filled with bubbles, and he was one, levitating and regarding himself below, a tall youth flushed with shock, cornered by his inquisitor.

'So you were expelled?'

'I was due to leave at the end of the summer term anyway, but the dishonour was great.' Bernard closed his eyes, remembering how it had been; the distress, the fury, the embarrassment . . .

'Why did Harold tell the headmaster rather than your parents?'

'I suppose because that way there was maximum disgrace.'

'What a vile person Harold was. I wonder why he hated you so? It makes me unhappy to think of someone hating you.'

90

He laughed and stroked her upturned face: 'Harold's hate did not bother me. In a way it was a challenge, particularly when I was younger.'

'What did your parents do when they learned of your disgrace?'

'My father was distraught. "You have brought shame to this house," I remember he accused me. "Shame upon the entire family."

'He wept. And many days went by when he would not speak to me. Even the punishment he selected for me was issued via my mother, and I well recall her pained expression when she relayed his instructions: that I was not permitted to visit Cramer, and that the piano was to be locked and the key hidden from me. My father knew he had struck me where it hurt.

'Harold did not dare show himself during that time. Needless to say Selina was banished, and I believe she would have found a job elsewhere in service, for my dear mother was a fair woman and wrote her a decent reference. Selina herself told me when she said goodbye. Her head was bent with shame. She wore her pretty blue bonnet, and her eyes were red from crying. As for my own feelings: I am ashamed to admit that my "love" for the girl disappeared with her person. I had enough to cope with – my father's reaction, the severity of my punishment . . .

'And I thought it curious, when I considered matters objectively a few nights later in bed, that the Jews should elaborately celebrate a pubescent boy's entry into manhood, and yet when that manhood is tested denounce it.

'I was without contrition, which did not help. I missed Cramer dreadfully. I wrote to him and told him what had happened, and when he did not reply I was desolate. I did not know he had written and that the letter was kept from me – until later; which proved to be too late.'

91

Chapter Six

It was an afternoon towards the end of March. Douglas received an unusual message to call upon Johann Baptist Cramer.

He had not seen the old man or visited the house for a year, and as he stood on the doorstep absorbing the faint warmth of spring, he remembered the previous times when he had visited for their musical sessions. The recollection of those moments made little Douglas hurt with nostalgia.

The door was opened by Cramer's wife. 'He is in bed, I'm afraid,' she said. 'But you may follow me.'

He followed her sad old shape, wondering why he was there.

Cramer greeted him from his bed: 'Hello, young Douglas. It is a long time . . .'

The sentence petered out; not because of the difficulty of forming the words, but because of emotion and its chain of memories. He who had toured the world, started a publishing firm, written books, founded the Philharmonic Society, met and performed with the greatest, was now struck with sorrow at the simple thought of two young, eager boys standing beside his piano, their faces alight with excitement and enthusiasm. Cramer loved young people. He loved their receptiveness, their eagerness for knowledge. Now this funny-looking, under-developed youth with his peering be-spectacled eyes, rabbity cheeks, and deceptively bewildered air stood before him.

His wife had quietly left the room and Cramer beckoned the boy closer. His eyes were rheumy and running, his lips dry and shrivelled in the shrunken face, but for Douglas, who was a firm believer in after-life, this only served to increase his awe and respect. The old man was dying – and what a life he had led! One could not grieve.

'It has been many months since I saw you. And many weeks since I saw the young maestro. He is, as you surely know, disgraced, and his punishment is that he may not visit me. It is my punishment also. He is greatly missed. He could not even inform me in person, it was not permitted. Instead he imparted the news by letter. I admired his honesty. I replied directly but I suspect my letter has been withheld from him. You must not tell your friend, young master Hamilton, for he must not know of this little visit of yours. I gather, too, that the piano has been locked and the key removed?'

'Yes, sir.'

'It – is – a – *crime*.'

Each word was softly spoken, but separately enunciated, with the emphasis on that final decibel, and Douglas was surprised by the vehemence in his tone.

Cramer hoisted himself further upright, the sinews in his neck becoming prominent with the effort. 'People, good, well-meaning, kindly and godly people can unwittingly commit the most ungodly sins through misguided outlooks . . . And how are you, Douglas? Does life treat you grandly?'

'Yes, sir. I am to go to the Paris Conservatoire in the summer to study initially under Henri Vieuxtemps. But that will be for no more than six months as he must return to Brussels.'

'Ah, remember me to him. You could not have a finer teacher – himself the pupil of Charles August de Beriot, and the master of young Henri Wieniawski. And you, Douglas, could go far in your chosen career. Are you anxious to travel?'

'I believe it is necessary.'

'That depends on the course you would wish your career to take. If you wish to perform as opposed to compose, then travelling is obligatory.'

'I am not interested in composition. I have no talent for it.'

Cramer made no reply. After a minute or so, he spoke in a quavering voice: 'If Bernard were to concentrate on composition he could possibly become one of his generation's finest young men – and believe me, young Douglas, there is much talent about. He is a fool. They – are – fools.' His voice broke and a wheeze caught his throat. 'I miss the young sir.'

There was another, more prolonged silence, during which Douglas again wondered why he had been summoned. After several minutes, when he thought perhaps Cramer had drifted into sleep and that he should leave, the old man heaved himself upright once more. He leaned towards the pot-cupboard beside his bed and fumbled around its top, pushing aside a mirror, oddments of paper, pens, and a book which fell to the floor. Eventually his hand alighted upon what it sought and he said to Douglas:

'Here, please take this.' It was a white letter of heavy quality, sealed with his family seal, and addressed to Bernard. 'The contents are confidential,' he explained, 'and the letter must, under no circumstances, be handed to Bernard before his eighteenth birthday. Is that a promise?'

'He and I are blood brothers,' Douglas said, by way of reply.

'Ah yes. I remember.'

He handed it to Douglas, and it trembled between them, vibrating from the irregular shaking of an old man's hand which would never again rest on a keyboard.

This time the silence extended beyond ten minutes and Douglas knew that the master was asleep and that he was dismissed, blessed with the honour of trusted mediator. He knew, too, he would never see Cramer again.

When he saw Bernard, true to his word, Douglas said nothing of his secret meeting. This was not easy however, in the face of Bernard's sorrow.

'I cannot understand,' he said, 'that I received no reply to my letter. I am so utterly disheartened, Doug. So utterly disheartened.'

'There is sure to be a reason,' was all his friend could say. 'He is a fair man.'

'Maybe he is revolted by my behaviour.' Bernard shook his head dejectedly.

'No,' Douglas said firmly. 'I am sure there is a reason — perhaps the letter has gone astray. I assure you Cramer would not ignore you.'

They were strolling beside the Serpentine, their coat collars turned up against the strong March wind. They passed a group of stern-looking nannies pushing prams. Then a girl rushed past them chasing a runaway hoop. As she ran her bonnet flew off, and her cry of frustration could be heard as she dashed first in one direction after her hoop, and then in the other after the bonnet which wheeled and took off into the air and eventually landed in the river, floating to the edge near where the boys were walking. Before it could drift again, Bernard grabbed it. It was sodden and dripping, and he handed it absently to the child. Glancing at her face, he was dismayed to see that it was distorted with the failed effort of not crying. He was always reduced to pity when confronted by tears, and his little sister had used to resort to them as her ultimate weapon against him.

'Oh, but you must not cry!' The seraphic smile divided his face. 'Here, have my handkerchief and dry your eyes. I promise that when your bonnet dries it will be as good as new, and see – here is your hoop! It has come to rest beside us of its own accord.'

Wordlessly she stared directly into his smiling face, the tears drying on her cheeks. Moisture bubbled in her little nostrils and she wiped her nose on her sleeve before remembering both her manners and the handkerchief. Slowly she took the initialled white cloth from Bernard and clasped it to her before blowing her nose heartily. Still staring, and very seriously, she reoffered it to him.

'You may keep it!' he laughed.

Somebody called her and she spun round, then back to Bernard, as if stricken. He noticed the little dimple in her chin. Her eyes, clear now, were the colour of a stormy sea, steady and serene. He wanted to keep looking at her.

'Anna!' the voice called again, on a note of impatience.

'I must go,' she said in a sweetly lilting voice, and then, 'what is your name?'

'Bernard.'

'Bernard what?'

'Foligno. Bernard Foligno.' He continued to smile.

'And mine is Anna. Thank you, Bernard. I shall keep your handkerchief forever.'

She walked away with great poise to join a woman who must have been her governess, the blue ribbons of her bonnet dripping beside her. She turned once to wave solemnly.

'What an enchanting girl,' Bernard exclaimed to Douglas. 'Was she not enchanting? She has quite pulled me out of my moroseness. You are right, there is surely some logical reason I have not heard from Cramer. When the furore has died down I shall visit him and he will explain.'

A few days later he was invited to join the Hamilton family in Gloucestershire. Douglas went a couple of days beforehand and Bernard travelled down by himself. He was met at Gloucester station by his friend driving a fine Brougham, and when Douglas took his arm it was as though someone had plucked a heavy and clinging garment from his shoulders. He felt free; ecstatically so. Gazing through the carriage window he was astonished by the racing sky, (it raced forever –) the wide, washed combination of air and cloud that shed itself into the folds of the hills which were dotted with windswept trees. The whistling wind against the carriage was intimidating in its display of power, the sound reeded and eerie.

He called to Douglas: 'Would you mind if we stopped just for a minute?'

Misinterpreting his reasons, Douglas called back: 'Won't do you much good, dear boy. It'll form lime-coloured icicles. Might drop off. Though on reflection that might please your family.'

'Very funny. I don't want to stop for *that* anyway. I want to – just look.'

Douglas halted the Brougham and Bernard stepped down. Around him the wind roared and, elated, he stretched out his arms. It bit into his lungs, pinched his nostrils closed, and when he sniffed to dilate them the air was different and wild.

The Hamiltons' estate, about half a mile from Bibury and about twenty-two miles from Gloucester, consisted of the old manor where the family and servants lived, a farmhouse inhabited by the estate manager, his wife and their brood of children, and six rather dilapidated cottages where the farm-workers and gardeners resided. All the buildings, including the barns, were constructed in the same gilded Cotswold stone and the entire complex was set in a bowl amongst the hills, with views across to Bibury church and of the tiny road that wound like palely coiled wool.

The Hamiltons treated him as their own son during his short sojourn, and Bernard told Douglas: 'I envy you, Doug.'

'Why is that, dear chap?'

'I envy you this lovely place and your relaxed upbringing. I envy you your supportive family and your future without barriers.'

And for once Douglas could make no retort.

The first few days were spent seeing the local sights, visiting friends and generally being sociable; partaking in a lifestyle foreign to him. London was remote in miles and in thought, his disgrace forgotten. Even Selina – her firm breasts and full round buttocks, and finally her tears – was almost callously dismissed from his mind.

It was over a week before Bernard touched the piano in the drawing-room. Until then he had avoided it as though it were a person with a contagious disease. One day, drawn by the sounds of someone playing, he entered the room. Elaine, Douglas's older sister, was seated at the piano and she turned round with a wry smile on her kind, plain face.

'I cannot play,' she excused herself. 'My heart feels that I should, but my fingers disagree. It is one of those unfair things.'

She gave a small self-deprecating laugh, and her expression relaxed. 'Now Bernard, you will play for me will you not, you unobliging boy?'

'I am not in the mood, Elaine,' he replied lightly, and stretched out on a rather uncomfortable settee.

'Come now, surely a truly disciplined artist does not have to be "in the mood" as you say. What would happen if a concert performer felt that way?'

'But I am not a concert pianist.' Bernard faked a yawn to emphasize his unwillingness to pursue this line of conversation.

'Douglas says you could be,' Elaine said firmly.

'Oh Lord, my friend talks too much.' But he shifted from a relaxed pose to one of hunched-up tension.

There was a faint scratching sound at the window, and a face appeared suddenly, pressed to the glass; an insane face with fish-eyes and a mouth which hung loosely open. Bernard leaped to his feet.

'Elaine, who on earth is that?'

'Oh, that is young Jonathan, the groundsel-seller. He is a mute, poor thing. His father raped his sister when she was fifteen and he was the result. He is harmless and only seeks attention. We buy the groundsel from him even though the canary died a year ago! Poor boy . . .' She waved, and the face broke into a gap-toothed smile before disappearing.

'Play, Bernard?'

Her compassion demolished his crumbling resolve.

'I shall. All right, I shall – or you will give me no peace,' he teased. But his fingers were tingling in anticipation and his eyes sparkled. 'What would you like me to play?'

'Anything. I want to hear what kid Douglas means.'

'You are quite a bossy lady, Elaine!'

'Me?'

Her tone seemed genuinely hurt, and Bernard, looking at the mouse-brown hair severely parted down the middle and the drab sage of Elaine's dress, said hurriedly: 'But I was joking, Elaine. Surely you knew that? Now, I think I shall attempt a piece by Liszt. You know Liszt? He is my favourite composer. It is rather lengthy, and if you become bored you may slip out in the middle, and I assure you I shall not even notice!'

He had played the revolutionary B Minor Sonata to Cramer about six months previously, and the master's comment by way of compliment then was: 'You could have performed that anywhere and faced the audience afterwards with pride.'

It was notably one of the most difficult sonatas with its many diverse moods in a single unbroken movement, and now Bernard tackled it as Liszt himself might have played it. He did not notice the Hamiltons and some guests tiptoeing into the room.

He played for about twenty minutes, entirely from memory and saw nothing before him except the white and black keyboard. When he eventually glanced up he was astounded to see an audience.

Nobody spoke: to have said 'Bravo' would have seemed ridiculously trite. Bernard rose to his feet stammering and apologizing, turning his neck in its tight collar from left to right in his embarrassment.

'Apologies? What for, lad?' Mr Hamilton asked. 'You play quite superbly. Bernard, this is Sir Alfred and Lady Leeming.'

'How do you do?' Bernard was uncertain how to address them, never having met aristocracy before.

'And this is Emma-Jane, their daughter.'

Sir Alfred was a big, blustering man. 'Emma-Jane plays the flute,' he told Bernard. 'Useless instrument. But her sister Miranda plays the piano. If you should ever consider teaching, please do not forget us. I mean that. Here is my card, or you can always contact me via these good people – even in the future. My second daughter is only twelve. I hope you aim to make music your career like young Douglas here. He is also a splendid musician, and all art must be encouraged, especially in England where we are known not to excel in that direction.'

'I am to be a stockbroker, sir.'

'A stockbroker! A businessman! How perfectly dreadful.' He coughed theatrically.

'Dear,' his wife admonished.

'But the boy's a musician, damn it,' Sir Alfred said heatedly. 'And no ordinary one at that. I know I am not minding my own business, dear,' he added to his wife. 'That may be so, but I believe in stating my mind. And speaking of that – what was it the good doctor said about a drink?'

'Lovely Sir Alfred.'

'Yes. A step nearer you, Anna.'

'Will we ever get there?'

'A little while yet.'

'I am growing impatient.'

*

On the seventeenth of April, Douglas and he were breakfasting together. It promised to be a fine day and the blossom seemed to have burst out during the night, spreading in a pink flurry outside the window. Bernard had declined Douglas's offer of half the newspaper, preferring to gaze through the mullioned window at the views. The smell of coffee was wholesome, the air warm, and the sounds of his friend gently rustling and folding the newspaper soothing.

Bernard became aware that the rustling had stopped; of Douglas's eyes boring into him.

'What is wrong, Doug?'

The newspaper lay rumpled on the table between them.

'Doug?'

He started to reach for the paper and Douglas gently laid his hand on his arm to prevent him.

'Bernard . . . Dear chap . . . Cramer is dead. He died yesterday.'

Cramer dead?

Bernard took the paper. He read: '*Johann Baptist Cramer, originator of Cramer Publishing, developer of the keyboard, brilliant pianist held in high esteem by Beethoven, and most respected composer, died yesterday, aged eighty-seven. His death will be a great loss to the musical world. . . .*'

'I did not say goodbye.' Bernard's voice cracked. The sobs rose dryly in his throat and the tears trickled silently down his cheeks. 'I loved him. I really loved him, Doug. How can I work without him?'

And with Cramer went the final embers of his childhood.

Chapter Seven

As soon as he returned, Bernard's parents gave him the letter Cramer had written in reply to his own. It was their gesture of forgiveness towards him. But for him forgiveness was hard.

The letter was brief, but it said all that was needed.

Dear young sir,

You have done nothing to be ashamed of, or that millions of other grown men do not do. But that is not my business. It is your family's. However, I shall miss my pupil. Dear young sir, God be with you always, and I think of you.

Remember music.

> *Yours ever, Johann Baptist Cramer*

The lump came to Bernard's throat anew as he read the shaky writing in the privacy of his room. Remember music. Remember me. Like Dido's farewell: 'Ah – but forget my fate. . . .'

Downstairs, Joseph said: 'As the Englishman says, "It is always too soon to die, but he had a good innings".'

Intended to offer comfort, these words only served to increase Bernard's feeling of separateness. The emphasis on the word 'Englishman' was yet another small demonstration of how Joseph regarded himself as different.

He looked at his mother's face, into her deep eyes, and saw her expression of sympathy. Her hand fluttered towards his cheek and he longed to lean against her. But he was a man, and the moment passed and was lost.

Cramer was buried at Brompton Cemetery. Bernard and Douglas stood together and paid their respects to the family. They were two of many, paling into the background, and Bernard had an awful feeling of insignificance. How could he have fooled himself that he had meant anything special to Cramer? He was just another follower upon whom the kindly master had bestowed routine encouragement and advice.

That summer Douglas went to Paris, and by coincidence Sophie went at almost the same time. But Bernard had long outgrown his childish infatuation, and could even smile about it now. Selina had erased Sophie from his thoughts. That episode, too, was now forgotten, and Bernard was back in favour once more. He became a stockbroker.

Every morning he dressed in front of the mirror, feeling a certain masculine pride as he donned his dark and sober clothes, buttoned the waistcoat, fixed his gold watch chain and – the final touch – set the outrageously tall top hat well forward over his bouncing curls, so that his features beneath the brim jutted forcefully and looked (so he was vain enough to think) both haughty and determined.

The early morning cab journey with his father took them through Fleet Street, whose office lights had burned throughout the night like the hot weary eyes of the reporters within, past St Paul's, and into the dark Venetian-like depths of the city, to be swallowed entire and undistinguished amongst the impressive fantasies of Victorian architects.

Bernard would trudge up the stairs at the side of the barber's shop, respectfully behind his father who had to stop every three steps or so to catch his breath – and into the cream office. The walls were lined with production charts and records and framed reports, and in pride of place behind Joseph's desk was an antique map of the City. Shelves overflowed with hundreds of books and on the floor were stacked piles of private files. The high barred window overlooked the street with all its activity: the old bootblack with his wizened face like a cork; a pair of newspaper vendors, one of whom was blind but knew exactly which coin was which; the tiny match-seller who could not have been more than seven years old . . . They stood there day in, day out, never varying their cries or their patter.

First thing in the morning Joseph and Bernard would have coffee and read through all the messages and papers. No day could be predicted in advance, and a quick but thorough reading was essential before anyone's duties could be assigned.

It was another hot summer, and it found Bernard venturing out on foot or by cab, gathering information and relaying it, neck swelling and sweating within the confines of the unyielding collar. In the evenings he could not believe its yellow ridge had come from himself. The soles of his shoes had to be replaced eight times within three months, and his feet were permanently as if on fire.

From Ludgate Hill up Old Bailey . . . turning into Newgate and Cheapside and thence into more obscure streets, Bernard hunted for the addresses his father gave him. He would accidently find himself in stinking back lanes whose gutters flowed with excrement, with an occasional rotting animal corpse, and with the dark deposits of composites no longer distinguishable and which people had discarded. Was anything except despair ever retained?

No experience is wasted: whilst Bernard complained bitterly to Joseph of the apparent triviality of his menial tasks, he was in fact gathering, piece by piece, an entire picture which would one day become the only opera he wrote. But then he saw only his grievances; that his daily life was glamourless, and that his feet burned.

'But what you are doing is vital,' Joseph said when Bernard complained. 'How else will I be kept informed? You must learn your trade from the bottom up. It is how everyone learns.'

Bernard thought, *Please do not mention music. It would be too unsubtle.*

'It was surely the same with your music. Once you had to learn your scales.'

After a couple of months, when the heatwave was over, Bernard developed an affection for the bewildering City streets. It began with the satisfaction of no longer becoming lost each day, and then with the lessening of revulsion at the smells of human life. Sometimes on a quiet day or during his lunch period he would visit the markets, noisy with raucous cockney voices, buzzing with flies and pungent with the smells of live animals. In particular he loved to visit Covent Garden, where the canopied stalls abounded with bright colours and gleaming shapes, and even the plainest seller looked pretty seated amongst her baskets.

Increasingly he spent longer periods in the smaller of the two rooms, which was his own 'office', and airless, despite the little window opened to its full extent. He would sit at his desk, assiduously writing reports or copying figures, and would frequently look dreamily out of the window and gaze upon the narrow crowded street, inwardly smiling at the men standing outside the barber's shop, self-consciously twirling a moustache or adjusting the set of a hat before entering the doorway.

Joseph always introduced Bernard to his clients.

'How lucky you are to have your son with you.'

'Yes, I am indeed fortunate.'

'And how are you getting on, young man?'

'It is all most interesting, thank you, sir.'

But he had received a letter from Douglas which was brimming with news and made him hurt with envy.

Dear Chap,

A hurried note. Already the end of September, and let it be said you should be here and that your companionship is much missed. Meanwhile café life goes on, and I must make do with the like of Hector Berlioz (!) and Charles Wilfred de Beriot who is as you know the pianist son of Charles Auguste (what a tragedy: blindness and paralysis of the left arm – surely a nightmarish prank to play upon a violinist). Charles Wilfred is a professor of piano here and I wish you could meet him. I have also briefly met Camille Saint-Saëns, a delightful and intelligent young man, not in the least conceited despite his success, and Meyebeer, the man Wagner so scathingly calls the 'Jew Banker who writes music'. In fact Meyebeer's real name is

Jacob Liebmann Beer. And you think you have problems!
Enough name dropping . . .

More truthfully these are persons I have only met
fleetingly, although I am greatly encouraged to mingle by
my teacher, Henri Vieuxtemps, who is doing his utmost to
involve me in this truly magnificent musical environment.
He is surely a genius, dear boy, and whilst he remains in
Paris I drink of his wisdom and knowledge. Someone I
HAVE met is your friend Sophie. It was by sheer accident:
I was basking in the glories of the Champs Elysées one late
Sunday, sipping a black coffee as only the French know
how to concoct, and dreaming of Napoleon and his Grand
Army, when I could not help but overhear the English
voices at the next table. I listened a while. The conversa-
tion, between two young ladies, did not appear to be of a
personal nature, and being a lonely fellow on his own I
ventured over to them. The one, a lanky redhead (very
badly dressed compared to the French demoiselles), was
less friendly, the other, dark and one could say rounded
in her physical form, was most charming and a shade
more fashion-conscious. When introductions were ex-
changed and I realized who she was I could not believe
such a coincidence.

Dear boy, she is surely not too bad. In fact you could do
worse. And naturally as you know she is Jewish. (She told
me she goes to the synagogue each Saturday. Synagogue
in Paris? I enquired surprised. Of course, she replied
with the simplicity which is typically hers.) Dear boy, you
lot get everywhere.

So when are you coming to visit? I would exhaust you with
the wonders of this city. I can see the Sacré Coeur from
my bedroom window. And the women – I have discovered
the Parisian women! I find that in this city my slight lack
of height is more than compensated by an English accent
which is apparently of unique appeal!

*Do I tempt you? Well then discard caution and come. I
will meet you at 'La Gare'. You name the date and I shall
be there. The times we will have will be rare, I promise.*

*I must close now. My 'hurried' note threatens to extend
beyond the allotted time limit, and I am being taken to a
Molière play at the Théâtre Français where my lack of
linguistics will no doubt mean tedious listening. Ah, but
life is rich.*

> *Love to you my dear friend.*
> *Yours ever, Doug.*

He always signed his name so that the 'Doug' sat beneath the
horizontal line of the initial 'H'. The familiarity of this stung
Bernard. He had a clear image of his friend sitting at a small
table writing frenziedly with the firm yet irregular hand that
denoted impatience. His mind was always ahead of his actions.
At school he had sat in front of Bernard because of his poor sight
and Bernard would see him hunched over his desk, his little
back rounded, and his right elbow sticking out sharply as he
scribbled. That elbow always came to rest by his side long
before any of the other boys'.

It was Shabat, entering with the failing of late summer's last
light, and secretly, with his kuppel on his head almost as a
gesture of apology, Bernard replied to Douglas. There had
been no time during the day, and he was long past that
particular guilt.

Dearest friend,

*Your ludicrous banter and vivid descriptions make it
seem as though you are not gone, however time lags
dismally, despite all the excitement courtesy of the City.
But you wait until your serious tuition commences! You
will wonder that once you possessed fingers. And how
is the French progressing? I cannot believe that even
you with your British charm will escape the perils of
ignorance for long.*

Now, would you believe that I have still not yet made it to 'Jew's Walk'! And you no doubt think at this point, 'Has the boy gone mad?' To which (hopefully) the answer is in the negative. 'Jew's Walk' is in fact the name given to a particular passage in the Stock Exchange which is occupied – yes, surprise – by the half-dozen or so Jews that are members. The brokers are known as Stockbroker Jews.

To be honest I was at first appalled by these attributions, but apparently they are not intended in any defamatory sense, merely as an explanation and even an assurance to Jewish clients. Nonetheless one is singled out and segregated by that nomenclature which taints the respectability with a seediness.

It is strange that my father never mentioned any of this that day when he proudly showed his son around a certain building in Throgmorton Street. He talked with animation of old coffee houses and Rothschild's pigeon – but no mention of these facts. Am I making an issue of something which is not an issue at all? One of my faults, dear Doug, as you have often delighted in telling me, is that on pointless subjects I dwell too long, and on those of consequence not at all!

I ramble on . . . I have come to know the City extremely well. It is a world of its own with so many corners and hidden areas you would not believe it, and I have by mischance forayed into many alleyways from which I doubted I'd emerge alive. You cannot imagine the contrast: the poverty situated only yards from where millions are being made.

My companion for the first few days was a young man named Arthur who has been with my father since he was younger than me. He is an East-ender with a dreadful pitted skin, strong cockney accent and the keenest sense of humour I have encountered. I missed him when I was on my own, and felt rather like a frightened rabbit as I strayed further and further into the warren which makes up these lanes.

I think of you so often, Doug, but am glad of your contentment. Convey my wishes to Sophie; how strange, as a child I fancied I was in love with her! . . .

After writing his letter Bernard joined his parents in the dining-room for Shabat dinner. He broke the Chollah and dipped it into his soup, and all the time he apparently took part in the conversation with his parents, he pictured Douglas in Paris.

After dinner his father went upstairs to attend to his toilet, and Bernard played the piano. When he had finished he hoisted Anna the cat from his lap and went to sit beside his mother, who was quietly working on an elaborate tapestry. The cat leaped once more onto Bernard's knee and settled herself, purring noisily. He stroked her absently.

'You are a musician, Bernard,' Helen commented sadly.

'No – a stockbroker, Mama,' he answered bitterly.

She looked at him with an expression full of remorse and spoke hesitantly: 'It is the right thing. I am sure, Bernard. Your future will be safe and assured. That is all your father wishes for you. He *knows* it to be right.'

She was pleading with her conscience, and it was the first time she had even vaguely broached the subject.

Bernard's brief anger was spent. He loved his mother. 'I know it too.'

He covered her hand and massaged her thin fingers that were the same shape as his own, and at that point Joseph reappeared and his heart swelled at the sight of them; whilst he could know nothing of the short conversation.

Time passed, and within Bernard developed a terrible dissatisfaction. He barely touched the piano and became a diligent, rather dour young City gentleman, purposeful and attentive to detail; and his father was proud of him.

Harold began to visit again and comfortably resumed his hold over the family, this time without challenge from Bernard, for the old energy required for battle was not there.

108

Every morning Bernard laid tefillin and every Saturday he went to synagogue as usual; but now he prayed avidly, concentrating on his prayer book with a new devoutness, reading works of a religious nature at home, and texts about the Jewish people. He read with an urgent zeal, searching for a meaning somewhere in something. He was permanently exhausted yet slept for ten hours a night, because his brain was worn out with dissatisfaction. Was this the life for which he had been groomed, this – desert?

Is it wrong to believe I am entitled to more than this? he wondered once. *Would I be content had I followed my own ambitions, or would I still find a reason for discontent?*

He had not replied to Douglas's last two letters. What was there to say? 'Today a client's affairs were entrusted to me to handle on my own.' And what of it? Soon there would be many more clients who would have to trust his judgement. It was not comparable to Douglas's news:

> *I am to perform in a concert with Vieuxtemps this
> Saturday at the Théâtre du Palais-Royal, after which the
> master is due to return to Brussels. We shall be playing
> Bach's Double Violin Concerto, and I cannot deny that I
> feel a few qualms. Dear boy, I wish you could be there for
> moral support. . . .*

Bernard was stung by sharp and useless jealousy, but he knew that he must simply accept the differences in their lives and that their discretions would diverge more and more. He saw no reason, therefore, to reply to Douglas's letters or even to prolong a friendship in which soon there would be no common link and only distressing reminders.

Just before Bernard's eighteenth birthday, his father had a heart attack. It happened on the way up the office stairs one Tuesday morning. Bernard was behind Joseph who had as usual stopped for his short 'breather', when the boy heard the little intakes of air become quicker and more shallow, catching in his father's throat. Suddenly Joseph swayed and gasped, and Bernard caught him as he was about to fall backwards down the stairs.

Joseph was under medical supervision for about a fortnight, and Helen barely left his side during that time. 'Dear, you must relax,' she insisted when he worried about the office.

'But Helen, it was just a small attack.'

'Nonetheless, it shows a vulnerability and you must not strain yourself.'

'I wish I could be at the office, just to make sure it is all right.'

'I am sure Bernard and Arthur are coping admirably, dear.'

'I hope so. It is a big responsibility. I thank God for Bernard, my dear. He has changed, become so mature. I am very proud of him.'

And Joseph looked long and lovingly into his wife's troubled eyes, and his own watered with emotion.

On the Sunday morning of Bernard's birthday the sound of the front doorbell was followed by a bang of the heavy brass lion's head. Bernard, alone in the family room, heard it but took little notice, continuing to read his newspaper.

There was a knock at the half-open door and the new maid (who was middle-aged and plain) announced: 'A Mr –'

'– Douglas Hamilton to see you, sir – and happy birthday to you!' the cheerful, dearly familiar voice announced over her shoulder.

'Doug!'

'Bernard!'

They went towards each other slowly. Bernard had intended that when he saw his friend again he would be cool and aloof but, caught unawares, he felt only the greatest possible joy.

'Doug!' he repeated, his face lit with pleasure.

They flung their arms around each other, and then Douglas held up his forefinger solemnly. 'Remember?'

'Of course.'

'You look terrible, dear boy.'

'Thank you.'

'The face of a suffering poet.'

'I shall ignore you,' Bernard retorted, smiling happily and

110

shaking his head in disbelief. 'How is Paris? When did you arrive?'

'I arrived yesterday morning. Paris is splendid as always. I'm a bit of a celebrity now, but I shall tell you that later.'

'You gave me no warning.'

'And deliberately so. I know you too well, Bernard. Where are your parents?'

'My father has been very ill. He's in bed. My mother is talking to him. He had a heart attack – didn't your father tell you?'

'My parents went to Scotland two days ago so I haven't seen them, and letter writing isn't one of their favourite pastimes. How dreadful, dear boy. Is your father all right?'

'Yes, but he has to take care.'

'Whilst your mother is upstairs I have something for you. I must give it you now, in private.'

'A letter – from whom?'

'From Cramer.'

'*Cramer*? Is this a joke? I don't understand.' Bernard brushed his hand over his forehead and felt momentarily giddy.

'May I pour us each a brandy?'

'Willingly.'

'The letter,' Douglas explained, with his back to Bernard as he quarter-filled two balloon glasses, 'was given to me by the old man last spring to be handed to you when you were eighteen. I have no idea what it contains.'

He returned, and sat in the chair beside the chaise-longue. 'And since today you are eighteen, what better day? Take a sip –'

He handed Bernard the glass, then withdrew the letter from a deep inside pocket.

Bernard stared at the seal and at the handwriting before ripping it open:

Dear young sir, (Oh, that achingly familiar form of address.)
Happy birthday! And so how is the businessman?

I write from my bed in my little house in Kensington, and as I lie here I have much time to reflect. I know that I have had

111

my turn in life and that my turn is now over. But young
sir, I can say to myself: 'Yes, you have indeed been
fortunate. You have directed yourself and have done all
and more than you wanted.' And this, I believe, is what
life is about; and it is an art to be learned; one that can
only be learned when you understand yourself and are
not afraid to discover that self. Then, after a life of
fulfilment, when death approaches as mine does now, you
do not feel deprived.

So my thoughts turn to you – the proud young sir who
pretended to disregard his old master, but who only
succeeded in disregarding his true self. We always had an
understanding you and I, did we not? I think of you, dear
Bernard, drifting in a sea of stocks and shares and
commodities; with figures and prices soaring and plummeting. Do they mean anything to you?

Remember music. Remember that once it was the sounds
of the piano soaring and plummeting that moved you.
   But it is not my business, is it? I tell myself this, and
then I think: 'But yes, it is your business, for you love him
like a second son, and have to watch his incredible talent
go to waste.'

For, dear Bernard, you do have incredible talent, and I
have failed you in that I have not managed to make you
pursue it, and you have failed me by not doing so.

Perhaps I am just a meddling old man, but I ask one
question, Bernard, and that is: when you attain my years,
do you think you will be able to sit by yourself in your
home and say as I can say: 'I have lived life as I wished and
no other way, and I can sleep forever without the burden
of regret in my heart?'

I wish I could have seen my young sir again before I died.
It is all a great, great pity.

  God bless you.
  Johann Baptist Cramer.

P.S. In case you should ever need to contact him, I enclose
the address of a close friend, Sir Edmund Moore, to
whom I have written about you. I expect you have
heard of him. He is a much respected music critic and
publisher of factual literature.
        Yours – J. B. C.

Bernard handed the letter wordlessly to Douglas and reached for his drink. The glass shook as he held it.

Douglas read the letter and gravely handed it back to Bernard. For a moment their hands remained linked by the sheet of paper.

Bernard said: 'It is as though he were in this room. I can hear his voice.' He closed his eyes and rested his head against the back of the chair, seeing Cramer's face, each line lovingly etched.

He sat in thoughtful silence whilst Douglas refilled their glasses. Bernard took his over to the piano and touched the keyboard caressingly. He had not played for many weeks and now he poured forgotten feeling into the instrument, and it yielded to him, responsive and alive.

When at last he pushed himself up from his chair, everything seemed bathed in silence.

He went and stood by the window where the sunlight made a halo round him. His fists were clenched at his sides, his eyes burning with excitement and he looked like someone who had just seen God.

He faced his little friend and his voice rang out, resonant and quivering with emotion: 'Douglas. Cramer. I am going to become a musician.'

PART TWO

Chapter Eight

Bernard had reached his decision in a moment that day in the family room, but it could not be acted upon instantly. While Joseph was at home regaining his strength and happily oblivious of Bernard's plans, Bernard held the fort at the office. He proved his worth and ability so successfully that it was only a matter of weeks before his ever-increasing workload made it necessary to hire another messenger. He had his room painted white, bought a more comfortable chair, and a shiny-leaved green plant which he watered each day and twice weekly coated lightly with milk.

Every evening when he returned home he discussed the day's activity with Joseph, whose eyes sparkled to hear his son talk. This was what being Jewish meant; this raising of children so that they might continue your ways. This was perpetuation. This was strength as understood by the Talmud; with it, nobody could ever penetrate the sacred circle of their race.

Joseph's recovery was now rapid, and he began taking gentle walks around the crescent, wrapped up with thick scarves round his thin neck, his top hat concealing his baldness, and doeskin gloves on his hands. Helen always accompanied him, her arm linked through his whilst he leaned towards her, so that despite his high hat he was still shorter than her. The contact of love flowed between them. They were bonded together afresh by the shock of the illness and the fear of losing one another, and they became newly precious to each other.

It was 1859, and for Bernard the months fled by. In early summer Sophie returned to live in London. She had visited briefly in the winter with Douglas, and an easy platonic friendship between her and Bernard had been established.

117

She was living once more with her family in a neighbouring crescent and often visited with her mother, a snobbish but kindly woman with poor vision, wiry grey hair and a hooked nose which seemed perpetually pressed to a lace handkerchief in an attempt to assuage its interminable sniffing.

In appearance Sophie did not in the slightest resemble her mother, her face was soft and round without any sharpness. Her years of singing training had lent her speaking voice a controlled clarity and the most beautiful intonation Bernard had ever heard in anyone, and of the girls he knew she was the one he respected most. He admired, too, the strength she had exhibited in the face of parental disapproval at her taking pupils for singing lessons. When he told her this, Sophie laughed in her down-to-earth fashion:

'I presented them with a far more depressing alternative – that of going on stage and becoming an opera singer! I thought dear Mama was going to faint.'

'But do you wish to perform on stage?'

'Yes, I believe I do. But it is not possible,' she added without rancour.

'But why not?' he said angrily.

'Why Bernard!' she berated him, laughing at the absurdity of it. 'You know it cannot be possible.'

He remained tight-lipped and silent.

'And now you are brooding. There. What have I said to make you brood?'

'It is not you. It is –'

'Yes?'

'No. I am being silly. So tell me your news.'

Their conversations were relaxed and natural and never now did he consider her in any light except as a good friend.

One person, however, had different ideas about Sophie, and that was Harold. He had decided he was going to marry her and that nobody would stand in his way. He was as single-minded in this objective as in everything else, and he saw Sophie as a prize he wanted to win as much for practical as for romantic reasons. In another year he would be qualified and had already been accepted to serve his apprenticeship with high-ranking chambers in Lincoln's Inn; as the wife of a successful barrister, Sophie would be ideal. And so Harold planned his tactics and set about his wooing.

After familiarizing himself with the parents he turned his attentions to the daughter, who until now had hardly been aware of his existence. The courtship began with the untypically romantic gesture of arranging for a lavish bouquet of flowers to be delivered to her door. They had cost a fortune. Sophie accepted her gift gravely and a little awkwardly for she was not a girl to be influenced or impressed by presents, and was not sure that she liked or trusted Harold. But Harold was persistent; the flowers were followed by weekly visits, and conversation was maintained on a light and civil note. If Sophie appeared at all strained, Harold convinced himself that she was merely a little awed by his intelligence and savoir-faire.

But the weeks were passing without much progress being made, and when he finally suggested that perhaps she and her parents might visit him and his father one Sunday afternoon, she politely declined, explaining how busy she was. Yet not too busy to be at the Folignos, on her own, on the very day he invited her. She was sitting beside Bernard and did not even blush when he entered.

'Oh hallo, Harold,' she said as though he were utterly unimportant, and continued talking to Bernard in lively tones that she never used with him.

Harold almost burst with rage and resentment. Seeing her and Bernard sitting together in easy camaraderie so incensed him that he longed to fling some object at them and storm from the house. But he was too logical and cunning for that. Instead he sat down opposite them, so close that his feet were almost on his cousin's, took a piece of fruit from the bowl, and between noisy munches began one of his monologues that obliterated all other conversation.

'He is dreadful,' ranted Bernard the second Harold had gone. 'I am ashamed to be related to him.'

Sophie suddenly gave a loud gasp.

'What is it?'

'I have just remembered something which could account for

his behaviour. He invited myself and my parents to his home today, and I told him I was busy. Oh dear. How perfectly embarrassing. What a terrible thing to do.'

'But it is wonderful!' Bernard threw his head back with gleeful laughter and flung himself onto the chaise-longue, where he continued to rock with mirth until Sophie was forced to join in.

Now that Joseph was in charge once more Bernard was able to relax a little, and he subtly tried to remove his influence from the business by handing more work to Arthur.

'Bernard – I am not doubting your reasoning, you understand, but why are you handing over so much to Arthur?' Joseph enquired.

'Papa, we are expanding the business so rapidly I think you must be prepared to delegate more. Arthur has been with you for years and I think perhaps you are too used to him to realize what a lot he knows.'

'Yes, perhaps you are right there,' Joseph said slowly.

Bernard gazed outside the window for a moment at the little match-seller. The child was picking someone's pocket – the speed of his action was unbelievable! He turned away with an amused smile.

'What is funny?'

'Nothing. I just saw something, that is all. Papa, to revert to Arthur, I think that beneath the quips and anecdotes is a sensible and knowledgeable man and that you ought to give him a chance to prove his worth.'

Even as he spoke Bernard thought: *I am as devious and sly as Harold.*

But Joseph, delighted by the sound sense of his eighteen-year-old son's reasoning, shook his head wonderingly. 'What would I do without you?'

'Don't say that, Papa.'

'Why not? I am surely able to pass such a remark, and I shall even repeat it: What would I do without you, my boy?' And he reached up and ruffled his son's thick hair.

120

'Oh Papa . . .'

At last Bernard felt the time had come to write to Cramer's friend, Sir Edmund Moore. He did not know how to begin the letter and was reminded of himself as a thirteen year old writing his bar-mitzvah speech. After many attempts, which veered between being too apologetic and too presumptuous, the final draft was completed – brief, formal and impersonal:

> *Dear Sir Edmund,*
>
> *I am taking this opportunity to write to you in the hope that my late professor of music, Johann Baptist Cramer, mentioned my name to you.*
>
> *I should be very grateful if you would be agreeable to making an appointment at your nearest convenience, and to this end I await your reply.*
>
> *I am, sir, yours sincerely,*
> *Bernard Foligno*

He then posted the letter and thought about nothing else. But it was a month before he received a reply during which time he had sunk into a mood of despondency. He had decided that there were three possible explanations: the first was that Cramer had failed to mention him after all; the second that Sir Edmund was disinterested; and the third that the letter had gone astray. This third possibility caused the most problems because he then debated whether or not to write another letter, which if the first had *not* gone astray would be a tremendous imposition.

However, just when Bernard had decided he had nothing to lose by writing again, a letter duly arrived from the address in Brook Street, Mayfair. He ripped it open as though his life depended upon it:

> *Dear Mr Foligno,*
> *Please forgive the delay in this reply to your letter, but I have only just returned from a six-week trip to Italy, and*

121

it arrived in my absence. It was, I admit, with considerable surprise, but also with great pleasure that I read it,
and most certainly I should be agreeable to a meeting
between ourselves, especially knowing in what high
esteem my dear friend Johann B. held you.

I would suggest you visit me at my house for tea on
Wednesday, 20th October, if this is convenient for you,
and shall look forward to seeing you then unless
I hear otherwise.

Yours truly,
Sir Edmund J. Moore

A couple of nights before his scheduled meeting, Bernard
went to a concert at the Hanover Square Rooms with Louis
Antone Jullien conducting Joseph Joachim, the virtuoso violinist. It was a splendid evening and Bernard felt rapturous,
imagining what it would be like to perform in such a place, and
to have such a receptive audience in his power. His future now
seemed like hillocks waiting to be climbed – offering him ever
greater rewards with each little summit attained.

During the interval he met a couple of young musicians he
knew, both struggling to survive. One was a clarinetist and the
other a cellist and they were 'useful' players as opposed to
remarkable ones. They waved when they saw him, smiling from
faces that were alike in their emaciated appearance. Around
their scraggy necks their winged shirt collars were yellowed and
barely stiffened, and the edges of their dress-coat cuffs were
frayed. Bernard hesitated before greeting them, not wishing to
temper his euphoric mood with doubts; and as he walked over
to join them, concealing the shame he felt on their behalf, he
smelled their stale breath and body odours and heard the
suspicious rasp in the throat of one of them.

As he had known he would, he returned to his seat dejected,
but after listening to Joachim play again, his spirits were
restored and he reasoned to himself: *I know it is a risk. I have
always known. But those chaps are fools with no brain to resort*

to. I can always revert to business if all else fails. And besides, they did not have a man like Cramer in their lives.

He could not fear the future. It had become too much of a friend to fear.

He decided to take a walk – he was far too overwrought to go directly home – and the night whilst cold was dry and clear, with a smell of soot in the air. His hands still burned from clapping so hard; his long legs ached from being cramped in a confined space; the excitement still thrilled in him, and he walked with no purpose in mind, in no particular direction, his thoughts churning wildly with the endless possibilities which now seemed within his grasp.

He found himself facing south down Regent Streeet, away from Oxford Circus, and with a kind of curiosity strolled across the boundary where the John Nash architecture divided the Hanover Square district from Soho. Into the narrow backwaters he wandered, where washing was strung outside windows on lines or across rusting railings – the casual exhibits of people's personal lives. White soul-less faces were illuminated harshly under street lamps, and the dull, beckoning eyes did not match the crude innuendo of the voices.

A taxi cab passed and Bernard was about to hail it when he realized it was already occupied. He stood back in the shadows of a building, and saw a figure lean out of the cab's window and point to a hovering girl with bright red lips in an ashen face. She shrugged indifferently to her colleague before sauntering with a swish of her skirts into the carriage. It was obvious from the action taking place that the person inside was no novice to such a situation, and Bernard caught a glimpse of him as the carriage moved off and the light shone inside it. There was no mistake. It was Harold.

Bernard felt no sense of shock; indeed, how many times recently had he himself thought of taking a whore? Sometimes in bed at night his body leaped with wakefulness and memories of soft, yielding flesh. To have been shocked, therefore, would have been hypocritical. Instead he was elated. He had a weapon to use against Harold for the future. Harold, the pompous would-be-barrister would not enjoy a public showdown.

It had been a good and fruitful evening in so many ways, and Bernard went home well-satisfied.

On the twentieth of October, Bernard stood on the polished step of the house in Brook Street and brushed the rain from his clothing. A butler greeted him with an inclination of his head, and he was shown in to a large square hallway with white and black marbled floor, a solitary centrally-placed library table and a single chair. The white-painted walls were broken by three pine doors, and gesturing to one the butler said:

'Would you care to follow me, sir?'

He was a little fellow with a strong Irish accent and lively, rather bloodshot eyes, and he opened the door for Bernard and ushered him into a fine, pannelled library.

Within, his hand outstretched in ready welcome, stood a commanding figure with a shock of white hair, whiskers and a beard, and from amidst this fleecy profusion his eyes fixed themselves on Bernard with a piecing blue gaze. Despite his bearing Bernard knew that Sir Edmund must be in his late sixties, and his appearance reminded him of the Commendatore in *Don Giovanni*. He was unsurprised to be greeted by a base voice so deep it almost rumbled, and containing warm humour and the faintest of Scottish accents.

They clasped hands and met each other's eyes, liking what they saw. Sir Edmund slapped his massive palm on Bernard's shoulder.

'So this is the prodigy! Grown up since my friend's last letter to me, I dare say. Did you know that you were his challenge?' He raised a shaggy white eyebrow questioningly.

'I realize it now. Perhaps I always did. I wish I could tell him he need not have been disheartened after all.' Bernard sighed heavily.

'I think, Bernard – may I dispense with customary formality and call you Bernard? – I think, Bernard, that we have a great deal to discuss, and we have plenty of time indeed, but first I should very much like to show you my favourite place, if you are willing.'

'I should be glad, sir.'

They were almost of equal height, Sir Edmund being perhaps an inch or so taller; it was in their bulk that they differed, the one being massive and heavy, the other lithe and athletic. Facing each other they seemed in that instant to reach an instinctive understanding, and Sir Edmund took Bernard's hand warmly in his.

'I am looking forward to knowing you, young man, and I am impatient to learn what prompted this meeting. And who knows, friendship apart, perhaps we can be beneficial to one another. So, Macduff shall lead on. . .'

With a purposeful stride he led the way into the music room, a vast high-ceilinged room flooded with natural light and dominated by the concert-hall-sized Broadwood grand. Two Persian rugs were spread on the parquet floor, but aside from chairs lining the walls, some stacked, a large gold, damask-covered settee, and a couple of card tables, the room was bereft of furniture. Colour on the walls was provided by two great tapestries, and the curtains at the windows were of the same gold damask as the settee and elaborately swagged, draped and tasselled. Clustered in a corner by the piano were flimsy music stands, and beside them an old oak coffer and a Canterbury. Both were filled, spilling with sheet music. Behind the coffer were various instruments in their cases.

'I am a poor musician.' Sir Edmund gestured to them with an apologetic expression. 'I dabble for my own pleasure and am master of none. In fact sometimes I can hardly bear to hear myself . . . Anyway, my own paltry efforts are not of consequence, for this is the room of wonderful soirées, when it is filled with the music of friends and selected people – people who care and have that common aim.

'And now – am I permitted to hear for myself what Johann B. meant? Do you by any chance know Chopin's Rondo in C minor? It was his first published work at the age of only fifteen and it is really delightful. I have the music for it –'

'I know it well, and actually I have no need of the music.' Bernard gave a small self-deprecating laugh and scratched his ear.

Sir Edmund smiled, remembering Cramer's letter:

He never needs to use music, and memorizes quite
formidably complicated and lengthy pieces. However,
I feel it is as a composer that his future lies.

He sat himself down in one of the balloon-back chairs which he positioned behind Bernard. He noticed the hunched set of the boy's shoulders, heard the intake of breath as though he were a singer filling his lungs . . . A few light experimental notes, and then – the revelation.

Old John had never been wrong. Now, was it up to him to carry on Cramer's mission? If it was, then Sir Edmund was prepared to dedicate himself to the task. He thought, *Ah Johnny B. I promise that you succeeded. Here is a giant.*

They returned to the library, where a butler's tray set with fine Georgian silver had been laid for tea and placed in front of the two large buttoned-hide chairs, behind which stood the little Irishman waiting to help them to their seats.

'Shall I pour, sir?'

'Yes please, Murphy.'

Bernard sat back comfortably, sinking a little into the soft leather cushion. Outside was gentle dusk and spasmodic rain and the thickening atmosphere of autumn, whilst within was the crackling applewood on the fire, the smell of smoked salmon sandwiches, and the sound of Murphy pouring tea into the green and gold cups. He was replete with sensual pleasure.

'Bernard, please help yourself to food – take a plate.'

Seeing him hesitate, Sir Edmund took a selection of sandwiches and biscuits and put them on his plate. 'There! You are far too polite – you hesitate too long. Now young man, after you have taken a sip of tea and at least a bite from every sandwich, perhaps you would be so good as to tell me exactly what is in your mind, and what it is you want from me . . . No! I said *after*, not before!'

Bernard obliged, masticating self-consciously and deliberately, his eyes submissive under the other's authoritative stare.

'Now you can tell me,' Sir Edmund laughed.

Bernard set his plate down carefully beside him and laced his fingers together earnestly: 'Sir, I wish to become a musician. I am at present in business with my father, but I cannot continue in that field.' He leaned forward tensely in his seat, and with an impassioned expression on his face continued: 'All my life I have contrived to be something I am not, but now I find I can no longer do so. I want, long, only to be involved with music.'

'I see.' The older man scrutinized him silently.

Bernard thought: *Oh God, he does not want to help me. I have confided in him and he has been kind and hospitable out of deference to Cramer; but he does not wish to help me. Oh, I am so arrogant and impulsive. They are such faults of mine.* He seemed to shrink with his feeling of humiliation and his head hung low. His demeanour was one of abject misery.

Sir Edmund looked at him almost tenderly. 'Then I shall help you all I can,' he said gently.

And at these words Bernard shot up in his seat, and the change in his face – the transition to joy – made him look like a child. He forced calmness into his voice: 'Do you mean that?'

'I never say things I do not mean, lad. I have no patience with falsity. Now shall we talk?'

They spoke of his future, of his potential, of ideas and ideals, and of course of Cramer. Then Sir Edmund Moore said: 'Soon you will have to break the news to your parents.'

'I know.' Bernard gritted his teeth. The prospect of telling them hung over him unpleasantly.

'So, when?'

'Well, not this month. My father has a new client by the name of Beavis to whom he wishes to introduce me. If Mr Beavis decides to accept our services our business could expand to such an extent that we would have to employ additional help, and possibly even move to larger premises. I have to work alongside my father here. I cannot let him down – it is far too important for him . . . And early December is the anniversary of my sister's death, and also my birthday. Then it is Channukah, which is an important Jewish festival. And, well, I think perhaps the New Year would be better.'

'And January? Whose birthday is it in January?'

'My mother's.'

'And February?'

'My father's.'

'And then?'

'In spring we have Passover –'

'You see? Bernard, Bernard . . . There will always be a reason *not* to tell them won't there?'

'But I *shall* do. I have decided that.'

'How long ago?'

'Almost a year. My father has been gravely ill. But I have not wasted time. I have been formulating ideas, and practising the piano for long hours.'

'I believe you, lad, don't look so agitated. And if a parent is ill, then that most certainly is not the right time for surprises, particularly ones which might not be received with pleasure. But now your father is recovered?'

'As much as he can be.'

'Then now it is. *Now.* You have been responsible, considerate and left matters tidy. *Now* is the time.'

'Yes, I know. I have needed somebody to push me. I think I shall tell my mother first. She is very understanding.'

When he arrived back that evening, he immediately asked the maid: 'Where is my mother?'

'I believe she is upstairs, sir,' she replid, taking his wet coat and hat from him.

Bernard bounded upstairs. Then he hesitated. From his parents' bedroom came the sounds of vomiting. The door was very slightly ajar and anxiously he pushed it open and peered inside. Helen was bent over the washstand being sick, whilst her old servant, Ethel, stood uselessly behind her.

'Mama?'

'Oh Bernard . . .'

She began to retch once more, and he walked over to her and gently supported her.

A week passed. Helen looked haggard and grey-faced, but Bernard tried not to notice, and as he had not seen her being sick again he convinced himself that all was well with her. He returned home early one day, having made an excuse to his father and wanting to find his mother by herself. He was prepared with his rehearsed speech.

They sat together in the family room and Bernard asked: 'How are you feeling now, Mama?'

'Fine, thank you, dearest,' she answered mildly.

How grateful he was for those four words. It was irrevelant that her face was as grey as her hair. She had said she was 'fine'.

'Mama, I –'

'Bernard, I –'

They spoke simultaneously, and each laughed self-consciously.

'You first, Bernard.'

'No, Mama. You tell me what you were going to say.'

'Very well. Bernard, I know it might come as a shock to you at my age –' She looked down at her fingers and fiddled with her ring, before returning her eyes to meet his. 'It is all rather embarrassing, dear, but the doctor has confirmed to me that I am – with child.'

'Good God!'

'Do not take God's name in vain, dearest.'

He stared at her slender body disbelievingly, and trying not to sound as appalled as he felt, asked: 'Are you happy about it?'

'Well –' she hesitated, smiling almost shyly '– now that I am growing accustomed to the idea I am quite happy. However, because of my age the first three or four months are crucial. I must be careful of my health.'

'Is it safe to have it, Mama?'

'Oh yes, dear. Mr Hamilton has assured me of that.'

'And Papa? How has he reacted?'

'He has concealed his shock exceedingly well!' She laughed girlishly. 'Now I do believe he is quite excited. Of course he hopes for a girl. I tell him it is too premature to hope for anything under the circumstances. There! I was dreading telling you – why, I shall be as old as many grandmothers! I thought you would look upon me with disgust. *Do* you, Bernard?'

'No Mama – of course I do not.' He took her hand in reassurance.

129

'What a kind boy. Your father is so proud of you, you know. Now, what was it you were going to tell me before?'

'Oh – oh I have quite forgotten. It cannot have been important.'

The pain scorched his heart. His hopes were like a fly beneath a heavy boot. How could he tell them now, with his mother's life in danger – whatever she said to the contrary? He wanted to shout with frustrated rage and disappointment at the way adversity continually thwarted him.

A few days later Bernard visited Sir Edmund Moore again, and as he relayed the news tears stood out in his eyes in unspilled loops and he turned his head, unbearably ashamed.

'But how unreasoning you can be for an intelligent young man, Bernard,' Sir Edmund rumbled. 'Your mother will not be with child or ill for ever. You have a couple of months to wait before you know whether a miscarriage is likely, then you tell them.'

'It seems so cruel. Sir – they are living this little idyll: a belated love affair, and my father in his false security indulges in fantasies of the future.'

'And what about your *idyll*? What about your fantasies? Are you not entitled to your own? Lad, you are not dying! You are not depriving them of your life. All you are doing is changing your profession. It is your turn now; your parents have had theirs. You belong to yourself, Bernard. Only yourself.'

That evening in a voice of barely concealed elation, Joseph announced that Mr Beavis had decided to utilize their services.

'On the strength of this, my boy,' he said, putting an arm around his son, 'we shall need bigger premises. And I promise you a smart room of your own. What do you think of that, eh? Ah, Helen dearest –'

He turned to his wife with that special look of caressing tenderness: Helen, whose swollen feet and ankles were soaking in a basin of tepid water. Her hands stilled from her needlework and she returned the look.

'It is really most exciting,' Joseph said. 'I feel as though my life is beginning and I hope you will feel like this at my age, Bernard. Mr Beavis was most impressed by you. He told me during our luncheon at Simpsons that your capacity to remember prices and facts was phenomenal. As you know he has many businesses including a printing concern, and when I told him that you have a slight interest in music he requested to meet you again – as soon as possible – apparently he wishes to venture into music publishing and feels that you might be able to assist him in various aspects. My boy, you must meet him soon. He could be extremely useful, and introduce us to many potential clients if he is satisfied with our firm.'

Bernard had rarely seen his father so excited, and this mood only increased his sense of deceit. He felt heavy with it. As he listened to the confident talk of the future, the plans for the next three years, Bernard wanted to cry out: *Stop, for goodness sake stop! You can take nothing for granted, you should have learned that by now.*

Days passed, during which his mother continued to vomit and heave and Bernard tried not to agitate himself with morbid reflections. The sense of his own selfishness never left him, and those transitional weeks were tainted with spuriousness. He felt like a guest about to spoil the party.

Chapter Nine

One day Joseph and Bernard went as usual to the office and found the barber's shop downstairs still locked, the blinds pulled down.

'That's strange,' observed Bernard. 'He is always in by eight o'clock, singing some Italian aria or other.'

They asked the blind newspaper vendor, and he turned in their general direction, his open eyes opaque white: 'Oh, 'e did 'isself in last night was wot I 'eard. 'Ung isself. Caught 'is missus wiv 'er lover. Upset 'im it did. So I 'eard. Did 'isself in. Upset 'im a bit see? One of them things.' He shrugged, and his expressionless face gazed into the gloomy sky. ' 'Ave a paper for my trouble?'

Joseph took a *Times* and paid him, and the old man briefly and expertly fingered the coin to ascertain its value.

'You'll be wanting change,' he rasped slyly.

'No, keep it, for your trouble.'

'Thanking you, sir.'

Within twenty-four hours Joseph had negotiated a deal for the barber's shop and they immediately set about altering it to their needs. This at least gave Bernard something else to think about, enabling him to feign a sense of permanence.

He met again with Mr Beavis over lunch at St James's Restaurant, which was attached to the Hall, and while Bernard conscientiously ate fish he looked enviously at Mr Beavis's grilled bones followed by roasted quails.

He was a friendly and charming man – small, rotund and balding, this compensated by his alarmingly hirsute eyebrows – and almost his first words were: 'I hear you were a pupil of Johann Baptist Cramer.'

At the mention of that name Bernard felt a leaping of his heart, and he knew for certain that this would be no ordinary luncheon. He listened to Beavis's plans, whilst all the time longing to tell his own. But the purpose of the meeting was to ensure business for his father, and he could not endanger that for a moment's self-indulgence. There seemed such irony in the situation. If only it could have been postponed for just a few weeks, then they could have talked on a different level. Instead Bernard was on his guard, forced to remain impassive as the other man spoke of his aim to encourage young composers and publish their first works.

'You must meet Sir Edmund Moore.'

'What – the critic? You know him?'

'Yes, sir. He is a – friend.'

'Then I should be most grateful for an introduction.' Mr Beavis sounded impressed and looked shrewdly at Bernard from under those bushy brows. 'Most grateful indeed,' he repeated, nodding his head emphatically.

They parted with great liking on both sides, though Mr Beavis was a little bewildered by certain enigmatic qualities about the young man.

A letter arrived from Paris.

Dear chap,

Surely you have told your parents by now; or am I to assume by your prolonged silence across the waves that the answer is still negative? I can imagine you tormenting yourself with guilt. For sure you are the guiltiest person I know!

Here in Paris, despite the easy availability and the lure of the female gender, I have decided to give those gracious creatures a miss at the moment, being as I am far too occupied in more cerebral activities . . .

Poor Douglas. So he had had no success as yet. Bernard could imagine his little friend being rebuffed, then attempting to dismiss his rejection with customary comic bravado.

*. . . And what of you? Dear boy, I have this fixed image
imprinted in my mind of you standing like Methuselah,
waving your arms and embracing enlightenment as if you
had already reached Nivarna! But you will, I promise.*

*What else? How is the dreaded toad? (This was their
nickname for Harold) Is he still wooing the voluptuous
princess? Give the latter my kindest and tell her that I
miss drinking endless petites tasses de café with her, and
also tell her not to succumb to the lure of the law.*

*It is damned cold here, and rather stupidly three days
ago I lost my coat. My nose feels like a dog's. However,
even the gloom of winter cannot remove the glory from
this place. . . .*

It was strange occupying the barber's shop. The big Italian's
ghost lingered, surprisingly graceful as he flitted between
customers, and the snipping sounds of the scissors was almost
audible. No longer could Bernard look from the upper windows at the men preening themselves outside, or at the street
and its traders. The scene's previous distance had held an
enchanted unreality, like looking at a story-book illustration; it
had offered him comfort and a reason to hurry back to the
office, to hang his head from the open window and inhale the
smells and sounds and activity. Now that he was on the same
level he was a part of that scene and it could therefore offer
him nothing. Upstairs Arthur had his father's old room, whilst
Bernard's little office was now devoted totally to the files,
books and general paraphernalia. Downstairs the shop had
been stripped, hastily refurbished, and partitioned so that
each had his own section. They had also invested in the very
latest typing machine for the new assistant who came in three
days a week.

'I cannot believe it!' Joseph exclaimed to Bernard. 'All this
space to ourselves. I am sad, though, that this only came about
because the barber died. But Bernard, how glad I am I do not
have to go up those stairs each day. You cannot imagine how

glad. They worried me every time I stood at the bottom and saw how many there were to climb. My son – before you, you see a contented man.'

The weeks passed. Sophie visited by herself one Sunday afternoon, and Bernard accompanied her as she sang. Her voice had developed into a powerful mezzo of wonderful tone-contrast. Afterwards they chatted companionably with the ease of shared childhood and shared interests. Acting as hostess in his home, Sophie poured him some more tea, and he sat back comfortably.

'When is it due, Bernard?'

'When is what due?' he enquired absently.

'The baby of course. Your parents' baby.'

'Oh. How did you know?'

'Goodness, Bernard! I *am* a woman.' As if it answered exactly how she knew.

He appraised her openly, this self-acknowledged woman with her full-blown, dark femininity, and was unembarrassed when she lightly reprimanded him:

'Really, Bernard!'

'I was just checking for verification.' He looked at her mock-seriously, and they laughed together.

'Oh, by the way,' he suddenly remembered to tell her, 'I heard from Douglas. He sent his kindest wishes and all that.'

'How very sweet. How is he?'

'Fine. He said he misses drinking coffee with you.'

'And I miss him, and Paris, greatly. It was a phase of my life I was fortunate to experience, and one not permitted to many girls of my sort. But now I must compromise – I believe it is an unfortunate component of adulthood. It is something we all have to do: mellow our beliefs and yearnings.'

Bernard shifted his position uncomfortably. 'But surely the compromise must not be detrimental to ourselves. We owe ourselves happiness.'

'It depends what you mean by detrimental. There is much that can be accepted, given time.'

In that instant he disliked her briefly, and stared at her with deadened eyes; while Sophie, unaware that the conversation was subjective and heedless of any change in mood, said: 'You have not told me when the baby is due.'

'In about five months – I think,' he replied vaguely.

'So the especially dangerous time is over then.'

'Yes . . . Yes.' His expression lightened as the realization dawned on him.

Sophie commented: 'Your mother looks so well now.'

'Oh *does* she?' He latched eagerly on to her words. 'Does she really?'

That Sunday night he studied his mother carefully. Certainly her face appeared to be less strained. She walked more easily, and there was no bowl of water near the chair for her feet. Joseph had just gone upstairs – he always took his time, washing and refreshing himself.

'How are you feeling nowadays, Mama?' Bernard asked in an unnatural voice.

'Why – completely recovered, thank you Bernard dearest. I become a little tired more easily, but that is to be expected.'

And she dismissed the conversation, because child bearing – especially at her age – was not a subject to be discussed.

'Mama, I have to tell you something before Papa comes downstairs. I have to tell you right *now*. It may shock you. But I *have* to tell you.'

They were seated opposite one another and the tension and urgency in Bernard's expression was answered by the loving concern in his mother's.

He had hardly begun to tell her – stammering with bursts of jumbled sentences and stories of Cramer, then of God's real purpose – when Helen interrupted:

'My dear, why don't you just say it: that you wish to become a musician?'

'I –'

He gazed at her, stunned into silence, and then leaped to his feet. 'I do not *wish* to become a musician,' he exclaimed loudly. 'I have *decided*. And I shall not be repressed.'

'My dear, please sit down. Do not be so angry. Sit beside me.' She patted his father's big chair and Bernard sat in it. His hands were clenched and she took them in her own, and prised his long fingers open, stroking them gently and lovingly.

'Oh, Mama. I am so sorry.' He leaned his head towards her.

'Ssh, my dear. It cannot be helped. It cannot. I see that. I thought this would happen sooner. Recently I began to hope it was not going to happen after all. But Joseph – Papa – he will not see the inevitability. He will see only that what he has striven for has lost its reason. Dear Bernard, I fear . . .'

'What do you fear, dearest wife?'

Joseph walked into the family room holding a small case that Bernard knew contained business papers. His expression was benevolent and unsuspecting.

Bernard bounded to his feet. 'I am in your cnair, Papa.'

'And are you anxious I beat you for such a sin,' his father teased good-naturedly, 'that you leap as if there were a nest of ants beneath you? So my dear, what was it you feared?'

'Oh, I forget! It has quite slipped –'

'Papa, I have something to tell you –'

'Wait Bernard, it is best I tell your father,' Helen interrupted.

Joseph looked from one tense, troubled face to the other. He set down the case and sat himself slowly in the chair vacated by his son.

'Such mystery! What is this? First my wife is afraid of some unknown force, then my son wishes to inform me of something which is so important that Helen wishes to inform me herself. What is going on?'

He tried to laugh to relieve the strange atmosphere in this most intimate of rooms. The little man suddenly felt cold and involuntarily shivered, stretching his hands towards the fire.

'Mama – it is up to me to explain,' Bernard said in a funeral-like voice. He confronted his father with a haughtiness he did not feel: 'Papa, I have decided I cannot continue in the world of commerce. It is – not to my liking.'

The terse words were wrung from deep within him. It was as though somebody had physically pushed him to speak; even as though he himself had pushed and someone else were speaking. Weakly he leaned against the mantelpiece for support.

He had to consider his father already as an adversary, and

tried to avoid seeing the small round head, shrunken amidst the big chair; his father – that good, simple man who loved him and never understood his son's very core; who had wept on those occasions he had administered corporal punishment as if he were inflicting it on himself.

I am re-shaping his life besides my own, thought Bernard unhappily in the ensuing silence, looking despairingly at the slow-motion change in Joseph's expression: from good-natured equanimity to bewilderment, to shocked anger and finally the impenetrable barrier of intolerance.

Joseph's face was now the colour of bleached cotton, crunched with lines, and he was leaning forward bulldog-like, his fists furled, while Helen watched helplessly, resigned to the tornado that would be unleashed.

'What do you mean, boy – the world of commerce is not to your liking? What rubbish is this?'

It was the word 'rubbish' that did it, that enflamed Bernard's emotions restricted by so many years of forced confinement.

'It is no "rubbish", Papa,' he answered coldly, afraid of the rising tide within him.

'The world of commerce is good enough for a Rothschild, but not for a certain young Bernard Foligno, is that it?'

'That is it, Papa.'

'What do you desire instead, Bernard? Can I hazard a guess? Perhaps I am not too insensitive to imagine. Possibly music has re-entered your youthfully romantic heart?'

'It never left it, Papa.' Icy politeness in exchange for sarcasm.

'Oh *Bernard*!' The exclamation, full of pleading and hopelessness, was closely followed by a choked sob, and in an instant of clarity Joseph saw Bernard as a small boy, his pale neck hunched over his table as he filled a page of manuscript paper with black dots and squiggles on the forbidden Shabat. The memory twisted his heart with pain. 'Bernard,' he moaned, rocking on the edge of his seat.

Fleetingly this grown child longed to rush into his father's arms, console him with love and assurance – and deny himself his future.

But Joseph's brief lapse of control was replaced once more by biting sarcasm and scorn. 'So you have decided to choose the minstrel's life in place of that despicable life which is commerce?'

'I never said it was despicable,' Bernard defended himself in a controlled voice, 'only that it was not to my liking. I am not suited to it. Surely I am permitted to say that?'

'So, having played your little tunes, and then having played with this alien monster that is commerce, you decide to revert to the former. Is music to be your panacea, boy? Your remedy for the world?'

The last words were shouted, and Joseph rose to his feet in his bulldog pose, his blue eyes glittering.

'Joseph –' Helen, anxious for his health, tried to restrain him, but he flung her hand from his arm.

'Don't interfere, Helen. Do not . . . Do *not* interfere. This is not your business.'

In reasoning tones she implored: 'You are my husband, Bernard is my son. You are both beloved to me. Is that not my business? Please dearest, be calm, listen to me.'

'Be *quiet*,' he roared, and then turned on Bernard: 'I forbid you to become a musician. Do you hear that? You are not twenty-one and I forbid it.'

'And I shall take no notice of you,' Bernard replied heatedly.

'How dare you speak to me like that?'

'Ah! It is all right that you may speak to me as you wish, but I am not allowed to speak to you as *I* wish.'

'Your wish, apparently, is to insult your father. Is that it?'

'No, Papa, that is not so. I should have preferred to discuss the matter sensibly, but you are not to be reasoned with.'

'Reasoned with! How dare you speak to me as if to a child? You have no gratitude. Your mother did not go through the agony and indignity of childbirth, nor I work hard and long as provider in order to be rewarded like this. And I – who have become a respected member of the Stock Exchange, a rare honour as a Jew – have I travelled so far in order that you might denounce it all and become a third-rate musician, one of the garret set, a nomad, a man of obscurity? I do not wish it for you, Bernard. I do not. I promise you would not be happy with such insecurity. This is mythical thinking, an allegorical fixation viewed from the safety of a comfortable home. You owe it to us to listen to mature wisdom.'

It was unleashed. The spring burst. 'I owe you nothing,' Bernard shouted. 'Nothing at all. No child owes a parent. The parent conceives and bears a child of his own volition. Do I have to reward you for conceiving me? A child need not be a mirror to his parent. Do you scorn Bach and Beethoven? Do you deride Leonardo da Vinci? Do you regard as worthless every inventor, scientist, artist? Because it is more than likely they were all innovators and defied their parents to be original. I am myself primarily, and not your toy to manipulate because it is what *you* had hoped for. All my childhood I spent seeking to be what I was not, in order to satisfy you, and Papa, don't you think *you* owe *me* my own life now?'

Flushed with passion he faced his father in the middle of the room, towering over him, not seeing the panic behind Joseph's intolerance, not seeing the helplessness on his dear mother's face, or her hand extended pleadingly to both of them. For a moment after his outburst there was silence which could have meant anything, could have gone in any direction: towards love and empathy, or away into the vastness of misunderstanding; and during this hiatus Bernard's facial muscles twitched frenziedly, registering all his feelings.

Joseph spoke eventually, in a voice of suppressed anguish, stuttering and stammering so that Bernard's heart lurched with sorrow: 'In this – great – macrocosm, Bernard, the-there will always – be those who progress with life and tackle it reasonably, and there will be those . . . the dilettantes who concentrate on – on n-nothing. They d-dabble. This is what you will surely – be. I cannot congratulate you on your choice. It is the wrong choice. You mention Bach and Beethoven so casually, as if you are assured of achieving s-such greatness, an-and I can only say one thing: that such con-conceit disgusts me . . . Oh my dear God, what has happened? What, *what* has happened?' He broke off, sobbing, covering his eyes with his hands.

Helen rushed to her husband's side: 'Dearest, sit down. Please. Mr Hamilton told you not to exert yourself.'

140

She tried to lead him forcibly by the elbow, but her interference apparently restored his strength and he said roughly: 'Go Helen. Go. Do not interfere. I am perfectly in control, I assure you.'

'Dearest, it is not good for you to –'

'Go, woman,' he bellowed. Then, in an agonized tone: 'Oh forgive me, Helen . . . And you –' he turned to Bernard '– who cannot accept the way of life of your father, whose life is not good enough for you – you realize that you are also in a sense rejecting Judaism? You will be alone in the field, Bernard, a man alone in the world. You might have music, but what about your family? What about Judaism?'

'What about it?' Bernard answered, his mouth dry, and fear huge within him. This was the great challenge he was unsure he could tackle, which was also his father's strength. 'I see no connection.'

'Ah, but there is. It is simple, Bernard.' Now Joseph's voice was like grey Northern stone. 'Judaism is based on the closeness of the family. All Jews are responsible for one another – and now you are rejecting your own family.'

'But I am not, I am not. It is the other way around,' Bernard cried, weeping openly. 'I am embracing something which has been a part of me all my life. I am not rejecting you. Don't you see? Without music my days have no meaning.'

But Joseph, aged, hopes shattered, his goals rendered futile and his whole life questioned, was steadfast. 'I see only that you talk in clichés. I see that Harold is more of a son than you.'

This was the ultimate betrayal: that his father should say this of Harold with his reptilian glance and contemptible ways. 'I do not believe you,' Bernard shouted, childish in his misery and jealousy. 'Harold is despicable.'

'I disagree. And of late I find him most charming. But you, Bernard, who mention that word "despicable", would appear more so.'

Bernard felt a sense of helplessness. 'You do not understand. Anything that does not conform to your way of thinking is too extreme for you. You see only repetition. And yet our ancestors wandered and sought and found many different openings.'

'They sought with their families as their roots. And you talk of understanding – do *you* understand that I have given my life, your mother her years and her body, and each of us our love to you, and you reject it all because you know better than us? Do you see the deceit in your objectives?'

'No, Papa. Because I never asked for anything.' He slumped before his father, who despite his diminutiveness seemed mighty in stature just then.

'But we would have given you everything.'

'Only on condition I conformed to your plans for me.'

'It is the same in all Jewish families. Perhaps I have been too liberal with you, Bernard. And your teacher – that Cramer – who filled your head with inflated ideas, he did not help. I am trying to be reasonable now, Bernard. I give you the chance to reject what you have said. We will never mention the matter again. We will continue in business as before – you have ability, and by all means play the piano as a pastime, like any normal man. Please . . .' His voice was humble. 'I entreat you, my son. Forget all the harsh words. So much is said in the heat of the moment. Everything I have, I offer you. We will strive together. It is all I ever hoped for. Please.'

Bernard was filled with weary hopelessness. He saw himself as a little boy at Milton Hall, and all around him, grotesquely distorted, were the taunting smiles of fellow pupils. *Jew-boy . . . You're different . . . Christ killer . . . Miser . . . Amputee, you're an amputee, you've only got half a . . .* Other phantoms from the past rose transparent before him and drifted away sadly.

Standing dejected and rumpled in the family room which had been the setting for so many happy scenes, Bernard could isolate himself from his body, so that it was another boy's dilemma he watched, and as such he could tell this wavering figure that it would do no good to oscillate:

You will not stay because of guilt. Don't stay. His life will be over in twenty years, and you will never have had yours.

His father's eyes were drilling into him imploringly and Bernard's disembodied feeling left him. He wanted to touch his father, hoped that physical contact might work where mental

142

rapport had failed. He reached out his hand, and the little man with eyes like crushed cornflowers looked up at his son, hope surging into his face.

'Papa, oh *Papa*.' He went to Joseph and clasped the slight form, and with that the father thought he had won and, feeling overwhelming relief, was ready to return the embrace; the tears were now of joy. But –

'Please understand, Papa. You will in time. I know that you –'

'*No*.' Agonized, Joseph thrust his son from him with such force that Bernard stumbled against the corner of the chaise where his mother sat, pale and trembling and nursing the frantic movement in her belly.

'Go. Leave the house at once. You are no son to your parents. You are treacherous and expect me to embrace you for it. Such minds make me physically sick. It is too much to bear. I cannot look at you. Go, do you hear? Take your belongings and *go*.'

'Joseph!' Helen leaped to her feet, horrified.

'I am the master of this house, Helen, sit down. Your son is rejecting what I have created for him, and with it he rejects us, his parents, and Judaism. You know the saying, Bernard: "Judaism is a way of life. A tree may be alone in the field, a man alone in the world, but no Jew is alone on his holy days." And where will you be? Playing in some music-hall or other to scrape together a living? You will be that tree, Bernard, severed from its roots.'

'No. You do not see –'

'I have perfect vision, Bernard. And I see plenty. I see a plethora of deceit, and I see that you were privileged to have a good education and you wish to misuse it. I see ingratitude and insolence . . . Now go. I do not wish to set eyes upon you again. You are dead to me.'

Bernard stood for a moment, numbed, trying to assemble his thoughts; surely such lack of understanding between two people who loved was not possible? Surely one should be able to discuss this rationally?

'Papa, cannot we talk sensibly as two adult men who care for one another?'

'Go from the house, Bernard,' Joseph's voice was quietly

authoritative. 'I have nothing more to say to you, you have made clear your terms. Now please respect mine.'

'Mama –' Bernard turned to his mother. Her face was distorted from crying. Bernard bent to kiss her. 'Oh, Mama.' Those two quiet little words held all his sadness.

Helen pulled his head towards her, kissed his cheek and was able to whisper quickly in his ear: 'I shall mollify him. Be assured it will blow over this –'

'Helen, are you to disobey me too? I told the boy to go. He does not belong here.'

Pointing a shaking finger, Joseph looked like an enraged mouse, and Bernard left the room, his eyes stinging and throat aching.

In his own room he gathered a few essential belongings. He had been banished! It was so ludicrous; so archaic; so unjust. But his mother had said she would console Joseph, and Bernard believed her. Joseph always listened to her. Soon he would welcome Bernard back. In the privacy of his room he became increasingly optimistic.

But now – where was he to go? The exile felt a moment's doubt before the answer provided itself: he would go to Sir Edmund Moore. He would make the boy welcome, and Bernard could remain there for the short while it took his mother to salvage the domestic situation.

Waiting in the dark for a cab, just a few yards from the house, he conversed with himself, consoling and chivvying himself that everything would turn out for the best. A cab passed and he hailed it, and as he climbed in he looked behind him. The curtains at the windows of his home were all drawn, seeming to close him out. He tried not to acknowledge his fear and instead to concentrate on his hopes and convictions, but the apprehension not only remained but grew, and his last view of the house was of those sealed windows excluding him from the life within. And not a curtain twitched.

Chapter Ten

Sir Edmund showed little surprise upon seeing his guest.

'Mr Foligno, sir,' Murphy announced, blinking and grinning his gap-toothed smile before leaving them.

The old man cursorily studied the strained face, noting the dark stubble exaggerated against the pallor, the flatness in the eyes . . . 'So the deed is done,' he commented quietly, clasping Bernard's hand in his strong and reassuring grip, and pushing him down gently into a chair. He went to the bureau where he kept the twenty-one year-old malt whisky which was reserved for special occasions.

Silently watched by Bernard, Sir Edmund Moore poured two extravagant measures into tumblers engraved with a coach and four on one side and his family crest on the other. He returned to Bernard's side: 'Now do you wish to tell me how your ordeal went?'

'It was terrible.' Bernard shook his head and gave a hefty sigh of despondency. 'It was far, far worse than I imagined. I never thought he would react quite like that. . . .'

As the alcohol took effect the boy became more garrulous and his reserve disintegrated. Words and sentences gushed out, and Sir Edmund did not interrupt except to replenish their glasses yet again.

But whisky was new to Bernard, and his inauguration was not without side effects; his voice became slurred and his complexion underwent a pattern of changes, from pale to cherubic pink, to pale again, and finally a jaundiced shade of yellow.

He lurched to his feet abruptly: 'I think . . . I wish to . . .' He ran from the room clutching his mouth, fumbled with the great front doors, and was promptly sick over the doorstep. Sir

Edmund, who had followed at a slower rate, gripped Bernard's shoulder as he retched, and then led the chastened figure upstairs to a spare bedroom where he virtually undressed him before tucking him in bed. He set a guard in front of the slow-burning fire and closed the door softly.

As he walked away, he mused: 'And this is the future king of the keyboard.' He nodded knowingly to himself and went to his own room.

During the next few days Sir Edmund's role became that of an uncle to Bernard. He advised, listened and suggested, but most important of all he offered constant encouragement when Bernard's spirits flagged.

'You did the right thing, lad. Trust me. You *did* the right thing. If you do not trust me, then trust our old friend, Glorious John.'

It was a Sunday afternoon. Exactly a week had passed and Bernard had not heard a word, despite having left a note with his address on the little gilded console table in the hall. Now, fortified by Sir Edmund's port, Bernard visited his home. The day was dismal: it was trying to snow, and spasmodic frail tufts drifted to melt on the pavements. He waited for his front door to be opened, stamping his feet to keep warm and repeating to himself: *It will all be fine, it will all be fine*.

He was shivering, as much with apprehension as with cold.

The maid came to the door: 'Why – sir!'

He acknowledged her without much enthusiasm, handing her his cloak. His hair was wet and curling and the odd drip trickled and ran down his forehead. 'My parents?'

'Are in the parlour,' she answered in her artificially cultivated voice. She meant the family room, but from the outset had frowned upon this title, having hailed from a much larger and more formal household before.

Bernard stood for several seconds outside the room, smelling his father's cigar and envisaging the cosy domesticity within. Longing and love overcame him so that he was weak with his need for his family.

They would be pleased to see him. Surely they would be so pleased. He opened the door with a half-smile, both eager and nervous, and three faces glanced up.

Harold was there. Already in the throne. The surrogate son.

Bernard felt his whole body rock in dismay. And dimly, in a haze he noticed a Menorah on the sideboard by the window with three candles burning.

They stared at each other, all four of them, and during that brief, suspended moment of speechless eye contact Bernard's vision was distorted and their faces shimmered, unrecognizable. Only at the dear sound of his mother's voice did they re-adjust.

'Bernard darling!' She stood with her arms outstretched, ready to engulf him.

Harold leered silently from his half-turned position. Bernard felt like the prodigal son.

'What do you want?' Joseph asked in a sour tone, immersed once more in whatever he had been reading. 'You are only welcome in this house,' he continued leadenly, 'if you have changed your way of thinking, and if you show some contrition for your chicanery.'

'Then I shall leave directly.' Anger rose within Bernard to replace his boyish yearnings. It circulated, sap-like, throughout his body. Now at least there was a conclusion; now there really would be no one to answer to but himself.

'Bernard, Joseph – please –' Helen still standing, made a beseeching gesture to both of them.

'No, Helen.'

'No, Mama.'

They spoke simultaneously and glanced at each other startled, taken aback by the fierceness in each other's tone. Momentarily their eyes softened – before glazing over again.

'I shall never forgive you, Bernard,' Joseph said.

'Nor I you, Papa.' He noticed his mother's lips were trembling, and said softly: 'I love you, Mama.'

And he left, with a kind of victory in his heart because he was completely on his own.

'You were so courageous to do as you did.'

'But dearest, I had no option. After Cramer's letter I knew

147

there was no choice. It was only a matter of timing, and there I was helped by Sir Edmund. But that Sunday, when I returned to Brook Street from my parents, suddenly it registered: the Menorah! It was Channukah, and I had forgotten. God forgive me – I had forgotten Channukah. The following day I rushed out to buy a Menorah, having no idea where to go for such an item, but finally I found one at a small silversmith's in Bond Street, and I remember I ran wildly back to Sir Edmund's, slithering in the slushy snow, clutching my silver trophy as though it were my link with God and my salvation.

'The following Saturday I went to synagogue. I walked from Brook Street to Wigmore Street and there was my father in his usual place. I thought he would at least be glad that I had not as yet renounced Judaism; but when I went to take my place next to him, Harold was already in my seat, and on his other side was my uncle. I stood at the back for three and a half hours. Harold turned once and glanced at me as though I were a carbuncle on someone's nose, but if my father knew of my presence he gave no indication.

'I decided then I would go to stay with Douglas in Paris, and when I returned I would join another synagogue – the break-away Reform one in St Margaret Street. It seemed logical because the Reform synagogue offered greater flexibility within religion. It also meant that I would not feel perpetually guilty (that I was a Heathen simply) because I couldn't adhere to the rigidity of orthodoxy!

'So I returned to Brook Street in a positive frame of mind, excited at the prospect of joining Douglas, and able to shrug away the pain. Youth is resilient.'

It was Bernard's last evening in London and he was having a quiet dinner at the Garrick Club with Sir Edmund Moore. Sir Edmund said: 'So tomorrow will see you in foreign parts, Bernard. I have enjoyed having you with me – you know that.'

'Yes sir, and I am so very grateful to you. I don't truly know what I should have done –'

'Utter rubbish.' Sir Edmund took a large swallow of red Burgundy, then pointed an admonishing finger at Bernard. 'And I certainly do not wish for gratitude. I shall miss your company, young man.'

'You have your family; so many of them!' He opened his eyes wide in emphasis.

They had all visited on Christmas Day, with the exception of one grandchild: five assorted grown children with their spouses – parents to their own broods, and two more babies expected. Bernard had felt awed by them all, conspicuous with his unusual darkness and distinctive features compared to their typical British looks.

'I certainly do have my immense family, and I thank God for that, but the problem, young man, is that I am a constant source of embarrassment to them. There is only one child with any spunk, if you will excuse the expression – my dead daughter's girl, Anna. This rather special girl is educated in Switzerland and is apparently asthmatic, which is poppycock as far as I am concerned. It is merely her father's excuse to send her away, because whilst he is a most excellent high court judge, he is totally inept at handling a high-spirited child. When she is not in Switzerland she spends a great deal of time with friends who live, I believe, in some kind of a 'folly' in Gloucestershire. She has often spoken to me of them, and I am glad she has been accepted by them so warmly because she has been shown little love by her own father. He is a fair man, you understand, but he is austere. Yes, that is the word. Austere.

'Anyway, I digress. As I was saying, to my own siblings I am an embarrassment because I remind them of earthy things which are best swept under the table. I disturb and disgust them although they are too polite to admit it. They regard me as a lecherous old fool, for whilst like all true Catholics they somehow breed children, I, you see, I have a certain friend who is female and rather modern, and who happens to be young enough to be my granddaughter!'

This news was certainly startling, and unsure how he should react to such a confidence from a man of Sir Edmund's standing, Bernard tried to look impassive. He wanted to say the right thing, so that it did not seem he was shocked. In a rather contrived way he swilled the wine in his glass.

'Is the age difference of great importance?' he asked carefully.

'Of great importance, dear Bernard? Yes and no – both, is the answer. The lady in question is an extremely capable twenty-four-year old singer with plenty of potential. She is attractive, articulate and witty, and whilst I dislike my own distrust, I am never certain whether she likes me, an old man, for myself or for the possibility that I can further her career. She could have any number of younger men, and yet she chooses to collaborate with me. I can only say that I did not seek such a situation, and would even have been scathing of another man in similar circumstances. But such hasty surmisings are to be made a mockery of. Never say, "I would never," Bernard; because you just cannot tell. And now I only feel a rather vicious regret that time has not been static, and that our births did not coincide more suitably.

'Another contrary issue (you see what an analyst I am) is that, assuming her affection to be genuine, there can be no future in a relationship with such an age gap, so I try to encourage her to remain away, and this *apparently* grieves her. What is the truth in such a relationship, Bernard? The peaks, the depths to which my life alternately ascends and descends are shattering.

'The final factor is that wherever we go together people assume she is my daughter, or if not they stare as if we were freaks in a fair. But possibly this aspect does not matter. It is she and I who are the "core" at the end of the day, and the truth must be discovered only in ourselves.

'The advantages of the relationship are that she has filled my life with simple joy and love, even if I am indulging in self-delusion, and I am happy just to think of her and know she exists.

'Young Bernard, seated opposite you you have an elderly, fairly well-respected man; a rather extrovert character who has fought for his refinements – and this same bombastic soul is reduced to the status of a dithering schoolboy by a slip of a girl.

Ah – but what a girl; endlessly fascinating and disrespectful of convention. And if I am ill, she is so tender it is hard to doubt her.

'But my children are probably right. Such passion in a man of my seniority *is* surely disgusting. My son-in-law, the judge, is appalled and has told me as much, and when I answered that my wild Celtic ancestry was to blame he was not amused. I find the legal profession a humourless breed on the whole.

'And there you have it, young man, and when you return from Paris, with your head full of its wonders, your mind emancipated with foreign joys, and your politics to the left of what they are at present, then perhaps you will meet her. No –' he held his hand up to prevent Bernard from speaking. 'Do not comment. I want no comment. I wanted only to talk. We are equal in that now I know a little about you and you know a little about me. Let us discuss other mattters.'

When they returned, the little Irishman handed Sir Edmund a note. 'It came by private coach, sir.'

It was from Mr Beavis, explaining he had been given Sir Edmund's address by one Bernard Foligno, a young man he had found most impressive and who seemed destined to go far in the world of commerce!

How long ago that meeting seemed, and to what a far-off world it belonged. And how astonished Mr Beavis would have been had he known the reason for Bernard's presence in Sir Edmund Moore's house at the very time his note arrived. Life: it could be delightfully unstructured.

'This man is searching for new young composers, I see.' There was a jovial glint in Sir Edmund's eyes, for he had seen another irony, and in his mind was already constructing his reply.

'Yes. I believe he feels it would be an obvious move on account of his involvement with printing.'

'Rather a novel idea.'

'Yes. And most encouraging to new composers.'

'I should very much like to meet him. It is a pity you will not be around, Bernard.'

And Bernard, who was not always perceptive, did not hear the playfulness in the tone, or the contrived casualness in the words: '. . . is searching for new composers'.

The following morning Bernard caught the train from Paddington to Dover, the only passenger in his compartment at this early hour and on such a dismal, snowy day. He secured his hat on the rack and drifted into a light doze. From grey and dejected Dover he took the steamboat to Calais, embarking with a very few other passengers, shivering uncommunicative forms like himself voyaging solely from absolute necessity on such a day.

The sea was magnificently savage – rhythmical, immense waves vaulted and dipped and spattered white foam as the vessel ploughed and lifted, seeming to make no progress. A mist shrouded any horizon that might exist, and the funnels ejaculated black smoke which shot into the atmosphere and was lost. The great paddles turned laboriously, cleaving a drunken path, and seemed as effectual as an elephant bound by chains.

Stray passengers staggered miserably below deck, only to decide that despite the comparative comforts there, the rolling and pitching were too severe – and returned to the deck, where they clung to the railings and vomited, before returning once more below, convinced that it must be an improvement after all.

For six hours Bernard remained on the deck. He knew only exaltation. It was as if there was nothing between him and the sea – no wood, no iron, no machinery. He was a dolphin, now riding high, now plunging, and the water's rhythm became his own; his mind was purged of all thought. Foam was hurled and splattered into the air, and the salt bit into his skin, whilst about the boat circled noisy gulls, wheeling tirelessly, diving suddenly and steeply into hills of water, accurate arrows that re-emerged with their trophies trapped in long bright beaks.

Bernard was conscious of a positive joy, a heady and thrilling feeling of independence, and he inhaled deeply through flaring nostrils so that the icy air grabbed at his lungs. *I am free at last*, he thought elatedly. *I am free, I am free* . . . He threw back his head and let the wind tear at his hair.

It was dark by the time of the boat's eventual arrival at Calais, and he travelled directly to Paris by the Chemin du Nord. A smell of garlic lingered in his train compartment, and a small, serious-faced boy sat opposite him, silently staring at him in a disconcerting way until finally, and much to Bernard's relief, he fell into a child's heavy sleep.

He had left behind snow in London, and now here in Paris it was snowing too. It was eleven o'clock at night and two figures waited on the platform of the Gare du Nord. One was a woman who with much fuss and joyful cries swept the sleepy boy into her arms; the other, dear and familiar, was Douglas, who greeted Bernard in his own typical way, a year since their last meeting.

'Under this light, dear chap, and without wishing to affront you, you look as ghastly white as Christ on the cross.'

A minute later they were embracing like brothers. However the physical contact was only for a second and they sprang apart, slightly ashamed.

Douglas took command of the situation: 'Food's at my place. Time for the streets tomorrow. Carriage waiting. All well-organized in your honour. *Mon Dieu*, but you are a ghastly ghostly white!'

His clipped English, his verbless statements were more exaggerated than ever and Bernard guessed that his friend had cultivated these affectations, along with his rather foppish clothes, to appeal to the French, to be remembered and talked about as a 'character'.

They passed through a tangle of wet dark streets with Douglas giving a running commentary: 'The Seine . . . Pont St Michel, and the outline of Notre Dame . . . Boulevard St Germain – Left Bank you know, or Rive Gauche as we say . . . My abode's off St Germain des Prés. Extraordinarily well-placed. Life begins in the St Germain area . . .'

The carriage came to a halt outside a tall grey building indistinguishable from the surrounding tall grey buildings with their black-railinged balustrades.

'Does one tip?' Bernard asked.

'*Pourboire? Mais sûrement*. Very eager-handed these fellows are. But my treat, dear friend. I insist.'

'No, Doug!' Bernard reached into his pocket hurriedly.

'But *yes*.' Douglas laid an allaying hand on Bernard's arm.

153

'You have plenty of time in which to become poor. You know how I have always despised talking about money, and the longer we stand arguing the more steamed-up my spectacles become. Come inside and see my splendid bordello, but I must forewarn you that the toilet facilities are not everything one would desire. Suspicious of cleanliness, I'd describe the French. Less pernickity than us British.'

They went up four flights of steep, cold, uncarpeted stairs, punctuated by the odd sombre engraving, and every few seconds Douglas would turn and whisper, 'Ssh, tiptoe,' on account of the other paying guests, and his landlady who went to bed by nine-thirty most nights.

In its own way Douglas's *apartiment* was splendid, for whilst it comprised only one room, this room was about thirty-six feet in length, having an elegant marble fireplace at one end, and at the other an alcove leading to a smaller area where stood a huge armoire – majestically ugly and imposingly solid in construction. The room itself, painted a tasteful olive green with the mouldings left white, was high-ceilinged with tall sash windows whose ornate brass locks did not seal them sufficiently tight to exclude the icy draught. However, there were internal shutters and these Douglas immediately bolted, and the change in temperature was instantaneous.

'Home,' he announced, gesturing to the heavy mahogany furniture and faded rugs. 'This is my home now. In the daylight the views are quite spectacular – over the staggered roof tops and across the Seine and *les ponts*, and to the Right Bank . . . You will see. And to witness the sun burst over the river first thing in the morning is a spectacle not to be missed. It is an experience possibly only surpassed by that of drinking coffee and sipping Cognac in St Germain des Prés. Talking of Cognac, I shall fix us both one. And if you wish to reduce your utterly unbecoming pallor by the morning, then I suggest that after some food you lay yourself on the day bed there at the far end of the room. It is wonderfully comfortable – especially if you care to remove the violin and the music stand.'

Bernard sank heavily into a marvellously yielding old chair whose original faded brocade was threadbare around the arms, and he fingered the paisley shawl draped decoratively over the back to conceal wads of exposed horse-hair. 'I am ravenous besides tired, Doug –' he gave a cavernous yawn '– where is this food you mentioned?'

'Here on the card table – by the way I've taken up cards. Really a most amusing way of passing time.' Douglas swept aside a lace cloth. 'Some cold beef prepared by the excellent Madame Becaud! She is really most kind – even left the gas-lights on especially for us – and some cheese and fruit. I had not the heart to spoil her amusement and tell her about your unusual dietary laws that forbid you to have cheese after meat, so if you like I shall indulge in your portion of cheese (and subject you to the resultant flatulence), and you can have my portion of beef.'

'I could have the cheese before the beef.'

'Biologically that makes little difference. At some point the meat and cheese will be in your stomach simultaneously.'

'You, Doug Hamilton,' Bernard said, flicking wine between his finger and thumb at his friend, 'jabber too much as usual. Am I to endure weeks of this verbal stream?'

'Well old chap, remember I only had your welfare at heart. I could not bear to derange your conscience.'

Bernard helped himself to cheese and bread, ignoring Douglas's incredulous expression. 'I *shall* have the beef afterwards. I do not think I wish to put your flatulence to the test. If I am driven out I have nowhere else to sleep. What is Madame Becaud like?'

'Too old even for such a man of the world as you.'

'Any daughters?'

' 'Fraid not, dear chap.'

Bernard pulled a face. 'No matter. Now tell me the news.'

'News in general. I can barely remember all that has happened. But did I tell you Spohr died? I shall follow his teaching, and were he alive he would be proud of my usage of his excellent invention, the chin rest. I shall be famous one day, Bernard. It is not so hard. All you need is talent.'

'And an inflated ego.'

'But of course. Doubt yourself and who is there left to believe in you? Do you want some beef now?'

Bernard eyed the meat and hesitated: 'Doug, I was forgetting – it's not kosher.'

'Bernard, you cannot possibly live in Paris for more than a day and avoid eating meat. It is not practical.'

'I can have fish,' he said airily, still eyeing the beef.

'Not every day! You will find it impossible. Don't look at me like that, dear chap. I'm not trying to make a pagan out of you. I'm only trying to say that religion should conform with modern life.'

Bernard considered this for a moment, reflected back to his own decision to join the Reform synagogue. Then he helped himself silently and almost angrily to the moist rare beef.

Douglas watched him with raised eyebrows, his mouth twitching annoyingly.

Bernard took a mouthful of food: 'You were speaking before of your future fame – and wipe that ridiculous smirk off your face.'

'Ah yes, my future fame. And I was serious.' He dabbed his chin with a napkin and his face was earnest. 'I am becoming known. People ask about me. I can show you reviews. I created a quite splendid cadenza two weeks ago and it was talked about everywhere. However I have something else I wanted to talk about, it is something especial I have lined up : . . Bernard – I saw you eat some cheese with your unkosher meat!'

'I did not.'

'I swear I saw it. Am prepared to lift my right hand in testimony.'

'Well, only the tiniest morsel. It does not qualify.'

'It certainly does. Downward path now. Taken a bite; bigger one next time.'

'As you said, one has to live in a modern world.'

'True. Only you can decide how to find your equator.'

'That is my problem. How far may I stray? Which rules may I bend for my convenience?'

'Oh dear – this eternal Jewish conscience. I see your point of course, dear chap. But you really must cease always to feel guilty.'

'I try, but –'

'Then be quiet. Let me tell you about this especial something. I have been asked to give a performance at a soirée in this

156

very grand country house about twenty miles south of Paris, belonging to the Comte de Boullery. He is, I believe, a relative a thousand times removed from Louis Napoléon, and the occasion is in just over three weeks. Well, of course I told them – being a considerate friend – that I could only consent if they permitted a Monsieur Foligno to perform also. All has been agreed, and arranged through the Conservatoire. I've also organized a practice room there. Well?'

Bernard clapped his friend so hard on the back that Douglas staggered backwards. 'But it is stupendous news, Doug!' He clicked the index fingers and thumbs of both hands simultaneously and gave a short laugh of excitement. 'And it is just the two of us?'

'Yes.'

'We don't want anyone else to detract from us, of course.'

'Exactly my way of thinking.'

'And are we to be paid?' Bernard was almost dancing from foot to foot.

'But of course, you unworldly boy. Although I admit it will be barely enough for a new bowtie. More the honour of being requested, you understand.'

'It will be the first time I have received money as a musician,' Bernard mused reflectively, sitting down once more and gazing into the distance.

'What a dreamer you are, Bernard,' Douglas said in his most supercilious voice. 'You sit there with such a seraphic expression!'

They continued to banter until Bernard, suddenly aware of his exhaustion, announced: 'Doug, I am very tired. I am going to sleep if you do not mind. Are there blankets?'

'Yes. And quilt and cushions in the armoire. I shall get them for you.'

'I can.'

'Must serve one's guest.'

'Fool.'

In their respective beds, the lights extinguished, little Douglas's voice came across from the other side of the cold room: 'I say – I'm most awfully glad you're here.'

'Me too.'

'Really?'

'But of course.'

'I was not sure.'

'But of course I am. You are my only friend. And Paris – I longed to see Paris. You made it breathe for me. I always received your letters with such excitement. Once I had made up my mind I was coming, I could scarcely wait.'

'*Really?*'

'Yes, idiot. Really.'

'I was not sure,' Douglas repeated. 'One cannot always say the things one wants. Too old, you know.'

'Fool,' Bernard said sleepily.

'Well, I am considerably cheered up now. I was a little apprehensive of seeing you, you know. Tomorrow will be fun! There is so much to do and to show you. Will you speak to me of your family now?'

'My family? I am dead to my father. The toad has taken my place. And the foetus in my mother's womb. Damn my father.'

'Steady, old chap.'

'Damn him, damn him, damn him. He has so badly let me down.'

Overwhelming fatigue and rather too much Cognac threatened to make him emotional. He had a sudden image of his father's pale, shattered eyes, and the vulnerable bald spot on his head, and he laughed shakily: 'Sorry, Doug. I find I cannot speak of my father right now. I suppose I cannot understand how a father who purports to love his child can behave in the way he has done.'

In the morning Bernard awoke before Douglas and padded silently over to his case from which he took his talett, straps and small boxes; then he pulled on some trousers and returned to the day bed to lay tefillin.

This small but significant ritual must at all costs be preserved. Somehow it seemed more imperative now: whatever other laws he let slip, whichever synagogue he chose to worship in, this most private act of prayer was his redemption. His back was to his friend and Douglas, awake now, reached for his round wire-

158

rimmed spectacles and lay quietly watching: the naked muscular shoulders, the pale skin exposed and goose-pimpled with cold between the folds of cream, tasselled silk; the tousled head bent in devout confusion and contradiction.

Douglas thought: *Maybe I shall never really know him. He is on another plane, so changeable. He is quite the most complex soul one could come across.*

They breakfasted at the Café Flore, sitting outside at a table on the pavement, with muffled necks and pink hands wrapped round small hot cups of dark, dark coffee. It was ten o'clock in the morning, and Bernard delighted in the scene about him: the wide and noisy Boulevard St Germain with its double-tiered omnibuses and cabs and energetic people skilfully dodging wheels and hooves; the unfamiliar accents and the cries of street sellers; fascinating shops and smells of baking; the church almost next to the café with a drunken tramp lying on its steps; the water-coloured sun in the grey haze of morning, promising to burst like the splattering of an egg yolk; the little pastries, gently dusted with powdery sugar – sticky in the fingers and smooth and crumbling in the mouth; the assorted customers clustered in groups – artists, musicians, writers, students from the Sorbonne, and the more formally attired business or professional men.

Douglas pointed towards three men sitting engrossed in conversation at a nearby table: 'You see those men – do not stare –well, on the left is Charles Wilfred de Beriot who is professor of piano at the Conservatoire; the other young man, on the right, is Camille Saint-Saëns of whom I think I have written to you, a curious and talented personality and an excellent pianist besides composer. He is organist at the Church of Madeleine in Rue Royale just across the Right Bank. And Saint-Saëns is a private pupil of the older man in the middle. That is Charles Gounod, whose new opera *Faust* has been such a stupendous success.'

Bernard, who had seen the opera, was awed to be seated so near such an illustrious man. He opened his mouth, about to say something, when Saint-Saëns caught Douglas's eye and called loudly: *'C'est le petit Anglais! Bonjour, Monsieur Hamilton. Venez-ici nous joindre, et votre ami aussi.'*

Bernard remained rooted to the spot, a rather wild expression on his face.

'Come on,' Douglas said impatiently. 'What's afoot?'

'They are all so famous. They cannot want us to join them.'

He had dreamed of this: casual introductions – a name here, a name there: 'Of course Berlioz believes . . .' or 'Whilst Saint-Saëns says . . .' Or perhaps even: 'Liszt told me . . .'

'Why ever not? They asked us, not the other way around. And we shall be at least as famous one day. Meanwhile – all mortals defecate, if you'll pardon the expression. And at least try and appear intelligent.'

Bernard followed Douglas's quick, jerky walk, loping behind him with what he hoped was a casual nonchalance, whilst his heart thumped out of control.

'*Messieurs!*' Douglas's high English voice made no attempt to adopt the French intonation to correspond with the word. '*Permettez-moi de vous introduire à mon ami, Monsieur Bernard Foligno. Un jour il sera plus connu même que vous!* Monsieur Foligno – Monsieur Saint-Saëns, Monsieur Gounod, Monsieur de Beriot . . . I told them one day you would be more famous than them,' he explained in an aside to Bernard.

'You didn't!'

Only Douglas could escape with such an audacious remark and raise a ripple of amused laughter at the same time. Possibly also at that moment the prospect of such fame seemed a little remote.

The three men stood up and swapped greetings, and Bernard was overcome with shyness and a sense of inadequacy. His talent was nothing besides this combined force.

'*S'il vous plaît – asseyez-vous, messieurs* – sit down,' Douglas commanded grandly, and like grinning lambs they all obeyed, including Bernard who was now placed between de Beriot on his right and Douglas.

'Cognac, Cognac. *Garçon*,' called Gounod to a passing waiter.

De Beriot enquired: '*Alors*, Monsieur Foligno, *vous êtes à Paris depuis quand?*'

Bernard's French failed him, and he faltered: 'Er, *je suis* . . . *Je suis* . . .'

Douglas rescued him: '*Mes amis*, Monsieur Foligno *ne parle pas très bien le français* . . . Told them your French wasn't up to much dear chap,' he added to Bernard.

Gounod said in excellent English: 'Then, little Monsieur, it is correct that we speak in his own tongue. Monsieur Foligno, how long have you been here?'

'Only since last night.' His nose felt pink with cold and his mouth frozen.

A waiter arrived with five balloons and a bottle of brandy, and Saint-Saëns poured large quantities into the glasses, frowning in concentration, then smiling quickly as each was filled. '*Voilà*,' and he handed one to every man.

'*Santé*,' the Frenchmen said almost simultaneously.

'Cheers!' Bernard took a large gulp, and immediately felt better.

'Good health, dear chaps.' Douglas sipped delicately from his glass.

Gounod, who as the best English-speaker amongst the three had taken it upon himself to be spokesman, said: 'Before you have arrived at our table we were not discussing music, but literature. The new book by this crazy Englishman, Darwin. It is entitled *Origin of Species*. What may you two young men think?'

Douglas answered: 'The man is a joker – a publicity seeker. Now look here, I think the idea of being descended from an ape enchanting, *mes amis*. I happen to have a great affection for apes. But I believe this showman is having an extravagant jest at our expense.'

'But Doug,' parried Bernard, 'why should everything accord with Genesis? The world is round, not flat and was certainly not created in seven days beginning with Adam and Eve, so why should there not be a pattern, a gradual formation, the way coal can be developed from a forest of trees? I cannot disagree merely on principle and I think that Mr Darwin has demonstrated much daring to have spoken out with such controversial views. I apologize, sir –' he turned to Charles Gounod, '– if I have offended you, but I do not believe we should close our minds to new thinking.'

'You have not offended me, Monsieur Foligno. You have answered honestly.'

'Dear chap – for sure you *have* changed your views lately. . . .'

And there followed much discussion, gesticulation and friendly argument, during which the contents of the bottle lowered and it was finally depleted.

The Café Flore was by now full. Inside, a man was sketching the stunning woman beside him. Nearby another man softly played a violin; smart young women dressed in the latest fashions surveyed the scene and spoke amongst themselves, glancing around frequently to ensure they were noticed. The lunchtime congestion built up in the street. Feet skirted their cramped table and passers-by looked askance at the eccentric group sitting outside in the extreme cold.

Bernard and Douglas parted from the others. 'I omitted to tell Gounod how much I enjoyed *Faust*, particularly the second act with its spectacular waltzes,' Bernard said, stopping suddenly and looking stricken.

'You will see him again,' Douglas reassured him, tugging his arm.

'However I was remiss.'

'Rubbish. He has sufficient confidence not to rely on minions. I daresay he will survive without flattery from you.'

'But my manners were remiss,' Bernard stubbornly insisted, stopping again.

'Forget it.' Douglas tugged once more.

Overhead the sky darkened. It began to hail.

'I cannot. He is so famous.'

They ran for the omnibus which had halted a few yards away, and were forced to climb the vertical ladder to the upper deck since the lower was full. The days of taking cabs were over, and they smiled at each other ruefully, resigned to becoming drenched.

*

'My love – that is what people say about you: "But he is so famous!" And you *can* look so intimidating!'

'It is not intentional. And I hope *you* do not find me intimidating, my Anna.'

'Only very occasionally.'

'My dear –'

'Yes?'

'Nothing. Nothing of great consequence.'

'Tell me anyway.'

'I shall miss you when you go tomorrow.'

'That is of great consequence. But it is only for two weeks, dearest.'

'I cannot explain it. I do not have good feelings. I feel – uneasy.'

'Touch me. There. Is that a good feeling?'

'Very good. Too good. Outside this house is a wisteria creeper which clambers up and grips the brickwork –'

'I have noticed, of course! You do say the strangest things!'

'But you have interrupted me. It is not so strange at all. I was going to say I wish you were the building and I the wisteria, and you could never escape me. . . .'

'I shall never escape you, I promise. Not spiritually. We have been separated so many times before, dearest, and for far longer periods than this.'

'I know. I cannot explain it. This time feels different. It seems as though it is for much, much longer. And my body is cold and alone suddenly. Snuggle as close as you are able, and if you are not overwhelmed with boredom I shall continue my story.'

Chapter Eleven

Bernard quickly adapted to the life of a student abroad, and on New Year's Eve he and Douglas attended a party. It was riotous and noisy, and Bernard found himself involved in a quarrel. It was with a middle-aged professor from the Conservatoire, an aggressive flat-nosed cellist who claimed to have played with Joachim, endlessly extolled Jean Louis Duport, and was prone to making sweeping statements which increasingly annoyed Bernard. He was an ox of a man, of mixed English and French parentage, who disliked the 'frippery' of Chopin. 'Ballerina's froth,' he termed it. 'Weightless, tinkling sounds created by an inferior musician who made no pretence to understand any other instrument besides the piano. . . .'

They argued for half an hour, stopping to take mighty swigs of red wine, and then, fortified, continuing the debate.

'You pianists are all the same. You think you are a breed apart.'

Bernard's heart sang: *You pianists . . . You are all the same* . . . He was accepted.

But Douglas, who had been drinking continuously throughout the evening and had heard the latter part of the conversation, interrupted deliberately loudly: 'Take no notice, dear chap,' he drawled. 'He is an embittered, choleric old bigot by the name of Gilbert who resents the fact that few of the great composers have held the cello in sufficient esteem to write anything half decent for it!'

'Sir, I resent your tone. I find you most impudent.' The other man moved threateningly towards Douglas whose cherubic little face stared back benignly and drunkenly.

Bernard said: 'But that is sad, if true; the cello is an exquisite

164

instrument. I think you will find that in the next twenty years much will be done to remedy the situation.' He nodded reflectively as he spoke.

Gilbert's enraged expression changed to grateful surprise, and he studied Bernard intently, his thin lips knitted together and sucked inwards. Bernard, half-leaning against the wall, looked steadily back, a small conciliatory smile on his face.

But Douglas continued, heedless: 'This man is one of the less attractive accessories of the Conservatoire, along with some of the rather dismal portraits, and the only reason he remains is that there is hardly a cellist to be found in Paris at the moment. Violinists and pianists – dear boy, we are two-a-penny, and it is survival of the fittest; but cellists are rare. Gilbert is the least popular man I know. Nobody likes him. Not even his wife. She left him, ha-ha.'

'You go too far, you arrogant little youth. The only reason I do not ram your oversized head into the ground here and now, is that I am in a position of authority and do not intend to abuse it.'

'Endanger it, you mean. They are waiting for an opportunity to rid themselves of you, so I heard.'

'Doug – you do go too far,' Bernard hissed in his friend's ear.

'I shall report you, of course,' Gilbert told Douglas.

'And what weight will it bear coming from you?'

'Hush, Doug. Apologies, sir. My friend has drunk too much. Take no notice. Goodnight, Monsieur Gilbert. I still believe you are greatly mistaken about Chopin, but I am sorry about your wife.'

And he left, half supporting the drooping, staggering figure of Douglas Hamilton, whilst the puzzled gaze of Monsieur Gilbert followed him.

The Conservatoire, situated in Rue du Faubourg and dating back to the eighteenth century, was a vast complex of buildings grouped around a courtyard, and the first time Bernard walked through the great arched doorway he was daunted by the sheer size of the place.

I shall never learn my way around here, he thought, thrown into a panic, whilst Douglas confidently showed him this and that and trotted about with the assurance of an old inhabitant.

However, inevitably it became familiar to him, and soon he was finding his own way there, taking an omnibus from the St Germain area, crossing the ancient Pont Neuf to the Right Bank . . . And then – through the noble, colonnaded entrance and past the myriads of rooms spilling out their wonderful diverse sounds. He might see a face or two that he came to recognize and who sometimes even nodded in his direction when he went to practice sessions, or for a lesson with the kindly Gounod, who had offered to take Bernard on as a pupil after hearing him play.

Soon all the intricacies of Conservatoire life were familiar to him: the politics, the petty squabbles and jealousies, the on-going dispute between the rather lonely, middle-aged Berlioz and the authorities.

'I am like a baby with a new rattle,' Bernard exclaimed to Douglas once. 'I am constantly thrilled and enchanted. I cannot become used to all this. There is nothing in Paris I dislike. I tell you, Doug – even the atrocious sanitation has a kind of drole glamour. Paris is so sophisticated, so free, so liberal in its attitude. By comparison London is sadly lacking.'

He did not see that his views might be coloured or that the life he was leading was the charmed one of a tourist, and he would vehemently have denied both these things. He had not lived through the crisis of 1848 or the harsh early years of Louis Napoléon's rule, and now Paris was a soft bed made by someone else in which he could luxuriate. His was the sybaritic life of the young artist or student who as yet had no serious troubles. It was smart in Paris to have a button missing or shoes whose soles were worn thin. It spoke a message. Even for fashion-conscious Bernard it became essential that he joined in to convey that message . . . And to walk amongst a group of friends with your head held high above your slightly fraying collar (albeit deliberately frayed), and your top hat gleaming impeccably: that was smarter still.

During this period Bernard wrote to three people: his mother, Sir Edmund Moore, and Sophie. Sophie, unbeknown to him, had been forbidden to have any future contact with the 'disreputable reprobate', but as it was she who took in the post each day she could guard her secret. She rushed to her room, locked the door and flung herself on her bed to read his letter:

Dear Sophie,

How wonderful it all is! I cannot believe my good fortune. It seems so far almost too easy, and I can neither believe nor quite accept that this can be so, or that something will not occur soon to sever my happiness. I am not yet ready to return, indeed have no plans to do so.

Paris is as I imagined – and more so. As you know from having spent so long here, the French are far more absorbed in the 'arts' than the British. But it is more than that: every experience, visual or sensory, is one to be savoured.

How are you keeping? I hope well. Now I am bursting to tell you my news, so prepare yourself: I have had an article written about me – yes, an article! It was entitled (in French naturally), 'The Englishman who would like to conquer Paris', and was written after a small performance I gave.

I am becoming quite used now to playing at little soirées and gatherings, though I am always surprised anew by the variances in tone between one piano and the next, and am learning to respect each for what it is, and to try and combat its shortcomings by developing my technique.

Life is very merry, and I think I have never been so content – so much myself. . . .

His letter to his mother was less informative, but very affectionate nonetheless. She also had to keep it secret. Her husband had become irrational in his attitude towards everything and felt himself to be a man without purpose who could look forward to little. All that he had done was poisoned by his son's disregard for his achievements, and Joseph was full of a choking hate. His behaviour towards Helen was a mixture of bitter resentment and contrite love, and he would vacillate between the two extremes, unable to speak of the pressure within him – which was grief as much as anger, and devastated love as much as hate. His boy was dead. There was nothing to speak of.

Helen's hands shook as she opened the letter. His news was already three weeks old.

Mama dearest, dearest . . .

And at that point his mama put her long white fingers in front of her eyes and let the tears pour through.

. . . I write to you with much love and wonder how you are, and hope you are not too concerned for me. I hope also that I have not made home-matters too hard for you to bear. Please realize I care so much for you – for both of you, and anything I have done has not been with the intention of inflicting wounds. Perhaps if you knew how happy I am then you would find it in your heart to forgive me.

Much has happened here and Paris is an endlessly fascinating city. . . .

Helen put the letter carefully in a drawer amidst her corsets and chemises. She had nobody in whom to confide her sorrow. She was lonely – for her old life; for her husband as he used to be; her son; and a small, Puck-faced girl. But there was another child in her and she must look to that. It did no good to brood. Life meant getting by, that was all.

For their 'evening' at the home of the Comte de Boullery, Bernard had adapted Paganini's famous theme from his Twenty-fourth Caprice for violin and piano. He had also decided to include in the programme a composition of his own:

the piece he had composed two and a half years previously during the 'Selina episode', and called 'Interlude'.

For three days and well into each night Bernard worked, adapting and arranging the Paganini, and after perhaps two hours' sleep he would rise from his bed and fumble in the darkness for his matches to relight the candle. He would sit, pale and engrossed, wool scarf wrapped thrice about his neck, his coat over his nightshirt, and commit himself to music, a charcoal-etched figure in the low light.

Douglas had never before seen anyone work with such ferocity. He would wake fresh and baby-faced and half-blind, reach clumsily for his spectacles, and find Bernard hunched over the table surrounded by manuscript paper and a half-expired candle.

'Sometimes I think you are not human,' he observed once in a wry tone.

'I have to get this finished,' Bernard replied absently, crossing something out and scowling over it.

'Plenty of time, old chap.'

'But it is in my head *now*, not tomorrow.' Once, as an eleven year old boy he had made a similar remark. 'Besides,' he added, 'if we are to rehearse and perfect the pieces together there is not much time.' Bernard glanced up at his friend as if just noticing him, and blinked a little.

'Dear fellow, without wishing to appear immodest I know the Paganini backwards.'

'Not now you do not!'

'What have you done to my Paganini?' Douglas cried. 'Have you massacred him?'

'I do not believe so. Calm down. You will hear tomorrow when we play it. Now quit fussing like an old woman and have faith.'

The next day, elated and glittery-eyed behind the thick spectacles, Douglas danced from foot to foot. 'Genius. You *genius*. Certainly you have not massacred him! You have even enhanced my Paganini.'

He calmed down a little, looked at his friend wonderingly and shook his head, seemingly lost for words. Finally he said seriously: 'Bernard, you might believe yourself to be foremost a pianist, but I believe you to be a composer, and from now will continue to think of you as such.'

Bernard rolled his eyes heavenwards: 'You may think of me how you like, my dear friend, but I shall be as *I* think of myself. And now, Doug, we have a week of practice in front of us. . . .'

Bernard and Douglas travelled to the Boullery estate with Gounod and de Beriot. Bernard could gauge Douglas's apprehension by his unceasing chatter, whilst his own nervousness was contained deep inside him as usual, and only by his clenched hands could one have told that he was anything but relaxed. The evening was fine and clear, and when eventually they arrived a demi-moon and thousands of stars revealed flat countryside and a narrow river snaking between fields where cattle grazed the sparse frosted grass. Poplars lined one side of the long straight drive where were parked probably two hundred horse-drawn carriages, and at the head of this drive was the great mansion where the coachman deposited Bernard and the others.

The building was long and low, and lights blazed from each window, the sounds of voices and laughter spilling out. Within, all was a-glitter. Chandeliers shimmered and their rainbow colours reflected the gilded Louis quatorze furniture, lush wall hangings and brocade curtains. Finely attired, important-looking guests mingled in the hundred-foot-long ballroom and were served drinks on silver salvers by red-coated white-wigged footmen. At the far end of the room there was a raised platform, and upon it a grand piano, stool, seat for the violinist and a music stand. Bernard's anxious gaze encompassed it all.

'We are amongst la crème de la crème here, dear chap,' whispered Douglas.

'It terrifies me,' whispered back Bernard, gripping Douglas's elbow.

'It should not. Some of the juiciest scandals in the entire country are mixed together in this pot tonight.'

They were briefly introduced to the Comte, a wizened, humourless old man, and at quarter past nine, against a background of clinking glasses, popping corks, laughter and chatter, their performance began, opening with the Paganini.

It was only a matter of a half-minute or so before not a murmur was to be heard from the audience, and every person present was enraptured by the loveliness of sound and impact of playing, while between the two young musicians there flowed such a reciprocal understanding that at times it was almost as if it were one musician playing two instruments. The recital ended with Bernard's 'Interlude', and the audience erupted into applause. At its sound Bernard's face broke into a spontaneous smile and a series of small thrilled ripples ran through him.

They were congratulated, patted on the back, hugged, and kissed on both cheeks. Many people asked Bernard who the composer of the last piece was, and he replied time after time with a gleeful sense of mischief: 'Somebody called Foligno.'

'Foligno? *Qui est* Foligno?'

I am Foligno. I am Foligno. I am Foligno.

'Doug – oh Doug, my friend, this is surely splendid.' He was flushed, his eyes shining, and his hair became wilder and wilder as he repeatedly ran his hands through it.

'We were splendid,' Douglas contradicted him.

'Yes, we were splendid.' Bernard could not stop laughing.

'So let us eat ourselves to madness. There is suckling pig and venison and beef. I shall have your pork. Oh, there is that ghastly man Gilbert. Permit me to hide behind you. Turn your back. Am I hidden, do you think? What is he doing here, the old has-been? Make your way over to the food. Don't want to be bothered by the likes of him. He will no doubt find something about our performance to criticize.'

A couple of days later Bernard answered a knock at the door of his practice room at the Conservatoire, and was surprised to see Gilbert standing there, looking awkward and embarrassed, his flattish face purple in colour.

'I am sorry to disturb you, Monsieur Foligno,' he spoke brusquely to cover his embarrassment. 'I wished to congratulate you, to say I was very much impressed by your performance two evenings ago, and – I wondered if you would do me the honour of accompanying me at a recital I am giving?'

171

He cannot find anyone else, that is why he turns to me, was Bernard's first thought. *Why should I? Why should I couple my name with a man like him?*

But something in the man's expression and attitude made him bend from his arrogance, and he replied instead: 'I should be delighted, Monsieur Gilbert.'

The other man's eyes registered both pleasure and relief, and Bernard immediately felt churlish at his own inflated sense of importance and ungenerous thoughts. He stood up to shake Gilbert's hand and repeated, 'I should be delighted.'

When they rehearsed together Bernard was amazed by the languid and sensuous sounds which Gilbert drew from the big instrument. He could not equate that clumsy, coarse-faced man with the transmitter of such plaintive tones, and he began to understand some of Gilbert's frustration that the instrument should be so little understood.

At first when they worked together they barely spoke, and when they did it was always concerning a relevant point to their music, but as the days passed odd personal remarks would be dropped in the conversation, and from them Bernard had the impression he was in the company of a lonely man.

A week elapsed, during which they had taken coffee together on a couple of occasions, and they were seated companionably in the practice room when Gilbert began to talk garrulously as though building up to something more important and more difficult. Eventually he paused and took a deep breath: 'My wife left me, as you know . . .' He started to explain, stammering pitifully, and gazing downwards at his cello.

'Please, Monsieur Gilbert. It is no disgrace. You have no need to explain.'

'But I wish to. People assume I must have treated her badly, but the truth is I worshipped her. She is a very beautiful woman (that is difficult to imagine when you see me, is it not?), considerably younger than myself – we were not married for many years – and she was a former pupil of mine. As you know, it is rare for a woman to play the cello, however she was most able. She was infatuated by me, her professor – how often do we hear that story, sir? – and mistook the emotion for love. I, being more mature, should have realized the illusory nature of her sentiments, but so besotted was I, so unable to believe my good fortune, that I made the grave error of marrying her.

'I became like a dog with my love. I must have been tedious . . . She left me for a Comte. He was rich and young, and I who had nothing and was of no consequence, could give her only promises. She mocked me and I became impotent with her. Great man that I am – I was reduced to soft, useless flesh.

'You are a young, handsome man with your confidence entire, Mr Foligno. You cannot imagine what it is like –'

'I am sorry, so sorry.'

Gilbert shrugged. 'I am sorry for unburdening myself.'

'A man needs to.'

'Yes, a man needs to. You are right. I like you, Foligno. It is a long time since I have liked anyone. You have barely left boyhood behind, but you are mature. You have substance. You weigh matters in your head and do not laugh at a man when he is down.'

'I have been laughed at many times.'

'You? A fine strapping young man like you?'

'I am a Jew.'

'Ah yes.' He sighed mournfully. 'When we gave our first gleeful kick in the world and began to march forward, we little dreamed what lay ahead, did we?'

'You are an excellent cellist, Monsieur Gilbert. Such art must have fulfilled your dreams?'

'To an extent. More often it has frustrated them. But I am a follower, not an innovator. I have to play another's creation. You are an innovator, Mr Foligno, besides an interpreter.'

'It is just something within me.'

'Do not use the word "just". Do not let the "something within you" go ignored or take it for granted as you would any of your body's functioning organs. Occasionally stand back and maybe speculate on its possibilities.'

Bernard laughed and stretched his legs. 'Everyone is trying to make me a composer. I enjoy composition, and I have composed since I was a child. But at the end of the day I must *play*. I am a pianist and that is my dream. What is yours?'

173

'I have none left, Monsieur Foligno. I breathe. I do not inhale.'

The following evening was their concert, a small but well-attended affair with many serious musicians and critics present. Douglas, who now grudgingly accepted Gilbert, sat in the front row blinking proudly at Bernard. The works included Valentini, Rossini, Paganini, and finally – to prove his point about Chopin – Bernard had included in the programme a Chopin prelude which he had adapted for the cello and piano.

That night Gilbert gave a superb demonstration of his instrument's versatility and was brilliantly received, and Bernard who as accompanist had taken second position, was also highly praised. Afterwards the three of them went out and got drunk.

They went from bar to bar, café to café, and Gilbert in the middle of them like a swaying ox, said: 'You have made me happy. Tonight that elusive word is mine.'

Douglas reached up to pat his back. 'There there, Gilbert, you're a sound sort really, aren't you? Isn't he Bernard?'

'A sound sort,' Bernard agreed in a slurred voice.

'A sound sort,' sniggered Gilbert. 'I like that.'

A few days later, on his way out of the Conservatoire, Bernard bumped into the cellist.

'Oh, Foligno – what a surprise.'

Bernard, shocked by the radical change in the other man's appearance, realized that the meeting was no accident.

'I wonder,' Gilbert began humbly, 'would you join me for a coffee? I need to talk with someone.'

'But certainly, Monsieur Gilbert. I should be delighted.'

They went to a nearby café, and Gilbert sat slumped in his seat, his face puffed and grey between red veins, and his chin covered with dark stubble. He wore no hat and his hair was like a mangy grey dog's.

'You asked me the other day what my dream was, and I think I replied I did not have one. But I should have told you that without dreams one can only survive if one clings on to a routine. Now my *raison d'être* has been taken from me: they have dismissed me from my post.'

174

He began to sob quietly, making no effort to hide his tears, his face crumpling in grotesque creases. Bernard watched horrified, his own eyes watering in pity, and tentatively he put an arm about Gilbert's shoulder. The big man leaned against him and Bernard could feel the heaving of his body.

'I have nothing left, you see. No friends. No music. It was my fault – I was drunk and I hit a fellow professor in argument . . . Do you see that there is nothing, Foligno? Can you think of one single thing that is good to tell me? For I cannot. I have not been a self-pitying man . . . But now, will I be on the streets? What have I – an ugly middle-aged, penniless and solitary cellist? It was a conspiracy on their part of course, but who am I, one man, to wage war against the strength and politics of the Conservatoire? I do not have the name of Berlioz. I am sorry, Monsieur Foligno. Please accept my apologies. You will go far. You are one of the lucky ones, and you are entitled to dream. I had the lion's share briefly once, and for that I must be grateful. Oh God, Foligno, what am I to *do*?'

And in answer Bernard could only offer banalities and continue to support the weight of the other man who leaned against him like a child. He felt helplessly inadequate and was devastated by Gilbert's plight, the more so because outwardly the man appeared so aggressive and strong. Of course he tried to boost his morale, and to speak of a bright future with new opportunities, but they both knew that the words of consolation held little reality. Eventually Gilbert stood up to go.

'Do you want me to come back with you?' Bernard asked in a concerned voice.

'No, no. I shall be fine.'

'And get drunk, no doubt.'

'What else is there to do, Foligno? I cannot listen to myself play the cello forever.'

'It is on account of the winter and the cold you feel so bad. When the –'

'Foligno, my problems do not disappear with the change of seasons.'

'I am sorry. I wish I could help; do something.'

'You are a very kind young man. You are quite the kindest and most sympathetic person I have met for a long time.'

'No, that is not so, I am sure. But are you certain I may not come back with you?'

'I am certain.'

'Perhaps it is best for you to be on your own,' Bernard said doubtfully.

'Yes, I am sure of it. You will go far, Foligno. Remember that. You are an innovator, remember that too. You are not a poor old Gilbert, a cellist degenerated to become a drunken thug.'

The next morning his body was found floating downwards in the Seine between blocks of ice. He had cut his wrists first.

When Douglas told him that evening Bernard went rigid with shock. He covered his face with his hands in disbelief. 'No. Oh no. How could he have done such a thing?'

'The hierarchy can be very cruel,' Douglas said quietly.

'And you –' Bernard swung round, suddenly angry with his friend '– you did not trouble to understand the man's soul.'

'That is not true –'

But Bernard had flounced off to the other end of the room. He sat with his elbows on the table, chin cupped in his hands, mulling over life's inconsistencies. The sorrow – Gilbert's sorrow – became his own, pressing upon him; and anger burned in him, at the pain human beings were capable of inflicting upon their fellows. Paris had developed its first flaw.

That night Bernard awoke after only half an hour, thinking of poor tortured Gilbert. He lay there, seeing again and again the defeated expression; a grey dog which had taken all it could stand. And he imagined Gilbert's body drained of blood and filled instead with the river's sludge, his wounds washed white.

A few moments later found Bernard back at the big carved table, lighting a candle. He scribbled all night, not noticing when daylight slid through the seams between the shutters, nor that his bespectacled friend was lying propped up on an elbow staring at him. Bernard completed his sonata for cello and piano, scrawled the title *Homage: In Memoriam* – became sufficiently aware of Douglas to mutter absently: 'Goodnight, Doug,' and returned to bed.

My life is a great theatre, he reflected, turning the cliché around in his mind as he drifted into sleep. . . . *a great, great theatre. I am learning a role. Other people – events – they are part of a huge experiment, pointing me in a direction. Stages. So many steps to the next one and the next . . . Poor Gilbert. Poor, poor Gilbert. . . .*

But he had done his best for old Gilbert. Gilbert was probably even better off dead.

The months passed quickly and it became spring. Intermittent between the rain were bursts of soft warmth and dappled sun, and the trees lining the avenues were like pink and white bonbons. Bernard and Douglas would stroll down the Champs Elysées with a group of friends, and Bernard's heart would be almost swollen with joy. Where had the days gone to – rapaciously swallowing their predecessors? They were never supposed to end.

The telegraph from England arrived in his fourth month. It was from his mother: *Papa gravely ill. Perhaps time to return home.*

At first that struck him more than anything: the usage of the word *home*. This was home now; Madame Becaud's establishment. This was *home* – with Douglas and his new friends and his new life, his *own* life. Then the significance of the message registered. It could only mean one thing: his father was dying.

The man who had mated his mother, created, raised and then disowned him – what did Bernard owe him besides creation?

'Papa is dying.' He repeated the words with different inflection and felt first the sharp sorrow of a small boy looking up to a straight-backed, fair-haired man, and then the bitterness of one strong-minded adult divided from another by misunderstanding. These two images could not be reconciled.

He packed his baggage haphazardly and Douglas hovered around unhappily, watching articles and clothing disappearing into the brown leather case in disorderly fashion.

'Leave something behind. That way you will have to return.'

Bernard had taken to smoking a pipe. He left it on the table alongside a sheet of manuscript paper and a half-drunk cup of sweet thick black coffee. He endured the awkwardness of 'goodbyes' – the sudden emotion and the Gallic embraces, first with Madame Becaud, then Douglas himself.

He set out on the long, uncomfortable voyage back to England, and with every sea-mile, with every curling wave, his strength seemed to be washed away, leaving further and further behind the cocky young buck and laying bare again the gawky Jewish son.

Don't let him die. . . .

He stood looking behind him all the way, as if the future lay in that short intermediary past; an enchanting foretaste of what could be.

Chapter Twelve

It was like it had been with Rachel; the smell of deterioration and medicament pervaded the house. Mr Hamilton was in attendance, reminding Bernard of his relinquished friend, and there were two nurses and a different maid – who had enquired who he was when she opened the door. He was so taken aback that she did not know, so travel-weary, that he was frozen on the spot and gawped idiotically, and Harold – it was inevitable that Harold should be there, active in the death scene – answered for him: 'He is the son of the house,' adding snidely by way of greeting, 'but which house is another issue.'

He had grown a luxuriant beard trimmed into goatee outline, and now he stroked it mockingly, running his finger backwards and forwards along the blunt edge almost sensuously.

'How utterly distasteful to see you, Harold,' counteracted Bernard in a civil tone, brushing past him, so much taller and more graceful than his cousin.

'Douglas sends his affection, sir,' Bernard told Mr Hamilton, who was in the family room writing something. 'Where is my mother? How is my father?'

'Ah Bernard, sad days. Sad days . . . very sad days, I am afraid. You are only just in time. Your father has, at most, a few hours left to him, and your mother, astonishing woman that she is, never leaves his side.'

Bernard was leaving the room abruptly when Mr Hamilton said gently: 'Bernard, do not be – offended by anything he might say. Mostly he is barely conscious, but when he is . . . He does not speak as he feels. He does not know of what he talks.'

With a bitter smile Bernard turned to Douglas's father and said: 'If he is aware enough to think, Mr Hamilton, then I am

179

certain he speaks exactly as he is thinking. You are most kind, but you have no need to protect me, sir.'

As he climbed the staircase he had to clasp the balustrade tightly for support. His hand was shaking, his body trembling in anticipation of the scene within, each step bringing him reluctantly nearer.

I want to be forgiven, Papa.

For what, my son? You did nothing. You wished to be a pioneer and follow your own route as did Moses. It is I who ask to be forgiven.

Oh Papa – I love you.

Bernard gave a short burst of uncontrolled laughter which tangled in his throat, and dragging his feet on the final stair he arrived on the landing.

His parents' door was closed, and although he knocked there was no reply. He crept in tentatively, and there was his mother, deeply asleep in the chair beside the bed, her hands folded palely on her seven-month pregnant belly, her head lolling slightly but not inelegantly. Her hair, in its loaf-like loop, was almost white, and seeing her like that she could have been sixty.

And the mound in the bed; did it breathe still, or as Helen slept had it eloped?

Bernard peered, dreadingly. The sparse wisps of peppered grey hair stood on end like insect legs above the stark white of the bedclothes, which rose laboriously with Joseph's stinking breath.

'Papa . . . Papa.' He felt beneath the many blankets, found a bony hand and clasped it. Could he instil in this withered, cold dry thing love and forgiveness? 'I am here. I am back. I am returned, Papa.'

Bernard's tears fell now, for certainly it was no time to ponder upon grievances. He was simply a son weeping over his papa.

'You . . .' The hand pulled away, and the single hissed word was like the sound of slipping stones. '. . . Do not belong.'

'Papa. Dearest Papa – I am back to see you. For as long as you wish.'

'I do not – wish.'

Now the whole tiny shrivelled face was revealed, horrific in its toothless unfamiliarity.

'Bernard, darling –'

Helen's loving voice called to Bernard gently and he felt a relieved gladness.

'Mama.' He went to her, crouching beside her and rocking her thin but bulky form against him. 'Poor dearest Mama.'

'I am so pleased you came.'

'But of course I came. How could you think otherwise?'

'Your life is so important to you now, I know.'

Before he could reply a voice from the bed interrupted, 'His – life – is – nothing.'

Could he hear? Could that thing lying there really absorb and listen? Now that he was rejected, his old stubbornness returned.

'Joseph.' His wife spoke in an imploring tone and sat on the edge of the bed. 'My dear, be calm. Bernard is here because he loves you. Surely that is the most important thing?'

'Love!' The scornful laugh was a thin searing wheeze. 'The love of – a – heathen with a – facile – turn – of phrase.' Joseph attempted to sit, but sank immediately, and for a few seconds seemed to be asleep.

Helen continued to hold and stroke and murmur, intermittently wiping away her tears.

'The heathen – has murdered his own – father.' The soft words were spat from the depths of the bedclothes.

'Papa, that is not fair, I must –'

'Bernard, Bernard . . . Ssh dearest. He does not know what he is saying.'

'I know – woman. Every . . . th . . . thing.'

'Papa. Every morning I lay tefillin. Papa, I love you. I sincerely love you. But love does not mean one has to be –'

'Bernard darling, your Papa is dead. He can no longer hear you.'

'And he left you nothing?'

'No. And had he done so I think I would not have taken it,

181

given as it would have been from obligation and not love. At least he was true to himself to the last. But Harold was looked after . . . However, before that there was the funeral and then the week of sitting Shivah. Harold was abominable and I had literally to push him from my father's old chair which was positioned beside Mama's. He told me I had no right. Can you imagine, Anna? He had torn his clothes as had I, and his beard was unkempt, and he thought as I had been outcast it was not for me to occupy that chair, but – God I would have none of it. My father had called me his murderer, and perhaps his death was precipitated by my actions, nevertheless he was *my* father. So I tilted the chair and told him quite cordially that if he did not vacate it immediately, then on another lesser occasion I would disfigure him.

'"You forget my profession, sir!" he counteracted. Lord, I could have howled with laughter! However, very grudgingly he gave me my seat, and throughout the week I sat beside my mother and gave her the support she needed. She was so brave.

'I had to handle my father's business. Harold wished to organize matters himself, but in this instance my courageous mother interfered. She told him that it was for me to do. Can you imagine the strangeness? There was I in the main seat so to speak, and all I had to do was to occupy it and take over. I examined the idea with the same detachment as a child examining a toy he does not want, and of course I discarded it. And so the business was brought to a close. There was a poignancy about it: the end of Joseph Foligno and his life's work. "Only a Jew", but a member of the Stock Exchange.

'Sometimes I tried to speak of my feelings to my mother – to explain why I had acted as I had, and to apologize. But she always prevented me.

'"I understand, dearest," she would say. "I truly do. Now we shall speak of the happy times or none at all."

'So we did speak of the happy memories and she seemed to be almost content on those occasions, as though the memories were the truth and the bad months had not intervened.

'Harold still came round, but my mother no longer made

him feel so welcome, and certainly I did not, so that he left us more on our own, and I think that during that time my mother and I became closer than we had ever been, and I was able to tell her something of my plans – such as they were – and of my hopes.

'Elizabeth was born, normally and without undue problems, thank God, and was fair like Rachel. A couple of months later, when I felt my mother to be sufficiently strong, I left. She wished to give me money, part of what my father had left to her. But of course I could not accept. We actually quarrelled over that, but I remained obstinate, and felt sure I was right to refuse.

'It was summer, and I was a precocious nineteen and a half years of age. I was certainly not a boy in my heart. I went to the Hamiltons in Gloucestershire where it had been arranged that in return for board and lodgings for the season I would play at various soirées they were giving. Douglas was in Leipzig for a spell, but Elaine was there and she was a very merry girl . . . And so I had my first real taste of society life, my dear!'

At first Bernard was impressed, and then doubtful of its merits, not caring for the hypocrisy and light chatter, nor for the attitude of some people:

'Foligno . . . Is that a Spanish name?'

'Yes, sir.'

'Are you a Spaniard?'

'No sir, I am English.'

'But you said your name was Spanish?'

How wearisome all this was . . . 'Yes sir, that is so. I am Jewish. My ancestors came from Spain.'

'A Jew, eh! Goodness me, fancy that.' And he stomped away, affronted.

But the Hamiltons treated him as one of their own family, insisting that the numerous invitations extended and accepted all included him.

There was also staying with the Hamiltons the younger of the Leeming sisters, Miranda. Her parents and elder sister were touring America, but at fifteen she was considered too young for such a trip. She was a pretty, frivolous little thing, tiny in stature and wild in her ways, with total disregard for convention, being both outspoken and forward. She also happened to believe herself in love with Bernard and, instead of being girlishly shy about the fact, was quite brazen.

'They can keep Boston,' she announced loudly after she had known Bernard a week and had unashamedly declared her undying love. 'I should prefer to be here in England with you!'

'Miranda, I think I am beginning to find this love of yours a little overwhelming.' Bernard gave an exaggerated sigh and crossed his legs lazily.

'Well, you shall just have to be overwhelmed then!' Miranda snuggled close to him on the sofa like a puppy.

Elaine, who dabbled in journalism, was in the room writing an article, and she glanced up and said mildly: 'Dear – whilst Bernard might be overwhelmed I fear you might be unrequited. Now move yourself a little for decency's sake. And pray be a little more subtle!'

Bernard laughed. 'Decency! Subtlety! It is too late for that. Miranda has obviously heard nothing of feminine mystique.'

Sometimes the three of them went for drives around the dusty little lanes, squeezing into the pony phaeton and taking turns to drive, but if they had a picnic with them there was not sufficient space, so Mrs Hamilton would insist upon the coachman taking them in the Hooper's wagonette with a harnessed pair.

Bernard had never known a family with so many vehicles. Apart from the phaeton and wagonette, there were also an old Russian Droshky lavishly upholstered in velvet and plush, a modern Brougham, a cabriolet made popular by the Count d'Orsay, and finally a Sulky which Mr Hamilton used for harness-racing.

'How many horses do you have?' he asked Elaine as they sat companionably by the river, picnicking on fresh salmon and summer fruits.

'Oh dear me, do you really wish me to count? Well, I believe we have more horses than we have servants; and we have plenty of them! Let me see: three harness ponies, four harness horses, and a fifth that Papa keeps only for the Sulky . . . And Douglas's old horse and Papa's two, and Mama's three – when you hunt as seriously as she, then it is not merely to be ostentatious, I assure you – and my mare . . . How many is that? I have not been counting!'

'Fifteen,' said Bernard and Miranda simultaneously.

'Goodness, is it really? It seems wrong really, doesn't it? Whilst we feed fifteen great beasts others struggle to feed their children. Still, that is the way of our world, I suppose, and I do not know that there is much to be done about it.'

'Marx would have it otherwise,' Bernard said. 'Much as I loathe his racism, one has to admire his theories.'

'But putting such theories into practice would surely prove impossible.'

'It does not have to be accomplished overnight.'

'And would you wish for such a world, Bernard?'

'And servants –' piped up Miranda before he could reply, alarmed at the boring route the conversation was taking. 'How many servants do you have, Elaine?'

'Goodness Miranda, the questions you ask me! Oh dear – I must begin to think all over again. Well, there is Papa's valet, Mama's maid, my maid, there are two housemaids and the cook . . . The kitchen maid, the butler, the footman . . . And then of course there are the coachman, the groom, the two stable lads . . . Is that it? Oh no, I forgot the two gardeners.'

'Fifteen, if you include outside the house. We have twenty.'

'Twenty!' Bernard gasped incredulously, thinking of his own tiny household.

'Yes, because my sister and I each have a maid. And we have two grooms, and two footmen and two cooks, and three gardeners. And so it makes five extra and that adds up to twenty, do you see?'

'Miranda, you really must learn not to boast.'

'But I was not. I was merely telling the truth. We *have* twenty servants – but it bothers me not a jot one way or another. Your turn, Bernard.'

'It is hard to count them. But – three! And a nurse who is

temporary, so I suppose that makes four, and no doubt she'll be replaced by a nanny.'

'Oh, how quaint!'

'Miranda!' expostulated Elaine.

'Yes Miranda,' Bernard agreed, 'you are really rather shocking.'

'Am I? Well I do love you, Bernard. I do, Elaine. You must not grimace like that – and I want no private little lectures later. You see how I read your mind. And Bernard, did you know that my papa only met you once and still speaks of you? He wished me to receive piano tuition from you, and I do think I could almost endure the tedium of practice if you were my tutor.'

In August Douglas arrived unexpectedly. 'Well I had to return your pipe, old chap. Revolting habit.'

And another month elapsed before the delightful season drew to its close. The fun was over, and now he must enter the next stage and channel his life towards its ultimate objectives.

Bernard found himself lodgings in St John's Wood – the entire ground floor of a well-kept boarding house. He had a separate water-closet for himself, and even with the additional cost of breakfast the rent itself was fair. His landlady seemed pleasant enough and was agreeable to his unusual requests: one being that he could keep a cat – for Anna the cat kept running away in his absence – the other that he be permitted to have a piano. To both of these she consented with good humour, her only stipulations being that he reimburse her for any damage the animal might do, and that he did not play the piano at night. But the most imminent problem was that Bernard did not have a piano, and without resorting to capital he could not afford to buy one.

The following morning, having settled himself and the cat in their new home, he decided on his course of action and went out and bought a copy of *The Times*. He took it back to his rooms where he studied the financial pages, scouring the columns until eventually he came across an article of interest: a rumoured takeover by A. and R. Wilfredson Corporation – the huge iron foundry – of P. and S. Steers and Sons, the steel manufacturers.

He lay on his stomach on the rug, pouring over the paper a while longer, then he leaped up.

'I shall sell my P. and O. shares, and replace them with Wilfredson's,' he said out loud. 'And then, Anna –' he stroked the cat winding itself about his ankles '– you shall have a piano upon which to sit.'

An hour later the transaction was completed, and Bernard stood outside the broker's office in a small road off Chancery Lane, well-satisfied with himself.

It was a mild September day and Bernard strolled contentedly for about half an hour with nothing better to do except stop and have his shoes shined.

The broker had asked him: 'What kind of musician are you, Mr Foligno?'

And Bernard had replied loftily: 'My aspirations are yet to be attained, sir.'

Now he smiled at the recollection and thought: *There cannot be that many pianists who have no piano, nor even a single plan. Maybe I should contact Mr Beavis. Yes, I think I shall do that. I have an idea he could help me. . . .*

Bernard's head was bent in thought and idle pleasure when he literally bumped into his cousin Harold.

'Do look where you are walking, sir.' There was a flurry of swirling black cloak. 'My goodness, Bernard! The bumbling pianist himself.' (Was he capable of being anything but obnoxious?) 'And what brings you to these parts?'

'You of course, Harold. I thought I would pay you a visit.'

'Me? Why me?'

Then he took note of Bernard's mocking expression, and the curly black head thrown back in scorn.

'You joke at my expense, I see. And now that we have exchanged such pleasantries perhaps you will let me pass.'

'I am not preventing you. You yourself choose to stand there as proprietor of the pavement. I confess I forgot I was in Harold-country here. Where is your wig, Harold?' he asked, knowing full well the other man was not yet entitled to one.

'Like you, cousin Bernard, I have yet to realize my ambitions. Unlike you, mine are not constructed of air. How are my aunt and her baby?'

'They are doing well, thank you.'

'I have not visited recently.'

'No,' Bernard said shortly.

'I shall call round soon. She must feel very alone.'

Bernard knew that this was indisputable and that just possibly Harold was demonstrating genuine concern, but even now he could only oppose him.

'She is preoccupied with my little sister and she has many visitors.' He felt a little guilty as he said this for as far as he knew the only regular callers were Sophie and her mother.

'Does Miss Sophie Romain still call upon her?' Harold asked.

'Yes.'

'I must visit Miss Romain again soon. I fancy that we might find a great deal to speak about now. Well Bernard, I suppose it would be civil for you and I to have a tea or coffee, but I am, as you can imagine, extremely busy even though obviously you are not, and –'

'And besides, when were we ever civil to one another, Harold?'

They parted and Bernard immediately took a cab to Sophie's home. It was an extravagance, but in his angry mood he did not mind. He was not sure, however, that by himself he would be made welcome by her mother, and was glad upon arriving to find that Sophie was by herself, Mrs Romain, by coincidence, having gone to visit his own mother.

'Bernard,' Sophie greeted him in the morning-room.

'Sophie, dear Sophie.' He kissed her round hand in affection.

She rang for some tea and then patted the seat beside her. She was twenty-two now, plump and matronly with very little girlishness about her.

'You look extremely wrought, Bernard.'

'I am extremely wrought. And soon you shall be also. I shall tell you the reason. I bumped – yes, really bumped – into my cousin Harold in Lincoln's Inn Fields just now, and he declared to me his intention of resuming his pursuit of "Miss Romain".

He considered you "might find a great deal to speak about together now".'

'Oh no!'

'Oh yes. So you will just have to find yourself another suitor quick.'

'Oh Bernard, you are quite dreadful. Well, at the moment there is no such possibility so I shall have to find other means of fending him off. Ah, here is tea,' she said, sounding slightly relieved, and used the opportunity to change the subject.

'I read in the *Daily News* this morning that Rothschild's house in Piccadilly has been equipped with a gas cooker for twenty thousand pounds! Can you imagine? It has hot plates, but no oven. I should have wanted an oven at that price!'

'And I a house!'

'So Bernard, talking about material things, what plans have you?'

'Well, tomorrow I have a meeting with Sterndale Bennett, the principal of the Royal Academy. Sir Edmund Moore has kindly sent a prior letter of introduction.'

'What would you do at the Academy?'

'Oh goodness, Sophie – anything. Anything they asked of me.'

'Are you nervous? Do you get nervous? You always seem so collected.'

Bernard laughed and shook his head. 'That is an illusion, Sophie. And yes, I shall admit it to you – I get nervous. If my well-being depends on a good reaction, then I fear the contrary.' He looked into her soft face and remembered how once his heart had leapt at the sight of it. Now he felt only the warmth of friendship. 'You are a good listener, Sophie,' he said. 'And you are a good friend.'

She laid her hand on his. 'I am so very glad of that, Bernard, and I do so hope for your happiness.'

The following day, at the Royal Academy of Music, Bernard played the piano for Sterndale Bennett. The latter listened with growing admiration and surprise as he played, but finally shook his head regretfully.

'I can offer you absolutely nothing at present, but I shall

certainly bear you in mind as soon as anything should occur, Foligno.'

'I thought perhaps as a friend of Sir Edmund Moore's . . .' Bernard left the sentence unfinished, the optimism fading from his voice.

'I am glad he referred you,' Bennett said.

'Then –'

'Sir, whom you know makes no difference to me. I judge on merit alone, and I admire your style of playing, even though it is a trifle self-indulgent. But I cannot invent, even for my own closest relative, a position which does not at this moment exist. You would not wish me to dismiss another merely to make way for you?'

It was precisely what he did wish – however he could hardly confess that. 'No, of course not,' he concurred politely.

'There you are. So what am I to do? But you must not be despondent. You are an impressive and individual pianist and I shall keep my word in that I shall consider you if the occasion arises. Meanwhile – please pay my respects to Sir Edmund Moore. Tell him he need not be ashamed of his judgement.'

Although he had been rejected, Bernard was not downcast, for he had been complimented by the great Sterndale Bennett, himself a pupil of Mendelssohn, and he returned home in reasonable spirits. There was a letter for him on the salver on top of the little table, and he opened it to find that it contained a card from Mr Beavis requesting that they might meet for dinner at his club that night at nine o'clock.

How curious, Bernard thought, *for I was only thinking of the man yesterday*.

He dressed himself with care, humming tunelessly as he buttoned his shirt with the pleated front, selecting a pale blue silk cravat which had a pre-formed bow and buckled fastening. The final touch, after the figured damask waistcoat and dark blue frock coat, was his new top hat in silk plush from Messrs Chapman and Moore of Old Bond Street. Bernard had a weakness for fashion: simple style – nothing ostentatious like Harold, or outlandish like Douglas; but beautiful

190

fabrics and a classic cut he found hard to resist, and he had developed an instinctive eye in keeping with his sensuous nature.

He surveyed himself in the mirror. *I look all right, I think. It is hard to tell how one looks oneself.* . . .

So attired, he set out to meet Mr Beavis.

'At last I have tracked you down!' Beavis greeted him. 'How very pleased I am to see you, Mr Foligno.'

'The pleasure is mine, sir.' He gave a small polite bow and had to prevent his mouth from twitching at the sight of Mr Beavis's amazing eyebrows – spiky dark wedges with long stray hairs that met his deep-set eyes.

'Well, well –' he was always cheery, and he rubbed his hands together to emphasize his cheeriness '– you are looking in exceedingly good health, young Foligno, I must say. And quite a bit been happening, I gather?' Not waiting for an answer, he continued: 'A drink is called for, I think. Whisky? Wine? Sherry?'

'Whisky sir, please.' Bernard had developed quite a liking for the drink since his inglorious inauguration.

The club was dark-pannelled and furnished with leather chairs and library tables, the windows hung with deep, maroon drapes to match the carpet, and the atmosphere was comfortable and genteel without being 'stuffy', refined without being too snobbish.

In a corner four young men who looked as though they had arrived in London from the country were playing whist, whilst another group of serious-faced men sat with documents on the table before them and were obviously discussing business. Two haughty footmen busied themselves carrying drinks on trays and offering cigars.

Mr Beavis had a dry sherry, and regarding Bernard's whisky, observed: 'My friend Sir Edmund's influence?'

'Possibly.'

'In moderation, I hope.' Beavis's expression was paternal.

'Oh rather,' Bernard agreed, his eyebrows knitting together in mock seriousness.

'Like everything – or nearly so.'

And Bernard, a little unsure as to the innuendo, gave a small nod.

'Are you happy to dine in shortly?'

'Delighted to, sir.' He was actually hungry. There had been no time for lunch during the day.

'You have not yet reached the "starving stage" in your career?'

'It has yet to happen! You know then that I am no longer in commerce.'

'Naturally. Sir Edmund informed me. What a delightful chap he is, and I am eternally grateful to you for the introduction. As regards yourself, let me say I was both surprised and unsurprised: surprised, because despite your extreme youth I considered you had the makings of an outstanding businessman; yet unsurprised, because you were strangely contradictory on the occasion of our last meeting. You seemed to shrug aside your achievements almost contemptuously. And there again, as a pupil of Cramer, you could have been no mean musician – yet I sensed a reluctance on your behalf to discuss music. And in your eyes, Bernard, was an almost painful longing which made me think to myself, "here is a malcontented youth." Now, of course, all is explained!' Mr Beavis leaned back in his seat, beaming proudly at his own cleverness.

Bernard's eyes sparkled appreciatively. 'It would seem, sir, you are something of an expert in psychology.' He licked the whisky from one corner of his mouth.

'Every man of business, if he is shrewd, must learn to apply psychology, Mr Foligno, if only so that he may remain one step ahead. Now, what say you we dine now? They do the most superb piece of beef here. I can thoroughly recommend it. But now I must ask a delicate question: as I recall when we were last together, you ate fish, and it now occurs to my most remiss mind that this might have been for religious reasons. Do you eat meat which is not killed in the special manner, Mr Foligno?'

'Yes, sir. It is considerate of you to ask; but recently I have modified some of my thinking towards religion.'

'Towards much else, it would seem.'

'Possibly so,' Bernard answered seriously.

'I am sure of it. And I believe a more relaxed attitude generally enlargens one's horizons, so long as one adheres to basic rules.'

'I hope so, sir.' Bernard frowned. 'It is an issue which constantly troubles me, for it is so hard to be objective. One is brought up to think of a subject in a particular light, and then, away from the old environment, one is forced to reconsider that subject. And the answers are not always clear.'

'Inevitably. But exploration is essential if contentment is not to be precluded for the rest of your life. Your father must have been exceedingly proud of you before he died.'

'No sir. He was not.' Bernard's throat constricted, and in him, as always, was sadness that the man who had mattered most had not been proud.

'How is that?'

'I went against everything he had hoped for me and which was familiar to him.'

But because of his father he had met Mr Beavis, and now over dinner his host put his proposition to him: it was exactly what Bernard himself had been considering the day before, and in a daze he shook the man's outstretched hand to clinch their arrangement and their friendship.

Much later, after brandy and cigars, and more pumping of hands, Bernard was driven back to St John's Wood in the Brougham, Mr Beavis having disembarked at his house in Belgravia. The night was cool, with that faint essence which heralds autumn. Bernard thought: *Now I have my entitlement. I am actually happy. I feel drunk – but I think it is only that I am happy.*

Back at his lodgings he opened the door to his room to find a new addition: in one corner stood a splendid Cramer upright piano in dark mahogany. On it was a note from Sir Edmund Moore:

Do not refuse this small token of affection and friendship. I cannot conceive of a more deserved usage for this instrument with its sacred name. The person of that name would also wish it.

193

And sitting on top of the piano, like an empress, was Anna the cat, sleekly middle-aged, purring audibly.

Bernard leaned against the piano and quietly cried. He slid to the floor in a gangling heap and just cried.

Chapter Thirteen

'It is raining even harder now. I hope the weather is not like this for my journey tomorrow.'

'And if it is – perhaps you will decide not to go.'

'Dearest, your face is as hopeful as a child's anticipating a sweet! Of course I shall go regardless . . . And now you look sad. Bernard, are you sad?'

'I am only a little tense.'

'Then please continue to talk to me, and I shall massage your neck for you meanwhile.'

'Well . . . I shall tell you of my efforts to become established . . . The passage to fame came in no illuminated burst for me, and during the next two years, despite Sir Edmund Moore's introductions and encouragement, I seemed rooted in a very unstartling career which only just kept me out of debt.

'My main source of income came from performing in small halls, churches – and before you look askance, I entered them with no thought other than that they were places of music – dancing halls, and at private soirées. And although Beavis published several works and paid me generously, these did not attract much public recognition.

'Yet throughout this rather static period I managed to retain my confidence. Perhaps that old inner arrogance of which I have so often been accused, was put to good use then; whatever – I became quite philosophical in my outlook, forcing patience into my impulsive nature and fighting my doubts when they threatened to take hold of me. I had friends, a roof over my head, and – dare I say it – the odd woman or two, and life was really rather fine.

'Then Harold's father went abroad for twelve months, and without a thought let his house. Harold, that newly-fledged barrister, was homeless. I recall he turned up one afternoon when I was at my mother's house, and immediately presented her with a box of Swiss chocolates. I was of course instantly suspicious, but my mother, bless her heart, thanked him delightedly. I waited all afternoon to see the reason for the chocolates, but eventually had to leave. The next day, when I called, I found that Harold had moved back into his old room. It was typical of him to wait until my mother was on her own and would not show any resistance, before asking her permission.'

'He has the hide of a rhinoceros, that man,' Bernard complained to his mother one day.

Helen, who had taken to wearing spectacles for reading, had been awkwardly engrossed in the *Family Herald* with Elizabeth asleep in her arms. She removed her spectacles carefully and smiled peacefully at him.

'Dearest, you must not take on so. Harold, as you know, is not my favourite person, I must confess it, but when I consider his childhood – why, his mother was really the most overbearing woman imaginable – then it is not surprising he behaves as he does.'

Bernard was about to burst out with his response – that he too had his own childhood problems, that he had grown up with the belief that his music was to be precluded him; and had his character, as a result, become twisted like Harold's? But his mother's expression was mild and sweet, and he stifled his reply for it would have hurt her.

Helen continued: 'Besides, I hardly see him. He is working during the day and out almost every night. I have no idea where he finds to go so regularly.'

'Have you asked him?'

'Oh well, it is his affair you know, Bernard. He has many friends, I daresay.'

'I doubt that, Mama,' Bernard answered scornfully.

'What are you saying, my dear?'

'I am saying nothing, Mama. However, I hope he is contributing towards his keep.'

'Well, Bernard dear – I do not need the money, and he *is* family.'

Bernard banged one fist into the other palm and his eyes blazed. 'That is absolutely irrevelant. It is the principle. He is using your home as a hotel, whilst his dreadful father skives abroad. He regards his presence here as an honour to you, does not pay you, and does not tell you where he goes. Well, I shall find out.'

'Dear, I do not understand this rivalry between the two of you. Anyway, I believe he has seen one or two houses which interest him.'

'He only needs one, Mama,' observed Bernard in an acid tone. 'And I want him gone within a month.'

Bernard had a fair idea where his cousin went in the evenings, but he could not be sure, and determinedly he devoted himself to the task of discovering.

We can all be devious, dear cousin. We can all have reptilian minds, he thought; *Papa, I am about to discredit your surrogate son.*

Having ascertained from his mother what time Harold usually set out, Bernard spent the next eight nights hiding like a thief near his own front door, waiting for his cousin's emergence, and then slyly trailing him. Of those nights Harold was out six, and of the six, five were spent appropriating prostitutes, two of whom were young children and one a boy of about fourteen. Harold's hunting ground was Soho and the Shepherd's Market where the little roads were literally lined with assorted beings, and where every kind of depravity had its price. Here was poverty without dignity, merchandise measured in human flesh.

Bernard was appalled, revolted and delighted at his discovery. His decadent cousin, always so outwardly virtuous, so devout in his religious beliefs, had handed him enough aces to win a life time of whist!

*

In the summer of 1863 Sir Edmund Moore announced his decision to marry his young mistress, Lilly Huckelby. By now Bernard knew her well and liked her – a tall wide-boned woman with a handsome, intelligent face and forthright manner. She was also obviously devoted to Sir Edmund, and her face would break into a smile of great happiness at the sight of her white-haired lover.

'Am I mad to marry her?' Sir Edmund asked Bernard over dinner at his house in Brook Street.

'You ask *me*, sir?'

'Yes, Bernard. You.'

'But I think it is wonderful news!' He clapped his hands together to emphasize his delight.

'But, Bernard, I am seventy now and she is still a very young woman. What, truly, do you think is her opinion of me?' He looked as anxious as a teenage suitor and Bernard laughed joyfully:

'Oh sir, she loves you. Of that there is no doubt whatsoever.' He helped himself to more wine and poured some into Sir Edmund's glass.

'But she could have anyone,' the other persisted gloomily.

'And she chooses *you*,' Bernard reassured him.

'That is what awes me so.' He sighed. 'I cannot believe it. It is now five years since I have known her, and still I doubt the validity of what she feels.'

'You will not when you are married, sir.'

'How wise you suddenly sound, lad. Ah, but I must stop my analyses, for really I am as happy as a man could be. Good God, Bernard – how shocked my son-in-law the judge will be when he hears the news.' Sir Edmund's eyes sparkled with sudden humour. 'Aye, how shocked the man will be!'

The date was set for August the twentieth, and on the evening of the seventeenth Bernard called on his friend.

Murphy opened the door, his face crumpled with weeping, and Bernard saw that the house was in a state of commotion, with various members of the family rushing about like ants.

'Murphy, what has happened?' Bernard grabbed the little man by the shoulder in his anxiety.

'Oh sir, oh sir . . . The most terrible thing . . . Sir Edmund is dead. He had a heart attack a few hours back.'

Murphy burst into fresh sobs and Bernard released his grip, his hand sliding away and down to his side.

He tried to speak and could not. His dear uncle, godfather and mentor was gone. It was an impossibility, but it was so, and Bernard was stricken.

There was no place for him now in the house in Brook Street and, unnoticed, he left to break the news to Lilly. It seemed he was engulfed by a great tongue of pain, and he gave little animal-like whimpers as he ran through the streets till he arrived at her place in Maddox Street.

Lilly was calm and self-controlled when she received his news, and Bernard, incredulous at her apparent calm, was unable to remain in her company. Dismayed and disgusted, he left.

Sir Edmund's body was taken to Scotland, to the private family cemetery, but the funeral service was held in the immense St Francis's Catholic Church in the City of London and attended by hundreds. Who had not known or known of Sir Edmund Moore – that enormous, ebullient and erudite man who was as true to himself as he was to others, despised falsity or prejudice, was impatient of stupidity, always had time for those whom he held in affection – and yet remained uncertain to the end of his place in a woman's heart?

And rightly so, as it turned out, Bernard thought bitterly.

Just a face in the massive crowd, he stood with Mr Beavis and his wife and Lilly. He could not forgive Lilly her calmness. Outwardly she behaved as if no catastrophe had happened, and he kept examining her profile for some revealing sign that within herself she was suffering. Finding none, he felt almost suffocated by his fury and disappointment.

From the scarlet and white robes came Latin words which meant nothing, and when the sounds of the vast congregation shuffling to its feet echoed massively he at first could not move with it; but then the choristers' exquisite notes blended with the grand organ and resounded throughout the building and a small lone boy sang *Ave Maria*, the reedy, sweet voice soaring, and they elicited from him the most raw, the most private pain Bernard had ever known. The sounds filled him and enveloped him.

. . . I did not think that I would lose him so soon . . . How polite everyone is in his grief. How sensibly it is tackled. . . .

He looked again at the calm profile of the girl who had been engaged to marry Sir Edmund Moore and felt suddenly faint.

'I am sorry, I cannot remain here,' he muttered to Mr Beavis.

The other man squeezed his arm in understanding, and Bernard forced his way past the pews of people, treading on feet, stumbling. . . .

Outside he stood gulping in the fresh air, the warm brightness of the day stilling the pounding of his heart. He took a cab home.

The next day he was visited by a policeman.

'Sir, I have come with a letter for you.'

'For me?'

'Yes sir. I have come directly from the lodgings of a Miss Lilly Huckelby who took her own life last night.'

'Lilly? *Lilly*? Took her own life? You must be mistaken.'

'No sir, there is no mistake unfortunately. I apologize, sir, that we had to open your letter.'

He handed it over to Bernard. The short note said simply: *Each individual has his own way of grieving.*

Bernard shook his head disbelievingly. 'No. Oh no . . . How –?'

'The usual, sir. Wrists. There is nothing suspect, sir. She left a brief suicide note.'

'What did it say?' Bernard asked dully.

'Only that she was taking her own life for personal reasons, and that nobody else was concerned. Well, I'll be taking my leave, sir, if you'll excuse me. I'm sorry to have troubled you.'

Careless of its occupants, London life continued as usual, and in early October Bernard's first real opportunity occurred. There had been a lull in his working life; despite pressure from Mr Beavis he had not felt inclined to compose, and during the last couple of months had rejected offers to perform, and declined invitations. The zest was gone from him, and his appearance was unkempt. He was filled with a feeling of monotony, and – worse – self-doubt.

The summons came completely unexpectedly: a message in the hallway of his lodgings to contact Mr Sterndale Bennett. For the first time since his friend's death Bernard felt a keenness, a rising of his spirits and return of interest.

He picked out a shirt collar which was the least frayed; shined his own shoes and took himself off to the barber's before going to his rendezvous.

Bennett shook Bernard's hand with a firm grip and appeared glad to see him. His sharp eyes did not miss the young man's paleness nor the faint lines of strain around his mouth: 'How have you been keeping, Mr Foligno, since we met two years ago?'

'Pretty well, thank you, sir.'

'I was sorry to learn of our mutual colleague's death. I refer to Sir Edmund Moore.'

Bernard looked at the ground. 'Yes, it was a tragedy.'

Bennett waited a respectful second or two before saying: 'Now, Mr Foligno, I wish to hear you play again. Afterwards I shall tell you why. You may select anything you please.'

Bernard chose to play Beethoven's *Sonata Pathetique*, knowing that its strikingly contrasting moods were ideally suited to his style, and that this essentially emotional work would give him the freedom he wanted to express and interpret every innuendo.

Afterwards, his fingers pink-tipped and tingling, he turned expectantly, but Bennett held up a hand as if to stall him:

'Mr Foligno – it is not what you think. I still have no vacancy here, even for a part-time professor, but –' again he held up his hand, this time in reassurance at the sight of Bernard's crestfallen expression '– I had something else in mind. I am, as you know, Conductor of the Philharmonic Society. We are to give a series of performances next month in the Hanover Square Rooms, and a pianist has yet to be found for an evening devoted entirely to Chopin.'

He looked at Bernard's face to gauge his reaction and saw in its smooth dark gaze nothing that indicated he understood.

But Bernard's heart was racing and beneath the curls on his forehead a pulse throbbed. The palms of his hands became sticky suddenly, and he clenched and unclenched his fists.

'What are you saying, sir?' He kept his voice steady.

'I thought I had made myself clear, Mr Foligno. I think you are a most accomplished pianist, and if you are not otherwise engaged on the evening of November the ninth I should like you to perform, with our orchestra, Chopin's piano concertos – one and two – at the Hanover Square Rooms.'

And Bernard, still seated on the piano stool, felt a great wave of thankfulness sweep over him. He put his head in his hands and began to laugh; deep laughter which shook him from inside to out.

Bernard began rehearsing for the concert. He practised for hours each day, both at his home and at the Royal Academy, where under Bennett's patient guidance he would go repeatedly over entire passages until they were correct.

'No, no, Mr Foligno! You might also be a composer, but this was Chopin's creation not yours, and certainly it owes nothing to Liszt. We are not in this game to break pianos. "Ff" does not imply that a hammer should be re-felted each time, or a string replaced. Passion – yes. But subtlety also. Think Mozart.'

'Cramer used to tell me that.'

'*Cramer*? Johann Baptist Cramer?'

'Yes.'

'You were a pupil of his?' Bennett's sensitive face wore an almost reverent expression.

'Yes, sir.'

'But you never told me.'

'You never asked me, sir.'

'It explains much.'

'Much?'

'I do not believe in scattering compliments, Mr Foligno. Suffice to say that Old John would not waste his time on an inferior pupil. Now will you please learn to keep a constant eye on the conductor – myself in this instance. I know old John

Cramer was never one to acknowledge the necessity of a conductor, however I am leading an orchestra and cannot have anarchy. I am not merely there for decorative purposes, and incidentally I do not follow Cipriani Potter's policy of no baton. I have always used one.'

'May I remove the score, sir?' Bernard smiled apologetically. 'I find it disconcerting to have it before me and concentrate on you also.'

'With respect,' Bennett told him dryly, 'I think you cannot yet have memorized the entire work, Mr Foligno.'

And Bernard replied equally firmly: 'I think I am able to, sir – with respect, and without wishing to appear contradictory.'

'Very well . . . Second movement. Taken from the end of the string passage . . . Da-da-da-daa-de-daa. . . .'

Bernard launched into the beautiful and gentle movement at exactly the right place, and now without the distraction of the music before him, he was able to abandon himself so that not only his hands but his entire body poured into the piano, and the hammers struck the strings with that positive lightness which can only be achieved by total body fluidity and relaxation.

'I think we have arrived, Mr Foligno,' Bennett commented quietly when, uninterrupted by a single remark from him, Bernard had played on until the end of the movement, keeping a perfect balance of awareness between his instrument and his conductor.

The experience of playing with a full orchestra was to Bernard at first terrifying, and then magnificent; that he should be at the core of such a volume of sound was intimidating, humbling and awe-inspiring, and that the orchestra should defer to him, a novice, was even more perturbing. Then, to listen to a piece of music as an entirety developing from what was initially, to use Bennett's expression, an anarchy of sound – that was surely the most exciting of all: like the revelation of a perfect flower. It was the coming together of entities into unity; the fact that it *was* 'we' as opposed to 'I'. And that he, Bernard Foligno, should be on the platform of the huge vaulted Hanover Square Rooms playing a Broadwood piano as soloist amongst the orchestra of the Philharmonic Society – wasn't it incredible? Wasn't it just incredible?

I cannot believe the evening will ever arrive, he thought to himself at the end of one afternoon's rehearsal. *I cannot believe it will actually happen and that this is not, after all, some kind of elaborate charade.*

The morning of the ninth of November was unusually mild. Bernard, seated at his piano, suddenly began to shiver violently. *I must have left a window open*, he thought, and got up to check. As he did so his legs buckled under him and he almost fell back onto the stool, frightened and shaking fearfully. He could see now that all the windows were perfectly closed and realized that the shaking was caused by the terrible coldness in his own body, as though his blood had stopped pumping. Aghast, he could only sit there helplessly, praying silently that whatever had possessed him so impetuously would leave him with the same abruptness. His trembling hands had turned a delicate pale lilac, and experimentally he laid them on the keyboard, tentatively picking out a passage from Chopin's first concerto.

Oh God. Oh God – I have no control. They are like rods, My fingers have become uncontrollable rods . . . Unjointed bones. I cannot . . . Oh God. What should I do? But it will pass. Surely it must.

Sweat broke out on his forehead; his eyes were enormous with alarm. Glancing at the carriage clock he could see that it was a little before ten o'clock. In just over ten hours he was supposed to be in the Hanover Square Rooms, adorned with the famous sword which hung over the chimney-piece in the artists' room and was always worn by solo instrumental players. In just over ten hours he was supposed to be giving a performance that would stun the audience with its brilliance, and at the very end, stirred with passion, every person there would rise to his feet and in total disorder scream for him.

That was what he had imagined and intended. It was to have been his chance, the event which would quite simply have changed his life.

And now – what was happening to him? This jerking of every

nerve, what was it? Why did he feel so disembodied, as though he floated somewhere above, surveying the whole horror?

He managed to stagger over to the settee, and heard Mrs Ford in the hall.

'Mrs Ford, Mrs Ford.' Even his voice had frozen and locked. 'Mrs *Ford.*' It cracked out like a broken whip.

There was a knock – welcome sound – at his door, and Mrs Ford entered tentatively. She took a single look at the figure flung on the settee and was crouching by his side. 'Goodness, I must get a doctor.'

'No!' He arrested her with his hand and breathing deeply, tried to form clear words. 'Please get a message – to someone – to Sterndale Bennett – Royal Academy of – Music. Take a cab now. Come back – with him. Please.'

'But a doctor. You must see a doctor.'

'Afterwards. Please. Sterndale Bennett.'

She was back within the hour, and meanwhile, by gripping onto furniture and leaning against walls for support, Bernard had made his way into the bedroom and thence to the bed. Feverishly he swaddled the bedclothes about him in an attempt to quell the shivering.

'Am I dying?' he wondered out loud.

'I doubt it most strongly.'

Lying on his belly with the pillows muffled about his head he had not heard anyone come in, and now he was confronted by Bennett looking at him grim-faced.

'Well, what do we do now?' Bennett said shortly, shaking his head with a growing sense of hopelessness. He sat down heavily on the edge of the bed, biting on his lips. 'Madam, please fetch a doctor this instant – any doctor,' he commanded Mrs Ford.

'There is one two doors away.' She hovered nervously.

'Excellent. Please fetch him.'

Bennett continued to sit on the bed brooding. He himself was well-capable of playing that evening – had actually performed the first concerto four years previously at Crosby Hall whilst he was still professor of music at Cambridge, but he had not played it since, and was not prepared to risk his reputation by performing inadequately.

The doctor arrived, talked briefly with Bennett, then ushered him and Mrs Ford from the room. After a shrewd look at the young man and an almost cursory examination, he asked casually: 'First major performance tonight?'

'Yes.'

'Nervous?'

'Not – in the least.'

'But you were excited?'

'Yes. Oh yes.'

'Looking forward to it, eh?' The other's expression invited confidence.

So much. Oh so much. 'Yes.'

'Not much sleep recently?'

'Well – I have been working. I do not need much sleep, doctor.'

'Poppycock. Everyone needs sleep, sir. Have you had any emotional traumas recently?'

'Well . . .'

'I want facts, Mr Foligno. In order to establish the nature of your problem, I need facts.'

'My father died two years ago. We – had quarrelled. He – did not forgive me. Then in the summer a much loved friend died, and his fianceé committed suicide.'

'How did you feel about that?'

'I was devastated.'

'Did you work during that time?'

'Scarcely . . . I felt barely able.' In between each word his juddering caused his chin to come forward emphatically.

'Why did you not feel able?'

'Because I was too – distressed. I had no residue left in me.'

'And then this chance came and it re-ignited your interest in life again?'

'Yes.'

'How did your quarrel with your father affect you?'

'I was – very hurt.'

'But you hid your hurt?' The doctor nodded knowingly.

Bernard did not reply. He closed his eyes instead, feeling once more the revival of that hurt.

'And then he died,' the doctor continued, 'and you did not know how to react to his death under those circumstances. Mr Foligno, I can tell you your problem is nervous mental exhaustion. You are also suffering from delayed reaction to shock. In other words your system has received just too many blows to cope with, and the excitement of being given this opportunity tonight was counter-productive; it has been the catalyst which has brought on this "crisis".'

'What can you do to help?' Bernard asked, thinking of the evening which was to have been his own. It seemed far removed now.

'I can give you some drugs which will have a calming effect, and the problem will shortly go of its own accord. I would say that without being aware of it, you have been suffering from extreme depression which has debilitated you. You must rest.'

'I cannot become warm.'

'The drugs have a tranquillizing effect and will help relax your muscles.'

'And – this evening?'

'Out of the question, sir. I am sorry. But you know as well as I do that it is out of the question.'

Bernard turned away from him to hide the sudden shameful tears in his eyes.

The doctor repeated the same to Bennett, who said angrily: 'It cannot be. He must perform.'

'I cannot agree to that, sir. You surely know of another musician.'

'No one I could locate quickly who would be capable of performing such works at a moment's notice. If I had wings, doctor, or could find a way of reaching everyone I knew quickly, then I might have success. But alas I have not. It is either Mr Foligno or no one.'

'Then sir, it is no one.'

Bennett remained with Bernard all day, hoping beyond hope that some miracle would happen, and almost possessively watching over him for any change. The boy would doze – or wake for a hot drink administered by Mrs Ford, and drift back into a yet heavier sleep. But the shuddering had stopped and the cold sweat had dried on his face, and though his colour was waxen it was no longer tinged with blue. By early afternoon he was able to sit up in bed.

'How do you feel?' Bennett asked solicitously.

'In a trance. As though I were someone else. Cold; though not so much as before. I am – sorry, sir.'

He looked so young and vulnerable sitting there that Bennett felt quite moved. 'It cannot be helped, Foligno.' But his reason for staying had behind it an ulterior motive and he asked: 'Can you hold your hands out steadily in front of you now?'

Bernard did so.

'Well done. Now flex them and work each individually – as if you were doing a Chopin run.'

Again Bernard obeyed.

'Good. Go back to sleep.'

He escaped with relief. But he awoke an hour later. Bennett studied him anxiously – was there actually some colour in his cheeks?

'Can you walk without toppling?' he asked.

'I shall try.'

'Round the room then, three times.'

He watched Bernard with a thoughtful expression, wondering if perhaps he was being tyrannical, but thinking in mitigation, what else could he do short of cancelling the concert?

'How do you feel now?'

'I suppose I am better than I was.'

'Good. I think you should remain sitting in a chair with a rug wrapped about you, and that Mrs Ford should bring some more tea. . . .'

After a further half an hour Bennett casually suggested that Bernard play part of the first movement from the first concerto, and Bernard, who by now realized Bennett's intent, sat hunched and drooping-eyed at his Cramer piano and placed his hands on the keyboard. Whilst they no longer shook, they felt like lifeless things that did not pertain to himself.

As he played Bennett thought, *Dear God, do I dare present him in this condition.* . . .

But certainly there was a huge improvement from only three hours before when Bernard could hardly sit up.

'I must sleep, sir. I cannot keep awake. My eyes shut of their own accord.'

'You sleep. You sleep.' Bennett watched Bernard shuffle into bed like an old man.

An hour later he was helping him into his clothes, half holding him up like a dummy.

'I am so tired, so tired,' Bernard kept saying.

'It is the drugs.'

'Yes, but I am so tired. How shall I perform?'

'You will not let us down.'

'I shall let myself down, Mr Bennett,' he replied, looking at the other man with a vanquished expression.

He is like a small boy who is waiting to be told he does not need to go to school after all, Bennett thought. *But go he must.*

Out loud he said: 'We shall make an announcement that you have been ill – we shall say that you are recovering from the flu.'

'I stood in the wings, and when the announcement was made I heard the audience give a huge combined groan, and even now I can feel how my heart thumped in sudden dread. Wearing the sword, I walked carefully onto the stage, and a polite, token applause heralded my arrival. I faced the audience briefly and unseeingly and knew that night I would conquer nobody. I could only pray I would not disgrace myself.

'The entire evening I was caution itself. I took no risks, and even remembered to look at Bennett. But to my own ears my playing was ill-defined and heavy and I could not help myself. I was slightly encouraged when I returned after the interval to find that no seats appeared to have been vacated, and I believe I played with a little more verve than previously. . . .

'When it was over there was a short burst of well-mannered clapping, and Bennett hit me on the back in his relief that there had been no great catastrophe. He made a humorous little speech to the audience in which he thanked me for not letting them down at the last minute, despite my illness – and I felt only a great weariness and sense of disillusion.

'The critics were not kind. J. W. Davison in *The Times* used the words "uninspired, clumsy, tedious"; whilst H. F. Chorley of the *Atheneum* was more scathing, deriding my excuse of illness and referring to me as an inexperienced student. He talked of my charmless performance, morose touch and lack of originality . . . And I read their reports over and over again, convinced that the same chance which could have made me great, had destroyed me; that I would be remembered only for my lack of ability.

'My Anna, I sank into such a state of dejection; and I could not extricate myself from it. Meanwhile Doug's letters kept arriving from all over Europe – his future was bright and already most people in musical circles had heard of him. And I could not bring myself to reply to him.'

After the Christmas period Mr Beavis visited Bernard at his lodgings. He had received no reply to his last couple of cards, and decided to visit in person. When he saw the decline in his young friend he was shocked: dark circles accentuated the pallor of Bernard's lean face, and there was a haunted expression in his eyes. Around the full-lipped mouth ran curved indentations – markings of his strain – and his black hair curled wild and untended around his head.

Beavis thought: *He is surely an unusually aesthetic, passionate-looking young man but how he* suffers.

He felt a surge of pity towards him, and his eyebrows worked frantically as he decided on his tactics. Finally he addressed Bernard severely: 'Bernard, either you haul yourself out of this despair, or you give up music. Your decision to become a musician was not because of Cramer or Sir Edmund Moore or any other ghost, but yourself. They are dead and others will die along the route, but you who once had courage are alive. Do something, boy, or abandon your music entirely. I had not credited you with such weakness of character and I must say I am most disappointed. And with regard to your disappointment at the Hanover Square Rooms – what, will you give up after one setback? Be a failure, if that is what you wish.'

'I do not wish that,' Bernard replied in a flat voice, fiddling with his lapel distractedly. 'But – it seems to be my destiny.'

'Rubbish,' Beavis counteracted scornfully. 'You talk of "destiny" at twenty-two? You say you do not wish to be a failure; then do something. A musician's life is never smooth-running, and you have always known that. You are in charge. So do something.'

'I wish I could, but it is like, it is like . . .'

'What is it like, Bernard?' Now he spoke gently, and his incredible eyebrows sank like low gables over his eyes.

Bernard stared for a second and wanted to laugh; a split second's hysterical laughter which changed into a gathering pain. 'I – I . . .' He felt tears come from some instant deep pool, and when the silent crying rose in him he could not quench it. It grew and grew until it burst from him.

Mr Beavis tucked him up tenderly in bed. 'Go on. Cry, my old son. You are going to make it, you know. By yourself. Only by yourself.'

During the following weeks Bernard endured the suffering and the hurt he had not expressed at the time of his father's rejection, nor later at his death. He experienced every feeling from rage to sorrow, and by finally recognizing these was able to exorcize them. He pondered over his entire life, recalling all the people who had featured in it then drifted out. He thought of Lilly who had killed herself and of Gilbert. He thought back to how he had sat up all night and written 'In Memoriam'. He had demonstrated strength then, resorting to his inner resources and drawing comfort through composition. He had survived, whereas Monsieur Gilbert and Lilly had not. One could not survive in the world and not be an egoist. Survival meant the ability to withstand sorrow.

It all comes down to solitude, Bernard thought. *In the end one has only oneself*. And what did a single mediocre performance mean after all? Let them think him inadequate – there was time yet to prove them wrong.

Daily he took himself to Regent's Park, wrapped in layers of warm clothes. Whatever the weather he could be found there, armed with a bag of crumbs for the birds, and when it was empty he would leave them squabbling and stroll leisurely, or sit on a bench, gazing around him and reflecting on the kind of person he was, the kind of people who influenced him and how that influence had affected him. Finally his thoughts turned to his role as a musician. For some years he had considered himself primarily a pianist, but now, as he re-examined the importance of composition, his reflections transported him back in time to a small boy frantically writing music early one Sabbath evening.

One weekend in mid-February, 1864, he paid a visit to the Hamiltons in Gloucestershire. Douglas, who was in England for just two weeks, greeted him joyfully:

'You look horribly well, dear chap. Was a bit worried, you know. Hadn't heard anything and all that.'

'Well, I am in excellent health as you see, despite not being as outlandishly fashionable as you.' He looked pointedly at Douglas's enormous spotted bowtie and purple waistcoat.

'It gets me noticed, d'you see?' the other drawled. 'It is so jolly boring to be the same as everyone else – you would look perfectly splendid in this bowtie, dear chap! Now tell me what has been happening to you.'

'Well Doug – and do not drop on the spot – I am composing a concerto. I began it two weeks ago and have almost completed the first movement. Mr Beavis wants it within three months.'

'But how perfectly marvellous.' Douglas's eyes gleamed delightedly behind their glasses. 'Always knew you had it in you, of course. But what about performing?'

'Things have just started to look up again. To be honest, Doug, I was a bit low for a while.' Bernard gazed steadily at his friend and that look conveyed that he had needed him and he had not been there.

Douglas shook his head sadly. 'For you, dear chap, I would have cancelled a trip to let you have one of my mighty shoulders. I wish I had known. But now you have come out of it and can only progress. Look – if you have nothing planned, the Leemings are still clucking about you. They are intent on refining young Miranda so that she does at least have one or two accomplishments. I think they would be delighted to have you for a few months, and there you could compose also and gather your thoughts. It is a rather wonderful place they live in.'

'Then if they will have me, I shall go. The sooner the better in fact.'

The mansion was more of a folly than anything else, being comprised of four tall Gothic turrets of differing heights and linked by a central square. Heavy thick-stemmed ivy clung to the pale gold stone and the bare branches of wisteria and honeysuckle intertwined and climbed round the studded arched door. The sunlight threw itself onto the red tiles of the turret roofs.

It is like some Swiss castle, was Bernard's first delighted reaction to the Leeming establishment.

Then there was the sound of barking, and it seemed he was surrounded by a dozen dogs of various descriptions joyfully leaping up and licking him by way of greeting.

The Leemings welcomed him not much less enthusiastically and there were introductions all round. Sir Alfred had a determined hold of his arm and led him to each member of the family in turn:

'My wife, Lady Isabel, whom you met at the Hamiltons at the same time as myself . . . My daughter Emma-Jane, whom you met also then and who still unfortunately has a passion for the flute . . . Miranda, my younger daughter and your pupil, whom you met more recently – and I gather subjected you to her usual –'

Miranda, a little taller and more womanly now but essentially unchanged, interrupted him: 'Papa dearest, Bernard has no wish to be reminded, I am sure.'

'Miss Leeming, I am delighted to see you again.' Bernard gave a small bow.

'Pooh! What is this formality, Bernard? I am Miranda, you know I am.'

'Miranda then!'

'Better, better.'

'And – ' continued Sir Alfred undaunted, and still hanging onto Bernard's arm, ' – this is a guest of ours. Miranda's closest friend. Lady Anna Charlton-Gray.'

The girl was extraordinarily beautiful, her proudly tall body clad in what was apparently a boy's riding habit. His eyes met hers and something akin to pain shot through him.

She said in a low, lilting voice: 'I have a handkerchief of yours, Mr Foligno, from many years ago.'

'A handkerchief?' Bernard ran a hand through his hair in confusion.

'Yes. There was an – episode – in the park.'

Her gaze continued to bore into him, willing him to remember of his own accord: eyes the colour of a stormy sea. A hoop. A bonnet. He remembered and his heart lurched.

Smiling gently, she continued to bombard him with surprises: 'And I believe you knew my grandfather.'

'Oh?' His mouth parted in a wide smile and his eyebrows raised quizzically as he wondered what was coming next.

'Yes. Sir Edmund Moore.'

'Sir Edmund Moore!' For a moment he felt almost dizzy – and then joyful. He could have swept this lovely girl off the floor and into his arms.

'Oh good God, you are – yes, he spoke of you – the granddaughter who lived in Switzerland! Oh, how very thrilled I am to see you!'

Delightedly they continued to stare at each other.

'Well, well,' trilled Lady Leeming, 'what a coincidence to

be sure. Now it is time for lunch. Come along everyone. It is certainly lunchtime.'

'We have met at last, then.'
   'Yes my darling, we have met.'

PART THREE

Chapter Fourteen

Bernard sat beside Anna as she painted: the early flushed light on the gentle green landscape. Using her fine brush swiftly and deftly she was nevertheless precise and detailed in her work, and was no longer self-conscious in his presence. He never tired of watching her sketch or paint and as he watched now – knees huddled to his chin, arms wrapped about his bent legs – he was filled with love for her.

The hesitant spring warmth briefly encompassed his body, deserting it as a slight breeze came up, and beneath him the grass was cool. He felt replete. His Anna sat on the small folding stool he had willingly carried for her, a rug covering her lap. He had insisted, having learned of her history of illness and she had reluctantly acquiesced, secretly relishing his assertiveness as with a serious expression he had tenderly tucked the rug about her.

Anna was an unpredictable mixture of contrasting moods – one minute tranquil and pensive, the next vivacious and animated. Sometimes she seemed wildly reckless and on other occasions submissive and timid, so that in asking her a question one could obtain an entirely different reply from one day to the next. Her voice, too, varied from being womanly and meltingly low to a more child-like tone that was higher pitched. Each mood offered a different aspect of her, like seeing exposed parts of the same body unveiled at intervals, and because she was well able to cope with the variances of her nature, perhaps was even unaware of them, it did not occur to her that others might not be able to adjust too.

During the past couple of weeks Bernard had witnessed most of them and loved each for itself, amused by Anna's different reactions to a stable situation and enchanted by her many facets. And if she had a tendency towards impatience it was usually self-directed.

Today she was in pensive mood, and it showed not only in her face but was also reflected in her manner of painting. Bernard, watching the developing picture, saw the landscape through her eyes, and narrowed his own to view the same lines and angles and horizon before they were transferred to paper. Her movements were gentle and his gaze followed them, noting the taut length of her body, the rapt concentration on her face, the clear far-seeing eyes and the sweet, calm profile. And if he could have painted, he would have painted Anna painting.

'I love you,' he said quietly in a tone of wonder. There was a great relief in saying the words. He had dreamed – tortured himself with the idea of uttering such a declaration, not imagining it would slip from him of its own accord as easily or with such lucidity. Now those words seemed insufficient to convey the strength of his feeling.

Anna looked up from the easel, placed her brush carefully in a container of water, and staring long at him answered: 'And I love you also.'

'I would not wish you to say that merely to please me,' Bernard said hurriedly. 'Nor would I wish you to say it if tomorrow you will not mean it.' He rocked backwards and forwards on his heels in agitation and drew on his pipe in short little intakes.

Anna laughed tenderly. 'You silly man. I say it to please *myself*, and I have longed to say it yesterday and the day before, and the week before, and long before you even knew me, and I shall continue beyond tomorrow, I do assure you.'

Bernard went and knelt to her level. This was a different love to anything he had ever known. Now he knew he had met the woman with whom, quite simply, he wished to spend the rest of his life. The thought was both beautiful and terrifying that it took another human being to make one feel complete.

'You are so young to know your mind,' he said doubtfully.

'And are you so old?' she retorted spiritedly, tossing her hair back. 'If you insult my emotions in such a way I promise that my love will tire very quickly!'

'I would not risk that.' Bubbles of effervescence rose to his throat and he laughed with his happiness.

'What would you be prepared to risk?' Anna asked softly.

Her expression, a potent mixture of love combined with sexuality, came as a savage attack upon him.

'I would be prepared to do nothing that would ever hurt you.'

'You could never hurt me.'

'Anna . . . Anna dearest –' He had never used the endearment before, and he wanted to linger over it. 'This conversation is too ambiguous by far, and we are evading issues. There are many ways of hurting and being hurt.'

'Would you be prepared to kiss me?'

Bernard drew away from her, trying to break the hypnotic effect of their closeness, and answered in a constrained tone: 'Anna, you are a young lady of – certain social standing. There are things one does not do. It would be wrong.'

'But those things are permissible with ladies of lower social standing whom you are not afraid to degrade,' she stated in a knowing voice.

He said nothing, staring confusedly ahead, whilst a moment ago he had been so confident.

'I am right am I not, Bernard?' she continued. 'You have kissed women for whom you possibly felt no love, yet the girl you claim to love, you refuse. Is that so?'

'Yes. *Yes*.'

'Well I do not *care* about my social standing as you call it,' Anna told him defiantly. 'You forgot the small girl you met in the park, but it was to me an incident of paramount importance and when, subsequently, I realized that the young man my dearest grandpapa spoke of with such affection was by coincidence the same person, I knew that somehow our paths would one day cross. I knew that you were to be part of my life. I *knew* it, you understand? Not just longed for it or wished, but knew it. And I dared to love the image of you I had created, because I was so sure.

'I did not see Grandpapa often; I have lived, as you know, most of my life in Switzerland, but whenever I was in England I visited him, and he spoke freely of you and I felt that I knew you

221

truly. I wish – *how* I wish – he had not died. My grandfather was the only man, the only person, who took note of my feelings and considered me as an individual.'

'He was a fine man. I missed him greatly when he died. I also suffered with his death . . .' Fleetingly, Bernard recalled that bleak period.

Anna took his hand. 'Kiss me, Bernard, please? I need you to kiss me. Please look at me instead of away into the distance. What good is it saying that you love me and then doing nothing about it?'

'Anna I –'

She pushed the rug impatiently from her lap and stood beside him, tall and assured.

'I understood you are to – become betrothed,' he said flatly, looking directly at her at last.

'Oh, that is the reason.'

'A very important one.'

'But irrelevant to you and I at this moment. The entire affair has been concocted by our fathers and is a package that has been neatly tied. I do not love Giles. I do not know that I even like him. But he is from an old Catholic family like mine, and my father – would be furious if I were to go against his wishes.'

Detecting the note of fear in her voice, Bernard felt the urge to protect her. 'You are afraid of him,' he commented.

'I could never dare defy him.'

'But you will be unhappy.' Bernard could not bear the thought of Anna's unhappiness.

But she replied with a hard-toned casualness which shocked him: 'I doubt it. I believe I will be merely indifferent.'

'So what is this then, Anna?' he asked her, anguished. 'A brief flirtation to kill your frustration as you wait? A kiss to assuage your curiosity and to complete your romantic picture of fate's intentions?'

'I do not know, I do not know. I only know I love you, and answered your declaration which you chose to make freely. You cannot deprive me of loving you, you know Bernard.'

Anna's voice had risen and now broke. Her eyes were opalescent with unshed tears and the long honey-coloured lashes were wet spikes. She was a young uncertain girl again, and with the unexpected weapon of her sorrow Bernard was destroyed.

'Oh God.'

He took her in his arms and kissed her, the first time he had kissed a woman whom he loved instead of lusted after, and the difference was extraordinary: the desire to become a single soul; the knowledge that the softness of skin was her softness and its scent, her scent; the sensation of their tongues curling and probing was sweet because it was Anna.

Bernard had no answers to the problems which might lie ahead, but for the moment, lying tangled with her on the grass, he was happier than he had ever been in his life.

'Have you ever blamed me?'

'No. Truthfully never.'

'I dictated the course of both our lives.'

'I do not know that that is true. One cannot say.'

'I wrecked our possibilities . . . But I was so timid of my father; so young; so used to obeying.'

'My love, I am not blaming you. When have I ever blamed you? Why all this self-recrimination?'

'I do not know. Suddenly I am uneasy. Before it was you, and now it is my turn. I am realizing how we have wasted our years. It is all most strange and disconcerting.'

Greystones Folly was situated in the tiny hamlet of Lower Fordlington in the Windrush Valley, between Cheltenham and Andoversford. Burrowing between hills, like a child's downy head cradled between its mother's breasts, the Leeming estate stood in its own private parkland with splendid stately trees shading softly sloping grounds. Peacocks strolled arrogantly across wide expanses of lawn, and a spring-fed trout lake was home to various species of ducks and swans. In the tiny wooded glades where wild flowers sprang underfoot, fallow deer kept mostly out of sight. A little path bordered by different heathers

223

and shrubs led from one secret wonder to another – from the balustraded terrace with its tiered fountains and statues and vine-clad pergola, through a series of gardens with 'themes'. It meandered to the elegant but neglected glass and wrought-iron pavilion tucked away amidst beech trees, and finally petered out at the little boathouse which housed a punt and two rowing boats.

To the left of the Folly and grouped around a cobbled yard were the stables, constructed in the same local stone as the main building and likewise red-roofed, and directly opposite – on the other side of the narrow lane – was a track which passed through fields and up the hill to the private gallop. But Sir Alfred was always happy for others to use it. He was a generous man with a keen sense of fun besides having a shrewd eye for art, and he had recently acquired a new toy: a Thomas McCall Kilmarrock bicycle with iron-ringed wooden wheels. This machine was a great novelty and nobody avoided being shown it since it resided in the hall, and each morning Sir Alfred 'exercised' it, his bulky body balanced precariously upon the saddle, his hands rigidly gripped on the wooden handlebar facing the decorative carved horse's head. However there was a small problem, for though the machine had a reasonably effective braking system, the saddle being placed sufficiently low for Sir Alfred to stop by placing his feet on the ground, he frequently forgot about this, and his shouts could be heard down the drive.

The Leeming household was to Bernard something from a child's fantasy. Colourful with disorder and droll touches nothing was as one expected, and this was further enhanced by Lady Leeming's passion for animals: they seemed to spring from a different nook and cranny in each room, to sweep from windows and roofs, landing on one's shoulder or at one's feet.

Apart from an array of dogs, cats and birds, there was a squirrel monkey called William who had two extraordinary habits, one being that he was an expert pickpocket; the other, that if he were given a nut he would take it very carefully in his tiny right hand and polish it on his long tail. He was also extremely fond of strong coffee and milky chocolate.

William was Lady Leeming's favourite and would sit perched on her shoulder for hours at an end, occasionally picking up items to throw at people from his safe height whilst his mistress smiled indulgently. He was usually dressed in minute velveteen breeches and a frilly white cotton shirt, but very occasionally he was 'naked', and then Lady Leeming swore that he was embarrassed by his state of undress and therefore more subdued than usual, not wishing to draw attention to himself.

This was a household in which each member cared about the others in it without caring what they did; where the vast delicious-smelling kitchen with its huge Dutch oven and clockwork bottle-jack was a room which everyone freely entered – even Sir Alfred, whose favourite pastime was to pull hunks off the bread as it cooled on a rack. He would stroll up and down, sampling from spoons, picking from joints of meat and teasing the servants. Finally he would pat one of the girls on the bottom before going into the cellar to choose some claret.

As soon as Bernard had arrived at the Folly he became part of the bizarre family, and he knew that here was an environment in which his creativity would grow. He was fertile with it; and in this enchanted atmosphere the love between him and Lady Anna Charlton-Gray flourished.

Perhaps it was as Anna said: that some force had decided the fate of these two particular human beings, and coincidence heaped upon coincidence had conspired to engineer their meeting, so that one could almost view them picturesquely as victims of a plot.

Anna was nearly eighteen years old. Her mother had died when she was seven, and almost immediately her asthmatic attacks began. From being a healthy, lively child she became sickly and withdrawn. The physician told Lord Robert Charlton-Gray that his daughter was unsuited to the English climate and that the Swiss air would be more agreeable for her. With a barely suppressed sigh of relief, for the prospect of raising a young, motherless girl was alarming to him, he packed her off – along with her old Irish nanny and a young English governess to a large house in a village near Morges between Lausanne and Geneva.

Deposited in a remote Swiss village, away from her old environment and everyone she had known, with only the superstitious old Irish woman and shy English governess for companions, the girl was obliged to look to her own resources and explore her own limits, learning to observe and listen to everything about her in order to guard against boredom.

It was not long before other families extended their hospitality – among them some English ones, and because of her attractive appearance and vivacious nature many invitations came her way; but amongst these people Anna felt there was no one who really cared or who understood her mind, and she preferred to mingle with the Swiss villagers, conversing with them fluently in singsong French.

She was, however, most content on her own, growing into a thoughtful, strong-minded and sensitive girl, unimpressed by most of the people she met, whilst nevertheless needing them as contact with the outside world.

She took up painting in watercolours as a hobby, and then it seemed she could be truly herself. When she painted, Anna was oblivious of time; pleasure would settle deeply in her and a feeling of utter peace possess her – a feeling of harmony with her surroundings.

Every so often her father would visit, awkward, stern and embarrassed – yet anxious to show how dutiful he was; he would take her shopping and buy whatever she could want and more besides. But his conversation was confined to strict advice or a command and always delivered in a tone which forbade contradiction and literally made her tremble. She both longed for and dreaded the prospect of his going home to England. Apart from her old nanny and grandfather, he was the only person who mattered in her life. He was blond and handsome and brilliantly clever, and she worshipped and feared him.

Periodically she would return to London, and during those times she would visit her beloved grandpapa Edmund in whom more than anyone else she could confide. She always felt slightly guilty about this, knowing her father disapproved of the old man, and from an early age learned to keep these two loves completely separated, whilst remaining steadfast and loyal to each.

She was a loyal person by nature – a Leo through and through, her nanny knowingly said, and it was from her own loyalty that Anna derived the most comfort and security.

At the age of thirteen Anna met Miranda Leeming, who was holidaying in the Alps, and from that moment another dimension was added to her life. Their friendship developed and blossomed, and it became the accepted thing that whenever she visited England she would spend at least an equal part of the time with the Leemings in their marvellous folly.

It was on one visit to London that the meeting with Bernard in the park had occurred. She had been feeling overwrought for several reasons: the first was that her father had made a disparaging remark about Sir Edmund which had cut her to the quick; the second that she had a new governess who was ugly and had halitosis; and the third that blood was mysteriously coming from her body in a rude place. Eventually that day, miserable and frightened, she told her governess who, frowning in a formidable manner, gave her a large white pad, explained it was something all women must endure – and told her never to mention the matter again.

It was in this frame of mind that the child-newly-launched woman first encountered, and never forgot, Bernard Foligno.

But her secret spiritual affair could not compete with the realisms of life, and while Bernard was in Paris staying with Douglas, Anna was introduced to the young Sir Giles Fotheringay, son of an acquaintance of her father, who immediately made it clear he considered that one day a 'match' between the two would be ideal. Fantasizing about a man was one thing, respecting her father another. It did not even occur to Anna that there could be a choice. She unquestioningly accepted that in all probability she would marry Sir Giles, and guiltlessly continued her reveries of Bernard.

Not long after Sir Edmund Moore's death Lord Robert Charlton-Gray realized that his daughter could not be an exile in Switzerland forever. She had not had an asthmatic attack for

227

two years, and there was no longer a pretext for keeping her away. Reluctantly, fearful of the young woman she had become, he told Anna it was time for her to return to England permanently and live with him in Belgravia. Foremost in his mind was the idea that she should be married to Sir Giles Fotheringay as soon as possible, relieving him of his obligations.

Everything suddenly changed again for Anna: her beloved grandfather was dead; she was uprooted from the pretty pink villa in the gentle hills of Morges where she had taught herself to be happy; she was ordered to remain in London with the father she respected but could not talk to; and her old Irish nanny was dismissed.

'It is absurd. You have no need for a "nanny" at your age.'

'But Papa, she is more than that. She is a friend to me.'

'She is a useless old woman with a mind full of tattle. You need a hand-maid at your age, not a doddering old nanny.'

Fighting back tears, she asked: 'But where will she go?'

'That is not my concern. She will be very well paid, I assure you.'

'But Papa, she will die of a broken heart.'

'Do not be so dramatic, child. Nobody has ever died of a broken heart. She will have enough money for a small place of her own. You may visit her, and she may visit you, should you wish it. It is all perfectly reasonable.'

'Oh please let her remain with us, Papa. Please. And I have *no* need of a hand-servant.'

She spoke wildly, becoming overwrought that she could not make him realize how she felt. But he was frighteningly cold, as she had seen him in court, and there was nothing she could do or say that would sway him. She feared his repressed anger and intransigence, and the forbidding expression in his eyes which told her she was a nuisance more explicitly than any words.

Her father was right of course: nobody died of a broken heart, and after an elaborate performance of protestation and flowing tears, the old nanny took the money, found her own place and settled down very happily to playing hostess in her own home, enjoying frequent visits from Anna.

Had her father been proved wrong in this instance, then Anna might have doubted his word forever and so found the courage one day to defy him, but as it was nothing had happened after all, except to prove that it was she who did not fully understand human nature, and when she met again Sir Giles Fotheringay she did not discourage his friendliness.

There was nothing she could pinpoint which she disliked about the young man. He was handsome and well-built, refined and from an excellent old Catholic family; but he reminded her of her father with his stiff formality and lack of perception, and though he went through all the right motions – complimenting her appearance, presenting her with flowers, and being generally attentive – she could not help feeling that this was a veneer. She realized she had been chosen for her suitability just as he had been chosen for his, and she knew also that by acquiescing she herself was playing an equal part in the matchmaking game.

Sometimes, if she felt unhappy she would read her favourite poem. This was Colonel Richard Lovelace's *To Althea from prison*, the last verse of which went:

Stone walls do not a prison make, nor iron bars a cage;
Minds innocent and quiet take that for an hermitage;
If I have freedom in my love and in my soul am free,
Angels alone, that soar above, enjoy such liberty.

After reciting this poem to herself Anna would feel replenished; she would remind herself that she had her hobby – her painting; she was in charge of her own body, her own heart and her own thoughts, and nobody could take these things from her.

She came to the Leemings shortly after all these changes, relieved to be somewhere she could behave as she wished – and away from pressures and the joylessness of her life with her father.

'We have a guest coming to stay – well, a sort of guest,' Miranda told her excitedly.

'Oh, who?'

'He is to give me piano lessons. A most romantic-looking man called Bernard Foligno.'

'Bernard Foligno!' Anna was dumbfounded with disbelief.

'Yes. Why, Anna dearest you have gone quite pale. Do you know Bernard? You react as though you do.'

'I met a Bernard Foligno years ago . . . How funny.' She tried to appear flippant, gauging correctly that Miranda would soon lose interest. Her friend was only inquisitive when she sensed drama or intrigue, and without those two ingredients she was quickly bored.

But Anna was thrown into turmoil that at last she was to see Bernard again – this figure round whom she had spun so many stories. Those stories had been safe as her own imaginings, but now she felt as though she were being flung into unknown territory. Then she calmed down a little, for wasn't this yet another example of destiny at work? And when things carried you along, you could only go with them.

She went riding that morning dressed in her new breeches, which meant she could sit astride instead of side-saddle – a delightfully unladylike indulgence Miranda had introduced her to.

Good time-keeping was never one of Anna's strong points, and despite her excitement the day had been so beautiful that she lost all sense of time and returned to the Folly too late to change her clothes; not for anything – certainly not vanity – would she miss the little 'welcome' gathering they had planned for Bernard Foligno, and she stood with the others, her heart thudding, quietly waiting to be introduced; and then when her turn came she said, 'I have a handkerchief of yours, Mr Foligno.'

In that moment of introduction he had noted every detail of her: her delicate, heart-shaped face and firm chin with its tiny dimple; her snub nose with its slightly flared nostrils; the darkness of her arched and fairly thick eyebrows which made such a contrast against her hair. Her skin was gold-tinged also, with a polished sheen which was contrary to the fashion of pale, fragile-looking complexions. Anna was startlingly unusual, exuding both innocence and sexuality, and Bernard had fallen instantly in love with her.

He teased Anna about her serious talk of fate, but secretly thought: *She believes it was pre-ordained, and how can I be sure it is not a reasonable belief? I may laugh at her – but what other explanation is there?*

Nobody took any notice of them or interfered, not even Miranda who was absorbed in a new relationship of her own, and so, unhindered, their friendship developed naturally as they spent an increasing amount of time in each other's company.

Anna taught him to ride, and Bernard confided to her: 'I have been haunted for years by the memory of a horse being shot outside my home. He had slipped and broken a leg. The driver cried like a baby.'

'And now – is that memory erased?'

'Erased? I don't know. But it no longer obsesses me. You cannot imagine how that episode lingered.'

'I can imagine. Knowing you I can.'

Bernard-in-love was a very different young man, and naturally it reflected in his work. He had told Douglas he had almost completed the first movement of his concerto, but how premature had been that statement. Why – he had merely excavated some ordinary bones; now he was discovering the flesh. Passages over which he had pondered became suddenly obvious and solutions arrived without a struggle.

The opening subject was based on a recurring triple quaver, and from this the whole concerto developed and Bernard treated it in masterly fashion. Where before he had been tempted towards flamboyancy, he realized that in fact subtlety was better; or whereas initially he thought the first movement must conclude softly, it now seemed to make better sense to progress through a series of chords and runs in gathering crescendo to a dramatic conclusion, in preparation for the contrast of the next movement's gentle largo.

231

He had never forgotten Cramer's advice to him as a boy:
'Understatement, young sir. It can convey so much more than
the other way round. Leave well alone – before it is murdered.'

Ruthless, Bernard put a line through much of what he had
written before he came to the Leemings. He tackled it anew
with splendid fervour. But the climax – there was nothing
understated about that.

Suddenly this composition mattered to him enormously. He
longed to be a person of calibre. And in that moment Bernard
knew that the satisfaction of music as an end in itself was no
longer sufficient.

Chapter Fifteen

It was Saturday. Shabat. It was also Yarzeit, anniversary of his father's death. He sat on the bed, embraced by his bands of tefillin – bones of the past – in his blue-painted room in this strange Gloucestershire mansion miles from any synagogue. The white memorial candle flickered steadily 'as he remembered Joseph Foligno, that loving little man who had believed in his own ideals. Who would have predicted that a man like Joseph would sire and ultimately disown a rebellious musician, who rejected his father's ways and seemed to pass most of his time blaspheming against all he had been taught?

And on this Saturday, this Shabat and Yarzeit, in the privacy of his bedroom Bernard would yet again blaspheme, defy the little man he was remembering with love and sorrow, and continue to write his concerto.

Papa, forgive me as I forgive you. I love you.

For an hour Bernard reviewed his past without regret, and honoured his father's memory. Then he went to the bureau and guiltlessly re-commenced his writing; and perhaps somewhere overhead a small man covered his eyes with one hand as he raised the other over a naked adult bottom.

Early the next morning Bernard sat at the piano in the music room. Through the French windows he could see the lake. He stopped playing and marvelled at everything that had happened: he loved and was loved, and it was incredible. He had sought nothing and had been rewarded when he least expected it – and to discover that caring for somebody else was even worthier than being cared for, was in itself an enlightenment. He felt enriched in a way he hadn't dreamed possible.

Anna's face peered round the door: 'May I come in?'

'Of course, dearest.'

'You do not wish to be by yourself?'

'Not if I could be with you.'

'You always say such beautiful things. You make me feel cosseted and safe.'

'That is how I want you to feel, would always wish you to feel. Cherished and protected.'

'What were you playing?' She came and stood beside him and he pulled her down so that she was on his lap on the stool. She laughed and took his face gently in her hands before kissing him full on the lips. 'What were you playing?' she repeated.

'Part of the second movement of my concerto.'

'But I think it is quite beautiful. I find it amazing to believe it came out of you – that your mind was its creator. I heard it from outside. I have never heard music like it; it is so new. It is sad, yet it is not sad, for it is also tranquil. I paint what I have already seen; that is not clever. But to compose – that to me is a kind of magic. I cannot read music, so when I hear it I can close my eyes and believe its origination lay in something magic, and not in a man's mind.'

'But is there not magic in a man's mind?' Bernard asked lightly.

'I would doubt it. Although I daresay there is in yours!'

'So you will give me the benefit of the doubt, then?'

'I should like to be inside your mind and to understand it,' Anna answered seriously, frowning a little, and Bernard smiled at her earnestness.

'You have such a beautiful smile,' she told him, tracing the outline of his mouth with her forefinger. 'I love your lips – their shape, their feel. And they taste good.'

'*Yours* taste good. Let me taste them again.'

'In a moment – but first tell me about your concerto.'

'What, am I to be rationed?'

'No –' She wriggled from him as he tried to kiss her. 'Just for a moment. I truly wish to know. What will you do with the concerto when it is finished?'

'I shall send it to a contact of mine, a man by the name of Beavis. He is a good friend to me, and you might say he has become my patron. However until recently I have preferred performing to composition. Of late I have become increasingly uncertain.'

'But you must compose. You are so good at it.'

'Oh dearest – if it were that simple! Besides, you just said you do not even read music.'

'I can tell when something is exceptional.'

'Perhaps you are a little biased?'

'No. I love you, but I am objective. You wait. Others will find it exceptional too.'

'You have such faith?'

'Yes.'

'Then I must have faith in your faith.' He stroked the strong lithe lines of her body lovingly.

'You know that this behaviour is outrageous,' Anna teased, nestling closer to him and sinuously arching her back, her hair tickling his neck.

'Since there is nobody else about, only you and I can decide what constitutes "outrageous".' But he moved away slightly, aware that he was becoming aroused.

'Why are you moving away? Have I offended you?' She sounded hurt.

'No dearest, of course not. I am only human, that is all.'

'What do you mean?'

She did not know: about the basic physiology of a man. To Bernard it seemed incredible that a woman of marriageable age should have been taught languages and literature, mathematics and embroidery, but that most important part of education was still a mystery – enigmatic terrors concealed by a sinister curtain, which were only ever spoken of in shocked undertones – if at all. Yet how could a woman purport to love part of a human being and despise that other part?

'Bernard?' Anna insisted gently. 'What did you mean?'

Now was not the time. 'Nothing,' he consoled her. 'I love you, and I wish never to stop saying it.'

'And I feel the same. But Giles is arriving later today for a few days.'

'Giles?'

'Giles. The man I am supposed to –' She could not bring herself to say the word 'marry'. The word seemed ridiculous in its context.

'The man you are supposed to marry.' He said it for her, with sarcasm.

'Yes,' she agreed, lifting her chin stubbornly, defying his sarcasm. 'He was there before you.'

But that was not true. Bernard had been there since the day in the park.

'I think I understand,' he said stiffly, moving completely away from her and standing up, the line of his trousers depressingly flat once more.

With the comforting closeness gone, Anna's brief mood of defiance was replaced by a weighty feeling of misery.

'I cannot help it. I did not wish for him to come, I assure you. There was nothing I could do. *He* does not know things have changed.'

'Have they changed?' he asked cruelly, glaring down at Anna and almost disliking her; blaming her for destroying the next few days and for encouraging their love when there was apparently no point. 'Whichever way you care to examine it our feelings would appear to amount to little,' he told her coldly. 'You are virtually engaged to this man.'

'I cannot help that. I cannot,' she insisted, tears in her eyes.

All the bitterness went out of him. He was dismayed by his own lack of sensitivity towards her. She was ruled by her father's influence – for years hadn't he also been?

It was his fault, for being a Jew. It made no difference that he was liberal and free-thinking in his attitudes. He was a Jew, and as such was an unsuitable candidate.

'Come here, my love. I am so sorry.'

'And I am too.'

'It is not your fault in the least. I had no right . . .'

'We are not to start blaming ourselves now.' She laid a finger on his lips. 'It is best forgotten.'

'I agree.'

But he could not forget. The thought was constant that she was not his to love. Wordlessly Bernard placed his hands on her shoulders, studying her face minutely, wanting to retain each feature in his mind. A shaft of sunlight made her mane of light-brown hair reflect with bronze and copper, and her eyes became momentarily green. With a sigh he averted his gaze and looked beyond her, through the French windows. He could see the shadows cast by the chestnuts and oaks, and the white bobbing blobs of the swans upon the lake.

He took Anna's hand and stroked it. 'Let us go riding,' he suggested.

In his imagination he saw them disappearing, the two of them, without a trace. . . .

They set off together, and rode up the lane towards the woods from where the views stretched to the valley and the Windrush beyond. The day was windy but clear, with thin sunlight filtering past light skeins of quick cloud, and the horses, instinctive creatures, caught the reckless mood. Their ears were eagerly forward as they cantered up to the clump of trees on a knoll which marked the beginning of dense woods.

Bernard, parallel with Anna, had the illusion that he was flying, and a feeling of intoxication swept away his previous moroseness. Turning, he saw that her face mirrored his own feelings.

'As a child I used to have a repeated dream I could fly,' he told her when they paused to rest the horses. 'It was so delightful that every night before I fell asleep I would will the dream to come to me. Naturally it made no difference: it happened or it did not, I flew or I did not fly! But the sensation – that soaring, liberating sensation – transcended anything I could ever hope to feel in day-to-day reality.'

'But I used to dream I could fly also! Isn't that strange? I used to flap my arms frantically at the top of the wooden staircase in our villa in Morges – faster and faster, flapping, flapping – and then this marvellous descent, swooping up again just before I landed, and out of the house in a streak.'

'Mine were swimming strokes like a fish. Not in the least like a bird's. They sound most undignified compared to yours. I would walk whilst laboriously moving my arms in a scissor-like motion, until finally I would ascend, and then the victory was very great.'

They were held in the grip of laughter at the imagery invoked by each other's dreams, and it occured to Bernard in a swift moment what a dour character his was and how rarely he laughed. Love made him lighthearted.

They rode into the woods, into the speckled dark, and there the bases of the tree trunks were shrouded in a ground mist. They picked their way carefully avoiding roots and treacherous animal burrows, hearing all about them the different calls and cries, mutterings and tappings of assorted wildlife. Flashes of colour escaped from the danger of their proximity: a pheasant, squirrels, rabbits; what might have been a fox. A young hare fled in front of them, then another, then two more . . . Scurrying after one another.

'How sad always to be in such fear,' Bernard commented.

Anna was silent.

'What are you thinking?' he asked her.

'That I am fearful. I dream that I would defy my father to be with you, yet I know I cannot do it, and therefore I fear the future – the years ahead when I will want to be with you and may not be. Now that I have come to know you I cannot be complacent.'

'Anna – do not be gloomy. Bring the mare closer, and kiss me. Darling Anna, kiss me and love me for now, and tomorrow will follow. Why, you are not even engaged yet!'

They walked back to allow the animals to cool down, and at the yard the old groom took charge. He alternated between brushes and curry-comb, polish for the hooves and sponge for the nostrils and eyes, and he finished with an energetic strapping session, sweating profusely whilst he pummelled the horses' coats into a burnished gleam.

'You gets the best shine on 'orse's coat after 'e's been worked,' he drawled in his West-Country burr. 'Sweat's all dried. Dust's come to surface, see?'

At that point there appeared in the yard a young man in his mid-twenties. He was in every way the antithesis of Bernard. Of medium height and build, his was a squarish, typically English face – straight-nosed, strong-jawed, light-browed and blue-eyed. The mouth was thin-lipped and edged by a neat moustache. The complexion was clear and healthy and the hair fine and blond, of a texture which usually receded early. It was a regular, unmarked and unlined face, handsome without specific character; a face whose owner had rarely been perturbed, who preferred the company of men to women, and would have little patience with the anomalies of life. It was the sort of face one would expect to find in the higher echelons of society, one that would smile easily whilst denoting little sentiment; the face of a reasonable man who would never understand the true meaning of soul.

The young man approached Bernard and Anna, hostility apparent in his eyes.

'Why – Giles!'

Anna had been assisting in brushing the mare, and Bernard had been intent on watching her – her actions and expressions already dearly familiar. Neither had noticed him arrive and for several seconds he had studied the pair of them together.

'You sound as though you are dismayed to see me, Anna,' he commented dryly.

'No, not in the least. I had not expected you so early, that is all.'

'I was told to come and find you. It is two o'clock.'

'I had not realized. We did not realize the time, did we Bernard?' Anna sought support from him – longed to take his hand to confront the other man.

Backing her up, Bernard answered: 'I am sorry, the time just slipped away,' before realizing it was the wrong thing to say.

He had never seen her timid before. All her confidence seemed to have ebbed, and her whole demeanour was changed into one of submission.

'Giles, this is Bernard Foligno. He is teaching the piano to Miranda and is –'

'A music teacher, eh? How do you do, sir?' Sir Giles cut across her.

He acknowledged him as he would any lowly servant, with a condescending nod, and Bernard barely inclined his head, pointedly standing straight so that at six feet two he could look down on the other man. His dark eyes were infused with the arrogant look which usually disquieted whomever it was directed at.

But Sir Giles did not react. He disapproved of and suspected foreigners, and this young man was either a foreigner or worse a Jew. He had come directly from visiting Anna's father to tell her that his blessing had been given to their marriage. She was therefore his fiancée, although she did not realize it, and that his fiancée should consort with this person was most disagreeable. In his opinion the Leemings went too far. They were too liberal for words, and as soon as he had any influence over his future wife he would discourage her from seeing them.

He removed his unflinching gaze from Bernard's and fixed it once more on Anna, pink-faced, breathing fast, wild-haired – and clad in her boy's breeches. Before he had been too agitated to notice what she was wearing. Now he was appalled.

'Anna, what *are* you wearing?'

She glanced down at herself with surprise, so accustomed to seeing herself dressed in this way that she could find nothing amiss. 'What do you mean, Giles?'

'On your *legs*. It is disgusting. You are dressed as a man.'

'Oh – ' she laughed. 'Don't be absurd, Giles. Miranda has taught me to ride astride a horse. It is far more enjoyable than side-saddle, and of course one cannot wear a cumbersome skirt.'

'I forbid it,' he blazed quietly, a man who would never raise his voice, but conveyed by inflection all he needed to. 'It is disgusting,' he repeated, giving vent to a cold anger caused more by the sight of that other man standing possessively by her side than by Anna's breeches.

Bernard could no longer remain silent. Resentment brewed in him. 'I cannot see that it is your business what she wears.'

'*She* is Lady Charlton-Gray, and she is my fiancée and therefore I regard all matters pertaining to her as my business.'

Anna was hit by a sense of shock. Her face lost its colour and she dropped the brush she had still been holding. Giles had obviously just seen her father, and if he had given his consent, then certainly she was his fiancée. But the timing of it was so unfair and sudden, burst out angrily instead of being discussed

240

in private. She bent wearily to pick up the brush, and looked at Sir Giles with a chastened expression Bernard hated to see.

His anger now mostly evaporated, and secure in his new officialdom, Giles recovered his affability: 'I have come from your father's, my dear, and he has given us his blessing.'

My dear . . . My dear. The words hung in the air like artificial bells.

Bernard looked long and hard at the woman he loved and who loved him, waiting for some protest or denial from her – a sweeping gesture of the arm: '*Here* is the man I intend to marry.' But the silence became protracted and he turned and walked away.

Morose days shattered what had gone before. He could not escape the pair of them. He watched with alienated vision and thought that he had never touched Anna, never stroked the length of her body, separated the strands of her hair, or felt her tongue twirling around his. He had never listened to her confidence or watched her for hours as she painted. And the network which had led them to one another was just sad chance.

He avoided her entreating glances; avoided her at all costs. He excused himself from the evening meals, feigning work commitment, so he did not have to hear Fotheringay speaking in his easy, charming manner. His jealousy consumed him, and he thought with his customary cynicism that he could almost laugh at the brevity of his relationship; but a sudden image of her snatched at him and played havoc with humour. Without Anna Bernard felt arid and deprived, and his sorrow settled solidly upon him.

For Anna they were almost the worst days of her life. She could not bear to think that she had lost Bernard already, and began to wish she had not re-encountered him, for at least she could have clung happily to her fantasies whilst continuing with the life planned for her.

A week and a half elapsed, the Leemings with their usual hospitality having extended their welcome to Sir Giles.

Anna went to the pavilion to paint. Giles was to spend the day shooting with Sir Alfred, and she felt a great upsurge of her spirits, revelling in the prospect of this temporary freedom. The last few days had been fraught with tension and misery for her; she had smiled her way through them with aplomb, but later in the seclusion of her room her face had sagged like that of a tired court jester. In bed she would lie awake thinking of Bernard – of what he might be feeling; of her own cowardice; about fate and illusion and delusion; about her fiancé whose company she found difficult to endure for half an hour let alone half a century.

Now, reprieved, she ran to the abandoned little building carrying her artists' materials. She surveyed the place to see where best to position herself, then decided that beside the diagonal line to the arch of the ramshackle doorway was ideal, because she could incorporate it in her picture, the cobwebs gracefully draping its curve.

Anna settled herself on her stool and began to sketch, quickly becoming engrossed, feeling the day's warmth rebounding from the glass of the pavilion and permeating her body. Shafts of light made long flared strips on the broken-tiled floor, and orange, curled dead beech leaves lay in small disorderly piles. The decomposed body of a bird lay in one of them as though in a coffin.

An hour passed, and the urgency had gone. Her elation was seeping from her to be replaced by lonely sorrow. *What is the point in painting*, she thought, *or indeed in anything else come to that? It is simply a pursuit to whittle away the tedium of time.*

She slumped in the shadows, unable to continue.

The iron and glass door rattled on its hinges and creaked open, then shut.

'Oh – I didn't know anyone was in here,' Bernard said.

She wanted to cry out: *I am not anyone. I am me, Anna.* But she replied instead with the same awkward formality, her hands twisting and turning with each other: 'I came in here to paint.'

They stared despairingly at each other, neither accustomed to playing games with his feelings.

Bernard backed away in misery, his arms dangling at his sides and his fists clenched. 'I do not want to trouble you. As I said, I thought the place was empty.'

'Oh, it is empty,' she retorted, gaily sarcastic now. 'I do not count. It is empty.' She stood up with a gesture of distress.

And Bernard, pacing backwards and then forwards, hit the side of his head on an iron bracket jutting near the door, and bent double in brief pain.

Without preamble she was beside him, hand pressed to his bleeding left temple, and his hand clasped hers, pulling it away, pulling her down with him onto the leaf-strewn floor. They kissed wildly – licking and nipping every exposed piece of flesh they could reach.

Very gently Bernard extricated himself from Anna's grip and stood apart from her, breathing quickly. He was hard, and aching with it, and she gazed at him only with utter trust and love.

'What is it?' she asked, confused.

'I want you so badly.'

'You have me, dearest. I am here.'

'Physically, Anna. *Sexually.*'

'Oh.'

She tried to imagine exactly what he meant, and although the act itself was a mystery to her, her own body was instinctively sexual and sensual so that there was nothing she would have denied him, or minded him doing to her.

'I know – a little, I think,' she fibbed doubtfully.

'Dearest, one day we shall both know what it is to make love to each other. But not now. *Not* now . . . Stand up instead and let me clean your face. It is covered in my blood.'

She stood obediently, little pulses throbbing throughout her body, and spat on his handkerchief with which he rubbed her cheeks and forehead. Then he smoothed her dress for her to brush down its layers.

'You are a young lady, Anna,' he teased. 'You must behave as befits one.'

'I love you.'

'And I too. I love you.'

'But –'

'Hush.' He put his finger on her lips. 'I know all the "buts", and let us not bother ourselves with them now. Let us not lose sight of our love.'

'I thought you had done.'

'No. Although I was wishing I could. But I cannot. I was merely jealous.'

'I am so sorry. I wish –'

'Ssh.'

'May I clean up *your* face?'

'I suspect the handkerchief is bloodier than my face.'

'I shall use my paint rag.'

'What an unromantic girl you are!'

'It is clean,' Anna protested, laughing. 'And I even have water.'

'I should rather have your spit.'

'Water will have to suffice.'

She was in the midst of tending to him when Sir Giles Fotheringay walked in. He barely gave them time to spring apart – the door swung open as Anna was pressing the rag to Bernard's forehead.

'Am I interrupting a little party?' he asked in a quietly furious voice.

'Why – Giles!'

'Why – Giles!' he mimicked. 'It seems, Anna, that you are forever surprised to see me, and you have this habit of looking not a little guilty.'

'But I thought you had gone shooting.'

'And whilst the cat is away, the mice do play, is that it?'

'No Giles. Bernard – Mr Foligno has hurt his forehead, and I was tending to it.'

'Ah, I see. How very domestic.' He turned to Bernard. 'It would seem, sir, that you enjoy the company of my fiancée.'

'Her company is most pleasant,' Bernard agreed, adding coldly, 'and you have no reason or right to speak to her in such a manner. Having the very great privilege of being her fiancé does not entitle you to such behaviour. Excuse me.' He brushed past, and strode away before the other could respond.

'My God, he is impudent and arrogant. A Jew, I gather. Anna I forbid you to collude with such a person. How dare he speak to me in that fashion? And you – what were you doing?'

'Painting, Giles. As you can surely see.'

244

'Yes?' He glanced at her work sarcastically. 'I do not see too much evidence of great industry.'

'I was not in the right mood,' she said wearily.

'And him?'

'Mr Foligno happened to pass by, came in when he saw me, and cut his head on the bracket near where you are standing.' Wickedly she wished he would do the same.

'I see.'

He pondered for a moment or so over what she had said, and Anna watched his reactions – the face muscles relaxing, the tension around the mouth easing.

Giles said gruffly: 'I am sorry, Anna. I did not intend to be angry with you. I was – jealous, my dear.'

She could not help laughing.

'What is wrong with that?' he asked indignantly, his pride stung, since the admission had been demeaning both to his authority and his masculinity.

She could not say that barely a half-hour earlier Bernard had declared the same. 'It is merely funny that you should be jealous.'

Doubtfully he joined in her laughter.

Looking outside Anna could just decipher Bernard's form. She stood half-turned from her fiancé, squinting through the glass doors for a glimpse of him – thought he saw her and that he waved. She felt invigorated, although nothing had changed. Here lay her future, with this man. She asked him: 'Tell me, Giles, why did you not go shooting?'

'Sir Alfred twisted his ankle on that ridiculous contraption of his. It failed to stop and he tumbled and caught his foot under the front wheel. Really I cannot say he did not deserve it. Anyway, the day was cancelled.'

How without warmth or humour he is, Anna thought; *how dry of life. But he is essentially well-meaning.*

'Are you coming to the house now?' he asked, wishing she would not stare in that way of hers and impatient to be out of the musty-smelling little building.

'No, I shall stay and paint.'

'But I understood you were not in the mood.'

'Well, now my mood has changed and I am inclined to paint.'

245

He was surprised and perturbed by the firmness of her refusal, but did not press her. He thought, as he so often did when certain of her actions displeased him: *When we are married she will change*.

He took her hand and kissed it quite tenderly. *She is so very young*, he excused her 'waywardness' to himself.

Spring became early summer, June. Bernard's concerto was finished at last and he sent it to Mr Beavis in London. Now that it was completed he was beset with uncertainty: possibly the work was too avant-garde, with its lack of formal structure; possibly it was crude; possibly he had introduced too many themes and had not dwelt sufficiently on a single one . . . And then he dismissed it from his mind much as one would an erring child with whom one no longer wishes to associate.

Anna and Bernard, left to themselves again, discussed life as though nobody had ever discussed it before:

'Life has no meaning or mission,' he told her as they lay by the lake. '*Oneself* has meaning. It is a matter of finding the dominant self and appeasing it, whilst satisfying the other subsidiary selves – who can occasionally mislead by attempting to convince you of *their* dominance.'

'But there must be a meaning. I need a meaning.'

'Ah, that is just it,' Bernard said triumphantly. 'You have created a fictitious meaning through need as opposed to belief, like everyone else.'

'Your views disturb me. Do you not believe in after-life?' Anna asked anxiously, her brow furrowed.

Bernard smoothed the furrow with his fingertips. 'As a child I was so certain of its existence,' he told her thoughtfully. 'But that was because it was what I was taught.'

'And then?'

'Dearest, I am an intelligent man. Should I believe everything I am taught?'

'So you *dis*believe.'

'Not necessarily. I neither believe nor disbelieve, and meanwhile I pray to God in case He is there.'

'Well, I believe He is and that He brought you to me.'

'Oh Anna.' He laughed tenderly. 'How can I dispute such sweet logic.'

Douglas came to England and paid them a fleeting visit. He saw immediately the situation.

'Who can blame you, dear chap? Perfectly splendid girl. Such a pity, mind. Damnable shame, if you ask me. I'll never let on of course, and if you ever need a friend and all that . . . Oh sod it, if you'll excuse the terminology, dear chap. Don't give her up. Just do not let her go.'

'I have no choice, Doug. It is not up to me.'

The weeks passed – hazy weeks of pale leaves and reflections on the water; of gentle tea parties and croquet on the lawn; lessons with Miranda and love with Anna; chess and whisky with Sir Alfred, whose temper had been impaired by his ankle which was after all broken and not sprained.

Then the letter came. It was from Sterndale Bennett. Bernard read faster and faster:

> . . . *Was delivered of your concerto by Mr Beavis* . . .
> *Greatly impressed* . . . *You can be proud. The music is*
> *original and emotive* . . . *An extraordinary diffusion of*
> *beautiful sound* . . . *You must alter nothing; let it be*
> *judged for itself* . . . *Wish to see you as a matter of*
> *urgency regarding the possibility of performing the work*
> *at the Hanover Square Rooms. You see, I believe in you.*
>
> *Yours ever, Sterndale Bennett.*

Bernard was in the library quietly smoking his pipe. Rain streamed down the window and he saw each drop as though it held a different image of his future.

This time, he was thinking. Just – *this time*.

He put the letter in his pocket and continued to gaze out of the window, his sculpted face peaceful and a far-seeing expression in his eyes.

247

A few days later he took his leave of the Leemings – and Anna. They said their goodbyes in the battered little pavilion.

'There are some precious truisms in life, my Anna, and our love is one of them. I cannot feel as sad as I ought, because I do not believe this is the end.'

Her smooth lovely face gazed into his, trying to draw hope. Her drooping body straightened imperceptibly.

'It is not the end,' he repeated, holding her chin, forcing it up almost brutally. 'Look into my eyes. It is up to you; my love will always be waiting to receive you.'

It seemed he was always waiting. All his life had been spent wanting and waiting.

Now one of the things for which he had long waited was about to come to fruition. Under the direction of Sterndale Bennett he was going to perform his first piano concerto with the Philharmonic Society at the Hanover Square Rooms, scene of his last disaster. Unbelievably he was being given a second chance, and it was Bennett who was risking his own reputation to offer him this opportunity.

You see, I believe in you.

And I shall not let you down.

Chapter Sixteen

November the third, 1864, the Hanover Square Rooms; and like that other time, not quite twelve months before, an official sword bearer adorned Bernard with the traditional weapon.

Bernard waited beside Bennett to go on the platform, encumbered by the weight and awkwardness of the sword, recalling his previous disaster and only too conscious that this time not just his piano playing, but also his creative ability would be open to judgement. Already he was flinching from the criticism, anticipating his sense of rejection. He imagined the audience as an antagonistic jury whose verdict was decided before hearing the case. Suddenly he was certain his music would cause anger and displeasure, that it was too 'different'. And it had been written with such love; that was what injured.

'They will all be there,' he whispered wildly to Bennett. 'Davison and Chorley . . . All those who previously slated me will be there. Is it not rather presumptuous of us to consider this so soon? Seventy years ago Haydn performed here in one of Saloman's concerts. What ludicrous trick do I play upon myself to believe I am ready to perform a work of my own in the same place – and wearing the same sword? Sir, it is the ultimate in conceit and presumption.'

'We are all presumptuous in our ways, Mr Foligno,' Bennett told him mildly. 'It is my opinion that you have produced a great work, or else I would not have invited you to perform here this evening. I hope I have made that clear to you.' He looked pointedly at the young man in whom he had put his faith. 'Now, shall we go on?'

Bennett walked in front, quick and assured, whilst Bernard

followed meekly, bowed briefly and took his place at the Broadwood. . . .

The dark uneven rows of heads were only abstract shapes after all. And what if they disliked him? Could he not shrug aside his hurt, and say that at least he had tried? Defeated by his own aims, he would return then to the City. . . .

Papa, you were right you see. I am back despite everything, in a cream room above another barber's shop, whilst below me there is another bootshiner and blind newspaper vendor, his fingertips worn from feeling coins. . . .

But – in the front row of the audience was Mr Beavis, his intrepid eyebrows visible as a solid line, and his wife. And beside her, Bernard's mother. He had not known she would come. Next to his mother was Mr Hamilton and – Douglas.

Incredulous, Bernard stared at his little troop of supporters. His mother's hair shone in its silver loop, and at her neck was the small cameo, the only jewellery she wore apart from her wedding ring. She smiled steadily at him: his own smile, rare and illuminating.

Their support restored his confidence. Eyes watering with emotion, Bernard gazed wonderingly around the auditorium; at the great chandeliers sparkling overhead. He turned to Bennett – who raised his arms and made a gesture with his baton – and he began to play: the triplet that heralded the shimmering strings.

So began the opening bars of the first major work by Bernard Foligno.

H. F. Chorley was ecstatic: *Can this really be the same young man to whom barely a year ago I was forced to listen delivering a lack-lustre performance of Chopin?* he wrote in the *Atheneum.*

This young man whom I have just heard is destined to become one of the greats of our century – both as a composer of enormous originality, and a performer of astonishing sensitivity. I have subsequently learned he was a pupil of the great Johann Baptist Cramer, and I am sure the latter would be proud of his student. Rarely am I moved to write in superlatives, but now I say: 'Mr Foligno, I welcome you to music's immortality.'

J. W. Davison in *The Times* wrote: *Tonight I was one of several hundred privileged to be present at what I must describe as an historic event in music, and for this we must thank Mr Sterndale Bennett, Director of the Philharmonic Society, for he has brought to our notice a gentleman by the name of Bernard Foligno. Only a year ago in these same rooms, we heard Mr Foligno denuding Chopin of his loveliness, and blaming his poor rendition on illness. I can now excuse Mr Foligno anything and only be thankful that Mr Bennett retained the courage of his convictions.*

The first piano concerto by this young man is a splendid example of innovative composition, ingenious both in its phraseology and its construction, deviating from strict form, but never wandering too far, and having some of the most exquisite interchange between piano and orchestra I have heard. As a pianist Mr Foligno's artistic dexterity is stunning yet loses nothing in the way of sensitivity. . . . .

Autumn 1864 progressed into summer 1865, and by early June Bernard, now aged twenty-four, had become a travelling virtuoso. He had stepped from obscurity into that musical hierarchy previously reserved for Europe. He was referred to as the 'Young English Jew', and when this description reached his ears he did not flinch from it, but revelled in this image of himself which hinted at mystery and passion.

He travelled extensively during that half-year, performing and composing, meeting people and accepting invitations, his reputation as he forayed deeper into a serious musical environment becoming firmly established. Bernard was one of the new young Romantics – Romantic in period, as Classicism in the arts digressed into something softer and less definable; and Romantic in appearance, with his dark intense looks, curling hair and tall graceful figure clad in immaculately-cut clothes. Women who were normally bored by music unaccountably developed a liking for it and begged to be taken to a concert so they could hear him.

From Paris he went to Rome, and from Rome to Weimar –

that unique small town which was the cultural capital of Europe. In Weimar he joined up with Douglas Hamilton, and over dinner in their hotel that first evening there was much to discuss. His little friend had barely changed over the years, but he had grown a moustache since Bernard had last seen him. This had the opposite of the desired effect:

'I grew it so they would take me seriously, dear chap,' explained Douglas. 'Now tell me, how is that wonderful girl?'

'Sophie was well when I saw her just before I left London.'

'I am glad of it, but actually I meant the splendid Lady Anna.'

A rod of pain shot through Bernard. 'How would I know, Doug? She is probably married.'

'Dear chap, you might have become a great composer and pianist overnight, but a great liar you have not. Am rather under the impression you're suffering.'

His comical moustache quivered as he spoke. His whole demeanour made one want to laugh – this diminutive man with his puffed cheeks and affected voice. Bernard loved him. The baby-blue eyes behind their glasses bore into him as he answered:

'Yes, Doug. I am suffering. Despite everything else I see her wherever I go, think of her whatever I do.' He shrugged. 'There is nothing to be done about it.' Wistfully he thought, *She was my lioness*. He had called her that when he learned she was born in August. 'I shall meet her again,' he said with conviction.

'Well *now* we are in Weimar,' Douglas said, 'and tomorrow night there is a rather special party. . . .'

This was in fact a fairly small gathering given by the Prince and attended by many high-ranking personages and guests including Ferencz Liszt. Liszt's friend and son-in-law, the hawk-faced Wilhelm Richard Wagner, was also there, junior to him by only a couple of years; and two other worthy musicians: the thirty-one year old, hard-working, bearded composer from Hamburg by the name of Johannes Brahms, whose first piano concerto had created a sensation three years before, and his touring companion, the supremely talented Jewish Hungarian violinist, Edward Remenyi.

But it was Liszt whom Bernard sought out: that straight-standing man of proud bearing and flowing hair who had been his hero since he was a small boy.

Liszt had been musical director to the Prince in Weimar until 1859. Now he was based in Rome, but was still active in Weimar hence his presence that evening. Beside him was the attractive Princess Saya Wittgensten, his constant companion and whom, rumour had it, the Pope refused him permission to marry, since her husband still lived.

Bernard bowed to the Princess and introduced himself to Liszt. 'I have been an admirer of yours, sir,' he told the great man, 'ever since I was a child. My early years as a student were moulded by your influence.'

'Ah, but I'll wager,' the maestro retorted with a twinkle in his eyes, 'that you have not broken as many pianos as I!'

'Sir, forgive me,' Bernard replied promptly and with barely a change in expression, 'but I have not had so long in which to try!'

'I like that, sir! Did I catch your name?'

'My name is Bernard Foligno, sir.'

'Ah, but you are already something of a celebrity yourself, are you not? Old Johann Cramer's pupil. I have heard your piano concerto in Rome. Mr Foligno, *you* are to be congratulated.'

From Weimar Bernard travelled to Leipzig, from Leipzig to Vienna, and from Vienna to Salzburg, and during all his time abroad he was unanimously acclaimed and treated with respect. He began work on a series of sonatas whilst in Salzburg which were unusual in that they were for piano, flute and harp, a much maligned instrument which, used with subtlety, could embellish a composition delightfully. After Salzburg he returned to England. He had been gone seven exhausting and thrilling months.

But at Mrs Ford's lodgings in St John's Wood, with his old cat for company and the Cramer piano and recollections of Sir Edmund Moore, he was lonely with longing for the latter's granddaughter. He was weary from travel and a little deflated after so much euphoria, and the pain of missing Anna seemed very great.

It is not knowing where she is that is the worst, he thought. *I cannot place her in a picture. In my mind she is still in the ramshackle pavilion where we said goodbye. Is it not ironic that, now that I have the one thing I have craved all my life, I am still unhappy? How will I ever feel complete without my Anna?*

A few days after his return Bernard visited his mother. She had taken his rapid rise to fame calmly and with little surprise, and when he questioned her about this over tea in the family room she replied:

'But dear, I always thought it would happen like this. Even as a child your talent was extraordinary.'

Bernard's face registered astonishment. 'But Papa – could you not have convinced him, if you felt like this?'

'When you were a young boy I tried to broach the subject with him, to warn him; then when you were in Paris I tried to explain again. He would not hear your name. I am so sorry, dear. I never wished that to happen. I could not even discuss you with him. His own son – our much loved son. Dear Bernard, you will never know how unhappy those months were, the deterioration in him as a man and in our relationship as husband and wife.' Helen's chin trembled and she glanced down swiftly at her hands.

'It was my fault,' Bernard muttered between gritted teeth, banging the flat of his hand against his thigh in a gesture of self-recrimination. He stood up, looking round the familiar room, his gaze encompassing his father's old chair still in its same place.

'Dear, it was no one's fault. Please sit down again.' Helen patted the seat beside her, lifting her daughter who was half asleep onto her lap.

'You could only be a musician, Bernard. I promise you that today your father would be as proud of you as I am. I speak for him as his wife, and I know it. He just – lacked imagination sometimes, that is all. He was a good man. Not always far-sighted. But a very, very good man.'

'Mama . . . Oh Mama.' He half sat, half lay on the chaise-longue, his legs stretched out on the floor, his head against her thin black-clad shoulder.

'What is it, dear? Are you sad?'

'Oh Mama – I love a woman.'

'Then she is lucky and I am sure she is very special.'

'She is very special.'

'So what is wrong?' Helen asked tenderly.

'I cannot tell you. I cannot talk about her,' Bernard answered brokenly.

His mother's expression was anxious, but she did not press him. She waited a moment and when he was not forthcoming she changed the subject.

'I hear Harold is seeing Sophie again.'

'Oh really?' Bernard tried to keep the annoyance from his voice.

'As you know he is well set up as a partner now with a couple of other barristers, and he has become a member of Lloyds since you were away. Of course this appeals greatly to Mr and Mrs Romain. After all, they are worried.'

'Why are they worried?' he asked irritably.

'Well dear, Sophie is twenty-seven, bless her, and still no sign of marrying.'

'She should be a singer.'

'But Bernard, she is a woman of breeding!' Helen sounded shocked.

Bernard scowled into his tea. 'Really Mama, that should not make any difference. And I can assure you that Sophie's going on stage would be infinitely preferable to her marrying Harold.'

And at that point the doorbell rang, reverberating through the house.

It was Harold, with his usual immaculate timing. Portly and stocky and balding now, he could have been ten years older than his twenty-six years.

'I thought I might find you here,' he told Bernard when they were alone, Helen having disappeared to settle Elizabeth for a rest. 'You are back from your gypsy tour then?'

'What do you want, Harold?' Bernard sighed to indicate he was not in the mood for sparring.

This seemed to please Harold who raised his eyebrows superciliously and cleared his throat before replying in his most

255

pompous tone: 'You may not know, Bernard, but I am courting Miss Romain in earnest and I must insist that you keep out of her way.'

'What on earth do you mean, keep out of her way? Is Sophie to be precluded all visitors because the great Harold is attempting to woo her? Or is this condition only imposed upon myself?'

Harold helped himself to a biscuit from the cake-stand, and the long, slow look he gave Bernard from under heavy lids was his most reptilian. 'I think you know the answer,' he drawled.

'If I am to interpret you correctly, Harold, I am afraid you will not find me compliant,' Bernard said in a tight voice. He had a sudden image of his cousin – this man who set himself up as a pillar of society – propositioning a young boy in Soho.

He longed to say: 'Your rabbi's robes are stained with dung,' but commented instead: 'When Sophie considers you are courting her and requests that I stay away, only then will I do so. Now if you will excuse me I have nothing further to say on the matter.'

'But I have, cousin Bernard –'

But Bernard got up and left the room. He called out goodbye to his mother and a moment later was out in the street hailing a cab.

A couple of weeks later he had lunch with Mr Beavis and Sterndale Bennett at the club he used to go to with Sir Edmund Moore and had subsequently joined himself. Bennett had just offered him a post at the Academy and Bernard had accepted on the understanding that he was free to travel as and when he wished. The lunch, whilst a pleasant social occasion, was also to discuss business, for Bernard had just completed his set of sonatas – ten in all – and he wanted Bennett to include them in the library of the Academy.

'I want these sonatas made available to all students,' he explained.

'Why?' Bennett asked.

'Because they exemplify today's music. Outside France, the harp is ignored and therefore the sonatas are educational. I understand what is required and what is needed.'

256

'Young sir, are you not a trifle arrogant?' Cramer had once said to him.

But Bennett, after a moment's hesitation, replied with an amused look in his eyes: 'Very well, Mr Foligno, I shall appraise them carefully and consider their merit.'

'Thank you, sir. I shall be playing them in Crosby Hall in a week's time which will help them to become known.'

Beavis took his package without comment. He knew that in Bernard he had a commercial asset. Then, the business discussions over, the three men sat back with a decanter of port and moved on to lighter matters.

The day was fine without being overly hot, and Bernard took a cab from his club only so far as Baker Street, preferring to walk the remaining distance to St John's Wood and rid himself of that excessive feeling resultant from too much food and alcohol at lunch.

When he arrived at his lodgings there was a carriage outside. The coachman was having a heated argument with Mrs Ford who was looking anguished.

Bernard went up to them and tapped her lightly on the shoulder: 'Without wishing to interfere, can I be of assist –' Then he saw the tattered piebald bundle in her arms. 'Oh no. . . .'

'Oh, Mr Foligno, you're back.' Mrs Ford burst out sobbing anew. 'He says it was not his fault . . . Poor mite ran right in front of his wheels.'

Anna the cat – music-loving, moustached, pink-nosed, nearly blind and nearly deaf – had gone out of his life the same way she had come into it: under the wheels of a carriage.

He took the body gently in his arms; it was pitifully light and still warm.

'It is over now, Mrs Ford,' he said quietly. 'Whose fault it was is of no consequence.'

His landlady stood beside him as Bernard dug a trough in the small back garden. He had removed his coat and unbuttoned his waistcoat. He worked silently, with that ferocious expression of his she had come to recognize as sorrow and not anger.

'I liked that cat,' she kept saying. 'She was a real character. I

257

never thought when you first asked me if you could keep her here, that I'd grow to like her. But I really did. Whenever you were away she used to keep me company. And the way she used to sit on your piano, Mr Foligno! She guarded that piano like it was her own.'

He finished digging and straightened his back. The little broken form lay between them.

'Tell me just one thing, Mrs Ford. Do you know if she died instantly?'

'Oh yes, Mr Foligno. She wouldn't have known a thing. It was over in a flash.'

'That is all that matters then.'

'I really liked that cat . . .'

Bernard removed the tiny velvet collar, lifted the body and very carefully with the spade, lowered it gently into its grave. He then replaced the soil, marked round the area with stones and went inside the house.

Her ghost sat on the piano, purring, and he sat on the stool staring into the distance, turning the collar over and over in his hands, remembering the circumstances surrounding her arrival at the house in Bayswater; the scruffy injured kitten, his distraught mother, dying Rachel on the chaise-longue, the billowy-sleeved tartan dress. . . .

And he thought, as he had so many, many times, how impermanent a thing was happiness.

He continued to stare into space and twirl the collar in his hands, impervious to the sounds of a carriage drawing to a halt outside, the knocker heavy on the door and a light voice . . . There was a brief interval then a knock at his own door. Mrs Ford was beaming delightedly, all traces of tears departed.

'You have a visitor who may cheer you, Mr Foligno. A Lady Charlton-Grey. She is handsome, sir.'

'Could you ask her to come in please, Mrs Ford,' Bernard told her – as though this visit were expected and an everyday occurrence; as though his pulses were not racing, nor his longing mingled with apprehension.

The door to his room was open and there stood Anna, as he had so often imagined her.

'I hardly dared call upon such a famous man,' were her first words. But a muscle in her cheek twitched nervously and her eyes were shy.

It had been a year since they had seen one another, and now Bernard was engulfed by emotion. He took her in his arms and stood with her in the middle of the room rocking from side to side, not kissing, not speaking; just holding her, inhaling her scent and feeling her preciousness.

Finally he said, his mouth muffled by her hair: 'You are beautiful. So, so beautiful.'

'I was terrified to come.'

'Terrified? Why?'

'I thought . . . Things might have changed.'

'Certainly some things have changed, but never my feelings for you.'

'Nor mine for you.'

They stood apart, having admitted their feelings, yet nevertheless faintly embarrassed and self-conscious.

'Your landlady said your cat has just died. I am sorry.'

'Yes, it is very sad. She was a nice old animal.' It did not occur to Bernard to say they had shared the same name.

For a few seconds there was a strained silence between them.

He tried to think of something to say. 'I am sorry. It is not very grand.' He gestured mockingly around the room. 'Nor am I very used to lady visitors.'

'Dearest, it is not important. It is all very fine. I assure you.'

He relaxed with her usage of the endearment. 'Oh *God*, I am glad to see you.'

'And I you.'

'I have longed for you . . . If only you knew . . .'

At last they kissed, tumbling to the floor, lost in one another after their twelve-month deprivation. Anna's skirts were spread everywhere, the crinoline cage hoisted uncomfortably towards her chest. Laughing, she sat up and adjusted herself.

'Bernard Foligno, is this proper?'

'It is absolutely proper. Now tell me what made you visit me? No – I shall make some tea, and then tell me.'

259

Anna reclined lazily on the settee and watched him being domestic – lighting the burner of the lampstand, spooning tea from the rosewood caddy into the silver tea kettle and setting the kettle on top of the stand. His waistcoat was still unbuttoned and his shirt had also come unbuttoned in one place, revealing quite dense black chest-hair. She was surprised by these hairs – outward signs of his masculinity. She had not considered men's bodies before, and now confronted by Bernard in this state of disarray she found herself aroused by sensations she shamedly understood for what they were, without quite comprehending all the implications.

They sat together on the sofa whilst Bernard served the tea.

'Now you may tell me why you are here.'

'I had to see you. It is that simple.'

'But you have waited a year.'

'Yes, and I have missed you so very much. It is just . . . Bernard, I am to be married in a fortnight's time.'

A harsh and silent coldness settled upon him; that sense of remoteness which made him retreat within himself.

'Bernard – don't,' Anna begged him, hating this rupturing of their communication, this exclusion of herself.

'Don't what?' he asked in a detached manner.

'Don't – sever me from you.'

'I am sorry.' He focused upon her once more. 'I cannot help it,' he said in a flat tone.

'But you knew a year ago that I was – engaged.'

'So why did you come to me? Just to emphasize what I already knew?'

'I wanted to see you,' Anna said, 'before . . .' Her voice trailed off into the tangle of sadness. 'I realize now it was a mistake,' she continued, pulling at long locks of her hair in a distracted way. Then she looked at him suddenly, narrowing her eyes: 'A year ago you said your love would always be waiting for me.'

'But what do you *want* from me?' Bernard asked, the disembodied feeling leaving him so that beside him again sat the woman he loved more than anyone in the world, but who would never be his wife.

'I do not *know*,' she answered in the same hopeless tone.

'Talk to me then,' he said gently taking her hand and stroking it, massaging with his thumb and forefinger. 'My little lioness, talk to me as my friend and tell me.'

'I don't know where to begin . . . I have been so very unhappy without you. It was as though I was mutilated. I never imagined that unhappiness could be so continual and prolonged. It was like an enduring illness; such hankering, *hankering* for another human soul to whom I felt a life's commitment . . . And all the while knowing I must marry Giles for whom I feel no affection.

'He is faultless in his manner to me, Bernard, and escorts me in a very proper fashion. He is determined that I shall become a part of society –' she gave a little laugh '– he tells me I am very unworldly . . . But the trouble is I am not in the least interested in becoming a socialite, and such people bore me. I long only to feel free. I do not feel like a girl any more, and I am continually oppressed, if not by Giles then by my father. The house where I live with him has for years been without a woman's touch and it is utterly cheerless – with dark panelling, heavy drapes and poor lighting . . . and austere portraits of my long-gone ancestors glaring down at me forbiddingly!'

She broke off to see Bernard's reaction, her gaze anxiously scanning his face. He kissed her eyelids gently and, reassured, Anna continued:

'It has all been so gloomy that I have not even felt like painting . . . Then I began to hear your name being mentioned, and soon it seemed I could go nowhere without hearing it; even Giles was impressed. I was bursting with my need to confide in someone: "Please let me tell you about this man I love; please tell me how to gather the courage to be with him; please help me to defy my father."

'But there was nobody, and I would never defy my father anyway. So – plans have been made for the wedding and a date set for early July, and I go along with everything, and it is as though it is all happening to someone else.

'Do you know that the other evening over dinner my father actually asked me if I was happy with the prospect of my future? His question amazed me and I waited an age before replying –

my heart beating with possibilities. I felt my mouth part then close. Dearest, the words were there, ready to burst through my lips . . . But my father's expression defied the truth, and I was cowed by it. So I answered that, yes, I was happy. Oh Bernard, can you believe I answered that? "Good," he told me . . . And I had jettisoned the chance with my cowardice.'

Anna leaned against Bernard heavily. She had become pale and her lips were dry. 'I am sorry,' she whispered, rubbing away a tear. 'I am so, so sorry.'

The front door slammed. 'It is Mrs Ford's night for visiting her daughter,' Bernard commented absently, stroking Anna's hair and supporting her weight with his arm.

'What are you thinking?' she asked. 'Please tell me.'

'I am not sure what I am thinking. So many things . . . I am thinking that I am sad for you and sad for me, and what a pity it all is. I am thinking that I understand *why* it is, although that does not help. And I am thinking that you are the only woman I shall love in such a way. I have never sought love, Anna, and I shall not seek it beyond you. The only thing I ever sought was music and I have incorporated that in my life at last and can at least take refuge in it. Mine is a difficult character; I know I am moody and too silent, that I can be unforgiving and arrogant. But I know myself and can finally exist with myself. It has taken a long time to reach this state. . . .

'I am explaining this so that you might understand a little about me. Why was I "removed" from you before, despite having told you to visit me whenever you felt inclined? Because I harboured secret hopes during our twelve months' interlude that a way would be found in which we could stay together. But it is not to be, and at night you will think of me, and I of you. And I want it to be *me* you remember and me who first loved you. Will you let me make love to you?'

'Yes.'

'You know what I mean?'

'I –'

'I am not talking about just kissing you.'

'I know.'

He led her into the bedroom. She was shivering with

apprehension, and her shoulders drooped. Very gently Bernard began to undress her. Slowly, and with such love, he removed each item of clothing, lingering to touch her tenderly, kissing her sweetly and reassuringly – the hollow at her neck, her shoulders, her armpits, the insides of her elbows. He unlaced her peach silk corset so that her breasts were exposed – voluptuous, and transluscently creamy, the nipples quite large and pale – and he took one in his lips and sucked it so that its smoothness became puckered and the little pimple projected.

'It is I, Bernard,' he said softly. 'Darling, I love you. I am not violating you. Everything I am doing to you is with adoration.'

In answer she took his head, hesitated – then held it against her, his soft black hair buried in her cleavage. She was breathing fast, her eyes bright, and the tiny hairs on her arms stood on end.

'Let me look at you, my Anna.'

With fingers and lips light as a moth's wings he kissed and touched her body; then, kneeling, he slid his hands over her, up and down, until he had covered her entirely. He undressed himself without self-consciousness, watching her all the while, noticing her eyes widen at the sight of his erect penis. He lifted her onto the bed.

'I must ask you, when did you last bleed?'

'I finished two days ago.'

'Then it is safe. Do you understand? You will not become pregnant.'

She nodded vaguely, not understanding, but trusting him.

'I do not mean to hurt you. I promise it becomes quite exquisite after the pain. Will you completely relax and remember I love you more than anything in the world?'

'Yes. I do too.'

'I know. But I want you to know that everything we do is natural and not in the least "dirty". Oh, you are shivering so. Let me warm you. Cuddle up to me, and just feel warm and happy. Bring your leg around mine . . . I love you, I love you, I love you. . . .'

*

263

Anna stayed with him for two days. Her father was in Edinburgh presiding over a case, and she had already forewarned the servants in the house that she was visiting a friend and might be gone overnight. Mrs Ford liked Bernard too much to criticize him, and thought Anna beautiful enough to forgive, and when he swore her to secrecy she answered:

'Bless you, I would not ever do anything to harm either of you.'

They felt ludicrously free and happy, playing at marriage, trying to make the most of every second, savouring rare moments and remembering a significant word or sentence so that they could be stored and recalled later.

They took a cab to Hampstead and breakfasted in the Old Bull and Bush Hotel, then they walked on the Heath towards Highgate and came to a vendor selling ices from an Italian ice-cream cart. He was singing:

> 'Oh! Oh! Antonio Oh!
> Then he's gone away
> Left me a-lone-io
> All on my own-i-o.'

The words caused them to glance at one another, and Bernard squeezed her hand and paid the vendor a halfpenny for an ice cream for Anna, whilst two small boys behind them cried because their nanny forbade them one.

'Why cannot we have one, why?' they cried in chorus.

And Anna said, deliberately loudly and in an angry tone, 'They are quite right. Why *cannot* they have one?' She glared at the nanny, who blushed. 'If you have not the money I shall pay.'

'No, no, I have the money.'

'Good.' Anna stood with her hand on her hip, waiting. The little boys, silenced, gawped at her, and Bernard's eyebrows were raised in amusement.

The nanny, her face and neck reddened with embarrassment, ordered two ice creams and the boys whooped and danced around her. Satisfied, Anna took Bernard's proffered arm and walked away from them.

'That was most admirable,' he congratulated her, trying to keep the laughter from his voice.

'Such unnecessary strictness makes me so *cross*,' Anna replied in an overwrought tone. 'Childhood should be happy, not laden with rules and regulations.'

They strolled back to the Village and down the little High Street, looking in shop windows, comparing taste:

'I like this, do you?'

'*Surely* not – what about this?'

'That? You cannot *possibly* like that!'

And laughing to find that they could appreciate different things and still love one another.

Two days of getting to know each other as a man and woman: waking up smiling in the same bed, without embarrassment; learning the miracles of pleasure one's body could give and receive; swallowing one's pride about needing the water closet. They learned about being natural, about the necessity for honesty in a relationship, about never feeling ashamed. In those two days they did not waste time with falsity and learned more about themselves than many couples of their era did in two years.

But the time came for her to leave, and they could make no arrangements for a future meeting. Bernard buttoned up the back of Anna's red velvet dress, touching each tiny pearl button, and fixing in his mind an image of her – her sleek back and strong womanly shoulders.

They faced each other gravely.

'Maybe we will have different partners in the eyes of the law,' he told her, 'and maybe we will in time come to respect those partners, but I shall always feel married to you. Possibly I am doing a dishonour to my future wife – whoever she may be. But that is how things are.'

'I cannot bear it,' Anna said in a desolate tone, as they waited outside for a cab. 'I cannot bear to be going from you.'

'You will bear it,' Bernard contradicted her with a firmness he did not feel. 'If you are certain you have to go through with this marriage, then you have to bear it.'

'Shall – I ever see you again?'

'Of course, my lioness. If you cannot contact me direct, then do so via Douglas Hamilton. I have let him into our secret. Tell Miranda if you need to. I am certain you can trust her, and she can liaise with Douglas if you are unable to.'

He hailed a cab and it stopped.

'I am terrified to leave you.'

Anna clung to him, and he enveloped her in his arms, smelling all her familiar scents – her clothes, her skin; bracing himself in advance for the pain of her absence. He prised her from him.

'You must be brave.'

Bernard studied her face, each endearing feature, each beauty and each imperfection. 'Oh God.'

He kissed her, bit her lips and sucked them until they were dry; then he pushed her from him. 'Please darling, don't you see? You have to go.'

'Yes,' she whispered.

She was calm now, the remnants of tears drying on her cheeks, and he helped her into the carriage.

'Knightsbridge,' he ordered the driver. 'Be brave,' he repeated, calling through the window, seeing her face and tumble of hair as a golden blur speeding away from him.

Bernard took to walking in Regent's Park each Sunday. It became a weekly ritual; watching the dissipating summer and the roses pouring their petals onto the grass. It was on one such Sunday he conceived the idea for his opera.

This particular afternoon was unusually hot. The pale sun created an incandescence in the sky, and there was a stillness in the air that even the piping of children's voices and yapping of dogs could not intrude upon.

He was walking into the sun's glare amongst the rose gardens and was musing about nothing in particular – curiously light-headed – when he came upon a scene that touched him:

A young urchin of perhaps twelve or thirteen years old was hovering around a bench upon which sat a very beautiful lady in her middle years, dressed in pale pink lace and silk. She was by herself, apparently unconcerned by the possible dangers, feeding crusts of bread and chunks of stale cake to the mass of pigeons which pecked about her daintily shod feet.

The boy stood watching, staring with huge tired eyes at this apparition of finery, then he transferred his gaze to the ground where the fat birds fought and scurried, and his look became one of craving hunger. For several moments he remained like that – staring first at the woman, then following her gloved hand delving into the large bag to scatter yet more morsels to the ground. She seemed oblivious to him all the while, yet she smiled a sweet and enigmatic smile.

Bernard sat on the bench on the opposite side of the narrow path to keep closer vigil, feeling as though he had wandered into an obscure play which was being enacted for his benefit. He was tense as he waited to see what followed.

Eventually the boy could no longer resist, and glancing directly at the woman, opened his mouth as though about to speak. He hesitated, then obviously thought better of it, and instead bent and joined the pigeons routing on the ground.

The woman looked at him with a tender expression for a second or two, then spoke in a low and kind voice: 'My dear child, are you so hungry that you must scavenge from the ground?'

He nodded from his position on all fours, his mouth packed full of bread and cake which spilled from the corners.

'Then you must return to my house for tea,' she said in a definite voice. 'Come.'

And she stood up, brushed her skirts, and led him away by the hand.

Bernard dwelt on this improbable incident for a long while: there had been a strange, dream-like quality about it, enhanced by the almost mystical aura of the day; and for some reason the episode became of great importance to him, grew out of all proportion, until he became obsessed with the idea that he had witnessed something that had never actually happened. For three days he considered the possibilities and wondered at the outcome of the incident.

On the fourth morning he woke up and decided: *I am going to write an opera. I shall entitle it, 'The Lady and the Urchin' – just that.*

'But what do you know about writing an opera?' Mr Beavis asked him; the first time he had ever expressed doubt.

'Since I was a child I accompanied my mother's singing pupils,' Bernard replied. 'I know all the limitations and the possibilities of the voice. It is an instrument which must not be abused and I understand that. I understand, too, how frequently the meaning of the music becomes lost during an extrovert display of vocal skill. There has to be a balance. I am confident I can provide that balance.'

'And therefore I respect your judgement. Go ahead and write your opera, Bernard. You have my full backing.'

The more he thought of his story, an English opera with its slightly Dickensian plot, the more excited he became, and he decided that the urchin's role should be taken by a woman – possibly a mezzo rather than a soprano.

The plot itself was simple: a young, intelligent boy, lives with his mother in a single damp room which they share with another family in a dilapidated East End building. The child longs for adventure and runs away from home, wandering the streets, encountering various people and troubles on the way, and begging for food. He is arrested for stealing, and taken to a workhouse from which he manages to escape – free to wander the streets once more. He is befriended by a wise organ grinder with whom he travels about, listening to the old man's tales and learning his philosophies. One day he encounters a gentlewoman in a park and she takes him to her house for tea. She is a widow and looks after him for several days before deciding she wishes to adopt him and they return together to his mother.

The boy must now choose between the mother he loves, but a life of poverty, and the affection of a stranger and a life of luxury. Remembering the organ grinder's teachings, he ultimately chooses to remain with his mother.

For a short while Bernard toyed with the idea of a fairy-tale ending in which the widow offered her home to both mother and son, but then he thought: *No, this is to be a realistic opera. And it need not be gloomy. Why – think of all the colours of the*

East End markets. There can be dancing and jovial choruses,
and drinking and brawls. . . .

Bernard sat at the piano puffing gently on his pipe, and
pondering over all the possibilities.

Who shall I approach as librettist? He must be able to
incorporate humanity, compassion and realism in the drama,
for I start with the disadvantages that the opera has no romance
to its story, is contemporary and in English! Oh dear, I can
already foresee the opposition I shall encounter! I wonder if
Adrian Gibbons would be prepared to tackle the task? He
would be ideal. . . .

Adrian Gibbons was a friend of Edward Lear, the artist and
humorist, and like Lear himself was a person of enormous
compassion and many complexes. But Gibbons had never
achieved the reputation he had hoped for, and harboured a great
resentment that his genius was not widely recognized. However, that he was a supremely talented writer and observer was
indisputable. He also held the advantage that he was illegiti-
mate, and his mother had been a servant in a large household.
Gibbons was a man of paradoxes: he bore many grievances, was
distressingly cynical and could be scathing to the point of offence.
But he was also a man who saw beauty where others failed to, and
optimism where it would seem wasted. He was loyal, kind,
erudite, and viewed things with absolute honesty.

And he liked the idea of Bernard's opera.

'*I* like it,' he told him over dinner, 'but it is not certain the
public will.'

Bernard poured wine into their glasses. 'They will – by the
time we have finished with the opera. But it is essential it is
treated in the right manner.'

'I admire your courage, Mr Foligno.'

'And I your writing, Mr Gibbons; and also your Bristolian
accent!'

Gibbons laughed. 'I was taken for a half-wit when I first came
to London on account of my accent. So then, Mr Foligno, let us
drink to the success of *The Lady and the Urchin*.' He raised his
glass.

Bernard raised his and clinked it against the other. '*The Lady*

269

and the Urchin.' And he felt a little anticipatory thrill ripple through him.

The following morning he began work on his score.

About a fortnight later he left Mrs Ford's establishment to rent a pleasant, recently constructed villa in the same neighbourhood. It was semi-detached and the building was painted yellow – which cheered him, and made him want to smile when he returned home and unlocked his front door.

It had seemed a sensible idea to rent an entire house now that he was beginning to meet and entertain influential people; and money posed no problem. His diary was full for the next ten months with engagements in England and Europe, and in addition to this he had a low but steady income from his part-time teaching at the Royal Academy, and he had just received a considerable sum for the publication of his concerto and the set of sonatas.

Bernard took the house furnished, but the first thing he did was to move some of the drawing-room furniture into the rather bare parlour in order to make room for his piano; he also, rather extravagantly, invested in a fine Queen Anne walnut bureau-bookcase. It was the first piece of furniture he had ever bought, and when he saw it displayed in the shop, he knew that despite its high price he must have it – and put it to use. The wood had a superb 'oyster' patina, and the mirrored doors opened to reveal three shelves. The desk part was a mass of compartments and drawers, and when he filled them with his own manuscripts and other personal belongings he had a tremendous sense of pride. Here he was, living in his own rented house at Number Four, Elm Tree Avenue; he had a housekeeper, a maid – and a piano and bureau-bookcase. And he had achieved all this by doing what he wanted.

So Bernard settled into his new way of life, and although he was reasonably satisfied most of the time, real happiness eluded him. He could never obliterate Anna from his thoughts for more than a few moments, and sometimes missed her and longed for her so badly that he would crunch his eyes shut as hard as possible, as though in doing so and by willing it enough, he would be able to conjure up her presence.

Towards the end of August the weather broke, and it was on a particularly showery and dismal Sunday afternoon that he took his usual stroll in the park. There was scarcely anyone about, and when he walked towards the pond, planning to sit on the seat nearby and take advantage of the momentary spell of sunshine between bursts of rain, he was startled to see a young girl sitting there alone.

He thought: *Regent's Park is full of surprises*.

He hesitated before sitting down beside her, then thought that he would have done so had she not been there, and rather self-consciously sat and lit his pipe. He turned his face to the sun – trying to be unaware of the girl, and not look her way. Vaguely he had had the impression of a small, waif-like face and black hair, but more than that he hadn't noticed.

'Sir, could you lend me some money?' the voice next to him asked unexpectedly. 'I would pay you back.'

Now he was entitled to turn and look at her: she had a pale, tight little face, and a tight little body. At her feet was a wet parcel which was coming undone and revealed its contents as clothes.

'I really would pay you back eventually,' she assured him, looking at him with very black, lively eyes that were small and extraordinarily long-lashed.

'Why do you need money?'

'I have nowhere to live. My landlord evicted me today.'

'Why?'

'He wanted to bed me. And he's fat and ugly.'

'How old are you?'

'Seventeen.'

'And what about your parents – don't they worry about you?'

'I doubt it. They're in Heaven or Hell, depending.'

'What's that supposed to mean?'

'They're dead, what else?' She grinned impishly, without filial sorrow.

'Oh . . . Well you won't find any lodgings by tonight.'

'I might – or if not, I might in the morning.'

'Might. Life is full of mights, is it not. Never mind. Stay with me tonight, and tomorrow we shall sort something out.'

'How do I know you're not a murderer?'

'As a murderer you were prepared to take my money,' Bernard reminded her.

'That's different,' she replied in a stubborn tone. 'How do I know you won't harm me?'

'Well in truth you cannot know that. You will simply have to take my word for it.' He laughed, suddenly light-hearted, and added: 'But I trust you will not harm *me*.'

Her name was Grace and she was an artist's model, and after two nights she became his mistress. She was not pretty, her features being too small and clenched, but there was a pertness about her which was immensely attractive, a cheeky sexuality. And he also liked the alertness and natural intelligence of her mind, her quick chatter and earthy lack of respect.

Bernard had thought he could manage without a woman, that he would never make love again without love, but he had not truthfully taken into account his own character and its needs. He had not foreseen the staleness of protracted solitude.

Grace made love like a small tigress. She had no inhibitions and cavorted about with him on the huge bed and told him ridiculous stories in her high-pitched cockney voice. In the mornings she helped him dress, and she left him alone when he worked. She did not complain when he travelled or went out without her, and neither nagged nor demanded. She was in every way the perfect mistress, and in return he gave her pocket money and bought her clothes. They co-habited, much to his housekeeper's disgust, for about six months, during which Bernard was kept busy with work and amused by Grace.

And he thought that perhaps he could eventually learn to be content.

Chapter Seventeen

It was a morning during freezing February, 1866. The long reigning Palmerston had died and been replaced the previous October by Lord Russell, with Gladstone still acting as Chancellor.

Bernard put away the latest in a series of letters from Anna. When the first one arrived he had unsuspectingly opened it in front of Grace, before rushing off to the privacy of the bedroom and closing the door. He had read:

Dearest love,

How strange to commence a letter with these words when I do not say them to my own husband. Yes, I am married as you knew I would be by now, and am recently returned from our three-month tour of Europe. I am trying to be a good wife, but Bernard, I am unhappy and I miss you so, despite knowing I have no right to say these things and that by doing so am being not only deceitful to my husband, but also unreasonable to you. Possibly you are doing your utmost to forget me.

Giles, of course, has no notion how I feel. He is, fortunately perhaps, an unperceptive man and he attributes my quietness to the fact that I have settled down in my new marital status, and actually it quite pleases him, since he was never at ease with my 'high spirits'. Now he feels he has 'tamed' me, and even mentions this occasionally with some pride! I feel I am becoming a really stuffy old matron and am sometimes terrified that along with my passions I am losing my identity.

How are you, my darling? It seems I am always seeing
your name in the newspaper nowadays, and I actually
heard you playing in a concert the other day – the one at
St James's Hall. You were marvellous, and it was tantaliz-
ing to be so close and heartbreaking not to be able to see
you privately. All the while I had to wear a polite smile
and chat to our guests about this miraculous musician!
As if I had never known miracles with him.

You said you wanted me to lie in bed and remember you.
You have what you wanted. Dear Bernard, I am thinking
of nothing else.

I hope you are happy. I know life is exciting for you and I
pray that everything lives up to your expectations. I hope
also that you are not angered by the receipt of this letter
or that it does not in any way disturb you.

For the moment please do not try and reply. It would be
too risky. It is enough to know that you are probably
thinking of me from time to time.

      Your loving Anna
P.S. I eventually confided in Miranda who informed me
you had moved, and gave me your new address. It sounds
very smart!

Bernard had received four more letters since, all requesting
that he did not reply, and he complied with her wishes, whilst
longing to make contact.

He put this latest with the others in a secret drawer in his
bureau which had a separate tiny key. Grace happened to be in
the drawing-room as he put it away. Curled up on the sofa, she
had been reading a woman's monthly journal, and now she
scrutinized him over the top of the page with her funny little
Eastern eyes. But Bernard offered her no more explanation
than he ever did. Grace was incidental to him. It was not that he
was callous, but she had entered his life as a kind of joke and he
could only regard her as such.

Without speaking he lit his pipe, and went over to the piano to play the final aria from his opera: that marvellous soliloquy sung by the urchin, in which Gibbons left the listener in no doubt as to the brilliance of his libretto, and Bernard's harmonies combined with the words in sympathetic beauty.

He recalled the afternoon they had worked on it together, mulling over the piece in the chaos of Gibbons's sitting-room.

'Mr Gibbons, I want the urchin's last aria to be a philosophical comment,' Bernard had said.

'In other words, though we must be careful not to glorify it, we show that to be poor does not mean to be without dignity.'

'Exactly so. The urchin has made his choice.'

'And as the urchin reflects on the luxuries he could have had, does he show remorse?' Gibbons asked.

'I think not,' Bernard answered after a contemplative pause. 'What do you feel?'

'I also think not. I think he must stand upright, proud; and he must sing with the gladness of profound discovery.'

They had looked at each other then, and smiled in mutual respect.

'I have liked working with you, Mr Gibbons.'

'And I, you, Mr Foligno.'

Bernard knew that together they had written a masterpiece, and today, with Mr Beavis, he was due to meet Frederick Gye and the manager of the Royal Italian Opera, Covent Garden, in the hope of finally persuading them to stage his work. Also present would be the musical director and the principal producer.

Mr Beavis had been acting as his 'mediator'. As a well-known benefactor of the cause of music, he contributed substantially to the opera house, as did about a dozen of his very influential friends; his presence at the meeting, therefore, was political, and Bernard had been happy to leave the negotiations to him. This was their second meeting, summoned by Gye this time and held at the luxurious Westminster Palace Hotel in Victoria Street.

Gye was the son of a tea and wine merchant and had taken over the management of the Royal Italian Opera in 1851, backed by Queen Victoria, the Prince Consort and members of fashionable London society. For the first time opera began to pay.

The five men shook hands in a perfunctory greeting, before immediately beginning their conference.

'Mr Foligno, how do you envisage yourself as an English –' Gye hesitated over the word '– composer with a single piano concerto and a set of sonatas to his credit, being able to draw an audience sufficient to fill a house nightly so that the enormous cost of putting on an opera is justified? You are known as a man of the keyboard.'

Bernard glanced at Beavis, then addressed everyone present: 'Gentlemen. Firstly, and with respect, I hope that at the age of twenty-five I am too young to have completed the range of my repertoire, and I cannot help what I am known as so far. However, in answer to your question and without wishing to appear immodest, I am, gentlemen, now fairly well-known, and people will come out of curiosity as much as anything else. I would also suggest hiring Mario for the part of the Organ Grinder, and Adelina Patti as the Lady. With the inclusion of those two great singers one could be fairly assured of drawing an audience.'

'Mr Foligno, what makes you think your work merits those particular singers?' asked the principal resident producer.

Before Bernard could jeopardize his position by answering angrily, Mr Beavis spoke:

'Gentlemen, Mr Foligno is unable to say this about his opera, but I can: it is a work of genius. It is profound and moving and highly original, and the libretto by Gibbons is undeniably clever. It would be a grave mistake not to stage the work, as I hope you will realize when you examine the complete manuscript, and I for one –' he paused significantly and looked steadily and meaningfully at them all from under the awning of his brows, '– would be most disappointed if it were not staged. At last we have a worthy opera of our own. Yet you prevaricate.'

The musical director said: 'Sir, we are not necessarily prevaricating. We only posed a question. As it happens we were impressed by what we have seen so far of Mr Foligno's opera, although a little disquieted by its bleak story.'

Bernard reacted hotly: 'But I was at pains to explain that with clever production – vivid scenery, bright costumes and so forth, and with the dancing properly choreographed, any bleakness would be alleviated. Besides, it is not actually bleak as you say, it is –'

Frederick Gye interrupted: 'Mr Foligno, I think you are perhaps being a little too aggressive, and becoming needlessly agitated. We are merely trying to examine all aspects of a situation. Putting on an opera is not like paying the tailor for one suit, you know. In fact we all endorse Mr Beavis's opinion. Your opera has great musical merit and potential dramatic interest.'

'You are prepared to consider it, then?' Mr Beavis asked calmly, scowling formidably and briefly at Bernard to prevent him speaking.

'Yes, one could say that, depending of course on this final draft.'

'I have just two stipulations –' Bernard burst out.

'Bernard, you are premature with stipulations,' Mr Beavis hissed in his ear to no avail.

'– that should the work be accepted, I be allowed to choose the singer for the role of the Urchin, and that I conduct the opera myself.'

'Are you not a trifle arrogant, Mr Foligno?' Gye enquired dryly.

'I have been accused of that before, sir.' Bernard smiled disarmingly.

Those tedious weeks of traipsing round East End back roads while he was apprenticed to his father had not been wasted after all, and Bernard had made use of them in his plot, recalling incidents and scenes with a nostalgia that at the time he never imagined he would feel, and describing them to his friend Gibbons so that the latter could incorporate them.

Who would have thought those wearisome days in the City

would merge with an incident in the park and become the basis of an opera?

Of course he knew his work would be accepted. It was an opportunity Gye could not refuse; the chance of making English opera respectable and worthy of accolade. It was not conceit that made Bernard think that, for he was still his own harshest critic, but he would have said it had someone else composed the same work: *The Lady and the Urchin was* brilliant.

From the start he had known who would be ideal for the role of the Urchin, but he did not know how he was going to persuade her. The day after the meeting he visited her at home. Sophie had just finished giving a lesson and was with her mother in the drawing-room.

'Oh Bernard,' said the older woman, disappointed. 'How nice to see you.'

She preferred his cousin Harold, and had never quite forgotten Bernard's treachery to his father. Still, he had ultimately become successful, and surely he must be earning quite a bit of money? She supposed musicians did earn money? Sometimes she thought that even Bernard would be preferable to no one, but there was no hope in that direction; he and her daughter were friends and nothing more. Still, she would tactfully leave the children alone just in case. As a mother of an unmarried girl who would soon end up a spinster, one had to hold out hopes. A little encouragement here, a little tact there. . . .

'Children, I have just remembered something,' she said vaguely, and drifted out of the room, sniffing.

'What did I do wrong?' Bernard asked in a mock-hurt tone.

'That is Mama's way of being subtle and liberal,' Sophie replied equably.

'Does that mean I am in favour?'

'Not so much as Harold!'

'Oh, that is surely too bad. Sophie, pour me a Scotch please. I have come about something terribly important and I want you to listen to me.'

Sophie poured his whisky and handed it to him, wiping the base of the tumbler with a napkin. 'How is the opera? Tell me that first.'

'It is that I have come about.' And he tried to cajole and persuade her – to no effect.

'My parents would never allow me.'

'You are twenty-eight, Sophie. Surely it is up to you.'

'I live here, Bernard. I cannot offend them and live off their hospitality.'

'But why do they mind so much?'

'You know why. Because the life of a singer or actress seems disreputable to them. I cannot help their opinions, Bernard dear. Do not get so angry with me.'

'But you would be perfect,' he insisted obstinately. 'Your voice has that mellow choir-boy tone and purity which are just what are required for the part. Once you wished you could be a singer.'

For a moment her expression became wistful. But she shook her head. 'Now I gain vicarious pleasure,' she said, still firm in her refusal. 'Bernard, you must not act like a spoiled child because I refuse. You surely knew I would.'

He looked at the large, gentle face he had known half his life. 'If you were my wife,' he jested without thought, 'I would make you. They could not object then.'

She stared back at him without reciprocal laughter in her eyes. 'You are joking.'

Bernard had thought he was joking. All at once he was unsure. What else was there? Who else was there? Anna was married, Grace was not of consequence. He liked Sophie, knew her. There were no surprises left. It made sense.

'I am not joking, Sophie.'

She moistened her lips with her tongue. 'I did – not know you considered me in that way.'

I do not. I do not. A pair of jade-coloured eyes blocked his vision. 'We know each other very well,' he said eventually.

'And love?'

'Love?' he repeated. 'What do you feel?' He turned the question on her.

'I asked you, Bernard.'

'Oh Sophie, that is unfair. You are my friend. I have always held you in esteem, you know that.'

279

How could he propose to a girl and not tell her he loved her? Yet that seemed the worst deceit of all; the admission of a sentiment he did not feel, debasing what he felt for someone else.

Sophie said: 'Maybe I am being unreasonable, Bernard. Perhaps it is equally important you like me, which I know to be true. Yes, I will marry you.'

She had made it easy for him, and Bernard whirled her into the air, whooping and leaping like a boy, ignoring the doubts that throbbed in his head.

The parents had not got the cousin they wanted, but when a girl attained the age of twenty-eight, was no beauty nor an heiress, one could not be too choosy; and certainly Sophie seemed happy.

'I give you my blessing, children,' her father said.

'Thank you, Papa.'

'Thank you, sir.'

And amidst the blessing and the drinking, Harold the would-be suitor arrived with an ostentatious bouquet of flowers, and so heard the news.

During the embarrassing hiatus he stood there, too dumb-founded to speak, the flowers suddenly absurd in his arms. He gazed almost idiotically at each face in turn, and felt they were laughing at him; the three of them with Bernard amongst them instead of himself.

'I had hoped —' Harold shook his head in a confused way. Then he flung the roses and carnations to the floor, appeared to choke — and left without a further word.

'He did not congratulate us,' Bernard commented, feigning a mournful voice, when he and Sophie were alone. He picked up one of the roses and handed it to her gallantly.

Ignoring it, she said: 'One cannot help feeling sad for him.' Then she asked quietly: 'Bernard, is this what you want?'

Her soft dark eyes were anxious and searching, and Bernard thought: *She is so kind, so trustworthy . . . And I am comfortable with her. Surely I am fortunate to have someone like her.*

He answered: 'Yes it is what I want, Sophie.'

'I am so happy then. I have loved you for a long time, you know.'

'Really? When I was thirteen, at my bar-mitzvah . . .' His voice trailed off, because he was no longer thirteen and his sentiment for her then was no longer valid.

The next morning, when they were still in bed and just five minutes after they had made love, Bernard told Grace: 'The time has come for us to part.'

'What?' She sat up alert, shocked out of the pleasant half-sleep she always lapsed into after sex. Pushing her straight black hair away from her mouth and eyes she said: 'You can't be serious.'

'But I am, Grace. You knew this was only a temporary arrangement.'

'But I thought –'

She looked like a forlorn child. A tear slid down her early-morning face and he touched it as he might an injured puppy which did not belong to him.

'Don't,' she spat at him, bolt upright in the wide bed, all white skin, hard tiny breasts and black hair.

'Grace,' Bernard said calmly, 'I am trying to be nice to you, to tell you gently. I am to be married.'

She sprang at him on all fours, snarling like a kitten. 'Oh, it's a fine thing for you to announce that, isn't it? I'm just some little whore you picked up, aren't I? Your little bit on the side. Cheap at the price. You thought you'd done your bit of chivalry by rescuing me, so then you could fuck me silly and go your own sweet way, didn't you? You never credited me with feelings, did you? What do you know about me or my past life? I was just your whore. I was, wasn't I?'

She was sobbing wildly and pummelling the bedclothes with clenched fists. He tried to pinion them, even to hold and comfort her, but – always quick in her movements – Grace snatched her body away from him.

'Don't you think I don't know about them letters you've been receiving? Do you think I'm so stupid? Oh you don't care do you, you with your high and mighty mind, treating me like bloody dirt as though I should be honoured to have you fuck

281

me. Don't you think I don't know those letters are from a woman?'

'If it makes you feel any better,' Bernard told her in a glacial voice, 'it is not her that I am marrying.'

'I don't care who you are marrying.'

All her gutter language came out now, and he listened impassively to the torrent of invective hurled at him. She was right: what did he know about her? And he *had* thought of her as his little whore. Certainly he had no inkling she had nurtured hopes of marrying him, or that he was the only person in her life who had ever been kind to her, or that while he was abroad she had tried to better herself by reading his books. . . .

'Bloody Jew!' Grace yelled finally. 'That's all you are. I'd been warned about you lot, and they was right. Bloody J –'

Bernard struck her very lightly but sharply across the face and shook her small body, his eyes blazing into her frightened ones.

'You may feel anything you wish towards me,' he told her in a constricted voice, 'you are perfectly entitled. But never call a Jew "bloody". Never. Do you hear me? Never dare say that again. It is a lie. A lie, you hear? Prejudice is evil and ignorant and your personal antipathy should not become confused. Now calm down, will you? And perhaps we could talk and remain friends if nothing else.'

He released her gently and she sat at the end of the bed, away from him and regarding him suspiciously.

'If I have hurt or upset you then I am sorry. It was never my intent, and perhaps you are right. I have not considered your feelings enough.'

She did not comment, and her expression was sultry and crushed.

'Grace – few of us are happy for much of the time, you know. You are not unique.'

'You always talk in bloody riddles, Bernard Foligno, that's your trouble.'

She wiped her nose on her bare arm and sniffed. Bernard smiled, and a smile quivered on her lips in return.

'Ah Grace, that's better.'

She thought – maybe after all they would not have got on; he was so moody. He would assist her in finding decent lodgings, she knew that. And she had all her fine new dresses. She was only seventeen – and you never knew who you might meet posing for an artist.

The housekeeper left that same day: 'All the comings and goings,' she accused. 'All the screaming. I've never seen such loose living. I cannot, but cannot cope with such goings-on, Mr Foligno.'

Two days later a cheerful new housekeeper/cook took her place and was delighted to find herself employed by such a nice young man, a quiet, clean-living young musician engaged to be married. He had explained to her that he was Jewish, but that neither he nor his future wife were religiously extreme, and she had replied in her expansive way that she didn't mind so long as she was paid on the nail, had her own room and a half-day off every week. Mrs Adams was a widow. She was stout, humorous, indefatigable, loyal to both master and mistress independently, and became part of the Foligno family with whom she remained for many, many years.

Bernard wrote to Anna via Miranda Leeming.

My darling Lioness,

I am just writing to let you know I have become engaged, and am getting married in a few months' time.

I do not know why I feel I should ask your forgiveness for this, but that is how it is.

I have known Sophie since I was a boy and have always looked upon her as a good friend. I respect her greatly. I find, however, that I am unable to lie and tell her I love her, and she seems to understand and to accept this regardless. It is a great disloyalty to her and an honour to you. I have a clear image of you in your red velvet dress,

*standing in my room at dear Mrs Ford's, and nothing I do
will shake this image.*

*Wrongly or rightly I still desperately want to see you, but
do not wish to intrude upon your potential happiness or
peace of mind, so I leave it for you to contact me. Perhaps
I am deliberately passing the guilt on to you. You see what
a devious husband I am planning to be – but I say this
with no pride.*

*Under these circumstances I have no right to be contem-
plating marriage, but I cannot help myself, darling.
A man needs to be married and perhaps have a family of
his own, and my liking for Sophie as a person has not
wavered over the years. She is a kind woman and from a
similar background to my own, and I believe she will
make me a good wife. Although I am unable to love her in
the way I ought, I shall try and make her the good
husband she deserves. If I commit injustices to her they
will not be intended with disrespect to herself or in any
way to wound. They will be because of myself.*

*You see, I make excuses for my behaviour already,
knowing that if you come to me, my dearest, I shall
instantly break one of the most famous of the ten
commandments and continue to do so wittingly.*

*This is my first letter to you, after your many to me, and
whilst I am glad you are still remembering me, you must
try and be as happy meanwhile as you can. It will not do
just to wilt away. Force yourself to paint, or ride, or to go
for walks – all the things you used to love which kept your
soul free. Remember Lovelace: 'Stone walls do not a
prison make', etc.*

> *Take heart, dearest Anna, and remember I shall
always love you.*
> *Yours ever, Bernard*
*P.S. I shall continue to live at this address after my
marriage.*

Anna's note in reply was brief:

My darling. Of course you must marry. Why ever not?
My love as ever – Anna

Four months later, on a sunny day towards the end of June,
Bernard and Sophie were wed.

They honeymooned in Italy for three weeks, then returned
to Number four Elm Tree Avenue and began their married
life.

Sophie's day started with breakfast in bed, brought in by the
doting Mrs Adams, and consisted of beaten raw egg and honey
which she drank for her throat, toast with jam and a pot of
lemon tea with more honey. She would then prepare and
dress herself simply and comfortably and go into the drawing-
room where she would, with interludes, practise singing for
six hours in preparation for her role as the Urchin in her
husband's opera. This was to have its première in mid-Novem-
ber at the height of the opera season. During the course of the
day she practised arpeggios and runs and scales, interval-leaps
and vowel exercises and breathing, until eventually after all
the 'limbering-up' she began on her songs – over and over the
ones already learned, and then onto another new one. When
Bernard was around he would sing the part of Widow,
Mother, Organ Grinder, Policeman, Beggar, in his funny flat
voice – making her laugh helplessly at his utterly music-less
tone – so that feigning great hurt he resorted to the piano for
all the parts.

Sophie had had no false illusions about marrying Bernard.
She was aware he did not feel about her as she did him, but
she knew far more about him than he realized, instinctively
understanding that he was a passionate man who could not be
content without love. She was wise enough to know it was
unlikely he would come to her for it, but she thought it equally
important that he liked her, and was confident that she could
fill a different kind of void in his life. They had each wedded
the other for their own reasons, she from love, he from

need, and each reason had attached to it its own importance.

Their days were companionable and sometimes amusing, and Bernard became accustomed to discussing matters with her, hearing her practise her singing, and asking her advice. He was neither so sad nor so lonely, and began to think he had done the right thing in marrying her.

The nights, however, were a different matter. Sophie was gripped with embarrassment by the sexual act and everything pertaining to it. She refused to let him see her naked, and limited lovemaking to twice a week when she submitted in an agony of suffering and self-consciousness. At his suggestion she touch him there, she was appalled, and when he tried to caress her she clamped her legs and was rigid and dry. They each came to dread Tuesdays and Thursdays, when the 'time' arrived, but Bernard was adamant about keeping to his routine, believing in his rights. Sometimes, with a slight pang of remorse, he thought about little Grace and their mad, uninhibited frolicking, and yet when he thought of Anna it was not in the carnal sense at all. When he thought of her, it was a reaching out of his being without an answer; he felt as incomplete mentally and bodily as an amputee.

Sophie had become a heavy-looking woman. Her beauty had blossomed too early and become over-blown in maturity; also she enjoyed her food – every aspect of it, from helping prepare it and having a pretty table laid, to consuming large quantities, much to the further detriment of her figure. She and Mrs Adams would pore enthusiastically over recipes together, discussing methods of cooking sauces and accompaniments, and Sophie would very often remain in the kitchen tasting and advising. She delighted in the creative satisfaction she derived from cooking – compiling unusual flavours and ideas and seeing if they worked. And then the presentation of the food, that was an art in itself. And somehow, too, food was the basis of home. The kitchen at its heart was her domain, and being in charge of it made her feel she was contributing to their marriage.

Despite all this feeding Bernard did not gain weight; the food passed through him without effect, burned up with his energy. But Sophie, always phlegmatic and slow, steadily grew larger.

Anxiously Bernard remarked to her: 'Sophie, you must not

grow any fatter, you will not be able to sing as the Urchin. He was starved and thin!'

'Bernard dear, nobody expects an opera singer to be thin.'

'I want my opera to be authentic, Sophie, to have dramatic visual impact.'

'I shall wear loose clothes to camouflage my shape,' she consoled him. 'Nobody will know what goes on underneath.'

During all this time Bernard was frantically busy with *The Lady and the Urchin* – attending meetings and rehearsals, liaising with orchestra and singers and director, pleading, coaxing, counselling, ordering, shouting and sometimes almost weeping with frustration. He had never dreamed that so much was entailed in the staging of an opera, and although he did not need to involve himself in all the aspects – and there were many who wished he would not – he insisted on supervising everything: the cast, the scenery, the costumes, the acting, the choreography, the direction. Each detail had to meet with his approval, and in the process he drove everyone to distraction. They were all experts in their field and resented the interference of a composer who knew nothing about their work and should confine himself to music. But Bernard knew what he wanted. It was his story, his idea, and he wanted it interpreted exactly and not in any way distorted. He was as inflexible as a possessive father.

Frederick Gye summoned him to his office: 'Mr Foligno, I really must insist you refrain from further involvement. It is unheard of for a composer to interfere with the entire production as you do.'

'Sir, if this opera is to be a success it must be done my way.'

'Really sir, you have ideas beyond your station.'

'Perhaps, but in the end I think you will be pleased.'

'I am beginning to dislike you, Mr Foligno.'

'Sir, I am sorry to hear that. But with respect, whether you like me or not is of no relevance to the success of my opera.'

It was a different Bernard who emerged: forceful, volatile, temperamental and impatient; continually annoyed by the apparent stupidity and laziness of nearly everybody except himself. He quarrelled with Mario and he quarrelled with

Adelina Patti. His days alternated between elation and rage, excitement and depression, and he wore himself out. For months he thought of little except the opera and became so insular that he seemed to be almost on another plane with his obsession. He felt omnipotent and lived in the temple of his head, saw nearly everyone outside with scathing eyes. He had become his own creation and could not separate himself from it.

Two nights before the première he told his wife: 'I shall never write another opera. It has all been too much for me.'

And a lot of other people too, she thought, but refrained from saying so.

'I cannot cope with everybody's stupidity,' Bernard complained. 'I cannot be stage director, set designer and goodness knows what else besides composer and conductor trying to put at least a feel of music into the wooden heads of an uninspired orchestra.'

'Are you satisfied now, dear?'

'Yes. Finally yes.' He turned to her, seeing her properly for the first time in days. 'Thank you, Sophie, for your support. I am sorry – I have not been easy, I know. You have been very patient and tolerant.'

'Are you satisfied with my singing?'

'More than satisfied, dear. You are superb. I hope I have never led you to believe otherwise. It is for that reason I was so adamant you accept the part.'

'And why you married me.'

Bernard was stunned and did not reply immediately, unsure in that instant what *had* been the reason behind his impulsive proposal.

Sophie was smiling, but in her expression he detected a look of hurt.

He touched her face. 'No dear, I married you for many reasons. I hope you realize that.'

'I do, Bernard,' she replied truthfully.

'I hope you do, because I have enormous respect for you, Sophie. Now I am going to rest. I am very, very tired indeed. Will you excuse me?'

He stumbled up to the bedroom and slept for eighteen hours.

*

The opera house was packed; there had been a great deal of publicity leading up to the event, and before the performance was due to commence the auditorium was filled with the roar of excited conversation. In the Royal Box sat the Prince of Wales, but it was well-known he was only interested in the dancing scenes of opera and slept through most of the rest . . . Everybody knew everybody, and in the audience were aristocracy, famous musicians, guests from Europe, critics, ordinary opera lovers and social climbers who came because surely this was *the* occasion at which to be seen.

Bernard had predicted to Sophie beforehand: 'Everybody will be there. There are those who will come out of curiosity and those who will want to enjoy an evening of music, but there are many who will come in the hope of witnessing my demise. There is nothing more boosting to the soul, nor better sport, than seeing the downfall of a man when he is not yourself.'

He strode into the orchestra pit. He felt almost God-like in his strength and with the force of his convictions. His head was proudly aloft, and he was not in the least perturbed when amidst the clapping, whistling and cheering somebody's voice rose clearly above the noise to shout:

'What do *you* know about opera, Mr Foligno?'

Bernard waited for the talking, shuffling, clearing of throats and rustling of programmes to die away, then raised his hands tenderly to beckon in the solo flute with the Urchin's theme, followed by the clarinets. The overture lasted ten minutes and comprised a slow, tranquil exposition section leading to the development and recapitulation, this being in the style of a bright gavotte. At this point the curtains parted to reveal a merry scene – a busy and colourful street market with dancing and juggling and a pair of live goats.

Sophie as the Urchin was wandering around the stalls picking up various fruits and setting them down. The cantabile singing of the crowd was interspersed by the cries of the marketeers, and Sophie's voice could be heard in brief bursts commenting on what she saw. Gradually she wended her way between the stalls and crowds to the forefront of the stage and glanced at Bernard who motioned her to come in.

A wave of something akin to love swept over him in that second's contact. She began the opening aria, her uniquely pure and ripe tones filling the auditorium, and Bernard, conducting his wife, felt a sense of all-embracing pride.

At the end of the first act the enthusiasm of the ovation was sufficient to convince Bernard that his opera was a success, but it was towards the end of the second act when Sophie, Adelina Patti and Mario sang their glorious trio that the entire audience completely lost its inhibitions and cheered and whistled so that the performance had to be interrupted for four minutes until things had quietened down.

The last act finished to tumultuous applause, and Bernard, holding hands with his wife, was called to the stage time and time again. He gazed wonderingly about him, exalted and thrilled and humbled by this wholehearted acknowledgement. He bowed deeply, then shrugged as though he did not know what was happening to him, and this little ingenuous act drove the audience even wilder, and as a smile broke on his face until he was laughing with joy, they shouted his name, chanted:

'FO-LI-GNO, FO-LI-GNO, FO-LI-GNO . . .'

Gibbons made one embarrassed appearance to loud 'Well-done's', and then the cast, including the four leading singers, stood aside to let the young composer take the curtain calls and accept what was his due.

Afterwards there were celebrations in the Crush Bar. Over a hundred people remained behind, audience mingling with musicians to drink champagne.

Sophie had changed into an evening dress which exaggerated her size, and naturally she looked weary. On stage she had given herself totally to her performance. Almost sacrificially she had offered her voice, her movements, her passion, and now she leaned slightly against Bernard, accepting the praise showered upon her and modestly insisting that all the credit should go to Adelina Patti. She was somewhat dazed by it all, and being an unpretentious person felt intimidated by the extraordinary happenings; she would have preferred to have gone home to bed, slept and awoken reasonably early and refreshed the following morning. There was another performance in two nights' time and she did not wish to be tired for it. But she smiled stoically, glad of Bernard's arm casually around her as he proudly introduced her to people and spoke to newspaper reporters.

A party of friends suddenly surrounded them and Sophie felt Bernard's muscles tense; then his arm was abruptly gone, and without it there she felt lonely.

Bernard had seen Anna.

Together with her husband she was with the Leemings and the Hamiltons, and at the sight of her, spectacular in an ornate apricot and white dress, his heart lurched. For a moment he was too overcome to speak, and all his movements seemed halted. Then she was rather pushed into the background as everyone else clamoured round Bernard.

Douglas Hamilton hugged his friend emotionally – standing back to look at him, then alternately thumping him on the back and embracing him once more. He had grown a beard, trimmed into a neat little point, in yet another attempt to look serious-minded, although as a musician of world-wide repute now this was hardly necessary. His spectacles were broken, and he kept pushing them back onto the bridge of his little nose from where they would slip forward once more making him sniff.

He beamed delightedly at Bernard: 'Dear chap –' the glasses fell onto his mouth and he readjusted them '– oh, but how splendid it was! Told you, did I not?' Thump, thump. 'Quite splendid. Unbelievable, in fact. It'll show 'em of course. At last England has its own opera. Pity old Cramer isn't alive. Sophie, dear girl – congratulations. Quite, quite superb. Always knew it of course. Waste of time teaching other people what you could be doing yourself.'

Then Sophie was cornered by Sir Alfred Leeming and Mr Hamilton and separated from Bernard who was talking to a fair-haired man and his ravishing wife.

'I think congratulations are in order,' Sir Giles Fotheringay said dryly. 'You have come a long way since we last met.'

291

'Thank you. I have been fortunate.' Bernard could feel the dampness on his forehead, and his throat was suddenly parched.

'You remember my wife of course,' the other said in a smooth tone.

Bernard found himself staring into that intoxicating face, unable to give any indication of how he felt. 'Yes of course.' He gave a quick mock bow. 'How are you keeping?' He could not bring himself to address her as 'My Lady'.

'I am well thank you, Mr Foligno.'

Anna had averted her gaze, but her cheeks were pink and he hoped Sir Giles did not notice.

'Your opera was magnificent,' she told him in a strained voice.

'Thank you, you are very kind,' Bernard murmured, thinking fearfully: *Perhaps she does not care any more*. 'Will you please excuse me?' And he left them abruptly to re-join Sophie.

His heart was pounding and his breathing felt constricted. *Dear God, I shall never recover from loving her*.

'I see he is as arrogant as ever,' Sir Giles said to his wife, failing to notice her silence and pallor now the flush had left her.

Bernard's mood had changed from its previous euphoria. Now he could only think: *I have to see her again, simply have to*.

Sophie was holding his arm, delighted to have him by her side once more. Poor Sophie – it had been her night of triumph too, and he had almost loved her.

'I am suddenly weary, my dear,' Bernard said. 'Shall we leave them to celebrate without us?'

He led her away from the party, not daring to look back at Anna.

Something has happened, Sophie thought. *In those few minutes something happened to change him*.

It was Thursday, the night for their bi-weekly ritual, but he could not bring himself to make love to the heavy form beside him.

'Perhaps we are both a little too weary, my dear . . . Would you mind if just tonight we missed it?'

She shook her head in the dark, relieved to be excused the mortifying ceremony, and pressed his hand and stroked his long fingers in the safe knowledge that this little display of affection would not be misinterpreted as a sexual advance.

They awoke late the following day, and Bernard was barely dressed when Douglas arrived at noon. They lunched together, whilst Sophie had hers upstairs in bed.

'Dear chap, before we go any further I have a letter for you. And this one is not from Glorious John.'

He hurriedly handed him the letter and Bernard tore it open. The writing was untidy and rushed:

My dearest,

How brilliantly clever you are – although you must surely know that by now. I wept through the entire performance last night. I could not help myself. I was so stunned to realize that it was really you who had composed this.

Bernard – it is no good my trying to forget you. I cannot. Believe me I have tried during the last months, for what good can come of a relationship between you and I? And now there are four of us.

Your wife is so extremely talented, and looks so very nice a person, the sort of woman I should actually like as a friend. Yet I covet her husband. I feel that I am very wicked; I made my own decision to marry, and yet I contemplate disrupting other lives. But dearest, I yearn so for you.

I am writing to say that this time I leave the choice for you. If you desire to meet me, send a reply via Douglas. If you do not I promise I shall understand and never bother you again.

As I seal this, I think that perhaps I shall not deliver it, and then – that of course I shall.

> *Your loving Anna*

Bernard put it with the small bundle in the bureau. 'How did you come by it?'

'She gave it to Miranda early this morning and Miranda brought it directly to me. What does she say?'

'She wants to see me. She leaves the choice to me. Oh Doug, what must I do?'

'Dear chap – impossible for anyone but you to decide. You know in your head what you ought not to do, but in your heart what you are inclined to. I cannot possibly advise you. Bernard, I have known Sophie since my early days at the Conservatoire, and I've always liked her as you are aware. But the other one – she is another matter again. She is superb. Dear chap, I understand your predicament.'

'The trouble is, Doug, it is not a predicament. I am married only a few months to a woman totally supportive of me, and my head knows what it ought to do, as you say. Yet there is no choice for me. There has only ever been one woman who mattered to me, and it will always be the same.'

Upstairs Sophie sipped egg and honey; downstairs Bernard took a sheet of paper and wrote his reply to Anna:

> *Dearest – Am playing with the Hallé Orchestra in Manchester on November the twenty-ninth. Can you arrange to be with me? We would be away two nights. Take the nine o'clock a.m. train from Euston, and if you see me on the platform make no acknowledgement. Buy a first-class ticket and go into the last carriage.*
>
> *I love you – B*

He sealed the note and gave it to his friend and accomplice. He heard Sophie moving about upstairs and felt a pang. The guilt had started.

Chapter Eighteen

Bernard and Douglas were at a club in St James's enjoying a lunch of roast beef accompanied by claret and catching up on each other's news.

Douglas asked: 'Tell me, dear chap, do you still think of yourself as a pianist, or will you agree now that you are a composer foremost?'

'Douglas, when we were boys you once asked me whether I considered myself English or Jewish, and I lost my temper because the issue was such an intricate one, and anyway I did not see why I had to choose, why I could not be both English and Jewish. This whole business of identity-seeking is so confounding, yet we all crave it in much the same way as we crave God. Now as a *musician* I am classless and have my title, and I am content with it. I trust you understand the gist of my response.'

'But of course. You were most articulate! And typically evasive. However you must learn that while music is to be taken seriously, we are not. We have been put on this earth as a joke. Talking of jokes, there is an article in this month's *Punch* called 'Pity the Poor Lawyers'. Very humorous, and naturally I thought instantly of the toad. You must show it to him when you get a chance. He will be enraged . . . And the princess – how is she taking her fame?'

'Very calmly all considering. But she has announced that after her role as the Urchin she will not perform again. I cannot understand it. It is what she always wanted. What will she do instead? She will teach the odd pupil without half her talent, and bustle about the home indulging in gluttony.'

'You must not be unkind, dear chap. She has formed her own conclusions, and that is commendable.'

'Oh, I accept and respect her wishes. Anyway she has two more performances left before she can retire to the kitchen.'

'Dear chap, she is a good sort.'

'I know,' Bernard said wearily. 'I know too well all her many virtues and merits. Perhaps I did her a grave unfairness in marrying her without love – but I can do nothing about it now. And she married me, knowing of all my shortcomings. And I must remember that I rescued her not only from the obscene clutches of my cousin, but also from spinsterhood, and have provided her with a good home away from her sniffing mother. I must not feel so guilty, Doug. As long as she does not know about Anna, it cannot hurt her. I have no wish to hurt her, you know, for I am fond of her in my own way. And I never lied about loving her.'

'Dear boy, as I watch your fork poised, about to enter your mouth with the forbidden, incorrectly killed beef, I think back to Paris and Madame Becaud's when you tried to justify that first evil bite!'

'Douglas, my friend, you are full of tedious analogies today. . . .'

It was Friday night. The traditional Shabat dinners were now held at Elm Tree Avenue, and they all sat round the big heavy-legged mahogany table which had come with the house: Bernard and Sophie at either end, Helen, Elizabeth and Sophie's parents either side. And two other guests – Harold and his father. Harold sat between little Elizabeth and Sophie, addressing the table generally in his barrister's boom, and pointedly ignoring his host who had been unapproachable since he had heard of the extra dinner guests.

'I refuse to have that man in my house,' he had told Sophie, raising his voice which was something he rarely did.

'Dear, your mother asked me. I could not refuse.'

'Why. *Why*?'

'Dear, please calm down. Your mother felt sorry for your uncle. Apparently since he has been back in England he has become very lonely and distressed, and virtually invited himself. And of course he insisted on being with Harold on Shabat.'

'I refuse. Besides, I despise the old man. The pair of them are as bad as one another – well almost – and equally manipulative.'

'Dear, you cannot refuse without putting your mother in a predicament.'

'I am the master of this house,' Bernard pouted, sounding like a small defeated boy.

'I know, dear,' his wife mollified him. 'It is just this once. They are family after all.'

'I would prefer to forget that. And I doubt it will be just this once,' he counteracted. 'Will my uncle be less lonely or distressed next Friday or the Friday after? You know how I feel about Shabat. Now it is ruined for me. Harold will preside over the table as if it is his home.'

Sophie was always mystified by Bernard's religious idiosyncrasies. He wrote on Shabat, took a carriage on Shabat, ate unkosher meat on Shabat (or any other day of the week), frequently missed synagogue attendance – yet he laid tefillin every morning, and since they had been married guarded his sacred Friday night dinners like a dog.

But for Bernard Friday nights were redolent with memories. He recalled those times as a boy, when they would all gather round the piano in the family room after dinner. Life had been simple and quarrels were far in the future. Now he wanted to recreate those nights and for them to be perpetuated. His father had been a traditionalist. In some ways he was too. And he would not have his Fridays 'desecrated' by his cousin.

The past few months had wrought a change in Harold. It was as though, since he had lost hope of winning Sophie, he had lost all vanity in his appearance. He had gained even more weight, his portly body degenerating into obesity. His lizard eyes were buried in pads of flesh, and the chin fell into multiple folds that merged without definition into the short neck. Now, too, there was a look of dissipation in his face, and harshly embedded lines around his mouth. From a resentful, bitter and spiteful boy he had grown into an embittered and vindictive man.

This Friday night, with Bernard sitting in silence at the head of his table, Harold expounded his views on religion. In his conversation he attacked the Reform synagogue which, as everyone present knew, was now Bernard's synagogue. Harold's implications were that the Reform breakaway was tantamount to converting to Christianity, and he had no time for these defectors who were little better than anti-semitic Gentiles, and probably read Karl Marx.

Harold's father had lately become very senile and his mind disorientated. The innuendos of the conversation were lost on him, and while everyone else listened in embarrassment, and Bernard's anger festered, the old man nodded his head continually in agreement, punctuating the commentary with a regular and proud: 'You see – my son knows what he is talking about. He is an important barrister now.'

Harold said: 'What I cannot abide about this new liberal-thinking breed is the way it superimposes its views over others.'

He looked pointedly from Bernard to Sophie, and at that stage Bernard got up from the table without speaking and went to his bedroom.

He boiled with rage. He would have liked to fight with this gross cousin of his who had inveigled his way into his house, could have pummelled him into the ground. Nothing compared to the dislike he bore Harold.

Eventually, for the sake of everyone else, and armed with a copy of *Punch*, he returned downstairs. Harold was drinking the last of his favourite port – refilling his glass until the decanter was empty. He was sitting in the large 'grandfather' chair, sinking into his own fat. He was depraved, this grotesque creature with his perversions.

'You go beyond the limit,' Bernard whispered fiercely to Harold.

'And you went beyond the limit when you married Sophie. You knew I planned to marry her.'

'But she did not plan to marry you, Harold.'

'I warn you, sir, you are too impudent. I am watching you, Bernard. One day you will make a wrong turning and I shall be there to expose you.'

'Are you threatening me, sir?'

'No. Merely warning you. If you are forewarned then you will not feel threatened.'

'Children, it is rude to whisper,' said Sophie's mother cheerfully, daubing her dripping nose with her handkerchief.

And they resumed, as far as it was possible, normal Friday-night proceedings.

'Such a lovely evening,' his uncle said when they departed. 'Such a lovely, lovely evening. You have made me happy by asking me, and Harold also. May I be invited again one day? It is so lonely, just the two of us.'

'Never again,' Bernard said later to Sophie. 'No, no, no.'

'Dear, just the very odd occasion.'

Bernard was about to answer when he saw the *Punch* lying on the table where he had left it, open at the relevant article.

'Damnation – I forgot to show him the article. It was his fault. I quite forgot. Oh, how frustrating that is. And it would have made him so annoyed.' Bernard banged his fists together in exasperation.

'What article, dear?' Sophie enquired mildly.

'Oh read it yourself, Sophie. It is there on the table. Mark my words – one day I shall get the better of Harold.'

And he stormed upstairs where she could hear him banging about.

A few days later Bernard left for Manchester. Anna was not on the platform and when he checked all the compartments in the end carriage she was not in any of them. He looked at his watch. Four minutes to go and she was not there. A gradual sense of resignation and inevitability came over him replacing the hot excitement he had felt earlier. It was not to be. Possibly she had thought better of it; possibly circumstances had made it difficult to get away. Whatever the reason – it was not to be. And when he returned from his trip, he would be able to look his wife in the eye and answer her honestly when she enquired: 'How was it?' Would the lack of guilt compensate for his disappointment?

Anna found Bernard slumped in the compartment staring out of the window, blowing smoke rings from his pipe and his collar turned up against the cold. She went silently over to him and he looked up with an old man's defeated eyes and saw her before him, wearing a silver-grey coat lavishly trimmed with fur.

He gave a great exhalation of relief. 'Thank God you came,' he said, so softly it was almost a whisper.

He stood up and very gently enfolded her in his arms, lightly pressing his lips to hers and keeping them there, just feeling their soft warmth, and closing his eyes.

'The horse went lame,' Anna explained when they drew apart. 'I am sorry. Of course I came, darling.'

'And your husband? What have you said to him?'

'He is away anyway, in Yeovil for four days on business. There is a combined cattle feed he is interested in. It is all he cares about – cattle.' Anna laughed wickedly. 'The only time I ever see a light in Giles's eyes is when he has brought some poor pheasant to the ground or when he is discussing cattle.'

Her gaze searched his face, and she traced its outline with a gloved finger. 'I have longed so badly to see you. It is terribly wrong, I realize, but I have longed for it nevertheless.'

'Hush – we will not speak of the wrongs. Now we have the whole compartment to ourselves for five hours and I want to hear what has been happening to you.'

'But your news is so much more exciting. There is so much I want to hear about you!'

'And hear it you will, in good time. But it is your turn first.'

Outside the guard blew his whistle and the engine echoed it. There was a jolt and the wheels began to turn slowly.

'How exciting this is, is it not, my Anna? Now dearest, put your hand in mine and tell me everything.'

The first months of Anna's marriage had been taken up with re-decorating the house in Brook Street. It was Grandfather Edmund's old home and had been left in trust for her until she married, or if she did not marry, when she attained the age of twenty-five. The day she took possession she visited it on her own and spent several hours in the empty building – the furniture had gone to various other members of the family. She went from room to room, her footsteps sounding exaggeratedly loud and echoing. Tears ran from her eyes as she recalled all those happy times. She remembered, too, that Bernard had been in this house, had stayed there. He would have sat in the library, and played the piano in the music room. Who had the piano now? She would have caressed the keyboard knowing Bernard's hands had embraced it.

Anna was careful not to destroy any of the original character, and left the music room and the old library untouched. But the rest of the house was too masculine for her taste, and she decorated it according to her requirements, keeping one room for her very own and transforming it into a restful, pale-blue 'boudoir'. Downstairs, adjoining the rear lobby, was a second small butler's pantry where Murphy had used to clean the shoes and polish silver. This area was full of light and it was here that Anna installed her paints and artists' tools. She had two sets of everything for she and Sir Giles divided their time fairly equally between London and the estate near Tetbury.

Her husband resented her painting. He resented anything which made her independent of him, she decided. Anything she enjoyed he would dampen with a sarcastic remark. Any ardour she expressed was treated contemptuously. If he did not love her, he nonetheless wanted totally to possess her; to have her pliable in his control. In bed, nightly, and often twice nightly, so that it would be hours before she fell asleep again, he took her without preliminaries, ramming hard into her, tackling her from all angles regardless of the person whose body he was invading. Never a word of tenderness was spoken during this loveless act, and had she been a virgin their first time together would have been painful and terrifying. Anna awoke leaden, aching and lethargic each morning, and only when he was safely gone from the house did she relax.

Oh dear God, why did I marry him? she thought over and over again.

She thought continuously of Bernard and how she should have had the courage to elope with him; that by not doing so she had gone against those paths of 'fate' she truly believed had led them to one another. She had only herself to blame for her dreadful mistake – and her married life closed in on her like stagnant water.

Sir Giles made her purchase all new clothes. 'I want you to be the most fashionable, talked-about wife in society, Anna.'

'Giles, I am quite happy with my wardrobe.'

'My dear, it is far too – ordinary. I want you to be completely reattired.'

'But my trousseau; I have only just had all those dresses made.'

'They are not grand enough, Anna.'

'Giles, I am not a "grand" person,' she pleaded. 'I like simple clothes.'

'You will dress as it pleases me, madam.'

She compromised. She took the name of his sisters' dressmaker, a lady renowned for her elaborate designs, and modified them a little more to her liking.

She could not object that Giles was cruel or even inattentive, but their conversation was unnatural and stilted and mealtimes a trial of polite discussion. When she attempted to enquire about his business he answered: 'You do not want to concern yourself with such matters, my dear.'

'Oh but I do, Giles. It is proper for a wife to interest herself in her husband's affairs.'

'I do not find it proper, Anna,' he rebuked her. 'I find it unfeminine. It is the duty of a wife to make herself attractive and look after the home, not to bother about masculine pursuits such as business matters or politics.'

'But I find such topics interesting.'

'I cannot help that.'

'So there is much conversation that is precluded me?'

'My dear, why must you always make such an issue out of everything? Incidentally I prefer your hair put up. It is not in the least sophisticated tumbling to your waist.'

'I like it the way it is, Giles. You must allow me some discretion in my own appearance.'

'Oh very well. You are always so contrary.'

Anna spent hours painting. Now she was experimenting with oils, and the scenes she painted were strong in colour and content; harsh scenes – of grief or of violence, of poverty or death, and she hid her canvases after each session, believing her husband would be angry if he discovered them.

They entertained lavishly – people whom Anna found superficial and wearisome. But Sir Giles was determined to introduce Anna properly into society.

'The trouble is, Anna, your upbringing has been so unusual you do not seem to know quite what is expected of you or how to behave. You are content to be a recluse.'

'Giles, you are always trying to change me.'

'No I am not. I only try to encourage you to mingle in society.'

'Then may I have Miranda to stay? I have not seen her for ages.'

'Miranda is not "society". The Leemings are outlandish.'

'Please, Giles. She is my dearest friend. And she has just become engaged.'

'Oh very well.' He grunted to acknowledge her thanks at this great concession on his part.

Shortly before Miranda's arrival in early December, Anna saw Bernard playing at St James's Hall; and when she saw all his passion and sensuousness transferred to his piano, when she saw and listened to him in his magnificence and was unable to go to him, she felt physically weak. She began to tremble throughout her body, yet all the while had to maintain a calm façade.

I love him, love him, love him. . . .

When Miranda arrived three days later, bursting with the need to tell her friend Anna at last confided her secret.

Miranda was thrilled. She clasped her hands excitedly and her eyes sparkled mischievously. 'But this is all perfectly wonderful!' She hugged Anna – and then stood back and pouted a little. 'Why did you not tell me sooner? It is bad enough I did not realize for myself. But at least you could have told me.'

'I was trying to forget him,' Anna said. 'And it is not in the least perfectly wonderful, as you say. I long for him. It gnaws at me, this longing. Miranda, you have no idea – it never abates. If it is wicked to have such thoughts then I cannot help it. Oh dearest Miranda, why did I marry Giles? He does not care for me, and nor does my father. I did it to please each of them, but it has resulted merely in Giles acquiring one more possession for his collection, and my father dusting the shelf where I sat troubling him. And in this mix-up *I* was the acquiescing instrument.

'I want at least to write to Bernard, but it would be so wrong. And besides, he might no longer wish to hear from me.'

'Dearest, I am sure from what you tell me he will always want to hear from you. I know Bernard of old. He is not fickle. And it is not wrong to write. Giles is a stuffy prig and he deserves it!'

It was just what Anna had wanted to hear, and that evening she wrote her first letter, never dreaming that Bernard might be co-habiting with another young woman. She felt better for writing, that at least a link had been re-established, albeit a one-sided link. A couple of months passed, and no word came from him – by her request; until that letter:

My darling Lioness . . . Am getting married in a few months' time . . .

Anna realized that this time their tenuous link must finally be severed.

Once more she declined into depression and took refuge in her painting – larger canvases this time, where giant mystical birds swooped with rats in their beaks and weeping children dangling from their wings.

Stone walls do not a prison make. Giles was her stone wall, and Anna felt herself withering under his suppression, becoming smothered by the weight she had taken upon herself.

Then, some months later, came the invitation from the Leemings to join their party at Covent Garden, and so – a year and half since she had last seen him – Anna came face to face with Bernard.

Once again it was as a result of Miranda's encouragement that she wrote her note to Bernard. At the end of the evening, almost in tears, Anna whispered to her: 'He did not even seem glad to see me.'

'Of course he was. He left because of it. He did not know what to do, poor man. You should have seen the way he was straining to catch glimpses of you. I promise.'

'I was too embarrassed to look. Oh, I long to see him again. I wish that I might just write.'

'Well do so,' her friend told her obligingly.

'And so now here we are,' Bernard said, adjusting his position on the hard seat, which was beginning to make his bottom feel numb.

Their hands were still tight together, as if bandaged, and momentarily he looked at the knot their fingers made, thinking that it seemed so symbolic of their love.

'You have been so unhappy,' he stated sadly.

'It is my doing,' she replied. 'And now I am making others unhappy.'

'Anna – listen to me. You are making no one unhappy. Sophie and Giles will not find out. But me, you are making me happy. Now let us have a pact: that we will not speak of either Sophie or Giles, but only of us. We will indulge ourselves and be greedy for each other, and we will treasure our time together, with no remorse or recriminations.'

From Manchester station they took separate cabs, arrived at the hotel within minutes of one another, and making no sign of recognition, discreetly checked in, in adjoining rooms. It was a new hotel, constructed in red brick in the oppressive style Bernard so disliked, featuring too much heavy mahogany, dark velvet, pannelling, stained glass and elaborate carving. He also disliked Manchester, and wished that he could have arranged somewhere more romantic for their meeting than a hotel near the station. However, they were together after a year and a half and that was all that was relevant.

He pulled the curtains in her room to shut out the grey street, and slowly began to undress her. Anna hesitated.

'What is it, darling?'

'Bernard . . . I have my – woman's time. It has just started this morning. I am so embarrassed.'

For a moment Bernard was stricken. In the Jewish faith it was

305

forbidden to have sexual intercourse when a woman was menstruating. But how many times now had he contravened the laws of his religion?

'It does not matter, dearest.'

'But it is – embarrassing,' she claimed, not knowing about the religious aspect. Her expression was shy, her eyes averted from his.

'Hush. Nothing is embarrassing between two people who love each other as we do. Everything that comes from you, from your body, I love.'

He lay her naked and smoothly golden like a prize on the bed. He stroked her with tender fingers and gazed at her wonderingly, almost reverently, and touched the spot of blood on her inner thigh. And then at last he entered her – to become part of this woman whom he adored spiritually and bodily.

Late that afternoon Bernard had to attend a rehearsal for the following evening. 'But we will order two huge dinners to be sent to our respective rooms for when I return,' he told Anna. 'And we will combine them and have a feast.'

'And then we will be too full for other activities.'

Anna, still in bed, rolled over lazily and scratched her fingers gently down Bernard's back. He sat on the edge, pulling on his shoes.

'Never,' he said turning to face here. 'We will make love all night and only be full of each other. Now I must go, my Anna.'

'Bernard – I am so happy with you. I am not entitled to such a happiness.'

'And I am so happy with you. And we are both entitled to it.'

The next morning they awoke late and passed the day leisurely, strolling in the park arm in arm whilst flakes of snow fell spasmodically from a yellow sky. Anna wore the same outfit she had travelled in, her hair tucked into the fur-trimmed hat, reminding Bernard of a Russian princess. They visited the fifteenth-century cathedral and the City Art Gallery and the port, and took a cab to the industrial area with its cotton mills and iron foundries and smoke-gushing chimneys. They ate continental-style cream cakes in a tea shop – and every moment they spent together made them increasingly aware of time hurrying by.

Charles Hallé, born Karl Hallé in Westphalia, Prussia in 1810, did not settle in England until 1849. He had visited the March before to hear Chopin play, and had himself played Beethoven's Emperor Concerto in one of the Gentlemen's Concerts in Manchester. He was subsequently persuaded by the committee of these Concerts to become their conductor, and from these beginnings the Manchester Orchestra was born.

He was a dignified man with neatly-brushed greying hair and deeply etched lines about his mouth – and more than any other musician in England Bernard respected Charles Hallé for his achievements. To perform with such a celebrated man, to have been selected by him in the first instance, was an honour.

Bernard took his place at the Broadwood piano and waited for silence in the auditorium. He felt the beginning tingles of familiar pleasure and his heart swelled with well-being. Somewhere in the front row of the Free Trade Hall sat his love, and the knowledge that she was there filled him with joy.

Of all the piano concertos, Beethoven's fourth was one of Bernard's favourites, and his ability to convey sentiment, his sensitive intimate touch, lent themselves to this work which he never tired of performing, and which seemed to wrench emotion from him every time he played it.

After the interval he was joined on stage by the young Parisian harpist, Isabel Lagrange, and the flautist Benjamin Wells, flute professor from the Royal Academy of Music and President of the London Flute Society. By now the atmosphere in the hall, already conditioned by what had gone beforehand, was one of camaraderie. The feeling of geniality extended to the musicians, and when the little ensemble played Bernard's ten delightful sonatas the empathy between the three performers was transmitted to the audience and drew a reciprocal reaction. They were noisily appreciative, and Bernard, standing beside Hallé, gazed around the hall with that same sense of incredulity and gratitude he always had.

He spotted Anna, beautiful in a discreet dark-blue gown. She was nearly as tall as the men who flanked her and was clapping so hard he could imagine the palms of her hands burning. A great spasm of love gripped him at the sight of her, and with it came the decision:

I shall never let her go again. There must be a way. I cannot let her go from me.

And with this illuminating decision life at long last had meaning.

Sophie had organized a huge dinner for Bernard's return. She had dressed especially for the occasion in an attempt to be attractive to him, and had chosen the rich green carefully to compliment her colouring. Predictably she asked: 'How was your trip? How was the concert?'

And Bernard found he was able to look tranquilly into her trusting brown eyes and reply: 'It was fine, my dear. Everything went well. Manchester is a quite dreadful and dreary city – damp, dirty and full of modern atrocities. But my concert was a success.'

'I know. Davison wrote most favourably in *The Times* this morning.'

'I did not know he was there. It seems he is becoming my greatest ally. What did he say?'

'He mentioned your "intensely intimate playing" as though you were "letting us in on his life . . ." He used words such as "mystical" and "entwined sounds" about your sonatas. I will show you the article afterwards.'

Do you like my dress? she longed to ask him. *Are you glad to be home?* Instead she enquired: 'You did not catch a cold in Manchester?'

'No, why should I?'

'Your room was warm? You had plenty of bedclothes?'

'Yes, Sophie.' He laughed at her concern.

'I missed you.'

'Dear, you must become accustomed to my absences. A musician travels a great deal and for long periods.'

'I realize that,' Sophie said hurriedly, not wanting to sound as though she was complaining. 'Of course you must be free to travel.'

She herself did not care for travel. She found it tedious and became sick easily.

'And how have you been, my dear?' Bernard asked dutifully.

'I – Bernard, have you forgotten – today is your birthday?'

'Goodness! Why did you not tell me?'

'I assumed you knew, dear! Mrs Adams and I have prepared a special meal to celebrate.'

'Sophie, you think too much of food.'

Her expression was hurt – she had looked forward so much to this evening and planned it in advance.

Bernard was immediately contrite. 'Dear Sophie, I was teasing you, and I am looking forward greatly to the meal, I assure you. My appetite is whetted at the thought.'

'You are sure?' she asked doubtfully.

He was not in the least hungry and extremely tired. 'I am sure,' he answered, kissing her on the cheek and noticing her dress for the first time. 'Is that a new dress?'

'Yes.' Sophie smiled at his belated observance.

'It suits you, my dear.'

'Thank you. Bernard – I have a small present for you, for your birthday.'

'Dear, presents are not necessary.'

'Well, I wanted to.'

'Then, thank you.'

She handed Bernard a large, heavy, wrapped package and he opened it carefully.

It was a beautiful walnut gentleman's combined toilet and writing box for travelling. Inlaid with ivory, it had concealed drawers and compartments and was fitted with pens, cut-glass bottles and silver-lidded jars. There was a small inkwell, seals and wax, and the writing tray which pulled out was covered in black leather.

'Sophie –' Bernard shook his head slowly and ran a hand over his face. What he wanted to say caught in his throat.

He lifted out and replaced each item in turn; opened tiny drawers and unscrewed bottles; peered at himself in the mirror which was inset on the inside of the lid; ran his fingers over the tiny seals, and locked and unlocked the box itself with the dainty little key.

He was as thrilled as a child. He had never possessed anything finer, and he liked it quite as much as a bureau! His wife studied his reaction intently.

'Sophie,' he said again, 'dear – you have been so extravagant.'

'But do you like it?' she asked impatiently.

'Like it? I think it is wonderful. Quite the most wonderful thing you could have bought me. It is so very, very splendid.'

'It is a small token of my devotion, Bernard.'

'Thank you. Thank you, dear.'

While he had been in Manchester with Anna without thought for Sophie, she had been planning his birthday, buying him this magnificent present, spending her money on him . . . And just then he was unable to meet her sweet gaze.

It was his twenty-sixth birthday, and it was also a Thursday night, Bernard realized reluctantly as he lay beside Sophie in bed. He clung to the memory of Anna and lay rigidly. Sophie's hand crept onto his. Mistakenly she thought he would want to make love, and this was her timid way of showing she was willing. His birthday treat! How selfless she was. Wearily and unenthusiastically he turned to her and rummaged beneath her cotton and lace shift. Her hair was concealed by a cap and he could smell the perfumed smell of cream on her face. He had never seen her body naked, but as he touched her he felt the folds of fat beneath his fingers, and her breasts were huge soft mamillas like the udders of a cow.

He thought back to the previous night when he and Anna had lain bathed in the glow of the street-lamp outside the window. Through a gap in the curtains it had shone in white patches on their skin, highlighting different parts of their bodies – their curves, their angles. Bernard re-lived each sensation and imagined her stretched out before him – supple and sensuous, her hair untidily tangled on the pillow. By thinking of her he was able to do his duty to his wife.

That night he fell deeply asleep and dreamed he was walking down a dark avenue of tall trees that gave him the sudden scent of childhood, and he became aware of a twinge of nostalgia. He slowly walked down this avenue, seeming to make no progress, and all the while he had a hankering to reach out to whatever was there and draw it to him as something that, if he let it go, he would never know again. What was it – this curious yearning? What in his mundane childhood had been so good that now he had to reclaim it? It was a mild sweet-smelling day and the chestnut trees in young pale leaf beckoned him on. He was so content. And he continued his lone passage down the long road with its hidden meanings.

A fortnight later, on the second day of Channukah, Bernard and Sophie attended synagogue. She sat beside him, as was the custom with the modified Reform regulations, feeling strangely conspicuous. The service too was different, being shorter, and some of it read in English, and Sophie wished she could be in her own synagogue with its traditions and familiar songs.

It was on the way back, when they took a short cut through a tiny cobbled mews off Baker Street, that Bernard saw the place: a humble cottage with a sign outside indicating it was for sale.

The next day he bought it. It was perfect; tiny, tucked away, and in an unfashionable area. A hideaway for himself and Anna.

PART FOUR

Chapter Nineteen

Two and a half years passed during which Lord Derby replaced Russell, and Disraeli replaced Derby, reforming parliamentary rulings and laws in his efforts to prevent the ascendance of Gladstone, and ending public hangings as 'entertainment'. But his term in office was short-lived and he was defeated in the General Election by the liberal Gladstone, who set about a programme of reform measures aimed at the welfare of the poor. It was a time of change: in fashion, in tolerance, in consciousness, in the rising of the Prussian army and reduction of power held by the British abroad; and most moderate people thought the changes were for the better.

It had been a busy period for Bernard. He travelled extensively in England and Europe, still taught part-time at the Academy, and composed a number of major works:

There was a symphony commissioned by Mr Beavis that had a moderate success, but not as much as Bernard had hoped; a song cycle written for Mario which had delighted the tenor; a set of variations; but most importantly, two other works which established him as one of the foremost of contemporary composers: a cello concerto whose second movement contained his 'Homage — In Memoriam' and was inscribed with the dedication *To Gilbert, that maligned, great cellist*; and a concerto for clarinet and viola — those two transposing instruments that had been his 'thorns' as a child. This work he addressed to *J.B.C.* with the words, *You see, your young sir finally mastered it*.

He became known as England's own composer, whose versatility proved that he knew every aspect of music, and it was said of him that the originality of his usage of each instrument was sheer inspiration.

Somehow during those two and a half hectic years when it seemed that every moment was accounted for, and he had not a second to himself, Bernard divided his time between his two women; between St John's Wood and Edgerstone Mews South, slinking from his marriage with its bi-weekly rituals and Friday night dinners, to the forbidden joys of adultery.

Yet neither Bernard nor Anna thought of themselves as playing the traditional lover/mistress roles. They saw themselves simply as two people who had been unable to wed.

Their 'love nest' was a secret, wonderful haven, a tiny place of happiness with its two small bedrooms upstairs and single reception room downstairs. It had previously belonged to an old lady who had owned a millinery shop locally and in a cupboard they had found dozens of hats and bonnets which Anna had gleefully tried on. They had the interior redecorated and bought a few simple pieces of furniture, and the outside was painted a rosy pink. Wisteria coiled and wound around the old shuttered windows and front door.

Here in this humble home Bernard knew peace of mind and a sense of bodily completeness. He called Anna, 'My very great love'. With her he felt that he had attained more than his quota.

'A man who is running and believes that he can go no faster,' Bernard told Anna once, 'and then his legs move of their own accord and he reaches another level that is sublime. That is how I feel. With you I am more than replete; I am brimming, spilling, overflowing.'

Sometimes, after she had left, Bernard would remain in the tousled bed. Anna's scent lingered and the smell of their lovemaking was still in the room. He would burrow his nose in the bedclothes and inhale all those odours, redolent of passion and of tenderness; and it seemed that her presence was still there.

Their biggest sorrow was that they could not go to public places together. He was too famous and she too recognizable. There was so much they would have liked to have shared, so many pleasures which must be precluded them.

'Shared memories are the foundations of a relationship,' Anna remarked wistfully, shortly after they had bought the cottage. 'Incidents become like old, tightly packed leaves. You can peel them separate and find another and then another.'

'We shall have our very own memories,' he consoled her.

'Yes, and we must surely make the best of what we have,' she agreed more cheerfully. 'We have our little base here, and though we are not free to go out and do things together, at least we no longer have to endure being separated.'

But privately Bernard dreamed of a life where she was always at his side. Sitting patiently as she sketched him; playing chess with her and watching her frown in concentration; lying in bed whilst she read poetry to him – always he was conscious of that rare magnetism she held for him. *She is exceptional*, he would think. *A truly supreme and complete woman*.

Sometimes they were parted for several weeks when he travelled, and when he was in England they were forever aware of the clock and of their responsibilities. There would be the rueful goodbyes, the hurried arrangements for the next meeting – then the going home to their marital partners and the effort of acting, the weariness of deceit, the very real guilt.

'A musician is not meant to have a smooth-running life,' Bernard told Anna. 'A musician must have a life which is a balance of tranquillity and tension. He cannot afford to be bland. I cannot believe he can compose effectively and lead an ordinary existence. You see – a musician is not an ordinary man. His music must be an extension of himself, and if that self is bland then what he expresses will be also. I decided a long time ago I would not be "small". I decided I would rather not be mentioned at all than mentioned in a small way.'

'And where do I fit in?' Anna teased him. 'My life is no more smooth-running than yours and I am not a musician.'

'You are an artist,' he said seriously. 'You are good enough to exhibit. You have talent.'

'I also have Giles,' she reminded him wryly.

In St John's Wood Bernard and Sophie now led a very social life. They had a wide circle of friends mostly connected with music in one way or another, and they entertained at home as regularly as they were entertained at other people's houses. Sometimes Sophie brooded over the fact they were seldom on their own.

But Friday nights remained sacrosanct to Bernard. Then the family gathered together to say Kiddush and usher in Shabat, to break Chollah and share the silver cup of sweet red wine. Occasionally Harold and his father intruded upon those evenings, and then it was always the same: the arguing with Sophie beforehand and the sulking during the meal. However Sophie was beginning to form the opinion that Bernard and Harold actually needed one another. In a strange way, she thought, each had to have someone upon whom to focus hate. They had long ago selected each other, and now they thrived on their antagonism and were as drawn to one another as if they had been lovers.

Each time Bernard saw Harold he was struck by his worsening appearance which had become increasingly dissipated, bloated and yellow-skinned. His temperament, too, had altered for the worse; belligerence had become aggression and dogma obsession. He was quicker to anger than he had been, and Bernard noticed how sweat would break out on his forehead and the skin become clammy. He thought to himself: *Perhaps the man is ill – but he shall not have my sympathy*.

Sophie was thirty now. All traces of girlhood had gone and she succumbed willingly to her role of home-maker and wife to a celebrated musician; was in fact ideally cast for the part. She was an excellent hostess and her sympathetic disposition endeared people to her. Those who had heard her sing could not comprehend why she did not wish to pursue an operatic career, but she had no desire to repeat her experience of being in the limelight. She could at least say: 'I tried it. But I do not want to do it again.' Her old ambitions seemed far distant and Sophie was happy to continue quietly with her teaching whilst giving Bernard the support he needed and remaining unobtrusive herself.

She suspected Bernard had a mistress. She tried to confront the issue dispassionately – not to feel cheated or to resent her husband's deceit; and if it was true that he was having an affair, then she had known from the onset he had married her without love and that hers for him would have to suffice for them both.

Sophie deplored the degradation of the sexual act, and therefore would not have resented Bernard seeking alternative pleasure, but she knew him. She knew that he needed love in his life, and this was what she found so destroying; not his body's infidelity, but the mental one. She was not interested in knowing the identity of the woman, and bore her no grudge, but her heart ached with the martyred pain of resignation. She resorted even more to the pleasures of food, raiding her kitchen and baking feverishly, becoming steadily stouter, and inwardly despairing of her own figure.

In June 1869, both women came to Bernard with their news on the same day.

From the sanctity of their love nest, with the glow of perspiration and aftermath of lovemaking still on her naked body, Anna quietly told him:

'Dearest, I am expecting a baby. I am about eight weeks gone . . . It is Giles's for certain, as it was when you were in Europe for a month. Oh Bernard, I am so confused.' She cried as though she had been told she was dying.

'Ssh, little lionesss; why are you confused? Of course you will have a family. It will change nothing.'

'You are positive?'

'Of course I am – that is, unless you wish it to change.'

'I do not.'

'Then it will not.'

He rocked her, comforting her; caressed her flat, moist tummy and kissed it, his lips travelling around its softness, his hair buried against her skin.

It would change nothing. But ridiculously he too wanted to cry, and fought against the urge: it was the impotence he felt in the situation; the fact that he would love the baby to have been his, to sire legitimately a child with this woman, to be a parent beside her. He wanted her belly to be swollen because of him, the embryo to be her egg and his sperm that had travelled to

319

meet it. He could almost feel his pride as she told him, *I am expecting your child*. Oh, the pain that it was not so.

That evening over dinner Sophie made her announcement.

'Bernard dear, I am so excited, so very excited. I have the most marvellous piece of news to tell you.'

And looking at her sparkling eyes radiating happiness, Bernard knew what she was going to say. The room spun round him. Such coincidences were surely not possible.

'It happened when I accompanied you on that trip to Europe. I am into my eighth or ninth week. I am so thrilled, dear. Our first child. I cannot believe it. Say you are happy, dear. Bernard? You are so very silent.'

'I am as happy and proud as a man could be,' he assured her, taking her hand protectively. And a door clanged shut behind him.

However, the idea of becoming a father was exciting, and Sophie's girlish mood was contagious. Together they made plans and considered names.

But as the months passed Sophie became ever more placid and her appetite for food was gargantuan. She plodded lethargically around the house wearing vast skirts in muted colours in an effort to camouflage what could not be hidden, and was embarrassed by the obviousness of her condition. Her swollen form was to her obscene. It seemed to shout to the world: 'Look, my husband and I committed that degrading act.'

As for those bi-weekly performances – she pleaded with Bernard to understand that they were out of the question. Reprieved, he willingly assented to her wishes. She also refused to entertain or to accompany Bernard to social functions where her body would be on public display and open to comment. At the thought Sophie blushed with shame.

'Where is the princess?' asked Douglas once.

'She has hibernated to the kitchen,' Bernard answered acidly. 'And if she is not careful she will be too huge to leave it again through the doorway.'

'Dear chap, that is a little unkind.'

'It may be. But it is true.'

'You sound a bit out of sorts.'

'Harold has just left. Sophie emerges from hibernation for Harold. He is round here the whole time. I cannot stand it.'

Harold had developed a proprietorial attitude towards Sophie, and whilst she had no fondness for him, she did not share Bernard's extreme antipathy and was too kind to turn him away. He would arrive, therefore, uninvited, irrespective of the time or whether or not she was alone, and frequently bearing flowers – a gesture Bernard seldom remembered. Then, after pouring himself a whisky he sat down beside Sophie and began immediately to fuss over her. If Bernard was there Harold ignored him and would direct his conversation to the woman he actually loved and would have married.

'He is behaving as if it is his child,' Bernard stormed. 'He inveigles his way into our privacy. He is like a serpent. Sophie, you are encouraging him. I am your husband. I am unable to work when he is in the house.'

'Dearest, I do nothing to encourage him, I promise you. He is lonely. He means no harm.'

'You are naïve. Can you not see it? He does mean harm. He means to disrupt our marriage.'

'Bernard, do not be so dramatic,' she chided. 'How could he disrupt our marriage?'

Bernard did not reply, and Sophie, stroking the mountain of her stomach, felt the surface ripple from the fluttering within and retreated into her seclusion.

Paradoxically, Anna, whose body was so young and lithe, was the one who was ill. From about ten weeks until her twentieth she suffered from nausea, headaches and depression, and vomited morning, noon and night. Dark circles ringed her eyes, she became thinner, and apart from a tiny bulge her pregnancy was barely discernible. Her husband was revolted by all this sickliness. He could barely hide his disgust, and the body which had before obsessed him and which he had impregnated, became repugnant to him. The sight of her drooping about the house incensed him and he was unable to offer a single consoling word to her.

During those weeks when Anna retched until it seemed that the foetus would not be able to tolerate such spasms, and her body felt as though it was being turned inside out; when her weariness made even walking up a flight of stairs an ordeal, it was Bernard who held her, soothed her and encouraged her – and did everything a devoted husband should do.

She said to him: 'I wish it were your child.'

And he who had been so careful not to say it to her before, replied: 'I wish it also.'

It was January the seventeenth, 1870, the beginning of a new decade. The snow lay several inches deep and was continuing to fall in thick, irregular flakes from a black sky, and in the cosy warmth of old Grandfather Edmund's house in Brook Street, after a short and uncomplicated labour, Anna gave birth to a healthy daughter.

A couple of hours later, after twelve and a half agonizing hours, a perfectly formed boy slid from Sophie's stretched and racked body. He was called Jonathan and his weakened heart gave just three beats.

The coffin was the minutest Bernard had ever seen, and its ebony form was lowered into the snowy trough near the bones of Joseph Foligno. The sky was a freezing blue, and gazing into its brightness Bernard knew that he had killed his baby.

He had willed this death without realizing it, and God had heeded his subconscious. It was irrational, but he believed this. He could not cry. He felt numbed and unable to communicate with anyone about him, annoyed by Sophie's mother's sniffing and – extraordinarily – Harold's tears. Harold was weeping as if he had lost his son.

Bernard wanted to shout to everyone present that it was his fault. He wanted to shout 'poppycock' to the rabbi who had just told them that 'God had his mysterious reasons'. He continued to gaze at the impossibly bright sky, and only because of its sharpness did his eyes water as though he cried.

Instead of celebrations there was Shivah, and sad, red-eyed Mrs Adams was continually answering the door to a stream of visitors who came to pay their respects. Sophie would visit the nursery and stare into the empty crib. She was so brave and

Bernard had such pity for her, yet he could not offer her the moral support he knew she needed, feeling hypocritical, believing himself to have been instrumental in their child's death. Nor could he say to her: 'There will be more babies.' He could not think that they would ever again mate to make those babies.

In a roundabout way he consulted Mr Hamilton: 'Sir, do you believe that if one parent does not wish the child to be born, even if it is a subconscious wish, it could be communicated to the unborn baby in some way?'

'Bernard, what are you saying? Of course I believe nothing of the sort and will not listen to such medieval gabble. In your case Sophie's labour was too long and arduous, and the baby became weakened. Bernard, thousands of babies die in exactly this way and there is nothing that can be done about it. You must remove all such gibberish from your mind and concentrate on helping your wife – and yourself – recover from this experience.'

Bernard visited the nursery for the first time and found Sophie sitting in the nursing chair beside the crib. Something in him dissolved. He went and stood beside her.

'I am sorry, sorry, sorry.'

'Why, dearest? It was nothing to do with you.'

'No, it was not. But I have not been much help.'

This had been pointed out to him a couple of days earlier by Harold. They had met in the front doorway as Harold was making his exit and Bernard his entrance.

'You are failing in your husbandly duties, cousin,' he accused furiously, sweat breaking out on his face, and the skin gleaming greyly.

'And you, Harold, are overdoing your cousinly ones as usual. Will you please leave me to manage my home, my wife and my affairs on my own.'

'It is the latter which concern me.'

'What does that mean?'

'Nothing, dear cousin. Good day to you.'

Sickened, Bernard mulled over the innuendo. He remembered standing before the headmaster at Milton Hall and being expelled because of an anonymous letter.

After a month the pattern of their lives was gradually resumed. Sophie took on new pupils and did a little voluntary work to keep herself occupied, but she could not avoid her thoughts: that she should have heeded Mr Hamilton's advice about eating less in order to keep her weight down; that perhaps if she had pushed harder, sooner, their son might have lived. He had lain in her womb and therefore she felt responsible. She told nobody of these contemplations, but she felt a great discrepancy in her life. She had yearned for a child, and now there was nothing to show for her nine months' gestation except an empty nursery and her colossal, sore breasts still oozing milk which should have nourished their little boy.

During this period when Bernard could reach out to no one from the island of his mourning, and could not go to Anna because even his codes of morality told him that would have been the grossest insult to Sophie, he composed his sombre little 'Nursery Pavan', with the covering words *Written in memory of Jonathan, for my wife Sophie*.

He presented it to her one morning when she was breakfasting in bed. Her lovely complexion was drained of its warmth and her thick, cloudy hair waved to below her sad sagging breasts. He saw beauty in her then.

He handed her the manuscript and kissed her on her forehead: 'Dear Sophie, I have composed this for you. Now we must start living again.' He looked long and hard at her and said: 'There will be more children, I promise.'

She looked wistfully back at her handsome husband sitting on the edge of the bed, the manuscript between them, and saw in his expression both affection and friendship. She knew she would have to make do with these sub-standard offerings – and should count herself fortunate in them. He would never leave her. He needed her too much – because she went with his Jewish home, and his Friday nights and his childhood.

After breakfast he played Sophie his Pavan, and then visited Beavis – now Sir David Beavis since his father had died and he had inherited the title. Bernard gave him the Pavan for publication and they lunched at their club, enjoying a game of cards and a couple of brandies afterwards. In the afternoon Bernard took a cab to Edgerstone Mews South.

Anna was already there. It was almost two months since they had seen one another, and he was struck anew by that very special kind of sexuality she exuded. There was about her a combined intelligence and raw animal power that was more magnetic than mere beauty.

'I have missed you,' Bernard told her, drawing her into his arms.

'We spend our lives saying that,' she replied wryly.

'Don't make me feel bad.'

'I am very, very sorry about your baby. I so wanted to speak to you about it. Douglas said your – wife was very courageous.'

'Sophie has been remarkable,' Bernard agreed, and changed the subject: 'And you, my Anna, what about your little Amy?'

'I love her. And she is such a very good little thing. Giles, of course, is disinterested in her. I suppose he had hoped for a boy, but he does not confide in me. I have done some watercolours of her to show you.'

'Whilst I long to see them, dearest. I long to have you stretched out upstairs even more.'

Anna laughed, and taking his hand, followed him up the tiny staircase and into the bedroom.

Things returned to normal, and in September Bernard received a surprise letter from Douglas:

Dear boy,

Some news for you all. I am getting married – to a perfectly splendid and jolly girl with the proportions of an ox. Would you believe she is five foot ten inches to my measly five foot four? She is also a violinist (what – a family of fiddlers?), and we are going to be married quietly here in Paris, and then intend to make our base in jolly London. Of course you will both come to the wedding. . . .

Bernard wrote back: *What has come over you, my dear friend? But seriously, I am delighted and excited for you and send my*

*warmest affection and congratulations. What do you want as a
present?*

The reply was short:

> *Dear chap,*
>
> *Many thanks for yours. In answer to your kind enquiry:
> why, a violin concerto especially written for me of course.*
>
> *Affectionately yours, D.H.*

It took just a couple of months for Bernard to compose his
violin concerto for his closest friend. The work was in the key of
D major and in it were passages alluding to incidents they had
shared as boys – the ritual pricking of fingers to become blood
brothers, quarrels, jokes, intimate confidences swapped. But
for all its lightness the work possessed marvellous lyricism and
beauty, and Bernard demonstrated yet again his skills at linking
a solo instrument with a full orchestra. It seemed his imagination knew no limits as he played with themes and tested the
versatility of instruments.

One evening Bernard and Sophie were sitting having a quiet
dinner when, in the middle of chewing on some chicken, he
began to laugh. He half-choked on the piece of meat and Sophie
got up to slap him on the back.

'Goodness, what brought that on?' she asked when he had
stopped coughing.

Bernard's eyes streamed. He started to laugh once more. 'I
was thinking, dear – you know I was a bit uncertain about the
ending of the last movement – my concerto, that is –'

'Tell me, the chicken has given you sudden inspiration!'
Sophie returned to her chair.

'Well, something has! I have decided to finish with a little
figure played by the violin: da-da-da-da-da-da-da-da-daaa . . .
using notes of the scale up and down in a quick run, followed by
an abrupt thump of the drum . . . And you know what it will
depict?'

Laughter shook him again and he wiped his eyes. Sophie
began to laugh also.

'No dear, tell me.'

'It will depict Doug knotting his bowtie – you know, that dreadful enormous green one with the purple lines in it – and the drum will be the final satisfied tug he gives to it! . . . Dear, would you excuse me? I must go and write it now.'

Sophie looked at his empty seat and the half-filled plate. She smiled with fond indulgence to herself and shook her head with a little sigh, then reaching for his plate she ate the remains of her husband's meal.

The wedding was, as Douglas had said, a quiet affair. The little bewhiskered groom (Douglas now had hardly any of his face uncovered), wearing fashionably shapeless trousers, stood beside his gigantic bride and exchanged vows, whilst swapping smiles of such outlandish complicity that Bernard was convinced, despite their unlikely appearance together, that they were eminently compatible.

The reception lasted all evening: a dinner was to be held in the Grand Hotel de Paris; but first was the performance of Bernard's violin concerto, given in the hall of the Conservatoire.

Bernard had hired the hall for the purpose, organizing the orchestra and a competent violinist, and the entire package was his wedding present to Douglas and Alexandra Hamilton.

They sat in the front row – bride and groom and guests of honour – listening to the work that later was to become so acclaimed and that Douglas would perform with major orchestras throughout Europe; and the little man, quite overcome, hid his face in his wife's shoulder and wept as he heard what his friend had written for him.

Bernard and Sophie returned to London the following day. Back home, Sophie began to bleed copiously. She had had stomach cramps on the boat crossing, but had refrained from saying anything. She had not even voiced to Bernard that she believed she was pregnant again. In the comfort of her bed, the embryo came away with her tears.

Chapter Twenty

'I happen to know you are having an illicit relationship, dear cousin.'

'And how do you know that, Harold?' Bernard's back was turned, and as he poured the whisky into two tumblers he had to concentrate on not spilling it, for his hand trembled involuntarily.

'Hear me out, will you, Bernard,' Harold said equably, enjoying the sight of his cousin's vulnerability, though even in his uncertainty Bernard had an elegance about him which enraged him.

'I am always hearing you out, Harold,' replied Bernard in a tight voice, passing him a glass and taking a gulp from his own before sitting down. He took his pipe from his stand and prepared it with tobacco, playing for time, biting on his lower lip as he tried to decide on his tactics.

'Well, this time really do so, because I have proof of what I have just told you.' Harold's tone was that deceptively kind one he used in court before he was about to slay someone. 'In my profession one meets many people, you see. And a fortnight ago I happened to have dinner with Lord Robert Charlton-Grey. It also happened that with him were a couple of guests – his daughter and her husband, Sir Giles Fotheringay. Now perhaps you see how the conversation is materializing?'

Bernard tapped his pipe lazily. 'Go on,' he said, his expression noncommittal.

For a moment Harold's eyes registered surprise at Bernard's composure, then he continued: 'During the course of conversation the subject of opera was raised and Fotheringay mentioned your name and that he had met you. He also mentioned that he found you rather disagreeable. Naturally I informed him you were my cousin but that I was entirely in accord with his character assessment.'

'Thank you. And I suppose you did not stop to consider that his dislike was rooted in anti-semitism, and that you will be no more in favour than I was?'

'It is of no interest to me, Bernard. Certainly I know the fellow is anti-semitic. What interested me . . . me . . . What interested me . . .' He began to sweat, the moisture appearing suddenly in patches on his face and settling in crevices of skin. His lips were dry and bleached of colour.

'You were saying, Harold?' Bernard inhaled long on his pipe and blew the smoke towards the other man, his dark eyes mocking.

'I do wish . . . I do wish you would not smoke that vile thing,' Harold shouted in a deranged voice. 'I *know* what I was saying. Do not interrupt me . . . I – know.'

He held the palms of his hands flat against his temples and sank further into the chair. His short legs were spread, and his belly was a giant egg resting on his podgy thighs. The perspiration ran in rivulets down his face which had become blotched with purple.

He breathed deeply and continued: 'As I was saying – what interested me was his wife's reaction. She flushed crimson, dear cousin, and spoke in the harshest voice. I recall her exact words: "Do not talk of him in that way," she said. "I will not hear him spoken of like that." And then she became embarrassed at her outburst and barely spoke again.' Harold was becoming excited and there was white spittle in the corners of his mouth. 'Do you . . . Do you not see, cousin, the implications?'

'I fail to.'

'But you are not a legal man like myself. I had long suspected you were having an affair. I knew you were not being faithful to dearest Sophie. Why did you marry her?' he shouted. 'You knew I loved her . . . So I had you followed, dear cousin, and I have conlu . . . conlu . . . con*clu*sive evidence that you and Lady Fotheringay are having an affair. Of course it will ruin your reputation. You disgust me. You are scum. Sophie is everything to me, and you took her from me. I can annihilate you now. Do you hear that? I shall succeed. You took Sophie from me. You did it deliberately. And I would have made her a good husband . . . A good husband.' He got up and staggered towards the sideboard where the decanter of whisky stood.

Now at last Bernard's turn had come: 'What – and give her syphilis?'

Harold spun round and some of the whisky splashed to the floor. There was the sound of spluttering and apparent choking, and he almost fell back into his chair. 'What are you talking about?'

'I know, Harold. You cannot deceive me. And it is you who are scum, as you put it – you with your perverted addictions. You see, you are not the only one who can play detective. *I* could annihilate you and succeed in doing so; and as a prospective Queen's Counsellor you would be in a more embarrassing situation than a musician. Musicians and artists are notorious for their unconventional behaviour. . . .'

He crossed his legs in a laconic manner and from under raised brows assessed Harold, who was greasy-faced and sunken in the chair like a deflated cushion. 'However,' Bernard went on, 'I have a better idea by far. What say you we have a truce, cousin –the truce of mutual blackmail? And I want it in writing, mind, that you will not arrange to have a letter sent posthumously disclosing my affair. If you cannot sign, then I shall not keep my part of the bargain. Is it agreed?'

Bernard's face wore its seraphic smile, and Harold, looking at him with venom and defeat, muttered: 'It is agreed.'

'We have not seen Harold for ages,' Sophie observed some weeks later.

'Thank Heaven.'

'I wonder why.'

'Are you sorry?'

'No. I only think it strange. Did you two quarrel?'

'As it happens, yes.'

'What about?'

'Sophie, we have always quarrelled.'

'But he has not stayed away before.'

330

'Sophie, I begin to think you miss him.'

'Definitely not. But I confess to having a little pity for him.'

'Pity for Harold! Sophie, do not waste your pity.'

'He is a good Jew.'

'He is a bad Jew. The worst possible Jew.'

Towards the end of February, 1874 Harold died. When Bernard returned home that day after having been with Anna, his mother was there with Sophie. They both looked so sombre that for a moment Bernard believed he had been discovered. He felt himself pale, his bones become liquid. He was ready with excuses.

Sophie said: 'Dearest, we have just heard Harold has died.'

Bernard was silent, his first reaction being one of relief that he had not, after all, been exposed. Following this, came his reaction to Sophie's announcement. So it had happened at last, a year and a half after their final conversation. At the age of thirty-six Harold's disgusting illness had finally beaten him. And alongside Bernard's gladness he knew a strange disappointment, a feeling that he had been cheated.

Helen interrupted his thoughts: 'Dear, I know you were never fond of him, but you should attend his funeral.'

'No Mama,' he said sharply. 'I shall not go.'

'Bernard,' exclaimed Sophie, shocked. 'But you must.'

'There is no "must", Sophie. I shall not attend the funeral. I do not believe in shamming.'

'Harold died a lonely man,' reproached Helen.

'He deserved to,' Bernard said. 'He deserved to die the loneliest man on earth.'

Bernard and Anna lay by the Serpentine in the mild end-of-summer sun. It filtered through the branches of the weeping willow which sheltered them. Beside them was the easel and stool, and Anna's little pug dog rested on the seven-month mound of her belly.

331

'I have a feeling about this baby,' Anna told Bernard, stroking the animal's flattened nose. She always joked that it was like her own.

'What do you mean "a feeling"?' Bernard asked in an amused tone, re-positioning himself so that he was stretched out with his head in her skirts.

'I believe it is your child,' she said calmly.

'My love, you cannot possibly know that,' he replied tolerantly. 'Besides we are always so careful.'

'Not when you returned from Leipzig.'

'But that was once!'

'It only takes once, darling.' Anna's eyes were bright with mischief.

Bernard sat up. 'Anna, if you had a child that bore no resemblance to either you or Giles –'

'My mother was dark.' She touched his lips caressingly. 'If the baby were dark I would say he looked like my mother. But it will really be because he is yours.'

'He?'

'Oh yes, he.'

Bernard lay back once more amidst the comforting silk of her skirts. His chest was tight with excitement. He saw no reason to doubt Anna's intuition or its frail foundations, trusting her absolutely. What extraordinary creatures women were – their intuitions were so different from men's! By comparison men were pedestrian and unimaginative beings.

That evening, inspired, Bernard shut himself in the drawing-room and finished the symphony – his third – he had been working on. It incorporated a single soprano in its last two movements, and the voice rose in celestial contrast like a lone bird.

'What is the significance of it?' Beavis had asked him once.

'It represents the power of gentleness,' Bernard had answered.

Eventually, when dawn was breaking he went to bed, satisfied in so many ways, and slept until almost midday.

Blearily he went into the newly-fitted bathroom. Sophie was in there being sick.

'Oh not again, Sophie,' he said with a touch of impatience.

332

'I am afraid so, dear.'

'How far advanced?'

'Three months.'

'Three months! But you have said nothing.'

'There seemed no point after the other times. I thought I would wait.'

'But still you should tell me. I am your husband. You should not have to worry about such things on your own.'

She did not say that he was not always approachable, or that he had a habit of looking stern lately. 'Do you want me to have a baby, Bernard?'

'Yes dear, of course.' He was becoming rather bemused by all this baby talk.

'Then this one will be born.'

'Will it be a boy or a girl?' he asked seriously.

And with certainty she replied: 'A girl.'

Two weeks before she had told her husband it was due, Anna gave birth to a black-eyed boy with a little crest of white-blond hair, and named him Rupert.

Giles was taken aback, and staring into the baby's eyes asked suspiciously: 'Where did this one come from then?'

Anna did not falter. 'My mother was dark,' she said equably.

Her father also commented on the baby's colouring but, shrugging, endorsed Anna's words to his son-in-law: 'My late wife was dark. I suppose the child must have inherited her eyes.'

But Anna knew otherwise and she rejoiced. She had Bernard's son. It was the greatest gift she could have been given, and much to Giles's fury she refused to have a wet nurse for him as she had with Amy, and every four hours undid her corsets and offered his voracious mouth her flowing milk.

As soon as it was possible she took him to the love nest to see his father, and Bernard, looking into his own eyes set in the minuscule face, at the tiny head with its cock's comb of pale silk, knew an overwhelming sense of fulfilment.

*

Four and a half months later, in March of '75, Sophie went into another protracted and tortuous labour, and it seemed likely that this baby too would die from a weakened heart.

Bernard sat by his wife throughout, refusing to heed Mr Hamilton's orders that he wait outside. His face pulled down with tension, he held her hand and suffered over Sophie's pain and willed the baby into the world.

Do not let it die. It would be so unfair. Do not let it die.

After fourteen hours, when surely no baby could emerge alive and no woman could survive such an ordeal, their daughter struggled out, reddened and furrowed – and shrieking gustily.

Bernard wept openly.

'No more babies, Sophie,' Mr Hamilton cheerfully told the exhausted woman as the midwife cleaned the screaming, black-haired infant. 'This little fighter will be enough to keep you going.'

Bernard allocated his days to extensive travel, performing and composing. His schedule was punishing and he was strict with self-discipline. His sleep-pattern had not changed and he could still survive well on an average of four hours a night, which was fortunate for he was greedy for time, impatient of every minute wasted when it could be used to advantage, and he found too that at nights he worked better than during the day when there always seemed to be some interruption.

Over the years he had written an astonishing number of works, most of which had been widely acclaimed. Bernard was an innovator. It had been said of him many times, and he never wavered in his conviction that music must progress continually forward. He was a fount of original thought, a constant spring of new ideas. It was as though he saw life interpreted through sound. Sometimes he was criticized for clinging to Romanticism, or for being self-indulgent or even pretentious, but every artist must have his critics, and at the age of thirty-five Bernard Foligno was generally considered to be one of the world's greatest contemporary composers.

As a pianist, too, he was spoken of with awe, and exaggerated rumours circulated that women in the audiences were so affected by his brilliance and in love with his handsome and poetic appearance that they were given to fainting.

But Bernard remained unaffected by this adulation. Firstly he mistrusted it, even feared its tenuous fragility, and secondly he was essentially a deeply serious man. He had never really changed from the yearning boy who had stood with a constant ache in his heart beside his old music master whilst the latter counselled him gravely. All this fame was merely a by-product of what Bernard strove for – to make music; to make near-perfect music.

He decided he could no longer teach at the Royal Academy. In the early days before he was firmly established, his post as part-time professor had provided him with 'back-up' income and a sense of security, but now, with so many other commitments, he reluctantly told Bennett he was unable to continue.

'I am becoming tired, Sterndale,' he explained, looking round the other man's familiar room and sighing regretfully. 'I find there is just not time for everything I want to do. The more hours I put in, the more I need.'

'I understand, Bernard,' Bennett said. 'But of course I am sorry – and to have your name de-listed from the professorship is a shame for all concerned. Perhaps you would consider taking up a directorship? You would not have to play an active role – only make an appearance now and again, pass opinions on major issues.'

'Sometimes I think I am a fortunate man,' Bernard said in a voice which held quiet emotion.

Bennett looked directly at the young man in whom he had put his faith. There were a few small lines about the eyes and mouth now, but apart from them he was unchanged.

'You are only what you deserve to be in life,' Bennett said a little wistfully, casting his memory back to that time when his own hopes had been without limit.

*

When Rachel was a couple of months old Bernard wrote his 'Sephardic Suite'. It was based on old Sephardic melodies – some merry and some sombre, and Bernard's treatment and development of the themes was so ingenious that each melody was vividly clear in its meaning and its beauty enhanced by the prominence of the woodwind and harp.

He dedicated the suite to 'the little Fighter and her Ancestors'.

He was known affectionately as the composer who always dedicated his music to somebody. There was Gilbert, and J. B. C, and the Fiddler. There was Sophie and Helen – and now there was 'the little Fighter'. Who was she?

'My daughter. She is my daughter,' Bernard answered, laughing at the eagerness of the reporters as he stood outside the St James's Hall.

'If you had to choose just one of your compositions, sir,' someone asked, 'which would be your favourite?'

'This latest,' he replied. 'The one we have just performed. My Sephardic Suite.'

'Why is that, sir?'

He reflected for a moment and they waited respectfully. 'Because it is steeped in history,' he said. 'Because it makes me feel humble.'

The Folignos seemed to be spilling out of the house. There were three of them, and four servants now including the nurse, and there were always endless guests. And furniture. Bernard had developed a passion for fine furniture which meant that whenever he saw a piece which caught his fancy he bought it. This necessitated continual moving around and upheaval to find a gap – but the gaps were becoming increasingly scarce, and the parlour, where Sophie had her own small piano for teaching singing, was crammed with discarded furniture which had come with the house.

'Dear, I cannot teach singing in here,' Sophie complained good-naturedly to Bernard. 'There is no resonance to the room whatsoever.'

'I have an idea,' he told her with that illuminated expression on his face which usually meant he was about to announce something impractical. 'We shall move to a bigger place.'

This was in fact a surprisingly good idea, but Sophie was reluctant. 'I am happy here.'

'Then we need not move straight away.'

'And meanwhile?'

'I shall organize to store some of the furniture, and buy no more from now on,' he promised.

And he meant it – until he saw a rosewood davenport he simply had to have.

He was the same with his daughter. Bernard was besotted with Rachel, and like all fathers was convinced of her exceptional intelligence and alertness. Every night, when he had finished working and before joining Sophie in the big bed where she always lay in deep immobile slumber, he would creep into the nursery to see his child. He would study her, learning the very outline of her body as if he were an artist, and listening to her sweet, light breathing. Almost each day he bought her a new toy, and soon the nursery was as crowded as the rest of the house; the shelves, drawers and cupboards overflowing with playthings – many so advanced that Rachel would not be able to play with them for years. But this did not matter to Bernard who derived immense pleasure from his lone shopping jaunts, and took a childish delight in discovering how the toys worked, or what their purposes were. . . .

Sophie watched all this spoiling with amused and patient indulgence, knowing it would be useless to say anything, nor wishing to dampen his joy. Her husband was like a small boy when he was in such moods and she loved him for the irregularities of his nature.

He bought his son presents too.

Anna said gently: 'Dearest Bernard, you are his father and we both delight in that knowledge, but to him you must always be just – a kind man. He will have to learn never to mention your name at home, and when I bring him to visit you I shall teach him to keep our visits secret.'

Bernard felt a moment's deep hurt. 'So I may not buy him presents?'

'Of course, dearest, but as he gets older you will have to be a little cautious, that is all.'

Her expression pleaded with him to understand, and he kissed her and then kissed their son. 'You are right. But how will Rupert learn to keep this "kind man" secret? He is bound to ask many questions.'

'Yes, but I shall find a way to manage. He and I will have a special relationship. The thought is always with me that he is your son.'

Bernard loved to watch Anna breastfeeding their child. This was to him the tenderest, most beautiful of scenes, and he was both profoundly moved and erotically aroused by the sight of Anna's ripe breast with its large pink nipple aimed at the little boy's mewed lips which sucked loudly, his fingers clawing at the soft flesh, making indentations.

'Look at yourself in the mirror,' he ordered her once, turning her about to face it.

She looked – at the curves of her breasts, the gracefulness of her shoulder, the arc of her arm, and her rippling hair, a lock of which was clenched by the baby. Rupert's long-lashed eyes gazed unblinkingly into hers and his small form fitted in the crook of her arm. The picture seemed compounded of curves and Anna saw herself through Bernard's eyes – a golden and sensuous woman.

But the time came when their son was formally christened the Honourable Rupert Edward Charles Fotheringay, in God and Jesus's hearing, under a Catholic roof, and Bernard paced his house all day, imagining the scene and filled with a black gloom.

I have an uncircumcised Catholic son with Jewish eyes who will never know who he really is, Bernard thought. *And he will more than likely be educated by that man he believes to be his father, to look down on his own race.*

Cynically he envisaged the future, when the child would be sent to Eton and learn to deride those he was told were different. He remembered his own schooldays – the taunts, the pain.

'It will not happen. I promise I shall not let it,' Anna consoled him the next day.

'I have no rights anyway.' He shrugged moodily.

338

'You have every right,' she assured him. 'And believe me – your son will grow up to be as remarkable a man as his father is. Now look at me and believe me.'

She tilted his chin so that he looked into her light eyes, and seeing their clarity and devotion restored his confidence.

That evening he sat reading a book while Sophie embroidered a sampler for Rachel's nursery.

'I do not understand it,' she complained crossly. 'My hands just will not work as fast as they ought.'

'Are they hurting?' Bernard enquired, not glancing up.

She considered. 'No. They are just stiff.'

'Then perhaps you are a little cold.'

'Yes, that is probably all,' she agreed, putting aside the needlework. 'Oh by the way, I forgot to mention we have received an invitation from the Leemings; it is there on the mantelpiece with all the others. They are having a party next month, and have suggested we stay the weekend.'

'Are you going?' asked Anna on a note of panic.

'We have already accepted,' Bernard said.

'But I have accepted for us. Oh dear, how did this *happen*?'

'Well, I assume that Lady Leeming does not realize you and I are lovers. However, it *has* happened, and does it matter so much? Surely we can put on a good act?'

Something about the irony of the situation actually appealed to him. Wickedly he found himself looking forward to the weekend, however he did not say this to Anna who was in a state of agitation.

'Oh dear. And Rupert – I am bringing him because of breastfeeding.'

'And we shall be bringing Rachel for the same reason.'

'Oh dearest, I am distraught. I do not like this one bit.'

'What a weekend that was.'

'I thought we did very well.'

'Well, I was continually under strain. I liked Sophie enormously – thought her so charming – and I never disliked myself, or you as much as that weekend, when our own deceit seemed to be laughing at us. Beforehand Sophie had been a remote person to me, but then I saw her as warm and real, and I felt appalled at what I was doing to her, knowing I was going to go on doing it.'

The Folignos were met at the station by one of the Leemings' coachmen who drove them to the mansion. It was as Bernard remembered it – even the dogs bounded out to greet them; different dogs, he supposed.

It was Friday afternoon, and normally Sophie would have been preparing for Shabat. The mysterious grey shapes of elongated shadows stretched between the huge trees, linking them abstractedly. The clay-roofed turrets of the Folly glimmered orange in the late June sun and a flock of doves suddenly flew up in the air, their wings beating and clapping.

They waited for the door to be opened, and Sophie commented: 'How extraordinary and wonderful it is,' voicing exactly how Bernard had felt eleven years earlier when he had first set eyes upon Greystones Folly. Incredible to think – eleven years. And he had arrived as Miranda's music master!

They were greeted in the drawing-room by Sir Alfred and Lady Leeming, Emma-Jane, who had not married, and Miranda and her husband. Sir Alfred Leeming had aged. He was perhaps in his late sixties and walked with a permanent limp now. His stomach was more rotund, his cheeks leaner and infused with broken veins, and his nose redder. His sparse hair stood wispily on end, and his eyes held a distant expression, as though his spirit were partially elsewhere. His manner was as effusive and genial as ever, but there was strain in the effusiveness, something overdone in the joviality, and Bernard who had known him well, thought, *He is in pain. He has that look about him, poor old man*.

Lady Leeming was as usual surrounded by her entourage of animals: William the squirrel monkey – Bernard presumed it was still William – crouched on her head like an outlandish hat; a parrot descended onto her shoulder, and the tails of several cats wound like snakes around her legs. She was as sprightly and cheerful as ever, and except for a little extra weight and a slight double chin, her appearance had barely changed. She had one of those smooth English complexions which never seemed to wrinkle, and her features, which Miranda had inherited, were small and neat.

Miranda had become a poised and pretty woman, still naturally coquettish and alarmingly frank, but her husband, a tall auburn-haired man with jutting ears and an enormous smile, obviously adored her and would have tolerated anything from her, and Miranda's flirtatiousness was innocent. They had two small daughters who were upstairs with the nanny.

'Bernard,' Miranda whispered hurriedly, when Sophie and Rachel were being made much of by Lady Leeming, 'you know that Anna is coming, don't you?'

'Yes.'

'Goodness, what a mix-up. Will it be frightful?'

'It need not be.'

'I wish my mother had told me before she arranged this. Still, she could not have known. How outrageous all this is! And I warn you – my father is expecting you to play the piano tonight.'

'I might manage that. Is your father ill?'

'He has severe gout and goodness knows what else. He is in constant agony, poor dear, and is quite short-tempered nowadays. I say, Bernard my sweet, you really have become terribly handsome. You are a most *romantic*-looking man.'

A piece of conversation drifted over to Bernard:

'We have another baby coming any minute,' Lady Leeming was saying to Sophie. 'Sir Giles and Lady Fotheringay are bringing their little Rupert with them. They were with us at Covent Garden the night you sang so divinely, dear. Bernard met her when she was staying with us years and years ago, and he was giving little Miranda piano lessons. Dear me, what a long time ago it seems.'

The bicycle was still in the hall, propped drunkenly against the wall beneath a portrait of a grim-faced lady in seventeenth-century dress. It was a remant of the boisterous past, left to remind Sir Alfred of his more reckless moments, when an ache in his body meant nothing more than lusting after one of the servant girls. The bicycle was decorated with little maps of rust and was broken in several places; it was like a child's neglected toy that nevertheless was still of enough sentimental value to be retained. Some works of art were missing and there were gaps on tables and pale rectangles on walls where ornaments and paintings had been removed – to pay the servants and the bills? Bernard wondered, as everywhere he went in the house he saw evidence of further deterioration.

'I am going to visit the stables,' he told Sophie. 'I think I shall ride before it grows dark.'

'Then I shall unpack.'

'Sophie, a maid does that.'

'Oh. Well, I shall rest a little perhaps. The journey was quite tiring.'

'Do you know – we are in the same room I stayed in eleven years ago? I wrote my first piano concerto in this room.'

And by the look of it, it had not been decorated since. He felt utterly dismal at the changes. The charming eccentricities of the Leemings had made them seem indestructable, and the Folly a stronghold.

He escaped to the stables; he had not sat on a horse since he had last stayed with the Hamiltons in Bibury, which was several years ago, and he felt rather apprehensive.

The old chief groom was still there, more grizzled and wizened and shrunken, but still able to instil fear into the stable lads, and strap a horse more energetically than any of them.

'Why sir! I'd recognize you anywhere.'

'How are you, Hobbs? You look fine.'

'I is as fine as I looks, sir. Miss Miranda sent word that Lady Anna'll be wanting to ride as soon as she arrives, and I believe as I heard them some minutes 'go. Will you wait for her, sir? That'll be a trip down the old memory lane, won't it, sir? You and she oft rode together. Why – here she be now, sir.'

They acknowledged each other formally in front of him, then rode up the old track into the woods where they had ridden so long ago. Anna wore breeches and sat astride; her husband had

342

given up hope of civilizing her, as he termed it, and this was only one of numerous issues concerning herself which infuriated him. The latest of her provocations was to paint for money. She was actually selling her pictures and accepting commissions.

In the glade Bernard and Anna dismounted and let the horses graze. The smell of the woods was pungent and far below them the valley was a patchwork of ripening fields divided by drystone walls. Between spaces in the trees the rosy-topped turrets of Greystones Folly were visible.

'I feel so apprehensive,' Anna said. 'Darling, I am as jittery as these rabbits which keep scuttling past.'

'We have only this evening to endure,' Bernard soothed her. 'Tomorrow during the day we will probably hardly see one another. You know how everyone goes in different directions here. And tomorrow night is the party. We shall be invisible amongst all the other guests.'

'You must not dance with me.'

'But is it not more obvious if I do not ask you to dance? I shall certainly dance with everyone else.'

'Please dearest. I shall blush to my roots if you ask me to dance. Already I palpitate at the thought.'

'Very well, very well. You have my word I shall not dance with you!' He laughed at her, happy to be in her company whatever the circumstances. 'Kiss me and stop fretting. I love you.'

'But don't you feel guilty?'

He replied soberly, 'I have been guilty for long enough now for today to be no different to any other. I have never minimized to myself the enormity of my deceit towards Sophie. But the question is, which is stronger – our love for one another or guilt over our deceit?'

'You know my answer,' Anna said quietly and with a small sigh.

It was already almost six o'clock, but as light as though it were midday; only the shadows were longer and the sounds different. Bernard and Anna rode back close to one another, their hands linked, and at the yard when Hobbs took the horses from them, they faced each other, leaning towards one another, smiling in a special and relaxed way.

Sophie, watching from the blue-room window, which was at the side of the house and partly overlooked the yard, thought how stunningly lovely the girl was. She felt an incendiary heat invade her body in a rush and for a few seconds she seemed frozen in immobility. This phenomenom had happened to her several times recently, and now, without analysing it she acknowledged it with fear.

'Did you enjoy your ride?' Sophie asked.

'It was most pleasant,' Bernard answered without looking at her.

'You – rode alone?'

'– No.' For an instant he had been tempted to lie. 'As a matter of fact Lady Fotheringay came too. I –'

'Yes?'

'She taught me to ride all those years ago.'

That evening Sophie took more care than usual over her appearance, but nothing she did could conceal the stoutness of her figure which was emphasized even more by the fashion for narrower skirts, and as she deftly coiled her thick hair which had once been so lustrous with its dark chestnut glints, there were more than a few strands of grey.

Before dinner she was introduced to the Fotheringays. Whilst Sir Giles shook Bernard's hand perfunctorily, the two women smiled graciously at each other and sat down side by side on the sofa, both apprehensive, yet instinctively liking the other.

How unusually beautiful she is, thought Sophie. *And what clear, intelligent eyes.*

She is so kind, thought Anna; *the sort of woman to confide in. She is without affectation. I like her. Yet I rob her of her husband.* She glanced anxiously at the two men but could not hear their conversation.

'I met your cousin a year or so ago,' Sir Giles was saying. 'I thought him a charming man.'

'He was odious, as it happens, but he has since died.'

'That is a loss –'

'Only to his equally obnoxious father and to certain whores.'

At Lady Leeming's suggestion the two babies were brought in for everybody to compliment and comment upon, and when Sophie looked at Anna's white-haired son she found herself looking into Bernard's eyes. The mystifying heat invaded her again and her body went rigid.

Anna, watching her intently, said softly: 'My mother had dark eyes like that.'

She spoke firmly and Sophie, stricken, studied the other woman's face for signs of deception, but instead found reassurance. Yet it was the reassurance of finding herself liking this woman, as opposed to reassurance that the child was not Bernard's. She covered Anna's hand with her own. 'Your son is beautiful,' she said gently.

'And your little daughter is too.'

'Do you have any other children?'

'A daughter called Amy. She is five years old now. She takes after my husband.'

'You are very fortunate. I shall never have more than one child. Our first baby – a son – died shortly after birth, and I have been told by our physician that I may not have more. But Rachel brings me such joy.' Possibly the girl knew all this, but it helped saying it; maintained the charade – if there was one.

'And I am sure you deserve that joy,' Anna said, tears prominent in her eyes.

Why is she so emotional? Are they lovers? She is so young and vibrant I could not blame him. And does she relish the act I deplore? What am I thinking? Please God, forgive my thoughts. I am hungry. I wonder when we shall eat. I wish we were at home for our Shabat dinner. I would have lit the candles by now. . . .

The morning of the party dawned fine. Last minute preparations of the ballroom were made and the kitchen was a flurry of activity that would have intimidated even Sophie. Throughout the house pervaded the smells of cooking.

The guests played croquet on the lawn and later strolled

about the grounds in the mild sun. Sophie noticed how rarely Lady Fotheringay and Bernard spoke. Certainly she never saw them touch or give any indication they were on intimate terms, and she wondered whether she was perhaps trying to fit a mistress into her husband's life, when there was not one. He had his music, after all. Perhaps it replaced the great love she had thought he needed.

However the uneasiness remained. She took the little path which led through the various gardens and towards the lake; a pair of young fallow deer grazed no more than ten yards from her, and hearing her soft plodding, pointed their wet noses and lifted their legs nervously before fleeing into the trees.

She came to the little pavilion, now completely derelict – a frame without a door and no panes to the windows – and stood under the skeleton of its roof feeling the presence of other people there.

There was the sound of approaching footsteps and when Lady Fotheringay appeared it was no surprise. Anna hesitated, then joined Sophie. She had come to be by herself and remember.

'I spent my childhood in this house,' she said simply. 'I used to paint in this pavilion.' *And it is where Bernard and I made up after our quarrel, and where we said goodbye.* Out loud she said: 'It is sad to see it like this.'

'It must be. So you paint? What kind of painting do you do?'

'Some watercolour, some oils. Mostly scenes of nature, but also portraits. It is only a hobby really, but I have recently sold some pictures and am sometimes commissioned. My husband heartily disapproves.'

'It must be lovely to have such an interest.'

'But you have your singing. You have such a lovely voice.'

'I have not performed since my role as the Urchin in my husband's opera.'

'Why is that, Mrs Foligno?'

'It is hard to explain. It is strange, is it not? Your husband discourages you your interest and your commercial endeavours, and mine positively nags me to resume mine! But I do not have the energy for it, Lady Fotheringay. I do not wish to be on stage or in the limelight. So I teach instead.'

346

'Well, I am sure it must be satisfying to pass on your knowledge.'

Was it satisfying? The only things that really satisfied her were being a wife and mother and keeping home. She looked at the young woman standing tall beside her under the wrought-iron structure, and felt faded and clumsy by comparison. Would Bernard have loved her more if she had become a singer?

'You are very beautiful,' Sophie said.

And Anna, taken by surprise, stammered and did not know how to reply.

They took the path back together and encountered Bernard coming towards them. Sophie knew he was on his way to the pavilion.

'I was on my way to the –'

'Have you been to the lake yet, Mr Foligno?' Anna interrupted him in a high, artificial voice. 'The wild life is greatly increased since you were last here, I imagine. And there are some swans nesting.'

'I was just going there. I shall see you back at the house, Sophie.'

'I saw a pair of deer, Bernard.'

'You will see plenty of those,' he replied.

Bernard went to the pavilion and kicked the piles of old leaves. How depressing it all was: this one little building was representative of the decay that was taking place on the Leeming estate. Sir Alfred, with his loathing for business, preferred to let the deterioration set in and sell his treasures in order to pay the bills. And Bernard, watching a peacock strutting by with its magnificent tail fanned out, was desolated by the irrevocable changes time had wrought – to see the degeneration of a fine place was no less sad than to witness the degeneration of a man.

Nevertheless, the party that night was lavish by any standards. About three hundred guests attended and were announced by a master of ceremonies dressed in full livery; the food was displayed in a spectacular and colourful buffet on tables along the length of the immense ballroom, and the French windows were open onto the illuminated terrace with its balustrades and fountains. The sky was just turning pink, the sun shot with red, and in this ruby light one could not see the moss between the paving stones, or notice that the statues were cracked, or parts of the balustrade were missing.

Inside, butlers served vintage Champagne from silver ice buckets, and from a raised plinth the orchestra played gay music by Johann Strauss. Already couples were dancing, and the evening promised to be memorable; a summer ball comparable to the smartest in society.

The women were dressed extravagantly; some – particularly the younger ones – were even outrageous, with revealing décolletés, absurdly clinched-in waists, and huge bustles with swathes of silk and organdie and artificial roses. Such dresses prompted much comment from the older matrons who gossiped between themselves with affronted expressions.

Anna wore a dress of cream and gold silk and lace decorated with ribbons made into tiny bows. It was elaborate without being ostentatious, and showed off her statuesque body and golden skin. Her hair was partly piled high on top of her head and woven with ribbons, whilst the remainder, left loose, rippled down her back, each strand a different shade of burnished copper and gold and brown.

Sir Giles Fotheringay was immensely proud of his wife's appearance that night and remained by her side a good deal of the time. Sophie tried to draw reassurance from this, and her glance repeatedly went from them to Bernard and back again. She was never happy at grand parties, and when Bernard deserted her, Sophie sought the company of kind, nature-loving Emma-Jane, and for the next half-hour learned about the mimicry of starlings, the nocturnal habits of bats, the reasons certain trees were evergreen, and the difference between animals and mammals.

She watched her husband out of the corner of her eye; and suddenly a memory came to her. It was of Bernard's bar-mitzvah party, and the gangling thirteen-year-old hero-of-the-day had awkwardly asked her to dance. His half-man's voice had wavered between a cracked falsetto and the baritone he was later to become. She remembered he had gone red with embarrassment. She thought of the incident now with a fond wistfulness.

He did not dance once with Lady Fotheringay. This fact was most disquieting. Why – after he had done his duty and danced with his own dowdy wife, coquettish Miranda, jolly Elaine, gentle Emma-Jane, and again with Sophie herself – did he not ask Lady Fotheringay to dance? But Bernard barely looked at her.

Sophie brooded over this incongruity and felt again that numbness in her limbs. Bernard was talking to Douglas and Alexandra and motioned to her to come over and join them; but she was suddenly overwhelmed by pain in her hands that brought tears to her eyes and stopped her in her tracks. It lasted only an instant, but it left her with a sense of isolation and the desire for another sort of comfort. She forced herself to smile cheerfully at him as she shook her head, and instead of joining him walked over to the array of food. She watched, her mouth watering, as her plate was piled high.

'I see Sophie had decided to sample the delights of gluttony instead of conversation, dear chap,' quipped Douglas.

And Bernard, looking at his wife, felt a wave of disgust and contempt for her.

Sophie was thinking: *Soon it will be time to feed Rachel. I shall tell Bernard I am going, and then remain away. Nobody will miss me.*

Back in the privacy of her room she loosened her dress and corset, and her flesh burst out, released from its constricting bondage. Perhaps that was all the pain had been: her body warning her that her clothes were too tight. She picked up Rachel and set her tenderly against her enormous white bosom with its blue veins. She stroked the black hair absently and began to relax once more. Suck, suck, suck . . . Now she was content. Now she was fulfilled. Once singing had fulfilled her, now it was her child and her home. She would be better again once she was home.

Chapter Twenty-One

The kitchen at Elm Tree Avenue was a large, awkwardly-shaped room with a quarry-tiled floor always wax-polished to the highest gleam, and a wide fireplace in whose deep recess was set the cast-iron and ceramic range with its four hot plates and large oven. There was always a thick-bottomed kettle full of water standing on it, and overhead, from a steel rail, hung all the implements – bottle-jacks, spits, ladles, wafer-irons, sieves . . . Greasy pipes snaked along the cream-painted walls and across the high ceiling, where steamy cobwebs eluding the tallest feather-brush, hung on victoriously. A capacious dresser and open shelves housed all the crockery, while the food was kept in the dark cold larder with its marbled shelves. A thick-topped pine table more than eleven feet long served both as work area and dining-table for the servants, and it was at this table that Sophie now stood, mixing ingredients for a cake.

Sweaty and hot, she was no different from any working-class wife with her hair tucked in a frilled cap and pinafore wrapped around her. In a corner of the room, never far from her, her daughter Rachel played with a saucepan lid, and from somewhere distant came the sound of Bernard trying out a passage of music on the piano. Sophie felt a deep sense of contentment.

In a few moments her pupil would arrive for a lesson, and she beat the mixture harder, using her entire arm in a circular motion – when it happened. Her hand was seized with a spasm and would not move. It froze like a talon, locked in position. She took several long breaths from the diaphragm as she instructed her students to do in order to relax their bodies, and gently tried to bend and straighten her fingers. This did not work, and she stared down at her hand with a detached pity and curiosity as though it did not belong to her.

'Mrs Adams, dear – might you see to the cake for me? I want to sort out some music.' Sophie left the kitchen abruptly and stiffly, and Rachel bawled lustily after her.

During the course of her lesson the stiffness began to ease and finally disappear, so that she could have almost imagined its presence were it not for the strange lightness left in her joints by the departure of the pain. Tentatively she picked out the notes of the aria on her piano, and the pupil's voice and Sophie's clumsy playing were heard against the muffled, crashing chords and runs of her husband.

Bernard had only returned from Vienna in the early hours of that morning, and had barely spoken to her since his arrival.

'I am writing a ballet,' he had announced, before shutting himself away.

Didn't he realize that it was these things which hurt her more than anything else – his dismissiveness and casualness? He never considered that she might miss him after three weeks' absence. *But I must not complain*, she thought, *after all there are so many good aspects of our marriage; better really than I ever hoped for*.

That night, Friday, dinner was at their house as usual, and around the table sat Helen, Mr and Mrs Romain, Elizabeth, and little Rachel in her high chair.

Helen, now in her mid-fifties, had become very thin, and this evening her hollow-cheeked face seemed solely comprised of huge almond-shaped eyes and mouth, giving her a clown-like appearance. Her hair, in the style she had worn it for as long as Bernard could remember, was pure white. Once recently, he had seen her before she wound it into its loop and he had had a fright. It hung heavy and straight to her waist and she had looked like a witch.

Perhaps because he had been in contact with death so young, Bernard had a horror of it that he could discuss with no one. He thought often about it – morbidly and with fear, and he hated the remorselessness of the ageing process constantly reminding him where it led. Now he was forced to confront it in his own mother.

Her shocking appearance struck him cruelly that night, and the black of her dress was inexplicably sinister, as though she were in mourning not for those she had lost, but for herself.

He thought: *She has always been there for me, and I have taken her for granted. What have I ever done for her? Have I let her down? She looks so old – far older than her years; so shrivelled and white . . . When did we last talk? Perhaps she does not even know I love her . . . Mama, I want to hold you to me and make you young again. . . .*

For some unaccountable reason he retained his kuppel after they had said Kiddush and shared out the sweet red wine, and he touched it on his head occasionally as if drawing comfort. He thought of his father and wished Joseph could see that his son had not strayed so far after all – that the precious Friday nights were perpetuated; that even Rachel's name was perpetuated, and the daughter he had never seen looked just like her sister.

As he was thinking these things he turned to his mother beside him and squeezed her hand impulsively. Its feel shocked him – the bones seemed to crunch under pressure, and it was icy.

'Mama?' Something was wrong. '*Mama?*'

He was enveloped by total silence except for the beating of his own heart. Everyone else's actions had been curtailed and only his great terror and his mother's face existed, and he mouthed again, barely audible: 'Mama?'

Her blue-grey lips opened slightly. 'My head . . . Dearest Bernard – my head. . . .'

She died in front of them all with the dignity she had always demonstrated in her selfless life, from what years later would have been diagnosed as a brain tumour. Her death left Bernard desolate, pining nostalgically for a past that was irretrievable. As was the custom he wore his tattered suit and did not wash, shave, eat meat or wear leather shoes for seven days. The smell from his body insulted his own nostrils, but this was an instance where he took his religion's rules as decreed, and he said Kaddish every day for the next eleven months and thereafter each Yarzeit.

It was the end of an era. His mother took with her the

gentleness of early Victorian England, a quiet goodness and a sense of justice that had always set an example for the family.

Young Elizabeth moved in with them; withdrawn, introverted and orphaned. At nights she sleepwalked, and several times Bernard had to carry her back to bed – this half-girl, half-woman who was his sister, yet a stranger, and looking down at her in his arms, at her smoothly pretty little face with its closed eyes like shells, he thought: *It is strange how a man has to take on responsibility – willingly or otherwise. It is expected that this is what a man must do.*

Reluctantly he left for a seven-week tour that included St Petersburg, Prague, Vienna, Strasbourg, Paris and Rome. Once he would have been thrilled and excited at the prospect – so many people to see, so many places to visit. Now he viewed the time ahead with a feeling of staleness: *I have done all this. Nothing is new any more.*

Seven weeks was a long time to be travelling, and not merely travelling but socializing, performing and composing too. He grew increasingly disenchanted, unable to clutch hold of anything familiar except his own music, whilst around him everything was impersonal and disconnected from him, and, apart from those basic essentials he travelled with, were someone else's choice or taste.

He was homesick. And he missed his Anna. His mind missed her and his body missed her. Bernard could not recover from loving this woman. He was certain that nobody loved as profoundly as they did, that no greater level of understanding could be reached between two human souls; that no man and woman could ever have discovered such sexual peaks.

He thought: *After this trip I shall not travel so much. I shall devote more time to composition. I am so beholden to others at the moment; at everyone's call. There is a limit to the time one can spend going from place to place, party to party, person to person – and always having to be civil for fear of being disliked. I am not cut out for this. I am not like Douglas. And I never feel so comfortable as when I am in England.*

With these thoughts still uppermost in his mind he returned to England – as excited as he once would have been at leaving it.

It was mid-June and when the weary traveller alighted at the station, red-eyed and dark-stubbled, he immediately took a cab to the little mews cottage off Baker Street. London was enjoying a rare heatwave. Bright sunlight showered the trees and the streets were dry and dusty. As usual the metropolis was congested with traffic, and the air filled with different cries and all kinds of odours.

When he arrived at the little cottage, as he had pre-arranged with Anna seven weeks previously, his heart beat ridiculously. He was fearful she might not have remembered, or that something might have arisen to cause a change of plan, and for a minute he stood trying to regain his calm. He smiled a little to himself that after all their years together the power of his love could still reduce him to such a state of turmoil. The wisteria was in full leaf – clambering around the little door, and an upstairs window was open. Bernard whistled – their special whistle – and she appeared laughing at the window, looking like a young girl.

He let himself in with his own key as she was opening the door, and embraced her fiercely. 'It will always be like this between us,' he said, his voice muffled against her throat, his fingers in the density of her hair. He wanted to stay holding her, to savour the moment.

But Anna pushed him away, laughing. 'Let me look at you, let me look.' When he thought about her in his mind she was nearly always laughing. 'Why, dearest, you have gone grey.'

'No!' he protested, horrified.

'Well, just a tiny bit. There are a few grey hairs I can see that I did not notice before.' She was delighted by his dismay, and at his peeved male vanity.

'I shall end up white like Mama,' he said, trying to envisage himself in years to come.

'Are you angry with me for telling you?'

'Furious. Now may I look at *you*?'

'I have so missed you. So longed to see and talk to you – '

'Ssh.'

'Why?'

'I *told* you. I want to look at you.'

'And I am not allowed to talk?'

'Definitely not.'

'You are a strange man.'

'So they say.'

Anna stood back, half-shy under his serious scrutiny which took in each detail of her. Then he stretched out his hand and she grasped it. She followed him upstairs.

The bedroom bore the scent of roses – she had filled a big Chinese vase with pink and white flowers and set it on the chest of drawers. A new lace spread covered the bed and some embroidered cushions were scattered casually on it; a shawl was draped over a velvet-upholstered chair he had not seen before, and there were different curtains at the window. On the wall were two new pictures she had done. One was a portrait of a black-eyed, flaxen-haired toddler, the other was of himself.

Bernard gazed at all the alterations and the paintings. 'When did you do everything?' he asked, touching the roundness of Rupert's cheek.

'Seven weeks is a long time. I had to do something which made you feel closer. I looked upon each day as an obstacle to be negotiated, and I came here almost daily to draw your spirit into me. Did you know your spirit is here? I talked to you. And I busied myself and bought or made things for the place we share. It was my way of being in contact. Can you understand?'

'I understand exactly.'

Bernard caught sight of himself in the mirror – eyes red-rimmed, face pallid and hair dishevelled. 'My God, is that me?' he exclaimed self-consciously. 'I do not know how you can bear to look at me. I am dirty and unshaven and must smell.'

'You are Bernard Foligno, whom I have loved nearly all my life, and probably in some other lives too.'

'You smell so feminine, perfumed –'

'You smell of man. Wonderful, wonderful man.'

Staring at him all the while, she unbuttoned her skirt and blouse and took them off. Then she lay on the bed, her back slightly arched, and opened her arms to him.

Afterwards, with the window open and the warm fresh air washing the room, with Anna's head in the hollow of Bernard's neck and his pipe set between his teeth, they talked and exchanged news.

'Rupert is speaking a little now,' Anna told him.

'What – already? How clever he is! What does he say?'

'Well, naturally he says Mama. But he also says "man". He repeats it – man, man, man – like a demented parrot. Of course, you are the man.'

Bernard returned to his little unit in St John's Wood. Sophie greeted him affectionately, but with some constraint. There were newly entrenched lines about her eyes and either side of her mouth, and if during his absence he had acquired additional grey hairs, she had also.

As usual he was armed with parcels – for Sophie, Rachel, Elizabeth, Mrs Adams, and each of the other servants – and everyone gathered around excitedly as he threw all the gifts gaily to the ground, calling jovially, 'Find your own amongst that lot.'

Amidst the flurry and sounds of paper being torn, the chattering, and the gurgling of Rachel over her toy, Sophie opened her package a little more slowly. Her hands were horribly swollen, but nobody noticed. Her gift was a pale lemon day-dress from Vienna made of the finest muslin, and even before she climbed the stairs heavily to try it on she knew that it would never fit; nor was there sufficient material at the seams to release it according to her measurements.

The bodice fastened at the front and terminated in a point at the waist, and she struggled hopelessly, until she was hot and red in the face, to make the fastenings meet, knowing full well that they would not. Her stiff fingers fumbled and pulled, and in her anger she was glad when the delicate fabric ripped into holes, and she could hurl the dress – hated now – furiously onto the bed. Even in its careless heap it was so tauntingly pretty, so obviously unsuited to her. Why had he bought it? Tears of physical pain and mental frustration careered down her cheeks as she gave way to the rare luxury of self-pity; but by the time her husband came upstairs her cheeks were dry and her hands had cooled a little, and Bernard found her sitting calmly on the edge of the bed in her decent layers of underclothes.

'Does it look wonderful, dear?'

He was so eager to please that she was contrite over her temper, and appalled at her treatment of his beautiful gift. Tears came into her eyes.

'I'm sorry, Bernard. But I am too stout for it . . . I –' She shrugged forlornly, then became aware of her immense, under-clad form and reached for the shawl at the foot of the bed and wrapped it around her.

He felt so sorry for her. She was always so dignified, yet her body had ceased to be a thing of dignity. He picked up the scattered dress before she could prevent him and saw the wrenched bodice.

'Oh Sophie.' The quiet exclamation held mingled exasperation and pity.

'I am sorry, Bernard,' she said flatly.

The vestiges of hurt remained in her lovely brown eyes and they shone with the embers of tears. He realized how tactless and thoughtless he had been. '*I* am sorry, my dear.'

'No, no. I must lose weight, I know. But meanwhile I shall have some extra material inserted in the bodice. You will never know it was not intended to be that way and it will look very pretty, I promise you. A panel of Chantilly lace perhaps?'

In July Bernard finished his ballet. It was called *The Beginning and Eve*, and was a lengthy outpouring of descriptive music and visual drama depicting the creation; but not as society was accustomed to seeing it portrayed. Bernard himself had devised the story, without thought to the consequences, so thrilled was he by the idea of showing on stage how man had descended from the apes. He had shut himself away nightly, his body hot with excitement as he visualized the work performed. But this time he had dared to be too controversial and England was not yet ready to greet such avant-garde ideas on the stage.

The ballet was performed in early November and audience and critics alike were horrified by the sight of dancers dressed as monkeys dismantling their disguises at various intervals and straightening their bodies to reveal that at last they had become human beings. One of these humans was Eve, who had clearly not been created from Adam's rib, and as she vented her joy in

357

her transmutation in an abandoned solo dance, people awoke from their stupefaction, stood up and jeered. Several moments elapsed before the performance could continue. After the first interval many seats were empty, and after the second half barely half the house was filled. Of those that did remain, some cheered and shouted their praise and support, whilst the others had only stayed behind to scream their scorn and abuse out loud.

The critics were scathing. There was an editorial commentary in *The Times* devoted to 'Foligno's disastrous misjudgement', and the letters page a few days later consisted almost entirely of outraged protests from middle-class moralists who had attended the ballet that night in 'innocent good faith'. For days the remorseless attacks against him continued, and became more vicious and personal. Letters were sent to him addressed care of the Royal Academy, and they shocked him with their venom and the fact that such hatred could be directed against him, when all he had done was stir up a little complacency.

Bernard had toppled from his pedestal and he felt betrayed, angered by the limitations of those to whom he had pandered for so long. It seemed that all the good, productive years were negated and counted for nothing.

They called him a Jew now, and it was without tolerance. In the same breath he was called a heathen. He was accused of desecrating his trusted position and using the vulnerable public to test his experiments; of disgracing all those who had given him the chance to succeed, and of misusing his advantages, daring to mock and insult church-going, God-fearing people.

This was what was being said of him, and if he believed he had been betrayed, the British public felt equally so.

Davison, his ally for so long and a staunch Christian, was brutal, but the *Musical Times* was more objective — its critic tentatively offered his support; however there was barely a comment anywhere about the music: his beautiful, lyrical and inventive score. Nobody even thought to remark on its value or genius. It was Bernard Foligno and the theories he had put forward that were being judged, not his music. After only that single disastrous performance the work was banned.

Enraged and embittered, Bernard nursed his disgrace and was inconsolable. Creativity lay like a dead foetus within him. He was convinced his career was destroyed, and he slouched around the house unshaven and untidy, refusing to see anybody who called and disregarding the continuing influx of letters. He ignored his daughter, was curt with his wife and impatient with his sister, annoyed by her ghostly nocturnal habits. He was rude to Mrs Adams, shouted at the new manservant, and reduced the nanny to tears. Even Anna did not escape his morose humour. In his suffering Bernard was utterly selfish and unreasonable, and unaware – or at least uncaring – of the hurt he was inflicting on others, for inside him was such hurt that nothing could banish it.

'Please dear – if you would only try and forget.' Sophie tried to mollify him, and laid her hand on his arm.

But he thrust it away as he would have a log onto the fire. 'Forget? How can I forget? I am merely a puppet who is one minute worshipped and the next stamped upon.'

'I know how you are suffering. Talk to me at least.'

'How can you know? What do you know about suffering? The extent of your suffering goes no further than having to wait between one meal and the next.'

And Sophie, whose body was never nowadays without pain, was caught in a paroxysm of another kind. His words stabbed her, made her gasp out loud, and she stared at him in disbelief, desperately seeking in his face something warm and familiar. He stared back blankly, and she got up and walked stiffly from the room.

One night Bernard dreamed of Cramer, and in the dream the old man spoke the exact words he had said to Bernard the child so long ago: *Some composers have to wait until they are dead before they are rewarded with a favourable verdict . . . They are the greatest: those who are prepared to dice with unpopularity.*

Oh Cramer, oh sir.

He awoke with wet eyes, a boy again, with hope and

359

optimism in his heart. The hard lump in him dissolved, and with its dissolution he recognized everyone around him again: 'I am sorry, sorry, sorry.' Repentant, he could not stop saying it.

The furore did die down; it was *because* of the fickleness of the public that they were as quick to forget as they were to condemn, and the memory of a single insulting evening did not last forever. But Bernard was slower to forgive and to regain his trust. He had felt his skin had been singed, and still it burned.

January 1877 was a memorable and emotional time for the Foligno family, for they left the yellow villa in Elm Tree Avenue and moved back to Bernard's childhood home in Bayswater. It was a period weighty with memories, redolent with images and recurring phantoms and voices calling out.

Bernard would sit in the family room with its dark, William Morris wallpaper and lapse into a trance in which time had been stunted. Caught in its convoluted infinity he saw his mother – still dark-haired – embroidering, and his father rustling the financial pages of the newspaper, his sister Rachel playing with a doll . . . and later lying on the chaise-longue in her tartan dress, bald-headed; he saw himself sprawled on the floor reading, and Selina stoking the fire, red-cheeked and bold-eyed; his old Hebrew master, whose sour breath he could almost smell. And Harold was there, splay-legged in a chair, holding forth with one of his homilies. . . .

It seemed the very building announced: *Here I am and nothing has changed.* Except that now he was master of it all.

He became quite passionate about the house. Here he knew he belonged, and it confirmed his decision that he had spent enough time travelling. From now on he would devote himself solely to composition, and this house would be his cocoon from where he would pour out music.

The white-terraced house had never been so vibrant. It reverberated with cheerful sound. People filed in and out freely, and Bernard, magnanimous, invited any number to partake in impromptu meals that had Mrs Adams complaining, whilst being secretly delighted at the restoration of good humour. There were parties and soirées, musical gatherings and poetry readings, and the Folignos' home became the focal point where everyone liked to gather, to meet and discuss and feel free.

Adrian Gibbons was a regular visitor, and Beavis and his wife, of whom Sophie was immensely fond; Sterndale Bennett, whose recent oratorio, *The Woman of Samaria*, had had considerable success; and the flautist, Benjamin Wells. Then there was the eminent pianist Edward Sydney and George Alexander McFarren who, despite failing sight, was professor at the Royal Academy of Music, composer and writer of text books. There was that outstanding young lady composer, Mary Alice; Charles Hallé whenever he was in town, Douglas and Alexandra; Miranda Leeming that was, and her husband . . . And visitors from all over London. The list was endless.

Couples usually left around midnight and then Sophie would retire, but men on their own would often stay much later, and these were the occasions Bernard preferred, when discussion and friendly argument would go on into the small hours.

'Have another drink!' he would cry, pushing his guest back into his chair if he appeared about to leave. 'You simply cannot go yet.'

In the end the guests would stagger out to their awaiting carriages, and Bernard would remain downstairs on his own for a while, inhaling the smoky atmosphere, enjoying seeing the leftover signs of conviviality everywhere – the displaced furniture, the empty glasses and decanters, the flowing ashtrays, flattened cushions . . . He imagined he still heard the voices of his friends and would go over pieces of conversation in his mind. Sometimes he dozed for a few moments in his chair, sometimes he padded into the family room and picked out a book to read. Then eventually he would make his way to bed and slip in quickly so as not to awaken Sophie.

However Friday nights were private still. These belonged to the family unit. Bernard sat at the head of the table where once Joseph had presided and knew the same sense of pride his father had felt.

Sophie was happy that Bernard seemed more settled, and she was pleased, too, because the relaxed atmosphere was good for Elizabeth and brought her out of her introversion. *At last*, she thought, *I can begin to feel at ease*.

There was so much to occupy her nowadays and she never had a moment to herself, but this Sophie did not mind; it prevented her from dwelling on the pains that were possessing her. The relentlessness with which the discomfort took hold of her was shocking and frightening, and no longer was it confined to her hands or arms, but spread rapidly to the regions around her hips and knees. However she had not said a word, because by being dismissive she was able to pretend that whatever it was would disappear.

Bernard could be criticized for lacking in observance and sensitivity, but it seemed to him that whenever he saw Sophie nowadays she was in a sedentary position, and when she *was* walking about he assumed her awkward gait to be due to the heaviness of her body. It simply did not occur to him that his wife, that uncomplaining reliable woman, could be ill.

Occasionally Sophie thought, *I shall visit Mr Hamilton*, and then she reasoned, *but he will tell me I am too fat and that I must diet. I do not wish to diet. I enjoy cooking and eating*. So she did not go, and although she did not know it, there was nothing to be done for her anyway.

In March Bernard planned a party complete with conjurer for Rachel's birthday.

'She will not understand,' Sophie objected. 'She is too young.'

'Nonsense,' he counteracted. 'Of course she will. What understanding does it take to delight in seeing a rabbit pop out of a hat?'

He was nearly always good-humoured nowadays. He had just submitted his latest work to Sir David Beavis – his magnificent Fantasy for strings, piano and orchestra, which was to restore him firmly and unreservedly back in favour – and he was full of vitality. He had so much to be thankful for: his lovely home, a successful career that was not after all destroyed, and a life which was varied and rich; but always interwoven with his general satisfaction was that single regret, that although he could not truthfully say his years with Sophie had been unhappy, how much happier, how ecstatically happy would he have been with Anna by his side.

She came to him, one day in early spring with a veil over her face, and in the subdued light of the little bedroom Bernard playfully lifted it. Horrified, he stared at her bruised and swollen left cheek and eye.

'What happened, what happened?' he moaned, covering his mouth with his hand in a gesture of shock, then taking her tenderly in his arms. Her silent shaking indicated that she was crying. 'Ssh, my dearest Anna, my lioness – it is all right. I am here. Hush, I am here. Tell me what happened.'

The shuddering of Anna's body gradually subsided. Sitting on the bed beside Bernard, her shoulder encased by his protective arm, she began to speak, her voice a dull monotone.

'I never told you about Giles's drinking. It started in a small way two or three years ago, but more recently has begun to be a real problem. No –' she held up a hand to prevent Bernard interrupting, '– what was the point in complaining about it? I chose to marry him and I suppose I have a strange loyalty to him which has at its roots my own guilt. Besides, I feel some responsibility for his tendencies, for previously he was only ever an average social drinker, and I believe it is his disappointment in me as his wife which has led to the change.

'He hated it when I began to take my painting seriously. As you know, Giles dislikes and fears the idea of my independence and believes that I constantly defy his wishes only to antagonize him. So he reaches increasingly for the whisky.

'Funnily enough, I think he loves me. He loves me wrongly and selfishly, but nonetheless he loves me. I think I frighten him with my liberal streak, and with my constant need to talk. In his opinion these are unfeminine traits. He calls me a Bohemian and his biggest disappointment is that he has not been able to mould me into the wife he wished for. In the early days, when you and I were apart, he thought he was succeeding – then suddenly he watched me revert to my wilful ways . . .

'You see how I analyse. Are you suprised by all this?'

'A little. This is all such news to me.' Bernard held her tighter. 'Go on.'

Anna resumed in the same flat tone: 'Lately Giles has taken to going out at night. I think he gambles. Certainly he drinks. When he comes back late, and often drunk, he wakes me up. He forces me to make love. He hurts me. I loathe it . . .' At this point Bernard's grip on her shoulder became so tight she had to prise it loose with her hand. 'Giles has never made any attempt to understand me for what I am, nor has he ever permitted me to become close to him. But there again, that is probably irrelevant in view of you and me.

'Anyway, his drinking nowadays is beyond control, and last night we quarrelled. It was over dinner and I told him that a gallery was going to exhibit my paintings. Giles said – and I quote almost exactly –' Anna gave a small laugh and cleared her throat '– he said: "I will not have you partaking in a commercial venture, Anna. We have no need of the money, and it is unfeminine."

'I argued, and this became a quarrel. In my dearest Grandpapa Edmund's dining-room we sat quarrelling until Giles left the house in the most frightful mood.

'I went to bed and slept – and awoke to shouting. I could not think what was happening, I was still so bleary. In my sleepiness I had forgotten our quarrel and could not understand this rage of Giles. He was drunk of course. My silence seemed to enrage him further, and he came over to me and shook me violently. My teeth actually rattled . . .' Her voice trailed away and she gave a little sob before continuing. 'My head jaggled backwards and forwards and I was terrified. Eventually I pulled away and huddled under the bedclothes. But he wrenched them from me. I fought. I really *fought*, Bernard, and I pushed the pillow in his face. That was when it happened. He pulled the pillow away and it split, scattering feathers everywhere – including into his eyes.

'He hit me. Several times I think. Then he raped me.

'When it was over he fell asleep, snoring, and I went into another room where I spent the remainder of the night. This morning I crept into the bedroom to get some clothes, and he was still asleep. No doubt he will be full of remorse when he knows what he has done.

'Anyway, I left the house and came here. Once it was such a happy house, Bernard. You remember when Grandpapa was alive. Now even my children cannot make it happy. Dearest Bernard – you look so distressed. I did not mean you to be so distressed.'

'I have failed you,' he said humbly. 'I feel I have let you down badly.' He held her tightly.

'But you have not,' she told him, astounded. 'How have you let me down?'

'All this time you have not confided your problems to me.'

'But that was because of myself, not you. I told you – I had a kind of loyalty to Giles.'

'So much for loyalty,' he murmured, and touched her poor face and felt rage. 'You must leave your husband.'

'I *could* not.'

'You could. Other people leave their partners. Your children would continue to live with you, of course. You have a private income, and the Brook Street house is solely your property if I am correct.'

'It is.' She looked at him from one wide-open eye, and the other watered pitifully.

'Oh my poor love.' Bernard shook his head in sorrow for her.

'It is all right,' she assured him. 'Really it is not so bad.'

He held her hands, turning them over and over in his own abstractedly, then stroked the blue-stained cheekbone gently. He hardly dared voice his idea out loud, this mad thought that suddenly seemed not so mad.

'What is it, my love? What are you thinking?'

'That you will go to your solicitor and show him your injury. That you live decently by yourself – with the children – for a year; and that when that year is up, we live together. I would meanwhile have separated from Sophie.'

He would watch his son grow and become a man and acknowledge his true father. He would have his lovely Anna beside him every night and listen to her breathing, and at last they would be able to share a life together.

365

Anna was so quiet. She was crying again.

'Darling, what is it?'

'Do not do this to me. It is cruel,' she burst out angrily.

'Why? What is cruel?' he asked bewildered, running his tongue around his dry lips.

'You present me with this enchanting picture at which I may look, but may not have. That is the cruelty. In the picture I see what I would dearly love more than anything in the world. In the reality I see you have a wife, Bernard, and a daughter. They matter.'

Bernard had barely considered them in his excitement and even now could dismiss them almost callously. 'Sophie would understand. We are friends. I believe she knows I do not love her. I would provide well for her, ensure she has a pleasant home for herself and Rachel. . . .'

In his egoistic enthusiasm he took for granted Sophie's assent to his plans and her accommodating nature; he was too transported to consider the heartbreak she would feel as she unprotestingly released her husband from his marital cage. Because he did not love her he could not conceive how much she loved him.

'Whatever you say, Bernard, it *is* a selfish plan.'

'And are we not selfish to one another in denying that plan? You owe your husband nothing – he has done nothing for you that is good. I owe Sophie a great deal, I realize, and I shall attempt to make amends in other ways, I assure you. Dearest – please think on it all.'

Anna lay back in his arms and contemplated what he was offering her. She had wasted one chance through her own cowardice, and now as a mature woman she was being given another. But their lives had been changed by that first decision and ruled by the responsibilities wrought by those changes.

She examined all the factors. She reflected upon her own situation, and upon Bernard's until the two became confused, and finally decided that she could only consider her own circumstances and not his also. *Oh please God, forgive me. I want this so very, very badly.*

Bernard was watching her intently. He saw the variances in her expression and every slight furrow and light in her face. He could feel the different responses of her body as it tensed or relaxed against him.

She sat up and he looked enquiringly at her.

'Yes darling. I shall do it.'

'Thank God.'

'I shall tell Giles tonight, whilst he is still in the wrong. And then I shall consult my lawyer. You see how capable of duplicity I am.'

'And I –'

The reality of telling Sophie no longer seemed straightforward. How would he tell her? He had no bruises to show her or accusations to make. It boiled down to this fact – that there was no 'right occasion' to deliver a blow. A blow was always a blow, whatever way it was dealt. 'I shall tell Sophie this evening,' Bernard told her.

When he left Anna, he was in a serious and apprehensive mood. He walked back slowly, preoccupied with his thoughts. *I have not taken much notice of Sophie lately*, he reflected with some contrition. *I must be nice to her for a while before I tell her.*

Like patting a dog before shooting it. He felt increasingly sober of spirit as he approached the crescent, and he thought of Sophie's loyalty, how she had stood by him through many stressful times, was the mother of his daughter, hostess to his friends, and had shared his youth.

I have some news I think you will not be happy to hear, he imagined himself saying, or, *Sophie, you and I have had many happy years together, but* . . . or, *Dear, you know how you and I have always been open with one another* . . . But that was a lie, he realized.

There was a coach and driver outside his house, and Bernard recognized him as Mr Hamilton's private driver. Hamilton was not a man to drop by casually. Bernard's stomach lurched, and he had a feeling of foreboding. *Perhaps it is Doug*, he reasoned. *Perhaps he has borrowed the carriage.*

The door was answered by the manservant.

'Do we have a visitor, Milnes?' Bernard asked, falsely cheerful, hoping to see his friend's face suddenly appear, whilst a sixth sense told him that this was not to be, that there had been a catastrophe.

'Yes, sir. I am afraid your wife –'

Bernard ran up the stairs, two at a time, to their room which had once been his parents' room, and where he had been conceived. Sophie lay in bed, dreadfully pallid; her hair was pulled back and seemed completely grey. *Goodness she looks so old*, he thought, shocked.

'I have bled her, Bernard,' Mr Hamilton said quietly, looking up when he entered, 'and given her some morphine. She has just fallen asleep, poor thing. I should like to talk to you.'

Downstairs he put his arm paternally around Bernard's shoulder and explained that Sophie was suffering from severe muscular rheumatism and inflammation of the joints. Her condition was rapidly deteriorating and she would shortly be completely crippled.

Sophie an invalid? Healthy, dependable Sophie? Bernard, scarcely able to absorb the truth, saw his future with Anna disintegrate, and within him a child's voice cried out, *It is not fair, it is not fair*.

To Mr Hamilton he could only say, 'I cannot believe it. She seemed so strong . . . She was so strong.' He shook his head in bewilderment.

Hamilton replied with some severity: 'She will have to be strong, Bernard, to continue to endure her terrible pain. Only her own resilience will make it bearable. God alone knows how she has suffered in silence for so long. And nobody noticed, Bernard. *Nobody* noticed.' His normally mild eyes glared pointedly at him.

Later on, when Bernard was alone in the family room, he could no longer restrain himself; he gave way to tears. Sprawled in his father's chair, in the unlit, night-time darkness, he put his head in his hands and cried his heart out.

Chapter Twenty-Two

'The boy has gone,' Charles Buckland of the *Musical Times* wrote in an article entitled 'Style'. 'Mr Foligno has indisputably been Britain's leading composer for more than a decade and rightfully acclaimed and respected for his contribution. Nonetheless, his music has always held that exuberance which is peculiar to youth, and – dare I say it? – more than a hint of arrogance.

'In Mr Foligno's latest two works – his clarinet concerto in B flat, and concert overture, "A mortal's dream", we at last see the simple humility which personally I felt his music, even in its most intensely emotional moments, previously lacked. Both these works are exploratory but never vague, and are as near perfect as it is possible for music to be. Manhood has come to Mr Foligno and I greet it with pleasure. I am only sorry to learn of what is no doubt a contributory factor: that Mr Foligno's wife has fallen prey to a painful crippling disease which confines her to a chair.

'Anyone who heard Sophie Foligno singing the Urchin's role in her husband's opera, *The Lady and the Urchin*, will surely recall her glorious mezzo-soprano voice and purity of tone which are still talked about even though Mrs Foligno has never performed since, preferring to devote herself to teaching, and shunning the public eye.

'I only recently heard of the tragedy which has befallen Mrs Foligno, and I wish her well. But meanwhile I should like to say that this second stage of Mr Foligno's career has come as an exciting leap in musical development. This most popular and sometimes controversial composer has managed to present us with new clarity and awareness, without resorting to gloom like a certain Bavarian contemporary I could name, beginning with B. . . !'

Sophie sat in her wheelchair becoming daily more gross, daily more immobile, daily more serene, as though her mind were in some way uplifted, and Bernard wondered if secretly she gloated over her victory from her exalted sanctuary of pain.

These were dreadful thoughts, and to combat them Bernard did everything he could for her. He assisted the nurse — an immense hefty woman — in her duties, brushed Sophie's once lustrous hair which had become entirely grey; and in the very early days when she could still just walk, shuffling along on flat feet, he would help her downstairs so that she could listen to him playing the piano or feel that at least she was involved in the activity of her own home. However it was not long before her legs were useless trunks to her. Such huge things as they were, they could not even take a step, and so Bernard and the nurse would lift her bulk down the flight of stairs and into her wheelchair in which at least she could be pushed everywhere. It glided with a whooshing sound which he came to loathe.

Some days Sophie would spend time in the kitchen amongst all the familiar paraphernalia and odours, that hub of the house which had been her domain, and she still planned menus and issued instructions, supervising the cooking from her seat. But her outward stoicism belied her inner frustration. It was so harrowing not to be able to do all the things she used to. Even if she needed to relieve herself, the commode had to be wheeled to her and she lifted onto it, like an obese child. It was so humiliating, and she felt like a smelly dog. But it was only another thing to adjust to. Little Rachel cried at first to be picked up, not comprehending her mother's disability.

Poor Rachel having a crippled mother who can no longer lift her or play games with her, Sophie thought. *But children adapt, and an invalid in the house teaches consideration. It is Bernard I am sorry for. He is trying to conceal his impatience, but he will grow bored. As soon as he becomes used to me like this he will long to escape. Oh dearest husband — I did not deliberately arrange this, you know.*

Bernard poured his energies into his duties as a husband. His disappointment was unbearably great, and his future lay bleak and unenticing. He viewed it despondently as he dispensed his soul to his wife.

But after the shock of her illness had lost its impact he began to think he had redeemed himself. It was not his fault Sophie was ill – only that he had failed to notice. Yet he had been sentenced to a life's punishment, and nobody would ever know of the sacrifice he had made. Her disablement binding her to the chair was as much his trap as hers; and her martyrdom was his also.

Sophie's illness began to provoke in him the worst kind of sentiments; yet the more he resented her, the more he did for her – and the more he did for her, the more he disliked her. *I wanted to marry Anna and I am forced to remain with this woman instead – who is old already and misshapen and moon-faced and smells . . . I can scarcely think she is my wife.*

Each night as he lay beside the voluminous hump of her he wanted to protest out loud: *I am with the wrong woman.* In the darkness he listened to the wheezing breath catching in her throat and imagined how it could have been.

Sophie, who had accurately predicted her husband's attentiveness would be short-lived, sadly recognized what was happening. She saw that he was trying for her sake to maintain his act, but that it was becoming increasingly difficult for him to do so. Poor Bernard. How dreadful to nurse a woman he did not love. She saw his sympathy become imbued with frustration, and that try as he might, he could not conceal his impatience.

Selfless as ever, she released him from the claustrophobia of her invalid's clutches. 'Bernard dear,' she said one day from her favourite position by the window in the family room, 'it is not good for you to spend so much time with me. I have Elizabeth and Nurse and Mrs Adams. You must get out more. *You* are not crippled, thank God.'

He objected of course – but how willingly he capitulated to her generosity; with what relief he left her, his steps lightening as he distanced himself from her; how carefree he was when he ran to his mistress's arms.

371

Fourteen months later, after a whirlwind courtship, Elizabeth left them to be married, and Sophie badly missed the girl's companionship. They had become close during the last year. It seemed that overnight the willpower which had kept her going was all used up. Her resilience crumbled and her condition deteriorated. Her suffering became continual, protracted agony which she could no longer apply the force of her concentration to defeat.

'I shall put her on a regular dosage of morphine,' said Mr Hamilton. And the drug dispersed itself in her system and temporarily eased the pain which monopolized her.

Now, with so much empty time to fill, Sophie turned inwards to contemplation and memories. They were all she had. Sitting there day in, day out, forever at someone else's kindness, unable to sing, embroider or plunge her hands into pale elastic dough, unable to play with her daughter, Sophie discovered that time held a different concept. As the hours dragged interminably she knew a frightening sense of tedium.

Her eyes grew weary from endless reading, until she could no longer concentrate. The book would slip from her lap to the floor and her head loll as she drifted into a listless sleep. She would wake and find herself still in the hated chair, her bottom sore and numb from its sedentary position, and would be overcome by a sense of pointlessness.

And regularly interwoven in the fragmented tangle of her imaginings was a clear memory: of a beautiful, tender woman and her son with eyes like mulled wine, Bernard's eyes. This memory was a thread flowing smoothly through the rest of her disjointed reflections.

On Friday nights they endeavoured to feign normality. Mrs Adams did her best with Sophie's coarse hair, and prepared clear soup and beige-coloured dumplings as Sophie herself would have done; then, after the meal they retired to the family room. For everyone's sake a great effort was made, and all faces bore expressions of forced jollity. But whom did it convince? It was only tiring, and served as an aching reminder of what Friday nights had once been.

Sophie's aloneness engrossed her and she frequently regressed into a fantasy world which was an amalgamation of her own reminiscences and fanciful visions invoked by the morphine. Sometimes these visions became wild hallucinations, but nobody understood that they were related to her increased use of the pain-killing drug to which she was becoming addicted.

In the grips of her enhanced imaginings, writhing figures were ripped apart by giant claws, which hauled out the lengths of their intestines in front of her before trying to strangle her with them. A large carrion bird beat its wing repeatedly over her head, pounding into her skull. Bernard stood menacingly over her laughing – his angelic smile distorted. Mrs Adams was poisoning her, squeezing lethal wild herbs and foxglove leaves into her lemon tea. . . .

Sometimes Sophie was so tormented in her struggles to escape these manifestations of her mind that she managed to rise from her chair and stagger a few steps before falling. Her loud cries would rouse everyone, and they would come running in to find her apparently throwing a fit of insanity. Any attempts to calm her were useless for she was aware only of her fictitious terror.

After these horrors followed a great peace and Sophie would sleep deeply, her features tranquil. When she awoke she recalled little of what had gone before, and was puzzled by the wariness of those about her, and the fuss that was made of her.

But in between the hallucinations and bouts of suffering were periods of calm which were relatively free of severe discomfort, when she could talk articulately and her concentration was unimpaired. Then one would catch glimpses of the old, vivacious Sophie, with her wry humour and aptitude for harmless gossip.

Sophie had been confined to her chair for about three years when she discovered her faith-healing powers.

It was the beginning of May and the weather was unusually mild, the air permeated by spring scents and the park beds bright with wallflowers.

A small group of friends sat on the bank of the Serpentine feeding the ducks and swans: Douglas and Alexandra Hamilton, Adrian Gibbons, Bernard and Sophie, two rugs spread over her and tucked under her arms. It was one of her 'good days'. A little away from their parents, and supervised by nannies, played three children: Rachel, and Carinthia and Emily Hamilton.

Douglas was speaking of the possibility that he might have to cancel a tour: 'Seems the old tendons are strained,' he said, holding out a crust of bread to a vociferous drake who drove all his colleagues away with small butts of the head and much quacking. 'The first three fingers of my left hand, you know. Dratted nuisance. Even my father cannot help, wizard that he is. Says things'll just have to run their course. Old girl was coming with me this time too, weren't you Alex?' He patted his wife affectionately on the back. Even sitting down she was inches taller than him.

Sophie spoke into the sympathetic hiatus: 'Douglas, may I see your left hand?'

They all turned to her in surprise; nobody expected much from her nowadays.

'May I?' Sophie asked again.

'But of course, princess.'

She loved this old endearment and smiled wistfully. Douglas moved closer to her and laid his hand on her lap, and it remained there for a second or two whilst she hesitated under the curious stare of the others. But Sophie felt herself driven by a strange impulse to set her own disfigured right hand upon his left one.

'Concentrate,' she ordered – and tremulously reached out.

Her hand was repulsive to look at, she thought objectively, as she covered Douglas's fingers with her own, allowing only the barest of contact. She closed her eyes. She knew exactly where his discomfort was, because the sensitive spot sent small sharp rays of warmth through her fingers. A prickling sensation then spread gently through the veins of her hand and wrist, travelling up her arm to her elbow. Sophie knew that it coincided with the ebbing of Douglas's pain. While she maintained her light contact, the strange and not unpleasant feeling continued and intensified, pumping currents into her, and the darkness behind her closed eyes became speckled with colour as she concentrated on the sensations to the exclusion of all else. She knew precisely when Douglas's pain completely left him, let her hand linger for a second or two, and opened her eyes.

Douglas was looking stunned, wriggling his fingers in disbelief. 'Good Lord, Sophie dear girl. It is impossible. Here chaps – I can move my hand again properly. I don't believe it. How d'you do it? Is this a trick, princess?'

'No, Douglas. I felt the – need to put my hand on yours.'

'Good Lord,' he said again. 'Remarkable.'

'When did you discover this, my dear?' Bernard asked, greatly impressed now that he had recovered from his embarrassment.

'Only now. The feeling came over me for the first time when Douglas mentioned his pain.'

'Steady, old girl. I only said it was a nuisance. I did not *fuss*!'

'Well, well, well,' exclaimed Gibbons. 'So we have a witch amongst us. Once you would have been burned at the stake for heresy. This really is most interesting and enlightening.'

They drank the champagne they had brought and discussed the phenomena for the rest of the afternoon. The episode gave each of them the chance to voice his opinions, be they related to science or religion, or something more enigmatic than either.

As word spread amongst their friends it quickly became known that Sophie possessed healing powers, and from her wheeled throne she laid her gnarled hands on all kinds of afflicted areas of the body, relieving them of headaches, stomach disorders, trapped nerves, strains, muscular aches, pulled ligaments, cramps . . . She could not heal herself. She remained as astonished as anyone by her talent and was mystified by its origins, for she considered herself such an ordinary and uninspired woman.

It amazed Bernard what an extraordinary lot of ailing people they knew. They came to talk, to play or hear music, to enjoy a good discussion – and then they surreptitiously, and usually rather shamefacedly, consulted Sophie about their latest ague.

During this stage of his life Bernard wrote a number of chamber pieces. He often spent evenings in the company of close friends, and those intimate, impromptu musical sessions prompted him to write a series of works specifically for such occasions. He dedicated them to various friends, alluding to them by their nicknames, so that the press wrote:

'Once again our pet composer is up to his tricks. Who is the Monkey for instance? And who is Twinkle?'

'Who *are* they, dear?' asked Sophie.

Bernard laughed delightedly. 'Why – the Monkey is Gibbons of course. You have heard of a gibbon monkey? And Twinkle is Charles Hallé . . . Halley's Comet?'

Sophie loved to hear Bernard laugh. He laughed so rarely nowadays. He had aged, she noticed. It was her fault.

'Would you like me to move your chair closer to the window, my dear?' he asked solicitously.

'If it is no trouble.' *That is all I am,* she brooded. *A thing to be moved about. I can take part in nothing.*

During those sombre years when joy could not be had guiltlessly and so much was changing about him, music was the single thing Bernard could control and place in order. Two people prevented him from lapsing into a degenerating self-pity: his Anna and his friend Douglas. The latter could still provoke him into a quarrel – which Douglas believed to be a good thing.

'Time is more important than melody,' Bernard observed once to his friend over luncheon at his club. 'Time is everything. It dictates an entire score. Take any note, repeat it thrice and hold each note for a crotchet, marking the piece "molto adagio", and you have something solemn and even menacing. Take the same note and apply semi-quavers, and you have pulsating excitement.'

'That is treatment, not time.'

'But time is treatment.'

'Time is a *part* of treatment.'

'Time dictates treatment.'

Douglas considered. 'You are as prone as ever to making sweeping statements, but possibly you are right. How can I argue with you anyway, dear chap? England's "pet" composer. Dear me, what will the press dream up next!'

'Don't you believe it,' Bernard replied, grimacing. 'And by the way you have just spilled green jelly on your quite ghastly bowtie. No – far from being a "pet", I am public property and therefore not permitted to put a foot wrong. Remember my doomed ballet? I have to conform or else there are outraged howls. It is enough being Jewish – I dare not step beyond that.'

'Your doomed ballet will become quite the rage in twenty years' time. And you always did have this damned obsession with your origins, dear chap.'

'But what I say is *true*.'

'They have accepted Charles Broadlaugh into the House of Commons – what more do you want?'

'He is an atheist, not a Jew.'

'Is there a difference?'

'I do not find that amusing, Douglas.'

'Dear chap – do believe you have had a sense of humour failure.'

Having known Bernard since childhood, Douglas was familiar with every nuance of his character. He knew him in all his imperfections, and never did two friends argue more, or accord better than these two.

They could go out together for the evening and have a fine time, and with him Bernard would think, *What a gay place London is after all. Life is not all gloom.*

And in the love nest in Edgerstone Mews South where Anna awaited him – there he could be himself and his great disappointments forgotten. His relationship with her had changed subtly over the last few years, for he was no longer the strong one. Where once he had been masterful and decisive, he was now beaten and without aim, and he looked to Anna to draw strength from her. He was cossetted by her, enveloped by her, and fed off her inner fortitude.

It was August, 1883 – and the shifting years had seen the ascension once more of Gladstone and the death of Disraeli.

The morning was oppressive and the sun hung grimly in a dark-patched sky. In Regent's Park a tall man walked hand-in-hand with a gangling, tow-haired boy who was subjecting him to a barrage of questions.

Bernard was now nearing the age of forty-three. He had mellowed lately, having perhaps finally adjusted to life's provisions, and his face, whilst a little lined about the forehead and eyes, was still boyish in contrast to his greying hair; his smile still radiated the same extraordinary quality that illuminated his features.

This for him represented happiness: walking with his eight-year-old son. It was one of those days which made him feel that everything was worthwhile and how much he really had to be grateful for; one of those days which enforced an illogical belief in God's existence.

Once a week Bernard saw Rupert alone. He met him with his mother and then took him off somewhere – to talk, to establish the rapport of a father and son, to learn his progress and feel pride.

Bernard reflected how different Rupert was from his half-sister, that volatile little creature with her explosive temper, cheek-stretching smile and perfectionist's eye. Rupert rarely argued, was naturally timid, and alert to the least change. He was as untidy as Rachel was immaculate, as disorganized and absent-minded as she was orderly and precise, and he was far more openly affectionate in his craving for love and constant reassurance. Rachel was sensitive to her own person, whereas Rupert was acutely sensitive to others and greatly affected by his environment. His unusual beauty endeared him to everyone, while Rachel's gnome-like appearance was rather deterring. Of course, they had never met.

'Why cannot I talk about you to my father? Why must I keep you secret?' the boy asked, tugging Bernard's hand down.

'Your father dislikes me, little Rupert, so it is better that we do not anger him, is it not?'

'My father dislikes practically everybody, and nobody else is kept secret,' the child answered in a reasonable tone. Then he frowned, considering possibilities and said: 'I think you and my mother are hiding things from me.'

'What sort of things, little one?'

'Oh – things. Things you think I shall not understand because I am too young. But I suppose you have your reasons.'

'I suppose we do,' Bernard agreed, wishing as always that he might divulge the truth.

'Besides, secrets are fun,' Rupert said, kicking a stone.

'I think so too.'

The ground shelved gently towards the lake, and on a little grassy hump the distorted stump of an ivy-draped oak tree stretched out a solitary branch in a pleading gesture. The boy leaped up to grab at it, then swung agilely back and forth before falling to his knees and rolling onto the grass. He looked up from his coiled pose, awaiting rebuke, but none came, and instead this big fine man looked down at him with dark eyes luminous with love.

Bernard reached out his hand and the child met it with his own, allowing himself to be hauled to his feet.

'You never become angry with me.'

'I do not see sufficient of you to become angry, besides I find very little that you do makes me angry.'

'I like you so much.'

'I like you so much too.'

'Like I was your son?'

'Yes. Yes, just like you are my son.'

This made Rupert very happy, and he gave a small hop and pulled on Bernard's hand.

'Do you like our days out together, Rupert?'

'So much. So awfully much. And I like holding onto your hand. Do you think me babyish for that? My father thinks so, and does not permit me. I do not believe my father likes me.'

'I am sure he does, Rupert. Some people are not very good at showing their affection, that is all.'

'But you do. You love Mama, don't you?'

Bernard hesitated. He looked down into the child's questioning face and longed to say: *I adore her. And together we made you.* 'Your Mama is a remarkable woman,' he answered carefully.

'But do you *love* her? I am sure you must, because you are so

379

nice to her and I never see you become angry. I don't imagine you ever become angry.'

The sky darkened and the sun vanished.

'Oh I promise you I do, Rupert. I am not always very nice. Sometimes when I have been working hard I am particularly horrible. I know I am being so yet cannot help myself. I am as dismal as the sky is now.'

'But your work is so important. You are very famous, aren't you?'

Bernard laughed – 'A little' – and felt a heavy drop of rain thud on his bare head.

'Do you like being famous?'

'Dear Rupert, you ask so many questions and not all replies are a straightforward yes or no. Why don't we go and have some refreshment in the pavilion by the rose garden before we are caught in the storm? The air has grown quite chilled suddenly.'

Some disturbed rooks were circling overhead and the boy glanced up at the sound of their raucous calling. He shivered.

'What is wrong?'

'I do not like those birds. They remind me of dying. They look like I imagine death to look, dressed in a ragged black cloak with cruel eyes and a long nose.'

Bernard stroked his son's white-blond head. Globulets of rain began to fall spasmodically and the sky grumbled.

'I do not think you need to worry about dying, little Rupert. Tomorrow you are going away with your Mama and sister. Come, let us hurry. I think after all we shall have to miss the pavilion if we are to avoid the storm. I shall put you in a carriage for home.'

'Will you run with me then?'

'Yes.'

'Now!'

They ran alongside one another.

'Are – you – seeing – Mama – this – afternoon?'

'Yes.'

'I – know – you – love – her. But – I shall – never – tell.'

Bernard saw his son off in a cab and waved to the figure waving back at him until it was out of sight, and then he took a cab himself to the love nest off Baker Street. Anna was already there.

*

'So we have caught up finally,' Anna said, lying entwined with Bernard.

'Yes, and I have spoken for hours.'

'How different it all could have been, yet I see now how impossible.'

'Why do you say that?'

'I say it because although initially it was I who could not marry you, you would not have been content married to me.'

'But I would have been more than content,' Bernard protested. 'I would have been ecstatic!'

'No, my love. You would have missed too much: your Friday nights, your Jewish roots, a whole way of life in which I could not participate. . . .'

'And?' he probed gently.

'You would not have been happy to see your Catholic children and myself disappear to church on Sundays.'

Bernard was silent. Outside the rain fled down and hammered on the slightly ajar window. The curtain billowed and deflated – in, out, in out. He felt depleted. He had regurgitated his past, calling upon old names and places, dredging a myriad of memories so that disjointed fragments had become whole and round; the belly of his life. He had spoken as he remembered the truth to be. One truth had stood out clearly amongst all the others: if he had been free he would have married Anna.

He had spent years with this conviction dictating his yearnings and disappointments. And now she was questioning it.

Anna's skin was light and fragrant against his. Beneath its texture was the substance of her body, and its familiar reality reached him. Theirs was a liaison of love; was it important, after all, that there should be a compartment for it?

Bernard thought: *Does it matter so much what I hoped or did not hope? Whether my illusions were spurious or not? Here we are still. Together. That is surely the only relevance.*

'Are you not speaking to me now?' Anna asked anxiously, propping herself up on one elbow, her hair falling forwards.

'I was thinking.'

'That I am right?'

'How can I know? It did not arise, so I cannot know. I know us only as we are. But I harboured such dreams for us. . . .'

'I too,' she murmured. 'I was bracing myself to tell Giles I was leaving him, when Douglas arrived with the news about poor Sophie.'

'I'll never forget my anguish when our plans were curtailed by Sophie's illness,' Bernard mused. 'Such selfish anguish in the face of her suffering. It was the same selfish distress I felt when, as a child, I had hoped Cramer would publish my Summer Overture. It could not happen because my sister was dying.'

'There, you have mentioned your Summer Overture again. You see how important your first work was to you. You must find it. When I return from Brighton I want to hear it.'

'I have said I shall find it, dearest.'

'And you will resurrect it?'

'Yes. It will be my present to you.'

'I must get dressed and leave. We are later than usual.'

'I wish I could be with you on your trip. And my son.'

'You will be in spirit.'

'To him I have always been that nice-man-who-writes-music, and nothing more.'

'What makes you suddenly say that, dearest? You sound so angry.'

'I do not know. I am sorry. It is just that he is my son, our son, and he will never know.'

'Bernard – we know, and that is all important. It is important that you value him and can be proud of him. When he is old enough to understand, when he is grown – maybe he could be told then.'

Bernard thought of that time in the future with longing – but this longing suddenly clouded over. 'Anna – my love – do not travel tomorrow.' It was absurd, his fear. They had been parted so often, for much longer periods.

'Darling, I have to. You are frightening me. You are so pale, what is troubling you?'

. . . I look into the sea of my lioness's blue-green-grey eyes

and I am desolated . . . 'I cannot explain. An ambiguous feeling. A morose feeling. A feeling of being very alone.'

'I am here. You are not alone. I shall stay another five minutes. Listen to that rain . . . How hard it rains.'

The following morning was overcast but dry, and at just before ten o'clock Anna and her two children waited on the platform of Victoria Station for the train to arrive.

A couple of shrill shrieks and clouds of black steam heralded its approach.

'At last, at last,' cried Rupert, jumping up and down.

The doors were opened and the porter took their luggage. Anna hung back as the others climbed in.

'Come along, Mama,' the little boy called to her impatiently. 'The guard is about to blow his whistle.'

Anna looked fearfully about her, trembling unaccountably.

'Mama.'

She moistened her lips with her tongue and mounted the two little steps into the carriage.

The doors were closed once more, and with a whistle from the guard and further squeals from the engine, the train chugged slowly out of the station.

Sophie was struggling to read the *Evening Standard*. She had had a 'bad day', and was drugged with morphine, but she could read the large headlines of the paper without too much difficulty.

Bernard came down from the attic, dishevelled and dusty. He had been searching for something. Now he appeared holding a large old box covered in cobwebs. It contained his Summer Overture.

'There has been a terrible tragedy,' announced Sophie, her voice slurred. She noticed the box in Bernard's arms: 'What is that?'

He ignored the question. The inexplicable sense of forebod-

383

ing he had had since the previous day, and which had kept him awake all night, became heart-racing panic. 'What tragedy?'

'There was a derailment this morning of the ten o'clock London to Brighton train. Fortunately it was not crowded, but everybody was killed. Those poor –'

'No. *No.*' Bernard let out an animal-like roar. '*No,*' he bellowed again, rocking in anguish. He was ashen-faced and sweating. He had an immediate image of Anna's eyes, of the compound colour of her irises, of the soft darkness of his son's; then came a fleeting vision of an oak tree crashing to the ground. He could not breathe. He was beneath it. Blackness descended. He swayed and fell heavily.

'Mrs Adams. Mrs Adams!' Sophie attempted to get up from the chair, tumbled to the floor, and mindless of her dignity, crawled on all fours to her husband. 'Nurse – Mrs Adams – Nurse! Dear God, what has happened? Bernard, Bernard . . .'

Her hulk was a solid mass on top of him.

The two women entered together. They managed to lift her off him and assist her back into her chair.

'Do not fret, madam dear – he has only fainted.'

'Why?'

Why, why, why? His people, His two people. His Anna. The tips of his fingers reached out, out to the tips of hers, trying to bridge the space.

'Bernard, Bernard . . . Mr Foligno?'

He was unable to breathe for the weight of the tree . . . 'Leave me. I am – all right . . . Leave – me.' His voice came in muffled gasps.

He struggled up and staggered up the stairs to his room where he sat on the bed, head in hands, emitting dry, broken sobs. He envisaged his agony as a comb of honey, its channels filled with bitter herbs.

She was an integral part of my life. Anna – I would write you, play you, listen to you, breathe you, drink you . . .

'*I do not like those birds. They remind me of dying.*'

'Oh God,' Bernard roared. 'Oh God, oh God, oh *God.*'

*

For the next three months Bernard isolated himself, closetted in the family room with his Cramer piano and reams of manuscript paper. Sophie was banned from the room whilst he was working. Nobody in the house existed for him and he made no attempt to pretend to care. He worked obsessively and was oblivious to his wife's concern, his daughter's bewilderment at her rejection, and to the fear of the servants for his temper. A hush of misery had befallen the Foligno household.

And what, as a child of eleven, had been written spontaneously, was now maddeningly difficult to re-structure. He longed to pour his emotions and sorrow into this work, introducing theme after theme which would eke out his insupportable torment – but such music would have been rambling and self-indulgent; instead he must modify his impulses and not permit their wildness to possess this work which he was determined would be the most brilliant of compositions, so that when he dedicated it to Anna it would be worthy of her name and memory.

But it would no longer be an overture. It would be a concerto for piano and violin. The Summer Concerto. Methodically he tackled the resurrection, and when he first looked at it after a space of thirty-one years, the neat black figures and signs were the dancing spirits of his past.

He was surprised at the Overture's maturity; recalled that first Shabat he had dared show disrespect – and then his father's wretchedness at the ensuing punishment which marred a Friday night.

Bernard divided the work into *four* movements, and each was rich in subject material and lavish with its development. Here was the river winding between its banks in the park – and bobbing on the ripples, the comical ducks; here the beautiful women with their parasols, strolling or sitting beneath the shade of immense trees. Here came little Rachel – represented by the flutes and oboes – tripping along beside him; he was the receiver, the laconic listener, played by himself. Here were his parents, represented by the cellos and double basses – solid and assuring. The clarinets combined with the strings to become the sun shimmering down, striking the streets like the spilling

385

yolk of an egg. Now he had met Douglas, played of course by the violin. And here once more was the opening theme, barely recognizable now as violin and piano joined to make it portray a train: a hopeful, rhythmical staccato, alternating between the two instruments, transporting him to further memories where a brother and sister played on a long beach.

The train theme recurred much later, in the last movement's long coda. Here it had a menacing air which became increasingly intimidating with the persistent and repetitious intensity of the rhythm.

Da-da-da-*da*, da-da-da-*da*-da-da-da-da-da-da-da-da-da-*daaa*. The train that took his two people away. There was a deafening and abrupt crash of piano and percussion, shocking in its force, and then a great hiatus. Following this came the peaceful, ghostly traces of the first subject from the opening movement, now in the minor key – sweetly and painfully evocative as phantoms trailing by without touching one another.

The work ended with the violin petering out into an imperfect cadence – 'as though it would wish to continue.'

The entirety was an intricate tapestry, a composite of blended and juxtaposed experiences and impressions. But it was not easy to write, and Bernard could be heard playing passages repeatedly on the piano. The family room had become his shrine to his Summer Overture, reborn as the Summer Concerto. Only Douglas could know what he felt. Only Douglas was allowed in the room while he worked. He needed his old friend, the sole link in his past, and was typically selfish in his demands.

'You must play this. I must hear it,' Bernard would insist.

'You can hear it in your head,' Douglas said.

'I must *listen* to it – listen how it is with the piano. I wish to be assured of its beauty.'

'Dear chap, you have been at it for five hours without a break. What about a bite to eat, eh?'

'No. I am not hungry. Ask Mrs Adams to prepare you something.'

Bernard could not eat. His work sustained him. He drank water and black coffee, smoked his pipe and worked. His pain was an irate, tormented bull inside him.

'You cannot go on like this, sir,' scolded Mrs Adams. 'You will make yourself ill. Look at you – so thin and drawn.'

'What is wrong with the master, madam?' she asked Sophie one day. 'It is almost as if his heart were broken.'

'He has been like it since the accident,' Sophie answered vaguely, her voice distant and expression remote.

'What accident, madam dear?' asked Mrs Adams tenderly.

'The rail tragedy.'

'But how should that affect him?'

But Sophie remained silent, and Mrs Adams thought, *Poor thing, her mind is really going. Oh what a sad house this is now. What will become of everybody? I can see no end to such misery.*

Douglas could barely bring himself to look at his friend nowadays. This dispirited, middle-aged, stooped and greying man was a parody of his former self, and his grief was also Douglas's. When he saw Bernard, he wanted to weep for each of them. It did no good to reason with him any more.

Once he said: 'Think of your daughter, dear chap; you have her. You have your music, your health, your friends, your memories.'

Bernard replied: 'I have nothing.' Only his obsession with his Summer Concerto.

It was completed at the end of November 1883, just before his forty-third birthday. He dedicated the work, 'To Anna'.

'Is it good, Doug?'

'It is brilliant, dear chap – quite the best composition you have written.'

'I am at their mercy.'

'Whose, old chap?'

'The public's.'

'They will love it.'

'They have to . . . I am quite, quite expired, dear friend.'

'*Please* Bernard –' Douglas took a step towards his friend, his arm outstretched in a begging gesture, and his thick glasses steamed up with wetness.

'I loved her so much, Doug,' Bernard said on a dry sob. He gripped the small hand of his oldest ally, his strong pianist's clasp squeezing Douglas's knuckles.

387

'Blood brother.' The funny little be-whiskered man with the receding hairline tried to smile. 'Remember?' His chin was wobbling.

'Yes,' Bernard whispered. 'Yes, of course.'

The work was performed five months later in April, 1884 at the Royal Albert Hall, and the immense round construction did not have an empty seat. In the Royal Box was the small stout Queen, and when the composer appeared on stage and bowed to her, she stood up and clapped loudly. A ripple of laughter followed, and then everyone was clapping. Beside Bernard, Douglas murmured: 'You see there is still some good left. Remember that.'

Gazing about him, Bernard thought: *I remember so much. I remember two young boys in a room in Kensington. I never imagined it would come to this.*

Sir Charles Hallé as guest conductor lifted his baton, and the huge audience – tier upon tier – rose to the anthem. This was followed by the usual scuffling, coughing, whispering and rustling of progammes, and Hallé waited patiently before raising his arm once more to motion in the orchestra.

. . . Here is Rachel . . . Papa, Mama . . . Ah, myself. I play myself . . . Doug, dear friend, here are you – something of a gentle comic. Now I am Cramer himself – are you proud, sir? The train. Weymouth. The glaring heat. I play myself again. Anna, I have met you. I play you now, my Anna. And our son – Douglas plays our son and then we play together. We are walking in the park. . . .

Bernard was lost in his playing, immersed in his creation, closing his eyes whilst the violin proclaimed itself or the orchestra came in, rocking his body in time to his memories. How delicate was this weaving theme, how prettily pastoral that passage. Douglas stood stocky and sturdy as he played his stupendous cadenza – and not a sound came from the auditorium.

Once we dreamed we would play together . . . Bernard's thin figure hurled itself at the piano, caressed and embraced it.

Cramer had said: 'Become music.'

I am music. Tears burned behind his irises. *My first work will be my last. Overture to conclusion*.

The straining of thousands of eyes concentrated upon the platform, and though everyone was aware of the extraordinariness of what they were seeing and listening to, they could not know that they were watching and hearing a man live his life.

Between this man and the flamboyant, portly violinist was a perfect rapport and Charles Hallé conducting could only go along with them. The atmosphere was charged with powerful emotion and they had no need of him. The orchestra had become a complete body and each individual instrumentalist was bound in the spell of the playing.

Finally came the recapitulation when all the themes mingled. The condensing of time. Lilting sweetness and haunting dances. Then the train again – pounding on the piano – killing his Anna and their son. There were the awful crashing chords, and Bernard seeming to fall upon the piano distraught . . . And Douglas turning to him, playing his dying traces with steamed-up glasses, leaving the questioning note to hang in the air, suspended on its imperfect cadence.

For a second there was a lull; a stunned silence. And then came a gigantic roar, a simultaneous exclamation from thousands of voices, and the enormous blast of clapping. The entire auditorium rose to its feet and the little Queen's 'bravos' were drowned amongst all the others. They screamed for more and continued to scream, but Bernard had no more to give.

Barely able to stand, he staggered against Douglas, and the two friends embraced, tears streaming down their faces.

'More . . . Encore. Encore. *Bis*. More . . .'

They did not hear him say, 'I shall never touch a piano again, nor compose another line.'

'*Encore*.' How insistent they were.

Charles Hallé, bowing beside them now, said: 'They will not abate until we have played again.'

'No.'

'But –'

'They are avaricious. Do they not realize when a man has given all he can?'

When Bernard came out he was an old man. He was immediately surrounded by a barrier of newspaper reporters:

'Sir, who is Anna?'

'Is it a pet name for your wife or daughter?'

'It is the name of a cat I once had, gentlemen,' Bernard replied.

'A cat!' exclaimed one. 'Ha-ha, sir. You have a ripe sense of humour. I shall write that down.'

Another persisted: 'Was she a childhood friend – an aunt – a sister – a pupil?'

'Gentlemen – I shall leave you to your surmising.'

The next day Bernard Shaw's column in *The Times* was devoted to a lengthy eulogy of Bernard's composition and performance. The article was entitled: 'TO ANNA' – ABOUT WHOM NOTHING IS KNOWN.

I knew everything there was to know.
She was magnificent.
She was never separate from me.
I knew EVERYTHING.

Sophie, mountainous, in pain and immobile in her chair, also knew; but she and her husband had long since ceased to communicate. She understood his grief, but could not heal him any more than she could heal herself. Now there was nothing left to salvage, and time would pass and come to mean very little.

'So Anna was a cat,' mused Mrs Adams, pushing the chair back and forth, back and forth, as though the occupant were a baby; whilst from the chaise-longue Bernard stared out of the window unseeingly. 'Fancy dedicating a piece of music to a cat,' she said, and continued to push her mistress's chair back and forth, back and forth, as Bernard continued to stare into vast, empty air.

Epilogue

Epilogue

Bernard Foligno was knighted in 1885 and died the year after, killed in a freak accident by a falling tree on a hot August morning.

He never wrote another line of music and became a recluse, hardly venturing from the house and shunning publicity. Many attempts were made to establish the identity of the mysterious Anna of his dedication, but without success. No letters or papers amongst his private belongings disclosed anything, and experts were sceptical about romantic connotations, believing Foligno to be a devoted husband.

If Sir Giles Fotheringay had his suspicions, his pride would not permit him to reveal them.

In the end it was concluded that Anna probably *was* a cat he had owned as a child, and that the work was dedicated to childhood. Evidence of early manuscripts endorsed this theory.

His wife survived him by twelve years; their daughter Rachel never married and became an active member of the suffragette movement; and the great virtuoso violinist, Douglas Hamilton, died on his ninety-ninth birthday. He lived to see his friend's ballet re-staged and euphorically acclaimed, and Bernard Foligno's name was the last word he spoke.

The Golden Cup
Belva Plain

At nineteen, Hennie De Rivera's dreams have no place for the suitable marriage her parents plan for her. Instead her thoughts are all of the young radical scientist Daniel Roth and their plans to change the world. But their stormy, passionate marriage will bring them into conflict not only with the establishment world of Hennie's prosperous family but all too often with each other . . .

From the riches and rags of turn of the century New York to the squalor and the slaughter of the First World War trenches, *Golden Cup* is another compelling novel by the

'Queen of family saga writers'
New York Times

FONTANA PAPERBACKS

Pamela Haines

Also available in Fontana

THE KISSING GATE

A grand saga, set in the beauty and pride of Yorkshire, with all the power and excitement of the Victorian era.

The Kissing Gate is at the heart of village life, and marks the beginning of the Squire's land. The rescue of Squire Ingham's son by an Irish servant-girl creates an uneasy bond between Sarah and the Squire's family, which in later generations will explode into forbidden love.

THE GOLDEN LION

Maria Verzotto is in her far-off home in Sicily, Dick Grainger is growing up in Yorkshire when they first hear the legend of the Golden Lion – the story of a heroic prince and how he wins his princess. But there is another Lion who is destined to influence Maria's life – the Lion of the Monteleone, a ruthless mafioso . . .

'Pamela Haines is now undoubtedly in a class all of her own' THE TIMES

'A born writer' Francis King, SPECTATOR

FONTANA PAPERBACKS

Teresa Crane

A Fragile Peace

It was a lovely summer's day – perfect for a garden party. Everything seemed at peace for the Jordan family. But by the time the party was over, the Jordans' tranquil, ordered existence had been shattered.

The year was 1936.

Molly

Molly is a fabulous saga set in London's East End at the turn of the century. It is about the struggles of Molly O'Dowd, a young Irish girl, who comes to London penniless and in search of a job, and who ends up running several companies. It is about the men in her life, about the family she raises. It is a marvellous picture of working-class life at that time, teeming with wonderful characters, and alive with the changes imposed by both industry and impending war.

The Rose Stone

When Josef Rosenburg, fleeing the Jewish pogroms of Imperial Russia, reached Amsterdam, he owned nothing but the clothes he stood up in. By the time he reached London, he had the price of prosperity in his pocket – a prosperity that had been bought at an appalling cost.

FONTANA PAPERBACKS

Fontana Paperbacks: Fiction

Fontana is a leading paperback publisher of fiction.
Below are some recent titles.

- [ ] THE CONSUL GENERAL'S DAUGHTER Erin Pizzey £3.95
- [ ] THE HAWTHORNE HERITAGE Teresa Crane £3.99
- [ ] UNDER GEMINI Rosamunde Pilcher £2.99
- [ ] GLAMOROUS POWERS Susan Howatch £3.95
- [ ] BEST FRIENDS Imogen Winn £3.50
- [ ] NO HARP LIKE MY OWN Marjorie Quarton £2.99
- [ ] TEA AT GUNTER'S Pamela Haines £2.95

You can buy Fontana paperbacks at your local bookshop or
newsagent. Or you can order them from Fontana Paperbacks,
Cash Sales Department, Box 29, Douglas, Isle of Man. Please
send a cheque, postal or money order (not currency) worth the
purchase price plus 22p per book for postage (maximum postage
required is £3.00 for orders within the UK).

NAME (Block letters)_____

ADDRESS_____

_____